THE FARMHOUSE FIVE
GO QUIZZING

THE FARMHOUSE FIVE GO QUIZZING

BY

DAVID LUDDINGTON

Return of the Hippy

The Money That Never Was

Schrodinger's Cottage

Forever England

Whose Reality is this Anyway?

Camp Scoundrel

The Bank of Goodliness

The Rose Well Files

The King of Scanlon's Rock

The Daily Sentinel

Breaking News

Following the death of eccentric Cornish millionaire Thomas Lovett, the details of his very unusual last will and testament have now been released.

Thomas Lovett was a direct descendant of William Lovett, the 19th century founder of the Chartist movement, and widely regarded as the driving force behind the creation of the Trade Unions.

Lovett, a passionate champion for natural Cornwall and the environment, has as expected, left most of his assets to family members. However, it is the Lovett Estate lands near Porth Cullen, which have been the subject of much controversy, and following the failure in the courts of several appeals, his final bizarre bequest can now be revealed.

The estate lands, consisting of 1,200 acres of forest and meadowland, along with a number of farm buildings, are to be donated to the winners of a gigantic quiz. Lovett, one time winner of the All Cornwall Brainbox of the Year, was well known for his love of quizzing and once came as runner-up in Mastermind.

The competition, entitled The Great Wessex Chase, is open to teams from across the United Kingdom and the prize is valued around £7,000,000. Entry is limited to the first 2,000 teams to correctly identify the location contained within this clue.

$$E=Mc2 \text{ over Pi sees the solution of } 7$$

For those who are reading the story of the competition, and wanting to take part in the fun, just solve the entry clue and you are in with the chance of winning a special hardback edition of the book, go to Luddington.com and click on the book for more details.

Good luck to you all!

CHAPTER ONE

TEAM FARMHOUSE FIVE

I GLANCED AT MY WATCH once more, still unsure whether to trust it or not. Seven fifteen, allegedly. I returned to my newspaper and studied the puzzle for a second time. It still didn't make any sense. So, giving up on the prospect of becoming a millionaire overnight, I turned the page in search of something I could at least comprehend. The pound was collapsing again, the Minister for the NHS had just resigned over some hooky deal with a US pharmaceutical company, and more coverage of the so-called Green Ninja's campaign of environmental terrorism. Same old, same old.

A crunching noise erupted out of the small speaker set up at the far end of the bar.

"Is this thing on?" Bernard Kerron, question master for the regular Smuggler's Arms quiz night, tapped the microphone. "Hello, hello. Can anybody hear me?"

The noise pulled me from my newspaper. "All okay back here." I folded the paper and pushed it to the corner of my table.

Bernard squinted into the lights, trying to locate my voice in the far dark corner of the bar. "Matt? I didn't notice you back there. You're early."

"The station gave me an Alexa as a retirement gift. It's got the wrong time and I've been running an hour ahead all day."

"I got a set of golf sticks when I left the railway."

"I didn't know you played."

"Never a stroke." Bernard tapped the microphone again. It howled and he dropped it. "I got a dog. Much more fun chucking sticks for him than waving them at little balls. You should get one."

"No, I never fancied the idea of a dog. Garden gnomes are far easier to care for. I'm trying to learn gardening. Been promising myself that for years. I've just bought a pergola, well, basically a giant Jenga set and some instructions in Swedish."

The door swung open, and Janet Sprigg stumbled in on a gust of wind and leaves. She pushed the door shut and resettled her green felt hat. As she wrestled with windblown hair and hat, her fingers found a small twig which had become lodged. She pulled it free, opened the door again and threw the twig out. Her eyes scanned the bar, and as soon as she spotted me, she gave a little wave and headed over.

"You're early," she said, as she settled at the table and dived into her Mary Poppins bag, dragging various items out onto the table.

"I've got an Alexa," I said.

"Oh, poor you. My granddaughter gave me one of those last Christmas. Though I don't suppose she went out and bought it herself. She's only five. Ah, here we are." She surfaced from the inside of her bag with a smile and a notepad. "We have some new stationery for tonight. They make very good little nightlights."

"Notepads?"

"No, silly, Alexa. She comes on when I walk near her. I've put her in the hall so I can find my way to the bathroom in the night."

I looked at my watch. "What time is it really?"

Janet lifted the sleeve of her jumper. "Oh muffins," she said as she looked at her bare wrist. "I forgot to put my watch on again. Never mind, let me see… it was exactly five past six when I left. I usually leave at six, but Tiggywumple wanted feeding, and it takes me five minutes to feed her."

"Okay, so how long does it take you to walk here?"

"Twenty minutes, unless it's raining and I have to find my umbrella."

"Right," I said. "Well, it's not raining, and you left at five past six. Twenty minutes, that means it would be about half-past six?"

"Yes. Except…" Her face took on a pinched look as she went away in thought for a moment. "I did stop to talk to Mrs Pomfrey. She wanted my recipe for raisin scones, they're very popular with the Church Ladies' Poker Club you know."

I drew a breath and forced a smile. "And how long did you talk to Mrs Pomfrey for?"

"Heavens above, I haven't the faintest idea. She can talk a double glazing salesman to tears. I've seen her do it."

The door opened again, and the wind blew in a small group of people, one of whom I noticed was Eddie Bishop, another of our regular team. A slightly rounded man, with a penchant for baker boy caps, exuberant waistcoats, and shiny bling. He spotted me, mumbled something to the others who split for a nearby table, then he headed over to join us.

"That wind's getting up," he said, and dropped his hat on the table as he sat.

"You shouldn't do that," Janet scolded, relocating the hat to the back of a vacant chair. "It's bad luck to put a hat on the table. Haven't you ever read the Shadowed Fedora?"

Eddie unhooked the hat and planted it on the back of his own chair. "This is a genuine Christy's 8-piece cap, and it's neither shadowed nor unlucky."

"It's probably about as genuine as that Gucci umbrella you sold me," Janet said.

"I did warn you not to get it wet," Eddie protested.

"What's the right time, Eddie?" I asked.

He glanced at his watch, a flamboyant gold affair with far too many dials, and said, "Just gone seven thirty, and we're twenty-two feet above sea level." He nodded towards my wrist. "Your watch not working? I can do you a deal on a nice Omega Speedmaster. Just getting a batch in from China."

"China? You do know I'm still technically in the Job?"

"Yeah, but you can't actually arrest people anymore. Um… can you?"

"No, but that's beside the point. And thank you, but my Timex is working fine. I just set it by my Alexa." I glanced at my ageing watch. "Now I've lost track of time."

"I've heard that can happen with the newly retired," Eddie said.

"Nothing to do with my retirement," I scolded. "It's my Alexa, when I switched it on, I thought I'd see how clever it was and asked her what the time was in Barcelona. It's been showing me the wrong time ever since and now she only talks to me in Spanish."

"Is that one of the ones with two Ls?"

"Huh?"

"Two Ls in Alexa. Written on the box."

"I never noticed. Why? Is it important?"

He shrugged. "No, just asking. You need to go into settings. You'll be able to change the language there."

"What's settings in Spanish?"

"How would I know? Ask your Alexa, they do translations."

Bernard's microphone crackled again. "Ladies and gentlemen, we'll be commencing in about fifteen minutes. And don't forget, the proceeds of tonight's quiz are going to the Little Didney Animal Rescue Centre, which is being forced to find a new site. There'll also be a collection at half-time, so give generously, people."

I looked around the nearby tables. Groups of people shuffled papers and pens between them and chatted noisily as they caught up on their weeks. Most of the occupants were regular Monday night quizzers, but a few tables hosted new faces, probably just in for a quiet, early evening drink. On a nearby table, a middle-aged couple leaned in closely to each other. Too wrapped up in themselves to be married, I guessed. Either courting, or illicit. Probably the latter. Forty years in the police had given me a keen interest in human behaviour. A bit too keen sometimes. A youngish man stood in the middle of the bar, looking slightly lost as he scanned the room. He looked as though his upward growth had left nothing to fill him out with. A failed beard traced his angular face, and he wore a battered denim baseball cap which struggled to contain an oversupply of hair. The way he watched Bernard piqued my curiosity. I told myself to stand down, and returned my attention to the incompleteness of our team, the Farmhouse Five. So called after the name of Janet's home, Farmhouse Cottage.

"Where're the others?" I asked Eddie.

"Dunno," he said. "I seem to remember Tom saying something about the Dorset Steam Fair, but I thought that wasn't until August."

"It is August."

"Already? That'll be it, then. He's gone to Dorset. I'll get the drinks in. Usual?" Eddie glanced at Janet and me. We nodded our assent, and he headed off to the bar.

"Dorset," I mused. "That's messed up our team." Tom was the only one of us who knew anything about football or soap operas. That left a big hole in our skill set.

"Any idea where Eric is?" I asked Janet. "He's not here yet either."

"Oh, yes. Now, he did say something. A bird, that's it, he's gone off to find a bird. Norfolk, I think. I remembered it because that's where Inspector Dalgleish solved the Whistler mystery in… let me think… Devices and Desires."

"Norfolk? That's a long way to go for a bird."

"Who's got a bird in Norfolk?" Eddie asked, as he returned laden with drinks. He planted our glasses on the table and resumed his place.

"Eric," I said.

"Very rare, so he told me. It eats bees." Janet sipped at her sherry and looked around the table. "Did you order my cheesy pasty?" She gave Eddie an accusing stare. "You know I always have a cheesy pasty with my sherry."

"Sorry, I forgot. We'll order you one with the next round."

"I can't drink sherry without a little nibble, it'll go straight to my head and then I'll get the giggles. Here," she pushed the pad to Eddie, "if he starts, you write the answers, I'll go and get my cheesy pasty."

"Are we all ready?" Bernard's amplified voice boomed across the general hubbub which filled The Smuggler's Arms, shaking the dust from the four-hundred-year-old roof timbers. "Nice to see a good turnout tonight, so let's dig deep and save the animal rescue centre. Here we go then, question one, which beverage was baptised by Pope Clement VII in 1600?"

"Wine," said Eddie.

"Are you sure?" I asked.

"Has to be. What else would a pope baptise? It ain't gonna be lager, is it?" He pointed at Janet's new pad. You need to write that down, wine."

"I thought *you* were writing down the answers until Janet gets back?" I said.

Eddie mumbled something, reached over for Janet's ballpoint, and clicked the mechanism a few times before scribbling a test squiggle on the pad.

"Coffee," called a voice behind me.

I turned to see the young man with the hair and almost-beard. He stood in the middle of the room and looked like a rabbit in headlights as all eyes in the room turned to look at him.

"Are you in a team?" Bernard squinted through the glare of the light in his face, straining to identify the voice.

The man looked around, then back at Bernard. "Me?"

"Yes, you shouldn't call out the answers. Keep them in your team."

"I ain't got no team. I'm not really here. I only came in for chocolate." His darting eyes and tight lips gave clear signs of building agitation.

I stood and approached him. He flinched as I neared. "I know that one," he said. "It's coffee."

"Come and join us," I said, pointing at our table. "You can be on our team."

"I've never been in a team before."

Eddie gave me a furrowed-brow look that spoke of his disapproval. "I think we should wait," he said. "Maybe Tom'll turn up yet."

"From Dorset?"

"Well…"

"I'm sure he can answer more questions than Tom's empty chair." I motioned for the man to sit down. "What's your name, anyway?"

"Oh, I'm Dylan," said the man.

"Like the rock singer, Bob Dylan?" I asked.

"Who? Nah, don't know him. The cool rabbit in The Magic Roundabout. My dad said it was his favourite TV programme. He used to watch it all the time."

I began to wonder if we should have stuck with an empty chair, but then decided that everybody knew at least some stuff that others didn't. Law of averages.

"Why did you say coffee?" I asked.

"Cuz I'm a barrister. Well, I was, that's how I know."

I studied Dylan. In all my years in the Force, I'd met many barristers, but this guy looked the perfect image of everything that wasn't a barrister.

"For the CPS? Or private chambers?" I asked.

"Huh?"

"Where did you practise?"

"Kupsa Koffee. Only we don't call it practise, it's training on the job."

It took me a moment to work out, then, "You mean you're a barista? You make coffee?"

"Yeah, what I said, barista. Just a trainee. Was, not now though. I got the sack. They didn't like me making up my own names for the customers when I wrote them on the cardboard cups."

"Hmm, Kupsa Koffee," said Eddie. "You'd think a company which sells a cardboard mug of coffee for five quid would have more of a sense of humour."

"What makes you think the pope baptised coffee?" I asked Dylan.

He stared at me. "He liked coffee. We had to take a test about coffee. I can tell you which country sells the most coffee."

"Hang on to that one in case it comes up," I said.

"I only came in to buy some chocolate. I'm not really supposed to be here."

"We won't tell," said Eddie.

"Cool. I've never been in a quiz team. Have we got a quiz team name?"

"Yes," I said. "We're the Farmhouse Five. Sort of a play on the Enid—"

"Question two," Bernard called loudly, cutting off my explanation. "How is this sequence of numbers formally known: 0, 1, 1, 2, 3, 5, 8, 13, 21, 34…?"

"Where's Janet got to?" Eddie muttered as he carefully wrote down the question. "She's supposed to be on writing duty tonight."

"That was number two," I said. "You've written it against number one."

"No, he said 0, 1, 1, 2."

"I meant the question number. You've written the question down against question one. That was question two."

Eddie pushed the pad to me. "Here, you do it. I'm not good with numbers."

"That's strange, I've seen you grossing down net of VAT for cash-in-hand for some knock-off Louis Vuitton bags often enough."

"That's not maths, that's discount," Eddie said. "And anyway, I don't do knock-offs, just alternatively sourced goods."

"The Fibonacci Sequence," Dylan offered.

"What?" I asked.

"It's the Fibonacci Sequence. That's my favourite number sequence. Along with the telephone number of the CIA, of course."

"Of course."

"20241850—"

"Yes, okay," I cut him short. "I'll take your word for that. How do you spell Fibonacci?"

"I don't know. I don't do letters."

I sensed movement behind me and turned to see Janet. "I've got us a dinger," she said, turning to indicate a woman just behind her. Short-cut blonde hair accentuated an angular face. She wore an overly large blue jumper and faded blue jeans.

"This is Robyn," Janet continued. "She was on The Chase once."

"I didn't win," Robyn said, with a smile.

"You mean a ringer?" I suggested to Janet.

"Oh yes. I knew it had something to do with telephones. We were both ordering a snack, and I said how good Sam Goodenough's cheesy pasties are, but of course he's run out and has to heat some more up, and then we got to talking about flapjacks which of course led on to quizzing, so—."

"Flapjacks to quizzing?" I interrupted, knowing I was going to regret asking.

"Yes, of course," Janet said, as if I'd missed the obvious. "Robyn had a question on flapjacks on The Chase."

"Oh, I see. Well, Robyn, it's nice to meet you, and great to have you on our team. Let's hope we get a question on flapjacks."

"Let's hope not," said Robyn. "That's the one I got wrong."

"Question three," Bernard called. "Who was considered to be the first computer programmer?"

"Bill Gates," said Eddie.

"No, Ada Lovelace," said Robyn.

"You sure? Wasn't she a porn actress?" asked Eddie.

Robyn fixed her eyes on Eddie in the way boxers psyche their opponents before a match. I'd seen that look many times over the years, and it usually presaged violence.

"You're thinking of *Linda* Lovelace." Robyn's eyes gave a hint of mischief, but the sense of threat never left. She added, "And anyway, she was nowhere near as sexy as Ada."

Eddie watched Robyn for a moment, as if trying to get her measure. Then he smiled and pulled out the spare seat. "You'd best sit yourself down then, love." Eddie caught the sudden flash in Robyn's eyes and corrected, "I meant, Robyn. Sit yourself down there, Robyn."

She settled herself at the table, planting her phone in front of her as if waiting on a call. "How does this work then?"

"Two rounds of questions with a break in the middle," I said. "We're doing this one to help the Little Didney Animal Rescue Centre. They have to find new premises, urgently."

"Don't hold out much hope of raising that kind of money," said Eddie. "Land around here is more expensive than London."

Janet sat back in her seat and retrieved her writing pad from Eddie. She stared at it. "Oh dear, oh dear. What have you been doing here?"

"We went a bit wrong." Eddie pushed the pad over to Janet.

"You've only had two questions." Janet tutted and crossed out Eddie's contribution. "How can you go wrong on two questions? And where's my pen?"

"It was here just a moment..." Eddie's eyes settled on Janet's pen, which now lay in front of Dylan. At least, its component parts did, all laid out in a neat row in front of Dylan.

"What's happened to my pen?" Janet asked.

Dylan fidgeted. "Sorry, I wanted to see how it works."

"It's a pen. It writes in ink, what's to see?"

"But the clicky bit. Some clicky bits have a little barrel which goes round, or a button, they're the best, and they're all a bit different. I've got a box of them."

Janet reached across and gathered the bits of her pen. "You can't just go taking people's pens to pieces without a by-your-leave." She looked at the bits. "How does this all go back together?"

I took the pieces, and after a couple of attempts, Janet had a working ballpoint again.

"Question four," Bernard called. "The Mysterious Affair at Styles is the first book to feature which detective?"

"That was Hercule Poirot," said Janet, writing down the answer without giving time for discussion. "And where's he got to with our cheesy pasties?" She looked around and spotted Goodenough heading in our direction. She waved a hand. "Coo-ee, over here." She turned to me. "A girl could starve to death waiting for him."

Goodenough slid between the busy tables and set the plate in front of Janet. "Had to warm some more up and I've put some House Salad on for you."

Janet looked at the single tomato sat next to the pasty. "That?" she asked.

"It's all the thing in that posh restaurant down Porth Cullen. That TV chef's place, whatshisname, Rupert Llewellen, he calls it Hot Cuisine. I'll add it to yer tab." He glanced round our table. "Got some nice meat pasties ready 'case anybody..." His eyes settled on Dylan. "'Ere, what are you doing in here?

You've got a court order to stay away from here." He flapped an arm at Dylan. "Sling yer hook."

"What's up, Sam?" I asked.

"It's him." Goodenough stabbed a finger towards Dylan. "He took my cash register apart. Just turned my back for a few minutes to get a fresh barrel, an' when I come back, there's bits of my cash register all over the bar."

"I got stressed. My doctor said I should find something to occupy my mind when I get stressed."

Goodenough looked at me. "You're a copper, Matt. Aren't you supposed to arrest him?"

"I'm retired. Besides, my station was Penzance, not... Look, I'll tell you what, I'll take responsibility for him while he's here. How's that?"

"You gonna pay for any damage he does?"

"You have my word."

"Hmm, well you mind he behaves. He should be locked up. It ain't right, going around destroying honest folk's property like that." Goodenough headed back to the bar.

"I said I wasn't supposed to be here," Dylan said. "It's what I said."

"You did," I said. "I remember you saying just that."

"I'm on bail, see? I'm supposed to stay away from here. And the sweetshop on Hill Street."

"Ah, you didn't mention that bit."

"I only came in for chocolate 'cause I'm not allowed in the sweetshop."

"But you're also... never mind, just keep your head down and answer questions," I said. "And don't break anything."

"I never break things," Dylan said, with a distinct sulk to voice. "It's just that I don't always remember how they go back together."

"Question five," Bernard called. "Outside of China, which is the largest bank in the world?"

"Morgan Chase," said Robyn, without a moment's hesitation.

"Never heard of 'em," said Eddie.

"I did some work on their computer systems a few years back."

"Wow, cool," said Dylan. "I'd love to go to America. They've got spray cheese. But I don't like their money, it's all the wrong size. The big coins are worth less than the little ones. Why would they do that? There's something wrong with a country that has big coins worth less than little ones."

"I wasn't in America," Robyn said. "It was remote work, sort of freelance. It's what I do. Data analysis."

"Ah, hence the answer to the computer question," I said. "Good knowledge to have on our team."

With our team now up to the required five, we were at least in with a chance of not disgracing ourselves. Robyn's knowledge proved eclectic and useful, but Dylan, after his initial promising start, had little more to offer. By the time the mid-point break came, we still had a few gaps in our answers, and we set about filling them in with best guesses.

Bernard appeared and rattled a collection tin at us. "Come on, open your wallets. Our furry friends need your help."

"I thought they were shutting down?" Eddie said, slipping a twenty-pound note into the tin.

"They're fighting the eviction. But to be honest, we're not holding much hope. Gwen's hoping to raise enough for the rent on a smallholding up near Trekenwryth, just temporary like."

"All for some fancy hotel, I heard," said Eddie.

"On the upside, it could bring more business to the village," I said, stuffing a matching note in the tin with just a touch of uncertainty. I was yet to receive my first pension payment and although I'd been told what it would be, I was still watching the pennies until it arrived.

"Not much chance of that. It's part of some huge chain. Melchester Hotels, or something."

"I think we should hold a bring-and-buy sale for them," said Janet. "I could bake some of my raisin scones."

"Can't they rent another place somewhere?" asked Robyn.

"They could barely manage the rent on the place they've got," Janet said. "It's been running on pixie dust and unicorn pooh for years, but now the owner of the land has to sell. Poor love, her father died, and the tax people are being horrible."

"And there's nowhere else they can go?"

"Not with the price of land round here," Eddie said. "Besides, who's gonna want thirty or so dogs yapping next door?"

"You should enter The Great Wessex Chase," said Dylan. "They're giving away a massive, big farm. It's 1,200 acres. That's 485 hectares."

"Chance would be a fine thing," I said. "We can't even win the weekly pot here, I don't think we'd stand much chance against the sort of people who'll be entering that, especially as it's only the first two thousand to pass the entry question who get in. I saw the thing in the paper, but I didn't even understand the question, let alone be able to answer it."

"What was the question?" asked Robyn.

"I can't remember. Too many numbers. I know it had something to do with Pi, but that's as far as I got."

"3.141592653—" Dylan started before I interrupted him.

"We probably don't need the whole thing, Dylan."

"It's my favourite number."

"I thought you said the Fibi-whatsit was your favourite number?"

"No, that's not a number, that's a sequence, like the CIA phone number, that's a sequence too, although everybody calls it a number, it's not really, it's a sequence. Pi is a number. 3.14159265—"

"Okay, I get the idea. Not helping the dogs though, whether it's a number or a sequence."

"I know some other numbers."

"Well, there you go…" I opened my newspaper at the page with the announcement about The Great Wessex Chase and slid it to Dylan. "See if you can solve that then. It's supposed to be a clue to a location somewhere in Wessex, but I don't even understand the question, E equals MC squared over Pi sees the… here, you have a go."

It should at least keep him quiet, I figured. And hopefully, keep him from dismantling the table.

Dylan studied the puzzle, and I turned to Robyn. "So, clever computer stuff then? Are you down here for work?"

"Just on a bit of a getaway, really," Robyn said. "I'll probably do a bit of freelancing while I'm here though, if I feel like it. The beauty of the internet."

"What's your name?" Dylan asked me.

"Matt," I said.

"I need your last name too." Dylan typed into his phone.

"Dixon. Why?"

"Cool, like the crossbow man from the Walking Dead, Daryl Dixon."

"I don't know him. Like George Dixon, the TV copper in the sixties."

"Who?"

"Never mind, anyway, why do you want my name?"

"For the competition. And your phone number, they need that too."

I gave him my number, and he looked at Eddie. "What's your name?"

Eddie looked at me. "What's he on?"

I tried narrowing my eyes a touch and giving the tiniest shake of my head, trying to send a secret signal to Eddie to play along. He gave me an inquisitive look, and I repeated my gesture.

This time he seemed to understand and answered, "Eddie Bishop, 07700 900428."

Dylan tapped the details into his phone with a blurred flurry of thumbs, then looked at Robyn.

"Robyn…" She seemed to hesitate a moment, then added, "Hedges."

Dylan's thumbs translated that into the phone, as Janet said without prompting, "Janet Sprigg."

"And…" Dylan tapped again as he carefully pronounced, "Farmhouse Five." He finished typing, slipped his phone back in his pocket, and looked up. "There we go, all done."

"Okay," I said. "Now, can we get back to filling in the gaps in our answers?"

"How exciting," said Janet, looking at Dylan. "When do we find out?"

"Oh, we're in," he said. "We're all entered."

"But don't we need to answer the entry question? This MC Pi squared stuff?" I asked.

"All done. I answered that."

"What? How?"

"Well, you see, if we take Pi, which is 3.141592653—"

"Okay, enough. I get that bit. But... are you saying we're in The Great Wessex Chase?"

"Yes."

"The quiz for a seven-million-pound estate? That quiz?"

"Yes. It was easy."

I looked round the shocked faces of my fellow quizzers.

Eddie was the first to speak. "I'd better get some more drinks in then."

CHAPTER TWO

"WE'LL START AGAIN WITH PART two," Bernard called. "Question twenty-one, which city used to be known as Byzantium?"

"So what's involved in this Wessex Chase?" asked Eddie.

"I don't really know," I admitted. "I read a bit about it in the paper, but the entry question made no sense to me at all, so I didn't bother reading anymore of the article."

Eddie reached for my paper and riffled through it. "Ah, here it is. 2,000 teams... chosen by entry question... maximum five in a team... can't change, add, or remove members once registered... Yada yada... we have to visit locations after solving clues."

"Where?" I asked.

"I don't know," said Eddie. "Wouldn't be much of a quiz if they told you that now, would it?"

"Istanbul," said Robyn.

"How'd you know that?" asked Eddie. "You ain't seen any clues yet."

"No, question twenty-one. The city that was Byzantium, it's Istanbul."

"Oh, right." He nodded to Janet. "Istanbul, the answer to question twenty-one. Have you got that?"

"I've already written it down," said Janet. "I thought everybody knew that.

It's where the Orient Express was going, you know, in Murder on the Orient Express?"

"What else do we need to know?" I asked Eddie.

He turned back to the paper. "Six clues… hey, that's not bad, only six. Ah, they're timed. So if you're over the time, you're out. And also, the slowest fifty percent of those who *are* within the time, are also knocked out at each round."

"Slowest to solve the clues?"

Eddie ran his finger over the paper. "No, the slowest to log in to the location, what? Oh, I see, we have to solve a clue, then visit the location and login with a special app on our phones."

"Where are the locations?" Janet asked. "Are they round here? Only, I hope they're not too far to walk."

Eddie studied the paper again. "Wessex, it says. I guess that means the southwest of England."

"Oh, dear." Janet looked worried.

"Don't worry, I can drive you."

"You can't drive, Eddie. Remember?" I said.

"I can drive," he replied. "It's just that the magistrate suggested I shouldn't drive. For twelve months."

"I think it was more than a suggestion, Eddie."

"It's only a formality."

"Okay, well, until things get a little less formal, it's probably best I drive. We can get five in my car."

"You'll have to make it four," said Robyn. "Or find a fifth. I can't go with you, sorry. I can't afford the time commitment. My work, I have to be available to leave at short notice."

"Who else can we find?" I looked at the others.

"No good," said Eddie. "It says the team entered can't be changed, added to, or members removed."

"Can't we just re-enter with different names?"

"Nope. We can cancel our place, but can't re-enter."

We all looked at Robyn. She shifted in discomfort and said, "What? I can't help it. I didn't realise I was being entered for this thing... whatever it is. I only came in to use the Wi-Fi."

"Well," I said. "It was a nice idea."

"Question twenty-two. Garden Gnomes are specifically banned from which event?"

"The Chelsea Flower Show," I said.

"How do you know that?" asked Janet, as she wrote the answer.

"I'm learning gardening, I'm starting with things that are easy to grow."

"Like gnomes?"

"No, I'm not growing gnomes, even I know you can't grow gnomes."

"Maybe you're planting them too close together," suggested Eddie with a grin.

"I just happen to like them, what's wrong with that?"

Janet studied me for a moment. "I'd never have had you down as a gnome person."

"Back to the point in question," I said. "What are we going to do about this Great Wessex Chase? Eddie, can't you find a loophole in the rules? You seem to be able to find a loophole in most things."

"If you're referring to my little contretemps with the VAT people, it's not my fault if they thought my lockup was in Luxembourg. Besides, from what I can see, whoever wrote the rules for this is far smarter than your average Customs and Excise lawyer. It's tighter than Boris Johnson at a Christmas party."

"Question twenty-three. What is the Malleus Maleficarum?"

"It's a book about witches," said Eddie.

"How did you know that?" I asked.

"I tried to read it once, when all my runner beans died soon after this weird woman moved in near me. Couldn't make head nor tail of it though."

"You read a book about witches because your runner beans died?" I asked.

"You can mock, but I don't believe in coincidence, not when it comes to spooky stuff. That's how they hide, by making people think they're not real."

By the time we had finished the quiz, we had answers to most questions, but we'd fallen short on our football and pop culture.

Bernard tapped the microphone to hush the room. "Ladies and gentlemen, we have the results. In first place, the Beer Necessities. In second, the Quizzee Lizzees, and in third place, it's the Farmhouse Five."

Third place wasn't a disgrace, so we didn't need to feel too bad about our performance.

But Bernard hadn't finished. "And a special announcement, the Farmhouse Five have entered, and been accepted into The Great Wessex Chase, which I'm sure everybody's heard all about. But for those of you just home from planet Mars, the prize is the Lovett Farm Estate lands at Porth Cullen. Over a thousand acres, worth about seven million quid, apparently, and the Farmhouse Five are doing this to support the Little Didney Animal Rescue Centre."

A round of applause ran round the room, and we cowered in our seats, just nodding and smiling.

"What are we going to do?" asked Janet.

We all looked to Robyn again.

"No, you're not putting this on me," she said. "I just came away for a few days to lay-low, the stress of my work and all that. Find somebody else."

We reluctantly accepted the undeserved back-slaps and offers of drinks from the crowd in the Smuggler's. We agreed to meet again in the morning when, hopefully, clearer heads would prevail. I slipped out before closing time and threaded my way through the narrow lane to my cottage. I settled with a nightcap, a packet of cheesy puffs and turned the television to BBC South West.

After ten minutes, I'd got bored with pictures of holiday traffic jams, drought-hit farms, polluted beach warnings, and the ostentatious spectacle that was the Porth Cullen Boat Show. No mention of The Great Wessex Chase, which was the reason I'd tuned in to start with. I turned to a movie channel and fell asleep in front of Once Upon a Time in the West.

CHAPTER THREE

TEAM BULLINGBOY CLUB

SIR JULIUS COMBERMERE HELD THE flat of his hand on the newspaper which lay across his expansive mahogany desk. His free hand fumbled for the intercom.

"Perkins?" he called, stabbing the button.

"Yes, sir?" returned a voice from the little speaker.

"I need you in here, now."

"At once, sir."

A polite double knock on Combermere's office door arrived within a split second of Perkins' reply.

"Yes, yes. Come in," called Combermere.

The door swung open and a tall, stick-like man in a grey pinstripe suit entered.

"Have you seen today's Sentinel?" Combermere asked as Perkins approached.

"No, sir. It's not one on my reading list."

"Well, it should be, damnit. It's your job as my private secretary to keep me apprised of situations affecting my constituency. I can't do everything, Perkins." Combermere slapped his hand on the newspaper. "It's a damned disgrace, that's what it is. They're like the plague of Pericles, infecting the hoi polloi with visions of grandeur."

"I see, sir. Might one ask what the problem is? Exactly?"

"That treacherous chartist, Thomas Lovett, damned communist. He owns... owned, the estate next to mine in Cornwall."

"Ah, yes, sir. I recall you were rather keen on acquiring this estate at one time."

"Indeed, it was going to be the finest hunting and shooting estate in the South, maybe even the country."

"I remember quite clearly, sir. You were negotiating a contract with a Polish factory farm for the supply of pheasant and partridge chicks. But, if I remember correctly, didn't Mr Lovett decline your offers?"

"He did, he did. But I would have won him over in time. Few men have virtue beyond reward. But now, in a final animus, the scoundrel has deliberately died and left the estate as some sort of prize."

"How terribly inconvenient."

"Inconvenient hardly covers it. The man has the treachery of Ephialtes. Telling me he would never part with the land, and now it's open season for any opportunistic Rachmanite to turn it into a ghetto of cheap rental housing for the feckless and drug addicts, and probably immigrants. Or even, heaven forbid, some sort of holiday camp. Who knows?"

"Forgive me, sir. I'm not sure I understand the issue. Surely, if the owner has deceased, then all that is required is to continue negotiations with his successor?"

Combermere pushed the paper towards Perkins. "Read the damned thing yourself."

After a few moments, Perkins looked up from his reading. "I see. Quite a conundrum."

"As you say, Perkins, quite a conundrum. Fortunately, the solution is at hand within the dilemma. You will enter the competition and win the prize. And this way, I will even save the initial investment."

"But this entry question, sir? E=Mc2 over Pi sees the solution of 7. I don't even begin to understand it."

"Nor do I. Fortunately, I have a chum in GCHQ, we're in the same lodge.

He's put a team on the problem," Combermere tapped the phone on his desk. "I'm expecting a call anytime now. Your job, Perkins, is simply to assemble a team who will travel to the various locations, and GCHQ will furnish you with the answers. Couldn't be simpler."

"But isn't that—"

The ringing of the telephone cut across Perkins' attempt at protest. Combermere held a finger to his lips to signal Perkins to remain silent.

"Nigel!" Combermere greeted into the phone. "Fortuitous timing. How did your people manage with our little puzzle?... They did? How wonderful! Tell me, what's the answer? ... Really? Who'd have thought? That's very clever... Yes, yes, of course. As soon as the budget request reaches my department, consider it granted. I know, we must meet up for a drink. Next time you're in town, pop along to the House. They do a very nice Guedes Vintage in the Stranger's Bar. My guest."

Combermere hung up the phone and scribbled on a Post-it note. "There you are, Perkins. That's your answer. Now, run along, there's a good man. Keep me apprised."

He switched his attention from Perkins to the newspaper laying across his desk. "Vagabonds, purveyors of half-truths and mischief."

He looked at the door as he heard it close. "Humph." He gathered the paper up, folded it into perfect quarters, then tossed it into the bin.

TEAM THE ALTER EGOS

The light on Stuart's phone flashed, indicating a waiting call. He slipped the headphones over his ears, pressed answer, and said, "Good morning, Ponzi Phone Tech Support Line. My name is Bruce, and it will be my pleasure to assist you. How may I help?"

He paused, listening to the caller, then said, "Have you tried switching it off and on again?... No? Okay, well let's try that to start with... Yes, hold the power button, then wait two minutes and switch it back on... I see, then you need to charge it first... The bit of wire that came with the phone...That's the big bit of wire which goes into the wall…That's right… Yes, it will take a while to come back… If that doesn't work, just call us back and ask for me, Bruce, and we'll escalate the response… You too, have a nice day."

Stuart clicked the button to terminate the call and turned to Nigel, seated at the next desk. "The idiots are out in force today. You'd really think somebody who could afford over a grand for a shit phone would at least have a few brain cells. You have to wonder how some of these people get dressed."

"Tell me about it," said Nigel. "Most of them wouldn't know the difference between a bit or a byte if it came up and bit them on their BIOS."

"Fun fact," said Stuart. "On average, serial killers have an intelligence quotient two points above the norm."

"Maybe Ponzi should only sell their phones to serial killers. At least they wouldn't bother us so much."

Nigel's phone lit up, and he stabbed the button without looking. "Good morning, Ponzi Phone Tech Support Line. My name is Clarke, and it will be my pleasure to assist you. How may I help?... Bruce? I'm sorry, he's on another call at the moment." He glanced across at Stuart and smiled. "Anyway, I'm sure I can help. What appears to be the problem? Tell me, what do you see on the screen? Have you put in the SIM card? The little piece of plastic that came with the phone... No, that's the charger. The SIM, it's about the size of a postage stamp... I see, well have you recently emptied your rubbish bin?... Oh dear. Well never mind, I'll arrange a new one to be sent out... No problem, now if you could just tell me your name and... Hello? Hello? Are you still there? He's gone away." Nigel clicked the button to terminate the call.

"Hey, did you hear about the Tower of Doom?" he asked Stuart.

"You mean the real place?" Stuart said. "Where they filmed the final battle between Raptoman and Gharial in King of the Waters?"

"That's the one," confirmed Nigel. "It's somewhere down in Cornwall, isn't it?"

"Porth Cullen way, I think."

"Well, the guy who owns the land it's on, somebody called…" He turned to his screen and pulled up a webpage. "Here we go, Thomas Lovett. Seems like

~ 25 ~

he's just died and left the land to be used as the prize in a competition. A mega quiz-chase thing."

"The tower and all?"

"Yeah. I happened over an email between our chairman and that tosspot Gregson, you know, head of land acquisition."

"Happened over an email?" Stuart asked, with a slight edge of suspicion.

"Hey, haven't we told them time and again that their internal email is unencrypted? Not my fault if they don't listen."

"Hmm."

"Don't give me hmm," said Nigel. "You're just as bad. What about that time when you intercepted the picture of the chairman's todger he was sending to his secretary?"

"Just a giggle."

"He didn't think so. Especially when it turned up on the staff noticeboard."

"So? What was in this email that you just… happened over?"

"They're entering a team in The Great Wessex Chase. They want the land where the Tower of Doom is, and this is the only way they can get it. Apparently, there are lithium deposits under the land."

"In Cornwall?"

"Seems so. And it can be accessed by strip mining."

"They'll never get permission."

"The money these guys have got? They'll have the politicians lining up to support it. But the point is, if they get that land, they'll get the Tower of Doom as well. Then they'll churn over the whole place, like they've done in Africa."

"We can't let the Tower of Doom fall, what can we do?" asked Stuart. "We're just a couple of techies on their help-desk."

"We have to win the competition. We're good at solving problems. It's what we do every day."

"I think there's probably a bit more to this than telling somebody to switch it off and on again."

"No, look." Nigel pulled up the quiz details on his screen. "This is the entry question, $E=Mc^2$ over Pi sees the solution of 7. I've already worked that out."

He pushed an A4 pad to Stuart. "See? We just need a couple more to form a team."

Stuart studied the scribbles on the pad. "That's very clever," he said. "How did you work that out?"

"It's easy. If you think about it, you just have to... Never mind, I'll explain later. Right now, we need a team to enter this before it closes."

"How about Chloe and Gerry, over in Networking? They're both members of IAN, the International Alliance of Nerds. And they do pub quizzes. I also happen to know that they're both into The Falconer movies."

"Perfect. What shall we call ourselves?"

"How about The Alter Egos?"

TEAM FARMHOUSE FIVE

We'd arranged to meet in the Courtyard Tea Room down by the harbour at ten. I arrived four minutes early, having corrected for Alexa Time, to find Eddie and Janet already there.

"No Robyn?" I asked.

"No, not yet," said Eddie. "Don't expect she'll come, is my guess. I think she's bottled out."

"We'll give her ten minutes," I said. "What about Dylan? Anybody seen him?"

"Nope, but I'm not convinced he knows what day of the week it is at the best of times."

I went over to the counter to order a cup of tea and some toast.

"Bit early for you, isn't it?" greeted Tilly, from behind the counter. "Going out fishing?"

"I don't fish. I spent my whole working life trying to catch slippery little creatures, I've no plans on spending my retirement doing the same." I turned my attention to the television high on the wall at the end of the room. The volume was on mute, but it looked like some sort of chaos going on at the Porth Cullen Boat Show.

Tilly noticed me watching it, her eyes bright with amusement. "That's all a bit of a to-do, I'll be sure."

"What's happened?" I saw several police cars and yellow tape strung between lamp posts.

"Somebody's been out drilling holes in them posh boats. One of them's gone to the bottom already. That Green Ninja fella is what they say. Good on 'im is what I say. Butter or marge?"

"Huh?"

"On your toast, dear, butter or marge?"

"Oh, butter, thanks."

I took my tea and toast back to the table just as Dylan arrived.

"Soz," he said. "Had an interview for a job."

"That's great news. Well done, you," said Janet. "What sort of job?"

"I'm going to be a chef."

"Well, good luck. I hope you get it."

"Oh, I've already got it. They told me. I start tomorrow."

"Well done, mate," said Eddie. "Which restaurant?"

"Krappi Burger. Out on the A30."

"Cooking burgers?"

"Yeah. No. Well, not yet. Just doing the fries to start with. Not actually cooking them, putting them in the cardboard funnel things. But when I graduate that, I move up to frying." He looked around the group. "Where's Robyn?"

"We don't know," I said. "I don't think she's coming."

"We can't do the chase if she doesn't come." Dylan's eyes flitted in a way I'd come to recognise as a sign of stress. "It says so in the rules. It says all team members must register their phones at each place. It's in the rules. A team member can't leave or the whole team is out. I need toast." He headed over to the counter.

"Eddie, you've had a good look at the rules. Any ideas?"

"Yeah, actually, I've got a plan. Dylan's got her phone number, and I've got a mate who can clone phones. All he needs is the number and—"

"Cloning phones is illegal, Eddie," I interrupted. "I can't be involved in anything illegal. It sort of goes with the job."

"Course it's not illegal. Besides, you're out now. Look, you get a new phone, you clone the new one to the old one, see? Everybody does it all the time. It's only actually illegal if you're doing it for nefarious reasons. And this ain't nefarious, it's for the good of the dogs, and cats, or whatever. That's the opposite of nefarious, it's anti-nefarious. It's not like we're trying to get at her bank, is it?"

"I'm not convinced."

"You worry too much." He emptied a sugar packet into his tea and attacked it with a spoon. "So, I've got one or two Poncy phones lying around, latest models with—"

"You've got Ponzi phones just lying around?"

"No, not Ponzi, these are Poncys. Same thing, probably made in the same factory, but just cheaper. Cutting out the middleman. I can do you deal on one, if you like?"

"No. Leave me out of this. I should be arresting you, not working out how to hack somebody's phone with a dodgy knock-off."

"You're not thinking of the poor dogs, are you? All gonna be chucked out on the street. Not to mention the seven million quid."

"I'm thinking of not losing my pension before it even starts. There must be another way."

Dylan returned with his toast. He carefully opened the little pat of butter and cut it into two halves with the precision of a gem cutter, and set each half in the dead centre of each piece of toast.

"In North by Northwest," started Janet, "the CIA set up a false character to fool the foreign spies. Only poor Roger Thornhill gets mistaken for… oh no, that won't work, they didn't have mobile phones in those days."

"Okay, moving on, does anybody have any ideas that don't involve secret agents or dodgy phones?"

As no more ideas seemed to be forthcoming, I was about to suggest abandoning the whole project when the door opened, and Robyn walked in.

"Um…" She paused just inside the door, as if unsure whether to continue in or not. "Sorry, everybody. I've had a bit of a think, and maybe this might do me some good." She watched us for reaction, but when all she saw was a collection of confused faces, she continued, "I remembered about the clues leading to locations all over the southwest. And, I thought… perhaps getting out and about a bit might be just the escape I need… and… well, if you're still up for it… I'd like to join you."

The stunned silence broke with Eddie pulling out a chair, and saying, "Good timing, you've just saved Matt having to sacrifice his conscience. And his pension."

Robyn smiled. It was a slightly odd look on her face, but I couldn't work out why. She settled into the seat. "What happens now? Do we know where we're going?"

"We were just about to go over the logistics and formulate a plan," I said.

"We were?" queried Eddie.

"We have to have a plan. If we're going to beat 2,000 other teams, we have to have a plan."

"1,999," said Dylan, carefully smoothing a layer of butter over his toast.

"What?"

"You said we had to beat 2,000 teams, but it's only 1,999, because we're one of the 2,000, and we don't have to beat ourselves."

"Thank you, Dylan," I said. "Of course you're right. 1,999."

"But we don't know where we're going yet," said Eddie. "How can we make a plan if we don't know where we're going?"

"I meant conceptually, at this point. Things like, do we use main roads or minor roads when we're going to a location. Do we use counter-surveillance techniques to avoid being followed, and do—"

"Counter-surveillance?" interrupted Eddie. "What do you think we're doing? Breaking into the Kremlin?"

"No, Matt's right," said Robyn. "2,000… 1,999 teams, some of them will be looking to cheat, you know, following other teams to locations. We have to think about that. We don't yet know how the clues are given out."

"I've got it here," said Dylan, holding up his phone. "They sent me the details." He squinted at his screen. "For each round, teams are given different clues. All clues have a time allocated, and each team is measured against that. Of those who solve the clue, only the quickest fifty percent to login to each location go through to the next round."

"A bit like golf," said Janet. "Like par ratings on a green, with birdies and eagles."

"I didn't know you played golf, Janet?" I asked.

"Oh, I don't. I just like watching it on the telly. I love the outfits."

"Makes sense," I said. "Can't have 2,000 teams all trying to get to the same place at the same time."

"Our first step is to minimise the travelling time as much as possible," said Robyn. "We don't want to be at the wrong end of Wessex when the clue arrives. That would double our travelling time."

"So we need to know where the central point is and start from there?" I asked. "Is that what you're saying?"

"Yes, but the problem is, in order to identify the central point, we need to know the perimeter. And we don't."

"It's the centre of Wessex, though, isn't it?"

"Yes, but Wessex doesn't exist anymore. And when it did, it constantly changed in area as various kings took, or lost, territory. Wessex, *when*, is the question."

"I don't see how we can find the central point of an area which doesn't exist, and which, if it did exist, keeps changing its shape."

"I can write a little programme to do that." Robyn pulled out a notepad and scribbled some quick notes. "It's fairly basic data analysis. I do that stuff all the time. I can calculate a mean external border, then work out the central point of the area from there."

"Sorry, I'm lost," said Eddie. "How does that actually help?"

"Because that gives us the place which means the shortest travelling distance to any possible location," I said, turning to Robyn. "That's right, isn't it?"

"Pretty much."

"You don't fancy writing one of your programmes to work out how a Swedish pergola goes together, do you?"

"Sorry, that's beyond modern computing." A flash of something resembling a genuine smile passed across her face. "I fear you might have to wait until quantum computers come along."

"When do we start?" asked Janet, dabbing crumpet-butter from her lips with a paper napkin. "I mean, when do we get our first clue? It's all so exciting."

I looked at Dylan and he fiddled with his phone. "Ah yes, I was supposed to connect you all to the app. Hang on…" he tapped at his screen. "Just a sec…" More tapping. "That should… no, wait a mo…" Confused staring at screen. "Oh, I see, I forgot… Here we go…"

My phone pinged, as did everybody else's. My screen requested I click 'YES' to join the Farmhouse Five's Great Wessex Chase team room. I clicked yes.

'Welcome to The Great Wessex Chase. Your first clue will be issued in 143 hours, 21 minutes, 49 seconds. Good Luck.'

"143 hours," I said. "That's… um… anybody got a calculator?"

"You'll have one on your phone, you dinosaur," Eddie said.

"Five days, twenty-three hours," Dylan said.

"That'll make it…" I counted on my fingers, "Wednesday, Thursday—"

"Next Monday at ten o'clock." Dylan interrupted my calculations.

"Right, okay." I put my fingers away. "That gives us some time to prepare."

"Prepare what?" asked Eddie. "Grab a bag and stick it in the back of your car. What's to prepare? It's not like we're off to the Costa Brava, and we're not gonna be needing posh togs or nothing."

"Good preparation can improve our odds. We have some information, and we can make some deductions. We know that we are going to be looking for locations across what was Wessex. We know the clues are going to be difficult, because that's the basis of a quiz. Therefore, the clues are probably going to be fairly cryptic, and likely to be hinting at obscure details of the location."

"Now you're beginning to sound like Sherlock Holmes. You missing being a detective by any chance?" Eddie asked with a grin.

"I've only been out a couple of weeks. I haven't had time to miss it yet. It's just that this is basic planning." I looked at Eddie, he seemed unconvinced. "Odds, like betting. The more you know about the horse, the better your chances of picking a winner."

"Ah, now I get you. But how do we shorten the odds on a horse we don't even know is running?"

"Think about this, the locations are likely to be reasonably well known, but they're not going to give away anything obvious. Like, if say one of the places is Stonehenge, they're not going to just say, a big circle of stones in Wiltshire, are they? Too obvious. It'll be more like, where the druids built a temple to the sun god. Or something."

"Only it wasn't the druids," said Robyn. "Nobody actually knows, but probably Mesolithic hunter-gatherers."

"Really? I always thought… never mind. But you get my point? And like Robyn says, about the Mesolithic gatherers, that's the sort of stuff that will be in the clues. I suggest we all spend the next few days reading up on any interesting places we can think of, and make notes of any relevant bits like that. The more of that stuff we have, the more likely we'll be able to figure out the answers, and faster."

"Jolly good idea," said Janet. "I love reading about interesting places. I once read a book about the house where John Lennon lived. Did you know they leave a light on all night in his old bedroom on his birthday every year?"

"Yes. Well, that's the sort of thing we need, only about places in Wessex."

"Oh, none of the Beatles lived in Wessex. Although John did buy his aunty a house near Bournemouth."

CHAPTER FOUR

TEAM FARMHOUSE FIVE

THE NEXT COUPLE OF DAYS I spent poring over library books and websites of all things Wessex. I learned that 'honest gene' is an anagram of Stonehenge, that there is actually a Merlin's Cave underneath Tintagel Castle, that Silbury Hill is the largest artificial prehistoric mound in Europe, and that a new species of Ichthyosaur was discovered in Lyme Regis. All of which went into my notebook. Forty years of police conditioning had ingrained into me the efficacy of handwritten notes in a little book, rather than trusting to electronic clouds.

We'd arranged to meet again on Friday morning in the Courtyard Tea Room. I arrived at ten o'clock exactly to find Janet the only one there.

"You alright for tea?" I asked. "Or do you need a refill?"

"I'm good for tea, but could you see if Tilly's got her flapjacks out of the oven yet?"

By the time I'd come back to the table with coffee and flapjacks, Robyn and Eddie had arrived.

"Anybody seen Dylan?" asked Eddie.

"He might be at work," said Janet. "Where was his new job? Oh, that's it, Krappi Burger."

"Krappi Burger," muttered Robyn. "Planet rapists. Did you know it takes sixty-five square feet of land and fifteen gallons of water just to make one burger?"

"No, I didn't," I admitted. "It's a good pub quiz answer though, but probably not much use to this project."

"You never know what's going to come in useful."

The door swung open, and Dylan came in. "Soz, I had an interview for a job." He settled at the table and scanned us all, as if weighing up if we were going to jump on him.

"I thought you already had a new job?" I asked. "What happened?"

"They said I was too slow."

"Filling cardboard cones with fries?"

"Yeah, well, they weren't even." He shuffled in his seat and looked at the table.

"Even? What do you mean, even?"

"They told me to put one scoop in each, but that wasn't always the same. Sometimes it was fifty, sometimes fifty-one. Even sixty-three once. But that was only once."

"You were counting the fries?"

"It wasn't fair, they're supposed to be equal. So I counted some, then it was an average of fifty-four. But I don't like fifty-four, I like fifty-five, that's a better number. It's a triangular number, so it works better putting fries into a cone."

"I can see how that might have slowed things down a bit. But, ever onwards, how did you get on in your interview?"

"Oh, I didn't get that job. He had a bit of a crab when I took his stapler to bits. Though, the good news, he said I could keep it." Dylan dropped a plastic carrier bag on the table. It clinked with the sound that only a dismantled stapler can make. "If you want anything stapling... when I've worked out how it goes back together, that is."

"I see. Well. I suppose the upside is that it makes it easier for you to be part of the team." I looked to the others. "How did we do on gathering key bits of information about locations?"

After a quick exchange of information, it seemed we'd accumulated a good number of potential locations. Although, we also realised the area contained thousands of possibilities. Robyn had calculated that the National Trust and English Heritage alone accounted for about a thousand sites in the area. Add to that, the thousands of private attractions like Eden, Land's End and so on, along with probably another few thousand geographic points, and the chances of any of our chosen ones being used were slim in the extreme.

"I've come up with a good central start-point for us," said Robyn. "I put in the changes in the Wessex borders over the years. They moved a lot, but I came up with a mean average, then found a central point from that." She took a map from her bag and spread it over the table. "Here." She pointed to an area just north of Tiverton. "That's the geographic centre of what was Wessex for the most significant periods. However…" She waved a finger over the eastern end of the map. "This area has no good motorway links between key points. Major A-roads, but slower to travel. Because of that, I used driving times, rather than miles, and that pushes the time-to-travel central point further east, to here…" She tapped a pen on Glastonbury. "That's the point with the best equidistant driving time to all possible locations."

"Glastonbury." I leaned over the map. "I was drafted there a few times to cover the festival. Nice town, shame about the hippies. And the mud."

"Ooh, we could hunt for King Arthur," said Janet. "He's supposed to be buried there."

"I don't think we'll have time for that," I said. "Remember, once we start, we're against the clock. We have to keep focussed."

"Oh, yes, of course. Focussed. I had an aunt who used to say that to me. Janet, she'd say, you need to focus. Unless you focus, you'll never… never… oh dear, I've forgotten what she said now, but she always said it. She wasn't a real aunty, of course. Just one of those pretend aunts. Come to think of it, I think she had a house near Glastonbury somewhere. I wonder if it's still there? We could go and have a look while we're there."

"I could do with dropping by Street to pick up some stock," said Eddie. "I heard the Chakrabarti brothers have just copped a container load of Prada leather jackets. Good price too, so they won't hang about."

"You're not filling my car up with your dodgy clobber," I said. "It's an ex-police car, not a white van. It's not right."

"Can we just concentrate on how we get to these clues quickly?" Robyn said. "I'm sure we can make time for visiting aunts, King Arthur, or shopping, once we've finished all this."

"Good point," I said with a sharp nod. "Let's drive up there Sunday afternoon. That will give us time to get settled and make sure we're ready for the off on Monday."

"I'd better go and sort out my packing." Janet stood, positioned her hat and gathered her handbag. "It always takes me ages. One never knows how the weather's going to turn." She started for the door, then stopped and turned. "Will we be dressing for dinner?"

"I hope so," said Eddie. "I don't fancy sitting opposite Matt in his birthday suit. Put me right off my steak and chips, that will."

I ignored Eddie, and turned to Janet. "I don't think you need to worry. Just keep it warm and comfortable."

***

We met on Sunday at the gravel car park at the top of the village. I'd spent the last two days checking the car over and removing the clutter everyone accumulates in a car over time. Several bottles of water, two jackets I'd forgotten I had, a box of old books I kept meaning to drop into the charity shop, and a steering lock I'd carried in every car I'd owned for the last fifteen years, and which had never fitted any of them.

Once cleared, I vacuumed inside and hosed off the outside. I stood back to admire my hard work. Not bad. One of the perks of 'The Job' was the option of buying ex-police cars at a discount when they'd reached the end of their service life. This one, a white BMW X5, had been a particularly good deal. Far too many miles on the clock, and noticeable marks and holes where police equipment had been removed, but still a bargain, and certainly not something I'd have been able to afford normally.

The others arrived on time and the X5 ate up their luggage with ease. By midday, we were on the A30, heading for Glastonbury.

By twelve-fifteen, we were parked in the Moto Chef car park just outside Whitecross, as Dylan took photographs for his collection of Moto Chef restaurants. By the time we reached the motorway at Exeter, we'd knocked up twelve such stops. I'd had no idea they were such ubiquitous entities.

Just after four, we passed a sign welcoming us to Glastonbury, ancient Isle of Avalon. Somebody had added underneath, 'Twinned with Narnia'.

Robyn scanned her phone for a suitable place to stay. "There's a Premier Inn just outside the town, walking distance to the centre," she said.

In the absence of dissenters, or alternatives, I followed Robyn's instructions and we pulled into the car park. After a torturous circuit of the overfilled car park, I gave up and found a rough pull-in on the side of the main road.

"We'll leave the bags in the car until we've checked in," I suggested.

As we climbed out of the car, Dylan handed me the ashtray from the rear passenger door. I studied it for a moment in wonder at how he'd managed to do that without any tools, then slipped it in my pocket.

The reception area boasted an ultra-modern check-in desk, flanked incongruously by a huge mural of the ancient abbey. The whole area thronged with people, and it took twenty minutes to reach the desk.

"Sorry to keep you waiting," said the receptionist. "How can I help you?"

"Five single rooms, please."

"Oh, I'm so sorry, we're fully booked for the whole week," she said.

I glanced around the foyer. Groups of people gathered and chatted with each other, cases and bags littered everywhere. We headed outside to see all the outside seating areas full, and a quick glance through the door to the bar and restaurant told a similar story.

"What's going on?" asked Janet.

"It's totally full." I scanned the building in front of me. "I'd say there's at least fifty rooms here and it's choc-a-bloc."

"Oh dear. Is it the pop festival?"

"No, that was a couple of months ago. I have a horrible feeling this is the competition."

"Looks like everybody else had the same idea," said Eddie.

"I should have thought of this," said Robyn. "The people who would have got through that entry clue are all going to be problem solvers. It seems like we all came up with the same answer."

"This is going to be a lot tougher than we thought," I said.

"What do we do now?" asked Janet. "Should we go home?"

"No, we just need to go further out. There must be somewhere else."

"Don't count on it," said Robyn. She held her phone and stared at the screen. "I've just been through several hotel booking sites, and they're all coming back the same. Everywhere close to the central point is full."

CHAPTER FIVE

FOR THE NEXT COUPLE OF hours, we slowly expanded our area of search, driving the roads and narrow lanes of Somerset. Each time we spotted a hotel or B&B which hadn't turned up in Robyn's search, we stopped and asked. The story repeated over and over, everywhere was full.

"I can't believe everybody had the same idea," I moaned, as we pulled back onto the road after yet another failed stop.

"They won't all have," said Robyn. "These will just be the ones who thought it through the way I did. I expect there are quite a few more in other places who've worked on a different logic."

"Maybe we should forget it," said Eddie. "What chance do we stand? We can't even win our pub quiz of a dozen teams."

"We're not giving up," I said. "We can't go back and watch those dogs being turned out without knowing we'd done our best."

"And cats," added Janet. "Don't forget the cats."

As evening shadows began to darken the ever-narrowing lanes, we passed a sign informing us we were entering somewhere called Trembly.

"Where's this?" I asked Robyn.

"I don't really know. It doesn't seem to be on satnav."

A small pub came into view as we rounded an overgrown bend in the road.

I pulled into the little gravelled car park alongside. A sign hanging above an oak door announced the place to be The Camelot. Not entirely original, given the area, but at least it looked quiet.

"You all stay here," I said. "I'll go check."

"Evening, squire," a man behind the bar greeted. "What can I get you?"

I glanced at a pump on the bar labelled Old Grumbler. I gave a quick look to the door, then, "I'll have a very quick one of those."

"Good choice, locally brewed with water fresh from the Chalice Well."

He pushed the frothing glass towards me, and I forced myself to take it gently, resisting the urge to snatch it. I drank deep, breathed, and instantly felt the stress of the last six hours washing away. "I don't suppose you've got any rooms, have you?"

"Funny you should mention that, I've just had a wedding party cancel. The bride and groom saw each other the night before the wedding. That's unlucky, you know."

"So I believe, but I wouldn't have thought it was serious enough to cancel the wedding."

"It is when the bride saw the groom in bed with her best mate and chief bridesmaid." He paused for a moment as if replaying events in his head, then added, "And they were two different people."

"Fantastic. Well, not so much for the wedding party, but fantastic for me. How many rooms do you have?"

"Three."

I pondered for a moment. Five into three didn't work. But then, it was all we were going to get. "I'll take them." I extended my hand, and we shook. "I'm Matt."

"Everybody calls me Arthur, on account of this being The Camelot, an' all. Albert really, but the tourists love it. Especially the Yanks."

"Pleasure to meet you, Arthur." I sank the last of the beer and headed out to tell the others the good news.

"We'll have to draw straws for who gets the single room," said Robyn. "It's the only fair way."

"We can't do that," said Dylan. "It's simple logic. If one of the girls draws a straw to have a single room, then the other girl must also have a single room. They can't share with a man. That would mean three men in one room."

"I'm not sharing with anybody," Eddie said. "I don't even share a room with my wife, so I ain't about to play cuddles with you two." He looked at me and Dylan.

Reluctantly, that left only one possibility. "Okay, so Janet and Robyn share, and I'll share with Dylan." I fixed Dylan's eyes. "And you, keep your hands off my stuff. I have no desire to spend my time trying to reassemble my laptop."

Arthur showed us to our rooms, ours being a compact, but modern and clean, loft conversion high up under the eaves. We sort-of unpacked, changed, and headed down to the bar.

"We're having one of our special Theme Nights," Arthur greeted as I approached the bar. "It's Indian Night tonight. Not Red Indians, of course. I thought about that, but my cook, Wojciech, doesn't know any Red Indian food."

"I'm not sure we're supposed to say—"

"All you ever see in the cowboy movies is a deer on a pole over a campfire. Well, I can't do that, I'd have the Health and Safety people round here faster than an MP at a free bar. So, the other Indian it is." He pointed to a chalk board behind the bar.

I scanned the menu. Steak and kidney vindaloo with pasta, Sausage Biryani, Tandoori pork chops, and the vegetarian option, Toffee Tikka.

"Is that supposed to be tofu?" I asked.

"Oh, you spotted that then? I sent Wojciech out for some tofu, but he came back with toffee. I was hoping nobody would notice and think it was a Kashmiri delicacy."

"I'll check with the others."

"Tell them we've got complimentary poppadoms with each meal. Well, not real poppadoms, I couldn't get those, but I'm opening a few packets of Pringles."

"I'll be sure to pass that on."

I ordered the drinks, then searched out the others at a table near the window.

I planted the drinks down. "We might want to think about eating somewhere else tonight."

"Why's that?" Eddie asked, grabbing his pint like a man just rescued from the desert. "I had a gander at the menu, looks good to me. Quite fancy the Sausage Biryani. Not too sure about the toffee whatsit though? Is that a spelling mistake?"

"Unfortunately, no."

The snack menu proved a little more normal, Lancelot's Baguette, a Holy Grail Burger, Merlin's Pizza, a Round Bagel, something called Guinevere's Secret, and a Fairy's Dingle, which turned out to be a vegan hotdog.

I toyed with asking about Guinevere's Secret but decided that whatever it was, it would probably be best kept a secret. Some things we just shouldn't know.

Arthur approached the table a few minutes later. "What can I get you, folks?"

I ordered a Lancelot's Baguette, as did Janet. Robyn went for a Fairy's Dingle, Dylan wanted to know if the anchovies on Merlin's Pizza would all be the same size, and Eddie had yet to decide.

"What's Guinevere's Secret then?" he asked.

I cringed, dreading the answer.

"It's a cheese and apple toastie," Arthur said.

"Apples in a cheese toastie?"

"It's the secret name of Glastonbury, the Isle of Apples, and we're right near Cheddar, see?" Arthur tapped the side of his nose. "Home of the cheese. Can't get much more traditional than apples and cheese. Goes back to Charles the Second's time, when he was down here hidin' away from the plague."

"Okay, sounds perfect. I'll have one of them, but swap the apples for a bit of bacon, will you?"

"But then it wouldn't be Guinevere's secret," Arthur protested. "Not without the apples."

"I know, but that'll be *our* secret."

After supper, I suggested an early night to prepare for what was to come tomorrow. It was met with a mixed response. Eddie said he needed to 'de-stress' before bed. His code for putting away a few whiskies. Janet agreed an early night was a good idea, and anyway, she had the latest Cormoran Strike novel to finish. Robyn said she needed to go out for a walk to iron out the knots of the long drive, and Dylan said he had to go and see a hole he'd spotted on the way in.

"A hole?" I queried.

"I like holes. They're all different, and they have different stuff in them. Some have cables or pipes, and some have roots and things. I don't like those ones. They look like they're alive."

"Where is this hole?"

"In the road, on the way here. Near the house with the wrong colour door."

"Oh yes, I remember. Some roadworks, wasn't it?" I thought it best not to pursue the idea of the house with the wrong colour door. "It'll be dark soon though; you won't be able to see anything."

"I've got a torch you can borrow," said Eddie. "It's a special tactical torch. They're all the thing with the SAS boys."

"What on earth's a tactical torch?" I asked.

"It's got fifteen settings, all the way up to 100,000 lumens. Have you any idea what 100,000 lumens looks like?"

"Not really. I'm still working in watts. How many 100-watt light bulbs make 100,000 lumens then?"

"Well, it's… I don't know. Ten."

"Ten 100-watt light bulbs? That'd be bright."

"It would be sixty-six point six," said Dylan. "Recurring."

"Sixty-six light bulbs?" I pondered. "That's mad. Why tactical, though?"

"Because it's got a strobe setting to disorient the enemy," said Eddie. "Or if you need to scare off a wild animal, and it makes a siren noise and can give an electric shock, like a Taser. I can do you a good deal on one, if you like? Just got a new delivery of them. I was going to knock 'em out to that bunch of preppers over Rose Well Park way. They'll go bananas for these." He reached into his pocket and handed a torch over to Dylan. "You lose it, you've bought it."

Dylan picked it up and pressed a button and suddenly all I could see was white. I screwed my eyelids closed, but still the white filled my head until I managed to press my hands over my face. I sat like that for a moment until I heard noise and sensed movement. The light stopped. I cautiously squinted through my fingers. Eddie had the torch in his hands.

"You wanna go careful with that, son," he said. "You could stand in for the Longships lighthouse with that."

I blinked my eyes and tried to focus on Eddie, but a glowing red blob covered his face. "Why don't you leave the hole till tomorrow?" I suggested. "See it in daylight. Wouldn't that be better?"

"No, there'll be people all over the place." Dylan stood and took the torch from Eddie. "Thanks."

"I want that back in one piece, mind."

I watched Dylan go, then headed upstairs. Shower and an early night. We had no idea what we were in for tomorrow, and I wanted to be ready. Not knowing how much alone-time I was going to get, I dived straight into the shower. Then followed a dance with the thermostat, which travelled through a temperature change of a hundred degrees on the turning of a hair's breadth of movement. Even then, it was prone to jumping from freezing to scalding each time I reached for the soap.

I'd half expected to see Dylan in the room as I exited the shower. Thankfully, the room was still empty, so I towelled myself dry and flopped on the bed with the TV remote for company.

I caught up on the news and had just settled into a repeat of Silent Witness when I heard the key in the door. I quickly pulled on some tracksuit bottoms.

"It's a four-footer," Dylan announced as he entered the room.

"What is?"

"The hole. It's a four-footer with straight sides. Probably made with a Bobcat digger. They're best for four-footers."

"I'll remember that."

"They had the lights in the wrong place though."

"The lights?"

"Yes, they'd put little orange flashing lights around the hole, but they were in the wrong place, they didn't line up with the street lights."

"I see." I didn't, but I figured I didn't need the conversation.

Dylan busied himself with getting ready for bed while I read a few pages from Tinker, Tailor, Soldier, Spy. A book I'd always promised myself I would read when I retired and had time.

Dylan settled in bed, and I put the light out. I pondered for a moment about Dylan and his odd ideas. A hole. I wondered how he found a fascination with something as prosaic as a hole. Something most of us would simply ignore. And the lights? Why were they in the wrong place? A thought niggled. "Dylan," I said into the dark. "Those lights…"

All was silent. I pushed the thought away. Just copper's paranoia, I told myself as I slid into a dark and dreamless sleep.

CHAPTER SIX

WE ALL ARRIVED DOWNSTAIRS FOR breakfast early, and with a sense of nervous anticipation. Arthur presented us with the breakfast menu, which consisted of the usual fare of sausages, eggs, bacon, etcetera, in multiple permutations.

Robyn asked if there were any vegan alternatives, and Arthur said, "I can do you a couple of boiled eggs and hot buttered toast."

Robyn settled for some hash browns and beans.

We made conversational trivia as we ate, while each of us kept an eye on the clock on the wall. We knew the competition was due to start at ten, but we had no idea how this was going to work. I never did well with uncertainty. In the Job, we always tried to eliminate as much uncertainty as we could. It was never possible to eliminate it all, of course, and some people positively thrived on the adrenaline rush of the unknown. Not me, I'd rather know if the flat we were about to raid, or the car we were going to pull over, contained a bunch of drunken lads out for a good time, or a crew of tooled-up drug dealers.

Dylan's phone buzzed with the announcement of an incoming message.

We all froze, me with half a sausage on a fork en-route to my mouth.

Nobody moved. Dylan just squinted at his phone without touching it.

"Well?" I said, after what seemed an hour, but was probably three seconds.

Dylan picked up his phone as though it was about to explode if he touched it. "It says, welcome to The Great Wessex Chase. Your timer for the first stage has already started—"

"How can they do that?" Janet interrupted. "We haven't had the clue yet. They can't start the timer till we've had our clue. It's not fair."

"Shush." I flapped my hand. "Let him read the message. Go on, Dylan."

Dylan continued, "Please each upload to the apps on your phones, a selfie of yourself and a group picture on the same background."

"I don't understand," complained Eddie. "What's all this about? Where's the clue?"

"This is a check to make sure we're all together," Robyn said.

"Why wouldn't we be?" asked Eddie.

"Because some teams may have thought it a good idea to split up all over the southwest so only the nearest person goes to the clue location. Fraction of the travel time."

"Oh, good job we didn't think of that."

"I did. But I also thought it too obvious a cheat, and that they'd have a way to counter it."

"They'll also be logging phones to faces," I said. "Come on, we need to do this quickly. The clock's ticking."

We each took selfies against the fireplace behind us. Although, I had to take Janet's for her as she had a minor panic and took several pictures of her feet, and one of her ear when the phone rang halfway through the process.

"I'm not very good with these things," she admitted. "But I do like the texty bit. My sister sends me pictures of her niece and dogs. I've got one here with—"

I held my hand gently over her phone. "Maybe later, Janet. Let's deal with this first."

"Oh good idea. You're always so organised."

We posed for the group selfie and uploaded it to our respective apps. Immediately, each phone received a message, *"Thank you, Team Farmhouse Five. Please ensure the full team is present at each solved location. Your timer will only stop when all members have logged in. Your first clue follows this message."*

We all stared at our screens.

"Ooh, this is so exciting," said Janet.

My phone pinged with the announcement of an arriving message. As did everybody else's. I drew a breath and opened the message.

"Good morning, Team Farmhouse Five. Here is clue one: - Did the King of the Tyrant Lizards get stuck in the hole by eating too much cheese? - Your team will be eliminated if the login has not been completed by midday, or you finish below the median. Good Luck."

An elongated silence was broken first by Eddie. "What the hell does that mean?"

"Let's get going," said Dylan.

"To where?" I asked. "We don't know where this is. It could be anywhere. And what's this median thing?"

"It's like an average, but not an average," said Dylan.

"Oh good, I'm glad you've cleared that up for us," said Eddie, adding an eye roll.

"The average of the numbers one, two, and five would be four," said Robyn, "But the median is the middle value, which would be two. So what they're saying is that if our time is greater than the middle time, we're out."

"We've got to be over the middle then?" said Eddie.

"Under."

"Why didn't they just say that?"

"I think they did."

I studied the clue again on my app. It still didn't make any sense. My eye caught a number at the top of the app. It seemed to be falling. Current Teams 1,623. The number dropped again, 1,617.

"Hey, what's happening here?" I asked, pointing to the falling number.

We all studied our apps for a moment, then Robyn said, "I think that's teams dropping out of the competition. I'm guessing a huge number didn't pass the entry check. Not all team members were present at the same place, wrong phones with the wrong face. Maybe some people entered but couldn't get a team together. Who knows."

The number seemed to settle at 1,598.

"That's nearly a quarter of the teams gone," I said.

"Well, that's just improved our odds." Eddie wrapped a sausage in a piece of buttered bread.

"It also shows how careful we have to be." I cast my eyes round our team. "Now, does anybody have any idea what this clue means?"

After five minutes of shrugs and blank looks, Robyn said, "I suggest we get busy on the internet. Cheese loving tyrant lizards can't be too difficult to find."

"Is that allowed?" Janet asked.

"Yes, it's fine," I said. "The rules clearly allow internet searches." I opened my laptop and searched for cheese eating tyrant lizards. At once, my screen presented me with a page of images that would probably stay with me long after this project was forgotten.

As I tried to engage some sort of filter to eliminate the most obnoxious of the results, I heard Janet say, "Well I never. I wonder how they got it to do that?"

I glanced over at her. She pushed her glasses lower over her nose and squinted at her phone.

"You probably shouldn't look too closely at that," I suggested. "You might never feel the same way about Dairylea cheese again."

"I've found a cheese influencer called The Tyrant Lizard," said Eddie.

"What's a cheese influencer?" I asked.

"I was hoping you'd tell *me*."

"Influencers are basically advertising prostitutes," said Robyn. "They make little videos promoting shit products for whoever pays them the most money."

"But cheese?" I queried.

Robyn shrugged. "They'll push anything if the price is right."

"A tyrant lizard is a tyrannosaurus," said Dylan, without looking up from his phone.

"Tyrannosaurus, of course," I said. "Well done. And king... that's Rex, isn't it? Tyrannosaurus Rex. That's it, we've solved it."

"Solved what?" asked Eddie. "They've been extinct for hundreds of years. Where're we gonna find one of them?"

"They've got one in the Natural History Museum," said Janet. "We had a day trip there with the Marc Bolan Fan Club back in the 70s."

"Marc Bolan Fan Club?" Eddie stared at Janet as if seeing her for the first time.

"Bit of a mix-up over tickets to see T Rex."

"Still not helping much, though. Kensington's hardly Wessex, is it?"

"Well, I don't know. I was only a teenager back then, and I was never very good at geography."

"What about Lyme Regis, or around there somewhere?" Robyn said. "It's known as the Jurassic coast."

"Look it up," I suggested. "I'm going to see if I can find any reference to cheese and Marc Bolan's T Rex. You never know."

"What about Guinevere's Secret?" Dylan said.

"Revolting idea," I said. "And haven't you just had breakfast?"

"No, I don't want one. It's too muddled up. I don't like any pies, they're too random. Food shouldn't be hidden inside other food, except for Smarties. But that's not really hiding, because you know what's inside each Smartie. They're all the same, apart from the colour. My favourite was the blue Smartie, but they changed them for a different blue. I don't like those so much."

"Cheese eating T Rex, Dylan," I said. "Remember? We're supposed to be working on cheese, or dinosaurs, not Smarties."

"The man in the pub said Guinevere's Secret was a traditional local thing. Home of the cheese, he said."

I paused in thought while replaying last night's conversation with Arthur over the menu. "You're right. Cheddar, of course. That's quite near here, home of the cheese."

"And the T Rex?" asked Eddie.

"I don't know. Maybe they found one round here somewhere. There's lots of caves there."

"According to Wikipedia," Robyn said, staring at her screen, "Tyrannosauruses were only found in North America."

This didn't make any sense. Follow the evidence, I told myself. "What was the clue again?"

Dylan flicked at his phone screen. *"Did the King of the Tyrant Lizards get stuck in the hole by eating too much cheese?"*

"Stuck in a hole," I said. "That could mean a cave. Tyrannosaurus, cave, cheese. Let's just focus on those three things. There may be some in the caves at Cheddar. Hang on, I'll ask Arthur, he'll probably know."

I took my empty breakfast plate up to the bar where Arthur was busy hanging glasses in the rack above his head.

"Thank you, that was delicious," I said.

"Local made sausages and bacon," he said. "Fresh from Putner's Farm over Wookey Hole way."

"Wookey Hole? Is that where they make the cheese?"

"Best cheese in the world. Handmade and matured two hundred feet down in the caves."

I froze as my mental memory book flicked through its pages. "You don't happen to know if they've ever found any dinosaurs or such-like over there, do you?"

"Don't know nothing about dinosaurs, but they've found bones of all sorts down there."

"Thanks, you've been a great help." I headed back to the others with my news.

"Right," I said, sitting down at the table. "We're off to Wookey Hole caves. It's famous for its cheese, Arthur says all sorts of bones have been discovered down there. He doesn't know about dinosaurs though, but it's a hole."

"It's a hole hole hole," Robyn offered.

"What's that?" asked Eddie. "A bad impersonation of Father Christmas?"

"No, Wookey Hole Caves," she read from her laptop screen. "It's a hole hole hole. Wookey is an old Celtic name for a hole, and cave means hole, so it's Hole Hole Hole."

"I knew that," said Dylan. "My grandad told me that when I used to stay with him."

"And where did he live?" I asked.

"Wookey Hole village, in a barge on the river Axe."

"You didn't think to mention this before?"

"Nobody asked. He also told me that Burrow Mump Hill means hill hill hill and River Avon means river river, and—"

"Can you stop him now?" interrupted Eddie, looking at me. "He's doin' my head in."

"Right," I said, in my best policeman's no-more-nonsense voice, "we're off to Wookey Hole. All at the car in ten minutes."

To my surprise, we were all at the car in ten minutes. Another minute, and we were out onto the main Glastonbury road. All went well for two hundred metres, when we came upon a hole in the road. Half in the hole, and at an interesting angle, sat a police car. A little piece of blue police tape fluttered between the rear screen wiper and a nearby lamppost. Neatly arranged along the edge of the pavement, stood a regimented line of seven orange warning lamps.

I glanced in my rear-view mirror and caught Dylan's eye. His face twitched as he noticed me watching him.

"Dylan…" I started.

"Pi is equal to 3.14159265358979—"

"Never mind," I said, stemming the flow of numbers.

I felt a pang of guilt as we drove away. I should really contact the local police and let them know how this had happened. But that would mean losing time, and therefore, probably the whole race. Besides, roadworks lights, or no roadworks lights, a competent police driver should never do that. My mind then drifted briefly to my first day at the Exeter Police Driving Centre when I'd managed to spin the training vehicle through 360 degrees and into the side of the Portakabin office. Apparently, they still had the photos of that on the wall in the centre.

"That's a new one," said Eddie, as we drove slowly past the hole. "That's gonna cost him his no claims bonus."

The drive to Wookey Hole took us just under half an hour. We parked up and headed for the ticket kiosk. The girl behind the window was very pleasant, but she was unable to conceal her puzzlement at five adults visiting together, and with no children. I paid for a group pass, and we made our way up the path, following the signs for the caves.

As we hurried along, Dylan slid alongside me and said, "What time are we getting back to Little Didney?"

"Little Didney? Depends, we might not be going back there until this is finished. Or we get knocked out. Why?"

He stopped walking and started plucking leaves from an overhanging branch. "I need to go to the police station," he said, carefully flattening the leaves in his hand rather than making eye contact with me.

"What's wrong?"

"I have to report in. I'm on bail. That means I'm waiting for a court—"

"I know what bail means, Dylan. Why are you on bail?"

"It's just a mistake. It's all about Mr Goodenough's cash register. It made a funny noise each time he opened it and I wanted to know why." He plucked three more leaves from the branch and aligned them with the rest.

"Ah, so that's when you took it to bits."

"He said I was stealing, and I wasn't."

"I see, but we can't go back to Little Didney. We don't have time. Come on," I started walking and waved a hand to indicate he should follow. "We need to find this dinosaur first then we'll have a think about your bail reporting."

"But…"

"Leave it with me, I'm sure I can sort something out. I'll have a chat with the local police later. For now, let's see if we can find our T-Rex somewhere in these caves and save our dogs' home."

I ushered him to catch up with the others, who were waiting at the cave's entrance.

"What's going on?" asked Robyn. "You only just made it. The tour group's about to go in and the next one's not for an hour."

"I'll tell you later. Where are we going?"

"There's a guide up front," she said, trying to point over the heads of a group of people. "We just follow her."

"Did you ask about a dinosaur?"

"Didn't have a chance. She's busy trying to stop small children crawling into small holes."

I heard the voice of someone I assumed to be the guide coming from the front, but couldn't make out what she was saying. The voice stopped, and the group moved forwards. We followed.

Discreet lights at floor level guided our feet as we headed down to an open cave where everybody stopped, presumably on the instructions of our invisible guide.

I did manage to hear her telling everybody to move forward and spread out a bit, after which we had a better view and hearing.

"This is the Witch of Wookey Hole." The guide aimed her torch at a piece of rock to her left. "It might be difficult to see but…"

"Nobody said anything about witches," said Eddie.

"You're not superstitious, are you, Eddie?" Robyn asked.

"It never does to mess with things like that. We had a woman down our lane who always had crows and magpies in her garden. Talked to them, she did. Dozens of the things, squawking and chattering all the time. There was this one time—"

I touched Eddie's arm, trying to stem the forthcoming story. "Can we leave that for later, Eddie? We need to find the location."

"Hmm," Eddie grunted. "What's a thing like that doing down here anyway?" He pointed to the Witch.

"It's just a rock," Robyn said.

"Focus, Eddie," I said. "Have you seen any sign of anything that looks like a Tyrannosaurus Rex?"

"Fat chance. Can't see nothing here. And she's not helping." He nodded in the general direction of the guide. "She's only interested in scaring the living daylights out of people with her ghost stories."

The guide continued her script. "Glastonbury Abbey sent a young monk, Father Barnard, to deal with..."

"You'd think she'd point it out, wouldn't you? The dinosaur," Eddie said. "I mean, we're down here and there's a soddin' great T-Rex down here with us somewhere. You'd think she'd point it out, instead of wittering on about witches and stuff."

"I think we have a problem," said Robyn, studying her phone. "How are we going to log into the app down here? I can't get a phone signal here, let alone a GPS location."

"That's a good point," I said. "I'm sure they've thought it through."

"... and please, no flash photography down in the caves," continued the guide. "We have some very rare bats here, including the Greater and Lesser Horseshoe bats, which are a protected species, and..."

"Maybe it's just a few bones," said Janet. "I saw an episode of Silent Witness once where they found these bones of a missing man. Only been dead twenty years and half the bones were gone."

"Probably dogs," said Eddie. "My German Shepherd brings home all sorts of bones. I'll swear she had a human thigh bone once."

"I hope you reported it," I said.

"No chance. Do you think I'm some sort of idiot? I'd have had your lot all over me. They'd have loved that, just the excuse they'd want to go through my cupboards."

"I don't think a dog is going to run off with a dinosaur bone," said Robyn.

"... If you'll all follow me, we're going down to the next cave. Please mind your step as..."

"Quick, we've got to find out if the dinosaur is here," I said. "Let's spread out to the walls and see if we can see anything."

"You still got my torch, son?" Eddie asked Dylan.

"Yeah." Dylan rummaged through his pockets. "Hang on."

The group started to drift away from us as they followed the guide.

"Hurry up," I said.

"Got it," Dylan said. "Here it is." He handed it to Eddie.

Immediately, Eddie let out a wild yelp at the same time as I heard a loud buzz. Sparks flashed from Eddie's hand. "You set the Taser," he yelled, dropping the torch to the floor.

The cave was at once filled with violent strobing flashes which bounced off every surface, augmented by the squeals of children. Then another sound joined in with the cacophony, the enveloping sound of bat wings fluttering through the still air of the cave. The strobing light froze individual bats in mid-flight, creating a weird imitation of a 1930s black and white vampire movie.

Parents gathered their squealing children around them as the guide called for everybody to remain calm, trying desperately to reassure everybody that the bats would *not* get tangled in people's hair.

Eddie scrabbled for the torch and finally brought it under control. "Sorry," he called.

Out of nowhere, and with alarming efficiency, two burly security guards appeared and homed in on our group.

"Right, you lot," said the larger of the two very large guards. "Out you go."

"It was just an accident," I said. "He just dropped a torch."

"No torches allowed. It scares the bats. Come on, off with you. Bloody hooligans."

"But we're treasure hunters," said Janet. "We have to find the clue."

"Treasure hunting's not allowed. It's an archaeological site. You can't be treasure hunting in an archaeological site."

"She didn't mean that sort of treasure," I said. "We just have to find a tyrannosaurus and get a photo with him."

"No tyrannosauruses down here."

"I know," said Eddie. "Not allowed?"

The guard studied Eddie for a moment, then said, "Now, if you would be so good as to walk this way, I will escort you safely to the exit."

"Are we going out through the gift shop?" asked Dylan. "We have to go out through the gift shop."

"You're *not* going out through the gift shop. You're going out by the nearest available exit. Which, in your case, is the same one you came in."

"But we have to exit through the gift shop. It says so in the leaflet."

Ignoring Dylan's continuing protestations, we were ushered out through the cave and back onto the path leading down to the entrance. As we moved along the path, I noticed a sunken garden on our left. In amongst the trees and paths, I noticed a life-sized model of King Kong and several dinosaurs. I nudged Eddie.

He followed my gaze. "Well, I'll be buggered."

"How did we not notice that on the way in?" I asked.

"We were in a bit of a hurry. Easy to miss things when you're in a bit of a hurry."

"But King Kong and several species of dinosaurs?" I paused, making out a shape between the trees. "And if I'm not mistaken, isn't that a tyrannosaurus right there?" I pointed.

I couldn't believe we'd walked right by it. Although I had been deep in conversation with Dylan about his bail. Still, I was a police officer, used to be, trained to be observant.

"Can we just stop off there for a moment?" I asked the guard. "A quick photo?"

My request was completely ignored, and two minutes later, we were all standing outside the main gates.

"Well, that's a bit of a setback," said Robyn.

"Bit of a setback?" Eddie challenged. "That's the biggest understatement since Noah told Mrs Noah to get the washing in, as it looks like rain. We might as well pack up and go home now."

"So, who had grumpy flakes for breakfast, then?" Robyn gave Eddie a condescending smile. "We just have to go with Plan B."

"I didn't know we had a Plan B," I said. "I was thinking it's time to head home and tackle my pergola."

"There's always a Plan B," Robyn said.

"Which is?"

"We sneak back in."

CHAPTER SEVEN

I WAS THE FIRST TO break the silence which had greeted Robyn's suggestion. "We can't sneak back in. That's illegal."

"It's only illegal if we get caught damaging property. Otherwise, it's trespass on private property, which is not illegal, it's civil."

"Hmm, that's splitting hairs a bit."

"The whole legal system runs on split hairs," Robyn said. "It's designed so the wealthy and connected can pay the fees of those who know how to split these hairs, while scalping the rest of us."

"That's a very cynical view."

She gave me the narrowed eyes and lifted eyebrow look which said, '*Prove me wrong*'.

"Okay, just supposing, how would you propose getting back in?"

"We could always just wait till the shift changes on the gate and buy new tickets," suggested Janet.

"We can't afford the time," said Robyn. "You all stay here; I'm just going to do a quick survey." She started to move away, then paused, turned, and said, "And try not to look suspicious."

We watched her disappear from the path and into a wooded area adjacent to the Wookey Hole park site.

I glanced around at my companions. We definitely looked suspicious. People even stared at us as they went past on their way in or out of the entrance.

"Perhaps we should move up the path a bit," I suggested.

"Oh yes, because four adults standing in a group up there," Eddie waved his hand up the path, "is *so* much less suspicious than standing here."

"We could sit on the grass and pretend to be having a picnic," Janet said.

"Slight problem with that plan, we don't have a picnic."

"That's why I said *'pretend'*, silly."

"You're the copper," Eddie nodded at me. "You should know how to not look suspicious."

"Retired," I reminded him. "And besides, not looking suspicious was never part of the job description. Only pulling people who *did*. We could read the noticeboard, though. That's the sort of thing we used to do on surveillance jobs." I pointed towards the noticeboards, which were festooned with brightly coloured leaflets.

I moved to one which held a welcome notice and started reading all about where, or where not, I could take a pushchair. I suddenly felt a sense of claustrophobia and realised the other three were all gathered around me.

"Maybe we should spread out a bit?" I suggested.

Just then, Robyn appeared. "What *are* you lot doing?" she greeted. "You couldn't look more suspicious if you had false beards and sunglasses."

"I was just trying to say—" I started, but Robyn cut me off.

"There's a dense bit of undergrowth over there," she pointed. "And an easy climb over a metal five-bar gate. Come on." She turned and headed off.

We followed her into the brush, pushed our way through some brambles and hawthorn, then came to the gate. An old, and rusting chain wrapped through the bars and was secured in place by a relatively new looking bronze padlock. Robyn slid over the gate with the ease of a liquid cat, and I followed, displaying all the grace of a drunken donkey. The ground on the other side of the gate sloped downwards at quite a sharp angle, but fortunately, various small trees and shrubs gave handholds to manage my descent. That was until we arrived at a near vertical two metre drop down a rock-face to the path below. There was no easy way down from here, other than a semi-controlled fall. Which wouldn't be too bad, other than the fact we were likely to drop into the path of visitors on their way to the cave entrance.

We all waited in the shrubs, hoping nobody would look up, until a break in the flow of visitors gave us our opportunity. I slid, crashed, tumbled onto the path in a small avalanche of loose stones and dirt. I spent two seconds making sure nothing was broken, then helped the others make it down in a slightly more gainly manner.

We dusted ourselves off and looked around. Nobody seemed to have noticed our sudden appearance, so we followed a track down until we arrived in the little valley below. King Kong towered above our heads, along with several different dinosaurs and a mammoth. Tyrannosaurus Rex stood taller than all the others and dominated what, incongruously, appeared to be a small English cottage garden.

"What now?" Eddie asked.

"We log our position into the app." I fiddled with my phone and found the right place. "There's a button for it, top right on the main screen. It says, Log Location. Do you think we all do it, or just one?"

"Try it and see what happens," suggested Robyn.

"What if we get it wrong? We could be disqualified just for not following procedure."

"I doubt they'd do that. Here, I'll do it." She opened her phone and stabbed at the screen.

I tensed and waited for the bad news. "Well, anything?"

"Hang on, it's having a think. Oh, here we go. *Upload a photograph of all Team Farmhouse Five using the phone registered to Janet. Ensure GPS is on.*"

"Just us?" I asked. "Or with the tyrannosaurus?"

"Didn't say. But I guess it doesn't matter, as it's going to get our location from the GPS."

"Okay, let's do it." I opened my arms to gather everybody together, and we grouped in front of the tyrannosaurus, just to make sure. "Just need somebody to take the picture now." I looked around for a likely recruit. "We need somebody who looks like they know what they're doing with a camera phone."

"What do they look like then?" asked Eddie.

"I don't know. Look for somebody who's carrying a posh camera."

"That doesn't mean they know how to use a phone camera. Just saying."

"Oh, for goodness' sake." Robyn took Janet's phone from her and marched over to an approaching family. She showed them the phone, pointed at us, and chatted with the daughter, who looked about twelve.

I couldn't hear what was being said, but both parents smiled a lot while looking at us while the girl fiddled with Janet's phone, then aimed it in our direction.

Robyn rushed back over to us and said, "Smile."

I tried smiling, but as soon as I told my face to look happy, I spotted the two security guards from earlier heading in our direction.

"Oi, you lot!" one of them yelled.

I felt my face shift from a half-formed smile to surprise, then panic, just as the girl said, "All done."

I wondered briefly which face had been immortalised. But only very briefly.

"We've got to run." I pointed at the approaching guards.

Robyn ran forward and retrieved the phone, then we scurried in the opposite direction, tossing appreciative waves and inaudible thank-yous in the direction of the family.

"What did you say to them?" I asked Robyn as we ran.

"I told them we're on an outing from the day-centre, and I'm the carer."

I stopped. "What?"

"It seemed like the simplest explanation. Keep running unless you want to be locked up with the witch."

"Uh? Oh, yes. Where's the way out?"

"The gift shop," yelled Dylan.

"No, we haven't got time for souvenirs."

"Exit through the gift shop. It's the way."

"Really?" I scanned the area. The way we'd come in was blocked by the guards. A sign pointed the way to the gift shop, so in the absence of any other plan. We followed that.

We rushed in through the door, causing heads to turn as we spread out, looking for the exit. Then I noticed a sign saying - *We hope you have enjoyed your visit. Please exit here.* "There," I pointed, and we ran towards the sign. We managed to slide through the exit turnstile just before the guards closed on us. We paused the other side to see if they were going to follow, but they just stared at us, one of them giving a slight shake of his shaven head in tacit warning.

Janet pushed strands of wayward hair back under her hat. "Ooh, I haven't had so much excitement since we went on the Colossus at Thorpe Park."

"The Colossus? That insane rollercoaster?" I studied her with new admiration.

"It was a day out with the Ladies' History Club. Bit of a mix up, really. We thought we were going to see the Colossus Computer at Bletchley Park."

Robyn came alongside me, holding Janet's phone. "Looks like it registered okay."

A notice on the screen said, "*Congratulations Team Farmhouse Five. Location correctly recorded. You have successfully completed the elimination round. From here on, you will be given a suggested start location from where your next clue will be within a 25-mile radius. Please note, you are under no obligation to start from the suggested location. Your clue will arrive at 10am. Your team will be eliminated if the login has not been completed by midday, or you finish below the median. Your suggested start location for tomorrow is tamed.yarn.domain. Good luck!*"

A silence hung in the air as we all studied the message.

Robyn finally broke the silence. "It looks like they're making sure everybody's going to have a similar travel time. That's fair, I guess."

"What on earth is this tamed yarn all about? That don't make no sense," said Eddie.

"It's What Three Words," said Robyn.

"What three words?" asked Eddie.

"It's a geo-location tool, more accurate and easier than GPS coordinates. Every three square metres of the earth's surface has a different set of three words. Hang on."

Robyn swiped and tapped at her screen. "Got it. Sherborne Castle. Dorset, isn't it?"

"Oh, how lovely," said Janet. "Thomas Hardy country. We can go and see Weatherbury, the town in Far from the Madding Crowd. Although that was made up, it's really Puddletown, where his family came from."

"I don't think we'll have time for that," I said. I pulled up the app on my phone. The message was the same. I looked at the team numbers. 748. I watched for a moment, and it clicked down again to 736.

"That's over half the teams gone already by the looks of it," I said.

Robyn studied her screen. "I'm guessing a lot of teams were caught out by the photo requirements. It seemed to be a too obvious cheat to be missed."

"What cheat?" asked Eddie.

"Each person carrying cloned phones of the other team members."

"Good job we didn't think of trying that."

"Again, I did, but I dismissed the idea. It was such an obvious cheat, and therefore equally obvious that the organisers would have a way of countering it."

"Okay, so what do we do now?" asked Janet.

"Let's go to the old penny arcade." Dylan pulled out a leaflet of Wookey Hole Attractions. "They use real old pennies. Each one was worth 0.416666 recurring of today's pennies. We can—"

"Were you paying attention when we got chucked out of there?" Eddie said. "Twice?"

Dylan looked deflated and folded the leaflet several times, ensuring the edges lined up perfectly, before returning it to his pocket.

"I think we should go back to The Camelot," I said. "I suggest we make sure we're all ready to leave at nine. Gives us plenty of time to make sure we're at Sherborne for ten when the clue arrives."

Everybody nodded or grunted, assent.

"Good," I said. "I need to fill the car up on the way, and I also need to drop in to the local police station."

"Problem?" Robyn's face took on a concerned look, bordering on panic.

"No, just routine stuff."

"Just routine is what they say when they're about to dump you in a cell on some trumped-up charges," Eddie said.

"Nothing like that, it really is routine. Boring procedural stuff." I gave a quick glance to Dylan and the tiniest of winks to let him know I was holding his confidence.

"Oh that's handy," Dylan said. "You can talk to them about my bail stuff while you're there."

I sighed. "And there's that as well."

"You're on bail?" Robyn queried. "What happened?"

"He can explain on the way." I flicked my head towards the car park. "Come on. Let's head back."

Once at the car, I interrogated satnav for the nearest police station. Apparently, there was a substation in Glastonbury. Closed on Wednesdays. "We'll be making a quick stop-off in Glastonbury on the way," I said.

"Oh good," said Janet. "We can pop in and see my aunt while we're there. If I can remember where she lives. I haven't seen her for years."

"We haven't really got time," I said.

"We could stop off in Street. That's nearly next door," suggested Eddie. "Got a pickup to make there."

"No, no aunts, no dodgy deals," I said. "We're stopping off at a police station for Dylan, and that's it. Anybody wanting to visit relatives, mythical kings, or Hooky Street dealers, you can get a taxi."

I followed satnav to a small car park near the abbey. The police substation was about a five-minute walk away, according to Open Maps.

"Come on then," I said to Dylan. Then to the others, "I don't know how long this is going to take, but there's a cafe over there, Merlin's Tea Shoppe, so we can all meet there in… say, an hour?"

I led Dylan through a narrow walkway and onto a side street inhabited by the kind of shops which can't quite afford the rent of the main road. Kookie's Magic Krystals, The Magic Pie Shop, Destiny's Tarots and a smattering of charity shops. I found the police substation tucked in a side alley between Wicca's Wands and Bob's Grow Shop. It looked for all the world like somebody's front door, apart from the typed notice declaring it to be Glastonbury Temporary Police Substation - Closed on Wednesdays.

"Leave the talking to me," I instructed Dylan. He nodded.

I tried the door. It didn't move. So I rang the bell.

I heard shuffling noises from behind the door, then a voice called, "Just coming."

The door swung open, and a man appeared dressed in black trousers and police issue blue shirt. He was struggling to pull closed his Tactical Duty vest over a stomach which had clearly expanded since the vest had been issued to him. It bore a blue tag reading, Police Community Support Officer.

"Good morning, sirs." He eyed us up and down. "What seems to be the trouble?"

"No trouble, officer, I'm ex-Job, retired." I held out my hand. "Matt Dixon, I was a Detective Sergeant down in Penzance until a couple of weeks ago."

"Oh, nice to meet you." He shook my hand and stood back to allow us entry.

The reception looked more like a small shop than a police station. A wooden counter cut the room in half, behind which a door led to what I presumed to be the interview room and possibly a cell. In front of the counter sat three institutional green metal chairs and a wooden coffee table with several copies of Model Railway Magazine. A small water cooler stood in the corner behind the door, along with a plastic cup dispenser.

"I'm Clive Proudfoot, PCSO. What brings you to my little nest?"

"Just a silly little administrative matter."

"Makes a change from all this terrorist business."

"Terrorists? In Glastonbury? I haven't heard anything about that."

Proudfoot tapped the side of his nose. "Need to know. Know what I mean?"

"No, not really."

He looked around the office as if expecting to see spies in every corner. "I'm only going to say one word, vehicle sabotage..." He paused in thought, then added, "...and Green Ninja. Okay, that's two words."

"It's four."

"What?"

"It's four words. Vehicle, sabotage, green, and ninja. That's four words."

Proudfoot counted silently on his fingers, then shook his head. "Never mind, it's terrorism is what it is. Destroyed my official police car with their road traps. I should be out there now hunting 'em down, only I ain't got no car at the moment."

I thought it best to stay quiet on the subject of police cars. "Anyway, my administrative matter..."

"Oh, yes. How can I help you?"

"This is my... acquaintance... friend, Dylan. He's on police bail over a very minor issue—"

"Police bail is never a minor issue." Proudfoot studied Dylan.

"Yes, I'm very well aware of that, but this probably won't even get to court. It's just a little... very little bit of property damage that—"

"Nothing little about property damage. You ought to see the state of my police car."

Calm, Matt. Calm. "I understand. However, the situation is that he's supposed to report in today before five, at the Little Didney police station. That's west Cornwall, and he's up here at the moment, with no way of getting back there on time." I looked at my watch for emphasis.

"I see. Failing to report in for bail is a very serious matter."

"I know. That's why we need your help. Could you contact PC Muchmore in Little Didney and arrange for the sign-in to happen here?"

"Can't do that. Not if it wasn't set up in the original bail conditions."

"Well... technically, it can be changed by the custody officer, which would be PC Muchmore, but the request would have to come from you, as you would be taking it on."

"So why's he running round up here if he's supposed to be on bail down Cornwall?"

"Um… an emergency. His grandmother, she's… not very well, and I drove him up here as he's the only relative." I couldn't believe I was doing this. If this came out, I could lose my pension.

"What's her name then? His grandmother? I might know her," he asked Dylan. "I know most folks round here."

I intercepted before Dylan could draw a breath to speak. "Oh, she lives in Trembly, just down the road."

"I know Trembly well. Grew up there."

Of course you did, I thought. But said, "That's lucky you probably know her then."

"So? What's her name then? Your grandmother?" He looked at Dylan.

"Um… Dina…" Dylan started, then paused. My breathing stopped while he pondered how to continue. "Diana, yes, Diana… erm… Saur."

"Diana Saur? That's an unusual name. Don't know any Saurs hereabouts."

"German," I said. "They're a German family. Sadly, she's the last."

"Apart from your friend Dylan here."

"What? Oh yes, he's the last, technically. Can you ring Little Didney? I'll give you the number."

"I'll have it on the system." He looked at Dylan. "You got any I.D.?"

Dylan dived into his pockets and came out with a crumpled sheet of paper. "I've got this." He placed the mess in Proudfoot's hand.

"What's this then?" Proudfoot held his hand still, as if the crumple of paper might explode with any movement.

"It's my barrister's certificate."

Proudfoot stiffened and looked at me. "You didn't say he was a barrister."

"He means barista, as in coffee."

"Ah, stay here a minute." He lifted a hatch in the counter and disappeared out the back.

I planted myself in one of the chairs and leafed through the magazine. Apparently, housing one's model railway in the loft is now seen as potentially hazardous due to the presence of some types of roof insulation materials. I was just perusing adverts for Intercity liveried rolling stock and Bachmann steam locos when I sensed movement behind the counter.

"All done," Proudfoot called. "Just need him to sign here." He slapped his hand on a sheet of paper on the counter.

"That was quick." I put the magazine down and waved at Dylan to come over.

After a quick scan of the paper, I pointed at the signature space for Dylan to sign and he inserted his scrawl.

"Thank you," I said.

"We're here to serve. Mind how you go."

As we started for the door, Dylan paused, then carefully placed on the counter several metal brackets, a couple of white plastic bits and some screws. "I'll just leave these here, shall I?"

Proudfoot glanced at the bits, then switched his gaze to what used to be the water cooler, then back to Dylan. "How…?"

"That probably needs looking at," I said. "To come apart like that, it must be a health and safety hazard."

We slid out of the police station before Proudfoot had a chance to process what had happened.

We arrived at Merlin's Tea Shoppe a few minutes later, but there was no sign of the others, so we continued on to the car to find them waiting, along with three large plastic crates stacked by the rear of the vehicle.

"What's this?" I asked.

"Just a bit of shopping while we waited," Eddie said.

"You've been shopping at…" I leaned down to read the label attached to one of the crates. "Chakrabarti Imports?"

"You said you wouldn't go to Street, so Ali came over to me while you were busy. Saved you a journey. Thought you'd be pleased."

"I'm not carrying counterfeit goods in the back of my car. This is still very nearly a police vehicle, and I'm only a couple of weeks out of the Job."

"How can they be counterfeit when they're made in the same place as the real stuff, and by the same badly paid workers? All they do is just keep the machines running for an extra shift here and there for themselves. These poor sods get a little extra money, and somebody gets a nice jacket for half the price."

"You're just a misunderstood philanthropist at heart, aren't you?"

Eddie shrugged. "What can I say? I'm one of life's givers."

"Just put them in the back. But I want them gone as soon as we get back to The Camelot."

He gave a big grin. "Deal. You sure you don't want one? They'd suit you. With your professional deportment, make you look proper dapper, they would."

I shook my head and climbed into the car. I waited until Eddie had finished loading his boxes in the back then we pulled out onto the main road. "I'm going to have to fill the car up before we get back. We have no idea where we're going tomorrow, and we don't want to lose time stopping for fuel."

I remembered seeing a Valdez petrol station as we were looking for somewhere to stay yesterday. That would do. I detoured off the main road as we neared Trembly, remembering that the petrol station was quite close to The Camelot but on a different road. It appeared in front of us exactly where I thought it should be, and I was just quietly congratulating myself on my navigational skills when I noticed a problem. Blue police tape fluttered across the entrance and a cardboard sign hanging from it, simply said, 'closed'.

I parked and got out of the car. The front of the pay kiosk had been spray painted with the words, 'Contaminated Fuel' and the green circle, black eyed logo of the Green Ninja had been painted alongside. Under the window, more words had been painted, 'Reject Greenwashing Lies'.

A man saw me parked up and wandered over. "Sorry, mate, we're closed."

"What happened?"

"It was like it when we came in to open up this morning." He pointed in the direction of a small manhole cover. "Filler valve locks were broken open, so we got the police, and they tested the fuel. Both tanks are contaminated with bleach."

"Bleach?"

"Kills petrol engines and can even explode diesel ones. This Green Ninja, whoever he is, needs locking up and the key throwing away."

"Is there anywhere else nearby we can fill up?"

He pointed back the way we'd come. "You need to get on the Glastonbury road. Couple of miles on your left."

"Thanks." I recalled PC Proudfoot saying something about the Green Ninja and terrorists. This must be what he meant.

"What's happening?" asked Janet, as I returned to the car. "Is it a murder? Should we help investigate?"

"No, some nutjob contaminated the fuel tanks. We're going to have to make a detour."

"Oh dear. Do you think we should stay and help? You're a detective, I could help you look for clues."

"I think they can probably manage without us. Just some lunatic calling himself the Green Ninja."

"How do you know he's a lunatic?" asked Robyn. "Maybe they have a point."

"A point? What's the sense in destroying people's car engines? It's as bad as those idiots who chucked soup over Van Gogh's Sunflowers. Just vandals."

"But no cars were actually destroyed. The Green Ninja gave a clear warning."

"That's not the issue. They could have been."

"Hmm, yes, I suppose."

I took the car back out onto the Glastonbury road and found the petrol station. At least this one was open. After filling up, we headed back to The Camelot where I fully intended to have a quiet pint and hide in a corner with Tinker, Tailor, Soldier, Spy.

But that was not to be.

We reached The Camelot just as the afternoon began to drift into evening. The bar looked surprisingly busy as I walked through to the stairs for the bedrooms. I dived into the shower before Dylan had a chance. I'd learned from last night that he tended to take a long time. I didn't know why, only that it involved counting. I pulled on a clean shirt from my bag, picked up my book, and headed downstairs.

My hope of a quiet corner disappeared immediately. Every table was occupied, and several groups congregated around the bar.

I slid into a space at the bar and studied the chalkboard menu while I waited. International Dogs' Day Menu. I scanned the menu with a degree of trepidation. Sausages and Chips, BBQ Ribs, Scrambled Eggs with Bacon, Cheesy Yorkshire Puddings. After a few minutes, Arthur worked his way to me, and I ordered a pint of Old Grumbler.

"Interesting menu," I commented.

"International Dogs' Day," Arthur said. "Celebrating our furry friends. Thought I'd do a dog oriented menu."

I studied the menu again. "I don't really see the connection?"

He pushed the pint towards me. "Tristan chose it."

"I thought your chef was called Wojciech?"

"He is." Arthur looked puzzled as to how I could possibly be confused. "Tristan is my Terrier. He chose the menu."

"Ah, hence the Cheesy Yorkshire Puddings."

"He loves them. His favourites."

I ordered sausage and chips, then wandered the room in search of a table.

"Matt!" I heard, above the hubbub. "Over 'ere."

I followed the sound of the voice to see Eddie and Janet sat at a table along with two men and a woman. Eddie stood and purloined a spare chair from a nearby table. "Sit yerself down. You look like you've just missed your last bus home and you've dropped your egg sandwich in a puddle."

I settled in the offered chair. "Thanks. It's very busy tonight."

"There's a few more teams in here now." Eddie waved an arm vaguely in the direction of the others seated at the table. "These are The Alter Egos. They've just arrived."

"I take it that's your team name rather than your secret identities?" I smiled at The Alter Egos.

"Both," said a fortyish, bespectacled man with scary sideburns. "I'm Clarke, this is Peter, and Bruce, and this rose betwixt the thorns, as one would say, is Diana. We're all members of IAN, the International Alliance of Nerds."

"I'm Matt. Nice to meet you all."

"Is that your secret identity name, Matt, as in Matt Murdock, Daredevil?"

"No, it's just Matt, Matt Dixon, as in Dixon of Dock Green."

"What powers does he have?"

"That's a secret. How did you manage to get a room?"

"Oh, we didn't," said Bruce. "We have a camper van in the car park. The landlord's let us stay there. Makes it easier to get where we want to be."

"Wherever we hang our camper van, there's our hat," said Clarke.

"We've just come up from Cornwall," said Bruce. "That's where our last clue was. Luckily, we'd worked out that Cullompton was the approximate centre of Wessex, so we were waiting there when the clue came in. Now, this is our starting point for the next one."

"Our last clue was—" Eddie started, then said, "somewhere not too far from here, as it goes." He nodded sagely.

"Now what do I do?" asked Janet, staring at her phone. She looked up at me, "Clarke's teaching me mojitos."

"Emojis," Clarke corrected. He leaned in, adjusted the position of his glasses, and studied Janet's phone screen. "No, you can't send that."

"Why not? Minnie could do with a smile to cheer her up. She's had that dog for fifteen years."

"But that's a smiley face. You don't send smiley faces to people who've just lost their dog. You can send a hug." Clarke caught the bewildered look on Janet's face. He took the phone from her hand. "Here, let me show you."

Eddie nudged my arm. "Pay attention, Matt, The Alter Egos have a proposition."

"I'm not doing propositions this week," I said.

"No, hear them out." Eddie looked at Bruce. "Tell him your idea, he'll love it when he hears it."

Bruce's eyes brightened as if somebody had just patted him on the head and called him a good boy, "We solved a clue today, and so did you—"

"How do you know that?" I asked.

"Because you're still here, obviously. So, with that in mind, we propose a trade, an exchange of information. A bilateral conduit of—"

"I know what a trade is," I interrupted. "Just what are we trading?"

"The answers to our respective clues. We tell you where we've been today, and you tell us where you've been."

"Apart from the fact that this is probably against the rules, it's my understanding, there are hundreds of different clues spread randomly about the teams. The chances of our two teams being given the same clues are about as likely as the king phoning me to discuss my knighthood."

My phone buzzed and rang in my pocket. I pulled it out, number unknown. I paused before hitting answer and then felt silly for doing so.

"Matt?" asked a female voice.

"Yes," I confirmed, cautiously.

"It's Gwen, from the Little Didney Animal Rescue Centre. Bernard gave me your number; I hope you don't mind?"

"No, not at all. How can I help?"

"It's silly really, but I have to ask, how are you doing with this quiz thing?"

"Well, we've done the first clue, that was okay." I glanced at The Alter Egos, shielded my mouth with my hand and whispered, "It was Wookey Hole, so we got lucky, it's just down the road. But that's all so far. Why do you ask?"

Silence hung for a few seconds, then, "They've moved the date when we have to quit the land. They want it vacated in four weeks. We have nowhere to move the animals to. I know it's a long shot, but… we have no other plan…" I heard muffled sobs. "Sorry, I don't know what to do. They'll make us… I can't… I shouldn't have rung, sorry."

"Don't panic, we'll sort something out. Even if we don't win this, we'll find a way."

"I know you will." Her voice said otherwise. "Sorry, I shouldn't have called. I know it's a crazy idea. We'll do some more jumble sales and raffles, we'll be alright."

The phone went dead.

"Gwen?" Eddie asked.

"Yes. She has to get the animals off the land in four weeks. She's a bit of a mess."

"No pressure then."

"How about the trade then?" asked Bruce.

"Let me think about it."

Arthur arrived with my sausage and chips, and I said to the others at the table, "Excuse me, I've got a bit of a headache coming on, and going to take this up to my room then get an early night."

CHAPTER EIGHT

TEAM BULLINGBOY CLUB

PERKINS SAT AT A SQUASHED table in a squashed corner of The Camelot bar. Two of his teammates, Barbie and Lothar sat with him, both totally focussed on their phones and oblivious to the world. The third member, Mario, the driver, stood at the busy bar trying to gain the attention of the barman. He'd been trying for fifteen minutes, but the place was heaving and for some reason, he'd failed to make his presence known. Mario was the nickname given to him, named after the Mario Kart video game due to the way he drove. Nobody was quite sure what his real name was.

Barbie, a six-foot five giant with a shaven head and a penchant for lifting heavy things as a hobby, wriggled himself a bit more space in the confined area. Lothar looked up from his phone and gave Barbie a look which cooled the surrounding air by at least ten degrees. Lothar, a slight man by comparison to his neighbour, had a look about him of a hungry wolf.

"Sorry, mate," said Barbie. "I'm on level twelve of Candy Crush. It gets a bit tense." He shuffled back from Lothar as far as the wall would allow.

They both resumed their phone studying.

Perkins thought of these three as his teammates, even though he wasn't actually registered as part of the team, and in reality, he had very little to do with them. They'd been chosen merely to be the field operatives for

Combermere's secret squirrel code-breakers, and each selected purely on their physical capabilities. Mario had once been a runner-up in the FIA World Rally Championship. His job was to get the team to the clue location as fast as possible.

Perkins had once had the dubious pleasure of being a passenger with Mario and had no wish to repeat the experience. Skilled, he may be, but he laced that with a total disregard for the lives of not only other road users, but his own passengers as well.

Barbie and Lothar between them offered physical strength and intimidation, should it be required. The three of them represented the public face of Team Bullingboy Club.

Perkins' job was to identify and keep an eye on other teams. Also, where possible, to gather data, such as car number plates, or where they were headed. And perhaps to create whatever mischief along the way as he could.

He looked up at the clock on the wall and decided he was going to be waiting some time before Mario returned with drinks, so returned to pushing pieces of sausage and cheesy Yorkshire pudding around his plate. He wondered briefly if he could manage any more, then decided his stomach would probably rebel and set the plate to one side. Somerset pub fare had proved to be a mildly alarming experience for a man who rarely left the safety of Westminster with its familiar Pret A Mangers, Tonkotsu Ramen, or Wasabi Sushi bars all within a few minutes eScooter ride of his office.

He took a paper serviette from the dispenser and spread it open across his plate, shielding the leftovers from view.

His phone buzzed quietly and danced a little jig on the table in front of him. His finger hovered over the green connect button on his phone as he stared at the name on the screen, Julius Combermere. He excused himself from his two companions, who didn't seem to notice, and sidled out into the hallway. Plucking up the necessary courage to connect the call, he drew a breath, held it, and stabbed the green button.

Combermere's voice reached through the phone the instant the call connected. "Perkins?" he snapped. "I hope you've got some good news."

"Yes." Perkins jolted, and the phone nearly slipped his grip. "A bit, the answer to our clue was right, so—"

"I should damn well think it was right," interrupted Combermere. "The amount we spend on these computer twiddlers in GCHQ, they should be able to solve a few simple puzzles between their cups of frappy-chinos and bean sprout wraps."

"Yes, so, it was Tarr Steps, as the GCHQ people said. The only trouble was your team took a bit too long to get there." Perkins tended to refer to them as Combermere's team when there was a problem. "They were still in time to log in, but... the traffic on the A394 was very bad and if they hadn't found a shortcut through Dulverton, they might not have made it."

"What are you trying to tell me?"

"That, well, it's good we have the help with the clues and everything, but the travel times can't be guaranteed."

"They'll just have to drive faster, man. Tell them it doesn't matter one jot if they pick up a ticket or two. It's a Civil Service fleet car anyway. Nobody checks. Just make sure we win this."

"With all due respect, sir, I'm a Parliamentary Private Secretary, not a racing car team pit stop crew. I have no control over traffic or road conditions."

"For heaven's sake. Look, if you get stuck again, ring me and I'll arrange a police escort. And if you don't win this, you'll be lucky to get a job as a tea boy in a pit stop. Now, what about the other teams?"

"What about them?"

"Are you following them to find out where the other clues are?"

"It's just me, I can't follow everybody. I can't be in several places at once."

"Hmm, yes, I can see that's a problem. I'll get onto the Chief Constable and get a list of nearby reprobates or lowlifes. He's bound to know which stones to turn. I'll ask him to have them contact you. Where are you?"

Perkins gave the details of the pub, terminated the call, and returned to the table just as Mario returned with two-pint glasses of muddy-looking liquid. "Was that him again?" he asked, settling the beers on the table.

"Yes, the Master. He wants me to follow other teams to find out where their clues are. What's that?" Perkins asked, nodding towards the glasses.

"It's a local beer. Something called Merlin's Special Brew. The barman said it's made with water from the Chalice Well."

Perkins picked up the glass and studied it. "Don't they have proper tap water down here?"

"I think it's meant to be traditional."

Perkins tried a sip. "Okay, it's not too bad. Anyway, the upshot is we're going to have help coming to follow some of the other teams. You three can just concentrate on getting to the locations as quickly as you can."

"How will they know who the teams are?" Mario asked.

Perkins looked around the room. "I'll help with that. It's just really a matter of watching for people looking at maps and stuff. There's a group with a White BMW X5 I saw. And another bunch with a camper van. There's also what looks like a team, but they all drive separate cars, Porsches, Ferraris and so on. Although, they might be a bit difficult to follow." He finished the last of his beer and pulled a grimace. "Anyway, I'm off to bed. Settle the bill will you? And don't forget the receipt for expenses."

CHAPTER NINE

TEAM FARMHOUSE FIVE

BREAKFAST THE FOLLOWING MORNING PROVED chaotic. I guessed Arthur had never anticipated such an influx. It also appeared that there were quite a number of camper vans recently arrived in his car park, and everybody wanted a good breakfast before their clues turned up.

Unable to find a table in the bar area, I ordered food, then took it to one of the outside bench tables. The sun played peekaboo with the morning clouds, drifting little patches of warmth over me as it danced with the shadows. Dylan and Robyn appeared from the patio doors and settled at the table. Robyn's breakfast consisted of beans, mushrooms, toast and tomatoes, while Dylan had opted for three sausages and three boiled eggs. They both stared at my Full English breakfast, each with their own reason for disapproval at my plate.

"Didn't see you two last night," I said to Robyn. "Early night?"

"Oh. I just caught up on some work. The beauty of being able to work from anywhere that has an internet connection."

"What sort of work are you doing?"

"Oh, it's for a financial institution. I'm testing the resilience of their data security. All quite boring, really."

"I'm sure it isn't." I eased my fried egg onto a slice of toast.

"Robyn was helping me," Dylan said. "I might get some unfair dismal money."

"Dismissal," Robyn corrected. "Unfair dismissal money."

"She's awesome. She helped me write this email to get me some money 'cause they didn't give me proper disciplinary procedures. Sent it to the big boss and everything."

"That was very good of you," I said. "Do you think it will work?"

"Hopefully," she said. "Had a bit of a to-and-fro with them, trying to get hold of the right department and the email addresses. They shouldn't think they can get away with stuff like that, just because they can bully the people at the bottom."

"I wasn't at the bottom." Dylan looked affronted. "I was a trainee chef. I had a badge and everything."

"Do you mind if we join you?" a voice said from behind me.

I turned to see The Alter Egos heading towards us. I slid a bit to one side to create space. "Feel free. It's still a bit chilly out here, though."

"Fun fact," said Bruce. "There's no such thing as cold. It's just a lack of heat. And the cold you feel is just a transfer of energy from a higher to a lower state."

I studied Bruce for a moment. "So why do I have to pay for energy to make my fridge cold?"

"Ah, that's because the second law of thermodynamics states that in a natural thermodynamic process, the sum of the entropies of the interacting thermodynamic systems never decreases. See?"

"No." I supped at my hot coffee and felt the warmth slide down.

Bruce looked puzzled. "Well, if you—"

Clarke patted Bruce's arm to stem the flow. "Did you think any more about the trade?" he asked.

"What are you up to?" asked Robyn.

"Not me," I said. "Something Eddie cooked up with these guys. He thought it a good idea to trade answers. Can't see the sense of it myself."

"It's probabilities," said Dylan. "I don't like probabilities. They're not real numbers. They're just might-be numbers."

"Probabilities are okay," said Robyn. "If there are two thousand teams to start then they would need two thousand locations for the first round and when we did our project to identify possible locations we came up with 1,179 but that was only the most obvious ones and we didn't even have our clue in the list, which is the only one we know for sure. We know that there will be six clues, which means we can divide that by six making 300, near enough, so if we—"

"Slow down," I interrupted. "They had a big list of clues. That's my point. Knowing what one of them is doesn't really help."

"Robyn's right," said Bruce. "If we each swap, we each have a one in 300 chance of getting an advantage, compared to a zero chance. Would you turn down a free lottery ticket, even if it was at 300 to one?"

"Well, no, obviously... But... Okay, I see what you mean. But what about the rules? I'm not risking our chances of being thrown out."

"There's nothing in the rules about that," said Robyn. "I've studied them thoroughly."

"Oh," I said. "I would have thought that would be in the rules. It seems obvious. I wonder why not?"

"Who knows," said Robyn. "Maybe they just didn't think anybody would actually do that. Or, on the other hand, maybe they don't mind teams helping each other."

"Or maybe they just overlooked the possibility." I looked at Bruce. He looked at me. "Well?" He held both hands out as if waiting to catch a beachball.

"How do we know we can trust you?" I asked. "You might not give us yours. Or you might make one up. You could even—"

"Oh, for heaven's sake," Robyn cut across me. "Ours was Wookey Hole, in front of the Tyrannosaurus Rex model in the little park. Clue about the king of the terrible lizards and cheese."

"Okay," Bruce said. "Ours was the phone box at Jamaica Inn, near Bodmin. The clue was, it's not in the Caribbean, but in the K6, the smugglers can get their money back by pressing button B."

"K6?"

"Don't worry about it, it's right." He checked his watch. "Sorry, we have to dash. Got to be in Yeovil by ten o'clock. That's our start point. Good luck." They headed off towards their camper.

After breakfast, I just had time to check over the car, then we reconvened in the bar to set out for Sherborne Castle.

"Those crates of dodgy coats are still in the back of my car," I said to Eddie. "You promised they'd be gone."

"Yeah, well, the guy who was going to take them has unexpectedly had to go away for a while."

"How long?" I asked.

"Twelve months."

"You see." I slapped my hand on the table. "I knew you were up to no good, Eddie. Get those things out of my car."

"It was nothing to do with the coats. It was just a silly case of mistaken identity."

"As in, the CPS have convicted the wrong man?"

"Not exactly. More like, he didn't realise the man he was trying to sell the speciality cigarettes to was an undercover Customs and Excise Officer."

"And by, speciality, I'm guessing you mean smuggled?"

"You say smuggled, I say cutting out the King's slice. He don't need it."

"Just get those coats gone."

"I'll get right on it. Trust me."

I shook my head in despair and looked around. Several other groups of people sat at tables and seemed to be killing time. I guessed these teams had this area as their start locations. One team, a group of young men all wearing blue T-shirts proclaiming 'The Cunning Stunts Quizzers', were already on the beer and joking loudly.

Next to them, a team of four expensively dressed youngish men had a large plastic pig on their table. It bore the name 'Money Boys'. I assumed they were banker types. Another table had a group of two men and three women wearing sweatshirts with the image of an estate agent's sign saying they were 'The Home Team'. We were certainly the poor relatives here.

One team, all dressed in khaki and looking set for the jungle, sat a few tables away, open laptops in front of each, notepads at the side, and a pile of Ordnance Survey maps in the middle of the table. I felt terribly under prepared.

Another glance at my watch, and just as my eyes settled on the clock the hands approached nine.

"We should get on," I said. "We must allow time for problems. They're minor roads to Sherborne."

We decided to not actually go to the castle, as that was all minor roads with no quick route back onto a main road. Instead, we parked up at a junction just south of Sherborne, but on the main road. A gamble, but as long as we weren't being sent north-east, it should give a slight advantage.

We sat in the car, idly speculating where the clue might be. There were a lot of potential sites in the area, Maiden Castle, Cerne Abbas Giant, a couple of minor stone circles, a dolmen or two.

My phone bleeped. As did the others'. A silence descended, just as if somebody had hit the mute button to the world.

I stared at my screen. The teams competing was now 733. That had dropped by three for some reason. I forced my eyes to settle on the clue.

"Good morning, Team Farmhouse Five. Here is clue two: Go through the Door on which the return of the Tenth stood, and observe the bull, and the cow, and the calf. - Your team will be eliminated if the login has not been completed by 12:00, or you finish below the median. Good Luck."

"Any ideas as to where this is?" I asked.

"A door," she started. "That suggests we're looking for a building. Maybe a farm building?"

"This is the southwest," I said. "There'll be a lot of farm buildings all over, and millions of cows."

"Why's he standing *on* the door?" asked Dylan.

Robyn's fingers beat a tattoo across the keyboard of her laptop. "The southwest has a cattle density of 147 per square kilometre."

"Wonder who counted them?" Eddie mused.

"The tenth has to be a person," said Janet. "Henry the Tenth?"

"I think they only went up to eight," Eddie said.

"What about prime ministers? There's been more than ten of those."

"Far too many of 'em, if you ask me."

"William Pitt the Elder was the tenth," Robyn said, reading from her screen. "Here we go, he had property in Cornwall, Boconnoc, near Lostwithiel."

"Yeah, but we're in Dorset," said Eddie.

"Ah, yes, of course. Good catch."

"Why's he standing *on* the door?" Dylan asked.

"Who?" I asked.

"The Tenth," Dylan said. "The clue says he's standing *on* the door, not *in* it. Standing on doors is dangerous. Unless it's laying down, then it's not so dangerous."

"Maybe it's a typo?"

"He's got a point," said Robyn. "They're not going to make a typo, not on the clues. *On* the door is significant."

"Whatever," said Eddie. "On, in, under, we need to find the chuffin' thing first, then worry about where this fella is standing."

"There's a Heaven's Door rehab centre near Yeovil," Robyn suggested. "We can try to sort out what the rest of it means as we drive."

"We could drop you off there for a little rest, Eddie," I said.

"Why did the ghost go to rehab?" asked Janet.

"I don't know," said Eddie. "Why *did* the ghost go to rehab?"

"Because he had trouble with the drink... Oh no, that's not it, tipple, no, I remember now, he had trouble with the boos." Janet dissolved into a puddle of giggles.

"It's the way she tells 'em," said Eddie. "So, when you've all finished taking the piss, are we setting out to this Heaven's Door, or what?"

"What if that's not it?" asked Janet, trying to stifle another onset of giggles.

"I agree," I said. "We shouldn't move until we at least know the location."

"How did the Tenth return?" asked Dylan. "It can't be a dead politician. Not unless he's a zombie, but I don't know any zombie politicians."

"There's a few I could name," said Eddie.

"If you name zombies, they have to go away," said Janet.

"You're thinking of demons," said Dylan. "Did you know the Pentagon has a plan to prepare for an invasion by zombie chickens?"

"Dylan's right," I said. "Not about the zombies, but about the return. It can't be a historical person."

"And why is 'Door' capitalised?" asked Janet. "That's bad grammar."

I studied the clue again. Janet was right. "It must be a proper noun, the name of a specific place."

I checked my watch. "We need to get a move on. Anybody making progress?"

"Ben Affleck was the tenth actor to be Batman," offered Dylan. "But there are only nine Superman actors. David Tennant was the tenth Doctor Who, Pierce Brosnan was the tenth Bond, if you count—"

"Wait, Doctor Who?" Janet said. "I loved David Tennant in that. He came back for a special episode."

"I saw that," I said. "Hang on, that's it! He regenerated on Durdle Door; he was standing on it. That's got to be it, Durdle Door." I pulled my map book open. "Here it is, Lulworth Cove. That's about..." I measured in thumb-widths, "Twenty-five miles in a straight line. Maybe thirty by road, give or take. We need to get a move on."

I put away my measuring thumb and paper map.

"What about the rest of it?" asked Robyn. "The cows and things, where are they?"

"I don't know. You can look that up as we drive."

My hunch about not waiting at the castle had proved sound as we were already on the road towards Dorchester. Robyn sat in the front with me this time, as she was the only one with the right skill-set for co-piloting. Mainly, she could read a laptop in a moving vehicle without throwing up, and she didn't need to change glasses between screen and road signs. Dylan read out road numbers and let us know when we were travelling on a prime number, while Janet practised her emoji skills by sending random texts to her sister.

Eddie, meanwhile, chatted noisily on the phone. I figured he was busy setting up some sort of deal and tried to ignore him.

Once on the main road to Dorset, the A352, which apparently is not a prime number, although all the digits added up to ten, which made it a favourite with Dylan.

Robyn turned from navigation to research and propped her laptop between knees and dashboard.

"There are some rocks near the Durdle Door," she said. "The Cow, the Bull, the Calf, that'll be them."

"Okay, that confirms we're going to the right place." I glanced at the satnav. "About thirty-five minutes, by the looks of it. We should be there before eleven. That'll give us an hour to log in. Looking good."

"We need to look out for Durdle Door Holiday Park. There's a car park."

Eddie finished his call. "We're gonna need a boat," he said. "My mate's got a car lot in Weymouth. He goes down there with his kids from time to time. Says we can go through the Door, but we'll need a boat."

"I don't do boats," said Dylan. "They don't stay where you put them."

As we settled into the drive, I took the opportunity to sate my policeman's curiosity about my travelling companion.

"What changed your mind in the end?" I asked Robyn. "You know, about joining us on this wildest of all goose chases?"

"Well... I thought it would keep me out of trouble for a while."

"Do you make a habit of getting into trouble then?" I glanced across to her.

Her lips pursed as she failed to control a smile. "No, generally I'm very good."

"Is all your work done remotely?"

"Mostly, yes. Sometimes it's not possible, and then I have to work on site. You ask a lot of questions."

"Sorry. It's the policeman in me. As they say, you can take the copper out of the Job, but you'll never take the Job out of the copper."

"Is that what they say?"

"In police stations, they do. Have you always done this sort of work?"

"Only since my husband died. I needed something to focus on."

"I'm sorry," I said. "Long ago?"

"Three years, two months, and fourteen days. We've got a tail, by the way."

"What?" I glanced in the rear-view mirror. A dark blue Toyota Corolla sat about fifty metres behind us. "The Toyota? What makes you think it's following us?"

"I've been keeping an eye on it." She tapped her screen and an image of the Toyota appeared. Clever, she'd obviously set the camera on the laptop to aim back across her shoulder.

"I'll make a loop off and back on again. Can you see on the map anywhere coming up that I can do that?"

"The road splits shortly. We're supposed to take the left fork, but if you take the right, we can loop left and back on again in about a hundred metres."

I saw the junction approaching. Good visibility into the side road, and no traffic there, "Going to make a quick detour," I called to the back. "Hold tight."

I kept the speed as high as I knew the BMW would be comfortable in a tight turn. Then, without indicating, I swung into the side road. I watched the mirror and saw the Toyota continue on down the main road. "Well, if he was following, he's gone now."

I'd spoken too soon though. As I pulled back onto the main road, I gave another glance in the mirror, and there he was again.

"Okay," I said. "We have a problem."

Eddie craned his neck back. "Couple of lads, by the looks of it. What d'ya think they want?"

Robin studied her screen, and angled it for a better view and enlarged the image. "My guess is a rival team."

"They're going to come unstuck with that idea," Eddie said. "If somebody's sent half their team to follow us, they're going to come up short when they're supposed to check in at their own clue."

"They won't be part of an actual team," Robyn said. "It'll be somebody hired to do this."

"Why didn't we think of that?"

"Do the sums. Even to hire a couple of lads, they must be on at least a hundred each for a day's work. Times that by at least a few hundred clues already given out, and as many yet to go. I certainly haven't got that kind of money. Have you?"

"There were some banker types at breakfast," I said. "Piggy Bankers, they called themselves. Could be them."

"Whoever, we need to lose them before we get to Durdle Door."

"Any ideas?"

"You're the copper, you tell me," Robyn challenged.

"I was often part of a tail team, but never the tailee. The usual shaking-off tactic used by suspects, was to drive like lunatics in the hope the tail would consider it too dangerous to pursue. And, before you ask, no!"

"Okay, I've got a plan. We need to trick them into the wrong location. We're going to be running close to Maiden Castle in about ten miles. There's a car park for it just off the main road. Pull in there, and we'll make it look like that's where we're going."

"Surely they'll just follow us on foot to see exactly where the clue is?"

"That's exactly what we want."

"I don't understand."

"Have you ever chased a suspect who decanted their car, ran up a narrow lane, then when you followed on foot, you find they had another car waiting at the other end and you're screwed?"

"It's happened," I admitted. More often than I'd want, I remembered.

"That's what we're going to do."

"I hate to point out the obvious, but we've only got one car."

"Damn, I never noticed," Robyn said, with a little shake of her head. "Just park where I say. I'll explain then."

"Yes, guv."

"It's ma'am."

We followed the main road until it swung round Dorchester. I watched the road in front, and the tail behind us, leaving Robyn to navigate.

"There's a roundabout coming up. Turn right off that and then take the first turning on the right," she said. "Should be a sign to the castle."

I followed the instructions and the turning and sign appeared almost immediately. I pulled the car into a narrow lane, and we followed this to where it ended in a large, gravelled parking area.

"What now?" I asked as we came to a stop.

Robyn slid out of her seatbelt and tucked herself low in the footwell. "I'm staying here. You four follow that track. It will lead you into the castle and out the other side. You'll find a lane there. As soon as these twats behind start following you on foot, I'll bring the car round and meet you. But don't hang about, the clock's ticking."

"Have you ever driven a—"

"Seriously?" she interrupted. "Do you want to check my papers? I'll just ask those guys to wait while you do a PNC."

"Sorry, it's just… I'll go now. Come on you three, we're visiting a castle."

"Oh good," said Janet. "I went to Nottingham Castle once with this very nice man I'd met when I was doing a battle reenactment at Slaughterbridge. Dirk, that was his name. Biggest arms I've ever seen. I shot an arrow at the Sheriff of Nottingham. He wasn't very pleased."

I looked at Janet, but stopped myself from asking. Maybe later. "Come on, we have to hurry."

"I don't like castles," said Dylan. "Castles are not really straight like they pretend to be. They're only straight on the outside where the flat stones are. On the inside, the stones are really untidy. It's not nice."

"I think this castle is nothing more than a few bumps and trenches in the ground," I said. "Before stone walls."

We left Robyn squatted in the car and ran up the footpath, trying to make ourselves look like five, rather than four. After a hundred metres, I stole a glance backwards. Two figures tagged along at a short distance behind us. One spotted I might be watching and signalled to his mate. They both dived behind shrubs which ineffectively covered only their heads as they ducked. That was a bit of a relief. These two were certainly not professionals.

As we headed in the direction of the southern end of the outer castle ring, an English Heritage sign caught my attention.

"This will do." I gathered a couple of rocks and planted my phone on them, aiming towards the sign. "Gather round."

"How are you going to take a picture?" asked Eddie.

"It's probably got an automatic setting. I'm sure it's a standard feature on these things."

"Did you set it?"

"No, this is only pretend. As long as Dastardly and Muttley over there think we're taking one, that's all that counts."

We made pretend happy faces, then each of us tapped on our phones, as if entering the location.

"That should do it." I checked my watch, just seven minutes since we'd left the car. "Okay, let's go."

We followed the track to the southern end of the site and just before we lipped over the hill, I glanced back. Our followers were still standing by the sign. They seemed confused. Good. We dropped out of the site where, with a slight sense of relief, I spotted my X5 parked in the lane.

"Slide over," I said to Robyn as I opened the driver's door.

"Not going to trust me to drive it to Lulworth?"

"You're not on the insurance."

"That didn't bother you just now."

"It did. But it was expedient, and now the expediency has gone, I'm driving."

"Spoilsport." She slid into the passenger seat and gave me a mock sulky face.

"Show them our tail," said Janet from the back seat. "They can bite dust, those... those little scallywags."

CHAPTER TEN

THE DRIVE TO THE DURDLE Door car park took just over ten minutes, and then another ten to scramble down to the beach. Five fully dressed adults traipsing across a sunny and popular beach in August was always going to gather attention, and we did. We didn't even carry beachgoer accoutrements, like lilos and cool boxes, to at least blend in. Heads turned towards us as we weaved between sunbeds and umbrellas on our way towards the Door.

We reached the closest point and stopped at the sea line.

"Well, this is tricky," said Eddie. "How are we expected to log our position under that arch without a boat?"

I scanned the beach. Lilos, inflatable crocodiles and pink unicorns seemed to be as good as it got in terms of seagoing vessels. None of which were likely to support five adults.

"We need to spread out and see if we can find anything suitable," I said. "Somebody must be renting rowing boats or something around here."

We agreed to meet back in ten minutes, then I headed east, Eddie west, with the others spreading out more inland. I found my way very soon blocked by the sheer rock face which reached out to the Door. I turned and threaded my way back along the shoreline, eventually catching up with Eddie. He was deep in conversation with a pair of lads. They looked fifteen, or sixteen, but well-built and wearing only roughly sawn-off denim jeans. The taller of the two had a garish gold chain around his neck.

Eddie caught sight of me arriving and turned. "Oh, there you are. I think I've solved our problem."

"How?"

He pointed to the water's edge where a blue and white rubber dinghy bobbed in the surf. One of the lads had his foot on the rope, securing it temporarily from drifting off. "They're from that yacht out there," Eddie pointed to an elegant motor yacht, at anchor about half a kilometre offshore.

"Mum and Dad are having a bit of a party out there," one of the lads said with a vague wave.

"We got bored," said the other. "They said we could take the dinghy to shore here to explore for the afternoon."

"And you're willing to let us borrow this for twenty minutes?" I asked.

"Your mate said *hire*, not borrow," said the taller lad.

"Eddie?" I looked at him.

"Well, I might have mentioned a tip," Eddie said. "A fiver, as a sign of our gratitude, like."

"You said twenty," the lad said. "Each."

"I never did."

"Anyway, it's forty, 'cause we didn't know there's two of you."

"Forty? Why does the number make any difference?" Eddie asked.

"Wear and tear. And that's forty for each of you."

"And for each of us," said the other lad.

Eddie paused as he worked that out. That's... that's 160 quid."

"Supply and demand. See any other boats hereabouts?"

Eddie looked at me. I shrugged. "Alright, 150 for cash," he said.

"Okay," the taller lad said, far too quickly.

Eddie pulled some notes out of his pocket and counted three fifties into the lad's hand. "Deal."

"Don't forget the deposit."

"What deposit? You never said nothing about a deposit."

"We never met you before. We dunno *who* you are. You might be boat thieves and doin' this all the time."

Eddie sighed. "How much is this deposit?"

"Two hundred."

"Two hundred?"

"You'll get it back, providin' you bring it back in good condition."

"I ain't got two hundred. You just cleaned me out." He looked expectantly at me.

"I don't carry that kind of cash," I said. "Probably twenty quid, tops. I use cards."

"That's a nice watch." The lad pointed to the gold monster on Eddie's wrist.

"That? That's an Omega Speedmaster. It's worth more than your dad's boat out there."

The lad shrugged. "Your choice."

Eddie muttered something unintelligible, then unhooked the watch from his wrist and dumped it in the waiting hand.

"Nice doin' business wiv' you, guv." The lad slipped the watch on his wrist and showed it to his mate, who nodded in approval. "We'll be 'ere when you're done."

I picked up the rope to the boat, and we dragged it along the shoreline towards where the others waited.

"Never seen you fleeced so totally," I said, suppressing a grin.

"Little shits. We're gonna divi that up, right? It's all of us in it, so that's… thirty quid each."

"Not sure you're going to get thirty quid out of Dylan. Or Janet, come to that."

Dragging a dinghy through the water's edge proved harder than I'd thought. I tried taking my shoes and socks off, then letting it float, which would have worked okay had it not been for the myriad of paddling toddlers and ball games going on. Eventually, we arrived back at the point closest to the Door.

"I don't like boats," Dylan greeted as we arrived.

"Yes, Dylan," I said. "You mentioned that before, but unless you fancy swimming out there, this is it."

"I'm not even sure that's a boat, is it?" Robyn asked.

"It will get us through the Door alright," I cast my hand seaward. "It's as flat as a mirror out there."

"Isn't that what the captain of the Titanic said?" Eddie said. "Just before he asked if somebody could fetch him a drop of ice for his gin and tonic."

"I went white water rafting with the Ladies' Twitchers Society once," said Janet. "It wasn't really supposed to be white water rafting. We were in a little boat on the River Dee at Llangollen, trying to get some nice pictures of the moorhens. I wanted some to turn into placemats. The pictures, that is, not the moorhens themselves. That wouldn't be very nice. Nobody told us that the River Dee is a bit fast there. It was all very exciting, a bit like that movie Deliverance. Only without the banjos. And the axe murderers. Edith lost her hat."

We all watched Janet for a moment, each of us processing those images in silence.

"Right." I pulled the rope a bit tighter to stop the dinghy bobbling. "There's only one set of oars, so I suggest I do the rowing, the rest, two up front, two behind."

"What makes you think I can't row?" asked Robyn.

"Sorry, would you like to row?"

"No, I've never been in a rowing boat in my life. I just don't like gender assumptions."

I glanced at my watch. We were wasting far too much time. "Of course, who would like to row? We can draw lots."

"I don't like boats," said Dylan. Nobody else spoke.

"Okay, it looks like I'm rowing then." I pushed the boat out until it floated, then settled in the central seat. "Come on, hop in."

"Shouldn't we have life jackets?" asked Janet.

"Probably, but we haven't."

"I think I should just go find a loo first," said Eddie, scanning the cove. "All this water stimulates my bladder. It was the same on the Isle of Wight ferry."

"We'll only be five minutes, surely you can hang on?"

"I don't like boats," said Dylan.

"Please, can we all just get in the boat? We're going to get timed out."

With muted grumbles, everybody squashed themselves in the tiny dinghy. Water already lipped at the highest reaches of the hull.

"Now, everybody stay still. This is going to be tricky." I pulled on the oars, but they just hit shingle. "Sorry, we've grounded. We all need to get out and try again a bit deeper out."

After much grumbling, splashing, and complaining, we were finally seaborne. The rowing proved more strenuous than I'd anticipated, and being this low in the water, what had previously seemed to be a mirror flat sea, turned out to be a rolling maelstrom. We felt like a ping-pong ball in a washing machine. To add to our difficulties, a strong current seemed intent on dragging us towards the western end of the cove when our target lay to the east.

"Budge up," Robyn said. "I'll take one of the oars."

"There's not really room for two on this seat," I said.

Ignoring my protest, she eased herself into an impossible space at my side. "I can't bear to sit here all day watching you rowing at a standstill."

We soon got into a sort of rhythm of moving our bodies as one, the only thing possible in this cramped space, and we started to make headway.

We finally covered the fifty-metre journey and sailed triumphantly under the arch of Durdle Door.

"What now?" Eddie asked.

"I guess we log our position," I said.

"What about the cow and stuff?"

"It's those rocks out there." I pointed to some black shapes just breaking the waves to the west. "The clue just said go through the door and observe them. We must be in the right place."

"Go for it," said Robyn, tucking her oar alongside her.

I took out my phone, checked the signal, then opened The Great Wessex Chase, and clicked the login button.

My phone bleeped, and a message flashed up. *Position confirmed.* *"Please upload a photograph of team member Dylan with the Cow, the Bull and the Calf in the background, using the phone registered to Robyn."*

"You're going to be famous," I said to Dylan.

Using one oar, I jiggled the boat until we had the rocks in the background and Robyn took her photograph. Nothing seemed to happen for a while, and I was about to suggest we try again when my phone beeped once more.

"Congratulations Team Farmhouse Five. Location correctly recorded. Clue number three will follow tomorrow at 10:00. Your team will be eliminated if the login has not been completed by midday, or you finish below the median. Your recommended starting point is client.they.rocket. from where the next clue will be within a 25-mile radius."

The top corner of the app showed the team numbers had now fallen to 223. "We're in the last two hundred, nearly," I said.

"Come on, let's get back," said Robyn, setting her oar in the rollock.

"We've got to find those little scroats and get my watch back," said Eddie.

The journey back to the beach proved much easier than going out, as now, we were going with the current. Although, we did hit the beach two hundred metres further west than our start point. We dragged the dinghy up onto the beach and I scanned the area looking for the two lads. Nothing.

I turned to Eddie. "Can you see them?"

"Nah, no sign."

I turned to Robyn. "You and the others stay with the boat. Eddie and I will go each direction. They must be here somewhere. Eddie, you go east, I'll head west."

I'd just turned to set out when I heard a loud shout. "Oi, you!"

I turned to see an overweight and over-tanned man puffing towards me. I pointed a finger to my chest and cocked my head.

"Yes, you. I want a word with you," the man called.

I waited while he marched up to me.

"What's up?" I asked.

"What's up? I'll tell you what's up. You stole my boat, that's what's up," he managed through gasps of air.

"I'm sorry, I don't—"

The man pointed to the dinghy. "That. That's my boat. You stole it."

"I did no such thing. I hired it from the son of the owner of that cruiser out there." I pointed to the big boat moored further out in the bay.

He followed my gaze. "That's *my* boat. We just came ashore for a picnic. I turned my back, and somebody had made off with our dinghy."

"But it was your son that—"

"I don't have any sons," the man interrupted. "Just my wife and me."

Eddie appeared at my side. "What's happening?"

"This chap says we stole his boat."

"We hired it," Eddie said. "All legal."

"I've done that bit, Eddie." I turned back to the man. "You really don't have any sons? Couple of lads, about fifteen or so. One with a thick gold chain around his neck?"

"I told you; we don't have any children. Certainly, none with gold chains. Now give me back my boat before I call the police."

I scanned the beach once more in the hope of seeing the lads, but there was no sign of them. "I think we've been done, Eddie."

We gave the man his boat and started out up the path to where we'd parked the car.

"Do you want to report this, Eddie?" I asked as we trudged up the path.

"What's happening?" asked Janet.

"Eddie put his watch down as security for the boat, and those scammers kept it," I said.

"Oh dear, was it expensive?"

"Six grand, wasn't it, Eddie?" I queried. "That's what you said." I managed to suppress a smile.

"Yeah, more or less."

"You should definitely report it," said Janet.

"I'll help you with the paperwork," I offered. "Have you got the original invoice?"

"Yeah, well, fortunately, it was my decoy. That's all."

"Decoy?"

"Yeah, the insurance company insisted I have a decoy for everyday use. That was it."

"Ah, I see. That will explain why the second hand ticked, instead of sweeping. I did wonder. Decoy, huh?"

"Well, that's it." Eddie shrugged. "Just like to see those little scroats' faces if they try to pawn it."

"So, what was it? A Chinese knock off?"

Eddie stopped walking and turned to me. "Look, can we stop banging on about my watch? Done deal."

We walked in silence for a while, then when I could resist it no longer, "Hey, Eddie."

"What?"

"You got the time?"

***

We stopped off at a pub in Dorchester for a well-earned pint and snack. It turned out to be one of a chain of cookie-cutter country inns. Generic house ales, and a menu designed to appeal to those who think potato wedges are avant-garde. But it was clean and efficient.

"Well, here's to the second clue down." I raised my pint glass, and we clinked for luck.

"Where're we off to then?" asked Eddie. "These client rockets, where's that?"

Robyn swiped and poked at her phone's screen. "Here we go, client.they.rocket is Tiverton Castle."

"Ooh, I like Tiverton," said Janet. "We stopped off there once on a trip to the North Devon Woodturners' Show in Barnstaple. Our coach broke down in Tiverton, which was a shame really, as I never got to see the man who makes vampire stakes. He turns them out of sacred ash wood, you know. But we did have a nice tea and cherry cake in the garden centre."

"Vampire stakes?" I asked.

"They make very good dibblers for planting my tomato seeds. Besides, you can never be too prepared."

"I suppose they would," I said. "But coming back to the competition, it looks like we've got to move to Tiverton."

"We could try to second guess the clue," said Robyn. "We know it's within twenty-five miles of Tiverton. What if we make a list of potential clue sites within that radius? We might get lucky."

"Twenty-five miles around Tiverton would take you coast to coast there," said Eddie. "Far too much stuff around, and neither of our clues were on our list. We'd be better off with a couple of pints and an early night. Fresh start in the morning."

"Early night?" I looked at Eddie.

"Might go for a bit of a stroll as well. There's a very exclusive craft distillery near there. I might pick up a case of their Glen Fiddlich. Old Sam Goodenough will be well up for a bit of that."

"By exclusive, I assume you mean illegal?"

"It's only illegal if you sell it, which I don't plan on doing. Sam's got a couple of antique Chinese foo dogs I've 'ad my eye on for a while. He's no idea what they are and uses them as door stops."

I shook my head, trying to erase the memory of this conversation. "Okay," I said. "But first we'll check out of The Camelot this afternoon and head down to Tiverton. Onward to the next clue!"

CHAPTER ELEVEN

WE APPROACHED TIVERTON JUST AFTER three. As we turned off the motorway and joined the North Devon Link Road, I spotted a sign to somewhere called The Nirvana Motel. I made an executive decision and pulled into their car park. A glance around showed a few cars, but it was by no means full. Maybe we had lost the crowd now.

"Why here?" asked Eddie.

"Why not? It's close to the suggested start point, just a bit closer to the motorway, and it seems to have vacancies. And it doesn't look too expensive."

"The Nirvana Motel at Tiverton," Robyn said, reading from the screen of her laptop. "A boutique hotel with motel convenience and budget prices."

"Sounds just the job," I said.

"What's a boutique hotel?" asked Dylan.

"It usually means they've got a fishpond in the restaurant and rooms named after poets instead of numbers," said Eddie.

As it turned out, there was no fishpond in the restaurant, but there was a large zen garden under a domed glass ceiling in the centre of the reception foyer. And the rooms were named after Buddhist philosophers. Fortunately, the prices were very reasonable and this time, we each had our own room. We agreed to split the cost of Dylan's room between the rest of us.

The receptionist took my details and swiped my card. "Would you like to book a session with our yoga master?" she asked. "He teaches Tandoori style. It was passed to him by a Tibetan monk who only comes out of hiding once every hundred years."

"No thank you."

"Or we also have a Tantric alignment practitioner. She can help free your channels of toxic vibrations?"

"I don't think so. It might not do anybody any good to go poking about in my channels."

She handed me the door card to my room. "Have a lovely stay." She put her hands together as if in prayer and said, "Namaste."

I studied the Zen garden while I waited for the others to check in. A large grey rock rose from one end of a sea of black sand. Three black pebbles lay on top of each other just to the left of the rock and four smaller rocks of varying sizes protruded from the sand across the centre. The sand held a raked pattern which looked vaguely like the sand on Newquay beach after the sand cleaning machine had been along there.

I took my bag up to my room, Batuo, on the first floor, and unloaded the essentials into the tiny wardrobe. The room was small, but well designed with a good-sized bed, desk, two chairs, a television, and a watercolour of a koi carp on the wall. I flicked on the television just to break the silence in the room and headed for the shower. When I came out, it was showing one of those seemingly endless series of reality bully shows. This one featured contestants painting pictures for a celebrity artist who then sets fire to ones he doesn't like while an audience chants, *"Burn it, burn it."*

I switched to the news channel and let it dribble away while I continued to dress. I decided an early evening walk might be nice later, so I was just trying to find something warmish to wear when a news item pinged my radar. It was a mention of the Krappi Burger chain. Not something I'd normally pay attention to, but it caught my interest because Dylan had just lost his job with them.

I turned up the volume and watched the screen.

"Today, every one of the tens of thousands of staff members of the international burger chain, Krappi Burger, received emails containing graphic images of the conditions inside Krappi Burger's intensive farms and slaughterhouses."

The news item went on to explain how thousands of staff had walked out from restaurants across the world. Video showed protestors patrolling outside restaurants holding placards about animal cruelty.

"Responsibility for the leak has been claimed by the environmental activist, the so-called Green Ninja. The resulting walk-outs have so far forced over half of the Krappi Burger outlets to close due to staff shortages."

I turned the television off and headed downstairs for something to eat. The Shambhala restaurant was at the rear of the building and, although quite small, it spread out into a glass covered extension. I took an empty table which gave a nice view over the fields outside and scanned the menu. I'd expected hand knitted tofu burgers or kimchi with hemp salad, but the choices turned out to be refreshingly prosaic and reasonably priced. I'd just finished my plaice and chips when I noticed Robyn coming in. I waved to catch her attention.

"Mind if I join you?" she asked as she approached.

"I've just finished, but please, I could use some company. I can recommend the plaice." I caught her look. "Oh sorry, I forgot."

She smiled. "No worries." Her eyes flitted across the menu. "I'm not really hungry. I'll just have a hummus and avocado sandwich, that looks nice." She caught the eye of the waiter and gave her order.

"Did you see the news?" I asked.

"I tend not to watch that. It depresses me. Why, what's happened?"

"Krappi Burger is having problems. Somebody leaked pictures of their farms and slaughterhouses and sent them to every member of staff. Quite horrific images, apparently. Mass resignations all over the world."

"Hmm." She lifted the lid of her sandwich when it arrived and gave an eyebrow twitch of approval. "Only a matter of time before that came out. Did you know their beef production alone produces more equivalent CO_2 each day than a million cars?"

"No, I didn't."

"People don't. Anyway, why the interest in Krappi Burger?"

"Nothing really. It just caught my attention because I remembered you saying you were trying to talk to their big boss about Dylan's sacking."

"Huh? Oh, yes. Never heard back. Tossers." She finished her sandwich and dabbed at her lips with a serviette. "Well, I'm going to take a walk before I settle. There's a canal that runs by here somewhere. Fancy a stroll?"

"I was thinking the same. My legs could do with a stretch. Far too much driving for one day."

We found the canal just a short walk out behind the hotel car park. A gravel path took us down to the towpath which ran along its western bank.

"This is all that's left of the Grand Western Canal," Robyn said as we walked. "A couple of hundred years ago, somebody thought it a good idea to join up the Bristol Channel with the English Channel. They got as far as Taunton and ran out of money."

"Sounds a bit like HS2."

"Only the canal builders didn't destroy ten thousand acres of wildlife land with their vanity project."

The canal cut between fields and bushes, and with nothing else in sight to reveal that we were slap between a large industrial town and a major motorway, it would have been easy to pretend for a moment that this was a different world. Had it not been for the shopping trolley peeping up from the murky water.

The last of the sun drew its long shadows across the water, and tiny ripples glinted their farewell. I watched Robyn as she paused under what looked like a young oak. She squeezed at a leaf, then sniffed her fingers.

"Do you do most of your work like this?" I asked. "Remotely, from wherever you happen to be?"

She stopped walking and turned to look at me, searching my eyes. "The beauty of the modern age. Fluid working makes for a better work life balance. It suits me."

She continued walking, and I fell in alongside.

"I see, I just wondered. It's a bit unusual, that's all. We had quite a few remote workers attached to the Force, but they mostly worked from home."

"Moving about gives me an edge over contractors tied to location. I can be close to whomever I'm working for, or when that's not necessary, I can just choose somewhere nice to be for a while."

"Sounds idyllic."

"Aren't you supposed to caution me before an interrogation, Detective Sergeant Dixon?" she said, with narrowed eyes and the briefest of all smiles.

"Sorry, I didn't mean anything. I suppose I can come over a bit... well, policeman-like. Too many years on the Job. Just ignore me."

She relaxed visibly. "No worries. Since I lost my husband, I've been unable to settle. I still have our apartment in Islington, but I'm rarely there."

"Yes, I remember you said earlier. What happened? If you don't mind me asking?"

"Covid. We'd moved to London for our work, we're both in computers, but John developed asthma soon after. Traffic pollution, the doctors said. Then, when the first wave of Covid hit, and... well..." Her eyes dislocated, and she seemed to go away for a few seconds and her eyes glistened. She hardened her lips, then a little shake of her head brought her back. "But there you go, it happened to thousands."

"I'm sorry," was all I could think of to say.

She squatted on the ground, picked up a stone and studied it for a moment before standing and tossing it in the canal. "Thank you. Anyway, how about you? How come a newly retired copper is running around the countryside trying to save the animals when he should be at home bouncing a grandchild on his knee and teaching them how to whittle spoons?"

"Okay, fair enough. I don't have any grandchildren, or even children. Just one failed marriage, the remnants of a career, and a pile of wood which one day is going to be a pergola. Oh, and I have an Alexa. Although, I do worry about her pedigree."

She stood, eased her knees in turn, then continued along the towpath. "You're probably better off with an Alexa than grandchildren anyway."

"Oh? Why?"

"Cheaper to maintain. Unless you do drunk shopping, of course."

"What's drunk shopping?"

She looked at me. "Really? You've never done drunk shopping?"

I shook my head. "Never heard of it."

"It's easy. All you need is a bottle of scotch, an Amazon account, and a credit card. The trick is to delete your history before you sober up. That way, you have the excitement of wondering what's going to turn up. It's a bit like Christmas for adults."

"I'm not good with surprises."

"Now, how did I not guess that? I ended up with a fantastic robot lawnmower last time."

"At least that sounds useful."

"It might be, if my apartment wasn't on the second floor."

As we continued walking, the sun turned burnt orange and sank behind some distant woods.

"We probably best turn back," I said. "This path could get tricky in the dark."

Robyn stopped and shrugged. "It's nearly at the end, anyway. This section is the last bit surviving of the canal. The rest of it has collapsed over, planted to rape seed, or been built on."

As we wandered back, I visualised nineteenth-century workers digging all this out by hand, and then the smoky barges chugging their loads along these waterways.

"How come you know so much about this place?" I asked. "It was a bit random that we ended up stopping here."

She looked at me as if I'd just asked why one and one make two. "Research. Whenever I go somewhere new, it's the first thing I do. I need to know what's there, how the place works, who the people are, quiet places, busy places. Find out where the roads out-of-town lead. Why? Don't you do the same?"

"Not really. Sounds a bit over-the-top."

She scanned me up and down. "Hmm, maybe you'd feel different if you were a single woman. Knowledge is power."

We took the gravel path back up the small rise and suddenly, we were back in the modern world.

I stopped and looked back. "Funny how there can be such a different place just round the corner."

She paused and studied me for a few seconds. "You need to get out more. The world is full of secret corners." Her eyes raked the landscape as the evening clouds drew across the horizon. "But best be quick, the light's running out."

An evening breeze ran cooling eddies around me, and I pulled my jacket closer. "Fancy a quick nightcap?" I asked.

"Hmm, why not? You can tell me all about your relationship problems with Alexa."

"Oh, don't get me started."

The Pilgrim's Cocktail Bar held a scattering of people, mostly couples, but one or two larger groups. I guessed they might have been other quizzers, but more probably company reps. We collected our drinks and settled at a table under a mural of a gold and red mandala.

A couple at a table in the corner caught my eye. Two young men, mid-twenties at a guess. One chatted on his phone while the other wrote in a small notebook. The one with the phone turned slightly to the wall in what seemed an unconscious attempt to shield his call.

I felt eyes watching me and glanced at Robyn. Her face held a distinct school ma'am look.

"You don't give up, do you?" she said.

"What do you mean?"

"The whole policeman bit. Let me guess, you've already pegged those two as drug dealers?"

"No, not really—"

"And those two over there?" She nodded to a middle-aged couple locked in deep conversation. "Adulterers?"

"Look, it's not—"

"And the men in suits, planning a bank job?"

"Okay, sorry. Old habits and all that." I twisted in my seat to face Robyn and cut off the distractions of the bar's clientele. "You have my full attention."

"Oh, there you are," a voice from behind me announced. I turned to see Dylan approaching. He pulled up a chair and planted his pint on the table. "I've been looking for you two."

"We went for a stroll along the canal," I said.

"Cool. Did it have barges? My grandad lived on a barge. It never went anywhere though. I don't think it even had an engine."

"No barges," I said. "Just a few ducks and a shopping trolley."

"What sort?"

"I don't know, they had brownish feathers."

"No, what sort of trolley? Was it full size or a narrow one, you know, for metro shops. I don't like the plastic ones."

"Um, I don't really know. Probably Tesco's, or maybe Sainsbury's."

"What colour was the handle?"

"Er…" I thought back. "Yellow, I think."

"Oh, that'll be Morrisons. Tesco's are Blue."

"Of course, silly me. Robyn and me were just—"

"Has anybody seen that nice young man from the front desk? The one with the David Niven moustache?" Janet asked, as she sat down at our table. "Only the cash machine has eaten my door key and won't give it back and now I can't get in my room." She planted her handbag on her lap and began emptying the contents on the table.

"You put your room card in an ATM?" Robyn asked.

"It was getting dark and the man behind kept making noises. Like he was sucking a toffee." A purse and a hairbrush added to the growing pile. "And now I can't find my bank card."

"You should ring your bank," suggested Robyn. "Just in case it's been stolen."

"I had it when we arrived. It must be in here somewhere."

A pink vibrator joined the collection and the sudden silence from the rest of us hung heavy.

At that very point, Eddie arrived. He stared at the table for a moment, then said, "Isn't that a Magic Bullet Dream? I can do you a deal on the deluxe version of that, if you're interested. It's got ten speeds."

Janet picked up the vibrator. "This? You mean my little pleasantry? No, this is perfect. It gets in just the right places." She switched it on and rubbed it behind her neck. "I get this terrible knot in my neck when I've been knitting for too long."

The collective sigh of relief fluttered around the table. Until Robyn said, "You do know what that's really for? Don't you?"

"Of course, dear," Janet said. "I may be gathering birthdays rather too quickly, but I'm not in my dotage yet. It's just that these days, I get far more satisfaction from being able to move my head through ninety degrees without it sounding like I'm eating bubble wrap."

I picked up the cardboard sleeve which the hotel provided with their key-cards. I opened it.

"Is this what you're looking for?" I handed her the credit card which had been tucked in the sleeve.

"Now, how did that get in there?"

As the promise of a quiet chat with Robyn receded into the general chatter, I decided an early night was in order and slipped away.

CHAPTER TWELVE

AS THE LIFT DESCENDED TO the ground floor, I idly contemplated whether to go for a full, all-in breakfast as opposed to my usual bowl of cereal. As I didn't know what was in store for us with the coming clue, or where we would be for the rest of the day, I decided all-in would be the way to go.

My contemplations ended the moment the lift doors opened and the sight of police tape criss-crossing the foyer greeted me. I had to fight my inbuilt programming that demanded I step under the tape and start questioning suspects.

Instead, I walked casually over to join the small queue for reception. The man at the front I recognised from The Camelot. Designer stubble beard and expensively blond tinted hair. One of the Money Boy team. Behind him stood Robyn. She hadn't noticed me, but was busy concentrating on her phone.

The Money Boy seemed to be arguing with the receptionist about something, but I hadn't caught what. I shuffled slightly closer and cocked my ear towards the man. He was complaining about a lost phone.

"I'm sorry, sir," said the receptionist. "We've had nothing handed in. Maybe the cleaners will find it later."

"The cleaners?" he challenged. "That's a £2,000 Ponzi Phone 13. They're not even available to ordinary people yet. What's the chance of some Albanian minimum-wage cleaner handing that in if they find it?"

"As I said, *sir*," she placed special emphasis on the word sir. "If it's handed in, we'll—"

"A Ponzi Phone 13?" Robyn pushed forwards and held out the phone she'd been playing with, and which I'd assumed was hers. "I just found this in the restaurant. It was by the coffee machine."

The Money Boy turned to look at her, then the phone. "Yes, that's mine. The coffee machine, you say?"

"Yes, just on the side. I assumed somebody had just put it there and forgotten it. I came here to hand it in."

"I don't remember putting it down," he said, taking the offered phone from Robyn's hand. "How did it get there?"

"I really don't know." Robyn caught sight of me behind her. "Oh, morning, Matt. I found this phone. Turns out it belongs to this gentleman."

"Charles," said the man. "Charles Digsworth. And thank you." He nodded curtly, then headed for the lift.

"Anyway," said Robyn. "See you in the restaurant?" She turned and walked away.

I moved to the counter. "Can I settle my bill, please?"

"Have you had breakfast?"

"No, not yet, but add it in anyway."

"Would you mind settling up afterwards? Only you need to validate your breakfast selection with your room card in the restaurant."

"Can't you just add in a full breakfast now? It would save me time later."

"No, I'm sorry, sir. We have a computer." She smiled that special smile which receptionists the world over know to indicate the conversation is over.

"Okay." I glanced towards the police tape. "What happened there?"

"Vandals," she said, waving an arm towards the Zen garden under the domed glass ceiling. "They've destroyed Akira's masterpiece."

I studied the Zen garden. I couldn't remember what it had looked like the night before, the layout of these things always seemed terribly random.

However, I was fairly sure that all the rocks had *not* been lined up in the exact centre of the black sand, and arranged by height order. Even the sand itself had been raked into uniform straight lines.

"Ah, I guess it's not meant to be like that. Who's Akira?"

"Akira? Akira Kazumi was one of the greatest Zen artists who ever lived. His works are treated as national treasures in Japan."

"I see. Can't somebody just put the stones back where they were?" I asked.

"Put them back?" She sounded shocked. "You can't just *'Put them back'* as you call it. That would be like…" she paused to think what it would be like. "It would be like chucking a bucket of paint over the Mona Lisa and somebody saying, *can't we just repaint it*? This was the last work he did in Europe before retiring to a monastery to Japan—"

"But surely somebody could just ask him—"

"Where he died four years ago," she interrupted. "It's even listed in the Tokyo Catalogue of Zen Art as a work of outstanding importance."

"Hmm, any idea who they were?"

"No, but they also threw all of our outdoor patio heaters into the swimming pool. They'll be ruined and we'll have to drain the pool now as well."

"What did the police say?" I nodded towards the police tape.

"That lot? They're about as much use as indicators on a Spanish car. Just gave me a crime number for the insurance and off they went. Didn't even bother to take fingerprints."

"Well, vandalism *can* be very difficult to prove without CCTV or eyewitness accounts."

She furrowed her brow and studied me momentarily. "You know, that's *exactly* what that idiot of a Community Support Officer told me. Can I help you with anything else?"

"No, it's just…" My words stalled, avoiding saying *I was just trying to find out if you'd got Dylan locked up in the basemen*t and settled for, "…um, so breakfast is in the main restaurant then?"

"Of course." Her helpful-receptionist mode clicked into place. "We do only have the one restaurant, there's a buffet and a coffee and tea dispenser at the far end. Where, apparently, it's a convenient place to lose one's phone." She switched on her smile. "Bon appétit."

The others were already eating when I entered the restaurant. I nodded acknowledgement as Eddie caught my glance, then collected a plate and set about gathering my breakfast items from the buffet. I was just trying to find an egg which hadn't been overcooked when a voice from behind me said, "Well, if it isn't the Farmhouse Crew again."

I turned, egg tongs in hand, to find Bruce from The Alter Egos standing there. "Farmhouse Five, not crew," I corrected. "It's a play on the old Enid Blyton books."

"Ah, I see." Bruce dropped a sausage on his plate. "What superpowers did they have?"

"None, they were just kids, out on adventures. They ate a lot of ice cream and drank lashings of ginger beer."

"Oh." Bruce paused with a second sausage mid-flight from buffet to plate. "I can see why that series never took off." He waggled the sausage. "Fun fact, Volkswagen produces more sausages than cars." The sausage finished its journey to his plate.

"I did not know that."

"Do you want to swap again?" he asked.

I glanced towards the table where the others were seated, wondering for a moment if I should consult. I forward wound the likely conversation in my head, complete with a lot of unintelligible numbers from Dylan, and decided that a fait accompli was probably for the best.

"Okay, we had Durdle Door, a clue about the return of the tenth, a bull, a cow, and calf. The tenth was all about—"

"Doctor Who, yeah, of course," Bruce cut me off. "The tenth Doctor Who, that makes sense. I remember that episode. It's the one where Ace wears the exact same bomber jacket as her character did back in the original Cybermen episode. Survival, that was the episode, back in 1989. I couldn't believe it when I saw that. Hope we get that one. I can take my sonic screwdriver."

"Watch out for a couple of chancers hiring out boats."

"Good tip. Our clue was a fatal union in a tiny lake, for a fee. Tolpuddle Martyrs' museum. Quite an interesting place. Fun fact, it's where the phrase Chalk and Cheese comes from. It's to do with the landowners fencing off good cattle land, leaving the peasants to farm on chalky soil."

He tried to shake my hand, but the combination of plates, trays, and sausages just turned it into a surreal juggling double act, and we gave up and simply nodded instead.

When I'd assembled enough breakfast items to see me through whatever the day held, I joined the others. Dylan studiously avoided my gaze as I settled at the table. I'd sat opposite enough miscreants in my life to know what that meant.

"Dylan?" I started.

He locked his eyes on his plate and busied himself by cutting up a sausage with the care of a surgeon. But he said nothing.

"Anything you feel you need to say?" I pressed.

"Don't know anything about nothing," he managed.

"The Zen garden?" I pressed.

"Lot of fuss about a few rocks." Eddie emptied a packet of sugar into his coffee, then paused and looked up at me. "But I'll say this, if one of the clues turns out to be Stonehenge, I think it's best we leave the lad in the car." He emptied two more sugars into his cup. "Just sayin'."

I looked at Dylan again. "The stones... well, I suppose I can kind of understand that. I don't see the point myself either. Not that I'd mess them up—"

"I didn't mess them up," Dylan interrupted, with an air of sulk as thick as Eddie's tea was becoming. "I just tidied them up. It was making my head fizz, them being all over the place like that. It's wrong."

"But what about the patio heaters? Dumping them in the swimming pool was hardly tidying up."

"What patio heaters?" Dylan looked genuinely surprised. "I don't know anything about patio heaters."

Neither his expression, nor body-language indicated he was being untruthful in his reply. I looked towards Robyn and said, "Have you any ideas?"

She cocked her head, eyes narrowing. "Why do you ask me?"

I paused, watching her expression. "Just wondered if you saw anything. That's all."

She studied me as if trying to see inside my head. "No, nothing. I had an early night and watched David Attenborough."

I glanced around the group. "Under the circumstances, I think it might be best if we checked out a bit earlier than we'd planned. By the way, I met Bruce, from The Alter Egos at the buffet, we've got another clue."

"Great," said Robyn. "That doubles the probabilities of us getting one of them."

"So, quick breakfast then checkout?"

"Suits me," said Eddie. "Maybe we could stop off near Exeter. I happen to know a bloke there who's just come into a job-lot of E-Scooters. I've got an option on a few of 'em."

"You're not filling my car up with more of your dodgy stuff."

"Well, if you'd let me drive my van, like I wanted, I wouldn't have to, would I?"

"It wasn't me that stopped you driving your van, it was the magistrates."

"You won't notice them. They're very compact and fold up like a pocket knife. Not quite as small as that, but still... and they're very green." He looked at Robyn for support.

"You mean those things which knock over old ladies on pavements, then keep bursting into flames?" she said.

"You're not putting those in the back of my car," I said. "Apart from anything, I'm not insured for exploding scooters. And you told me those coats would be gone by now."

"Just waiting on a phone call. Anyway, there's plenty of room in the back of that thing, I put a case of Glen Fiddlich in there and you haven't even noticed."

"I've got an E-scooter," announced Janet. "Well, it's not really mine. It belongs to Kevin, my grandson. Only his mum doesn't know he's got it, 'cause he leaves it in my shed. I use it to pop into the village to get my Radio Times, but don't tell Kevin."

Silence descended over the table for a moment as each of us wrestled, in our own ways, with the image of Janet on an E-scooter clutching her Radio Times.

I checked my watch. "Okay, we have just over an hour before the next clue arrives. I suggest we pack our gear now, check out, then meet up by the car."

Twenty minutes later, I was sitting in the car waiting for the others to arrive. Robyn was the first to appear.

"You were quick," I greeted.

"I'm used to living from a suitcase," she said, climbing into the passenger seat. "These days, I only buy clothes which still look good after being squashed and abused. I wonder where we're going to end up today?"

I glanced at her, taking in the jeans and black T-shirt with an open white shirt over. She was right, not a crease or a scrunch.

She caught my gaze and gave the briefest of smiles. "Any ideas?" she asked.

"What?" My mind stalled while it tried to put the question into the correct context. "Oh, where we're going? No, not really. Let's hope it's somewhere without a Zen garden."

"I didn't like this place." She stared out of the window. "It's a Potemkin village. I don't like companies who use the trappings of religion or social conscience just to sell their product." She turned to look at me. "It's the worst kind of dishonesty."

"Potemkin village?" I queried.

"Grigory Potemkin, a Russian minister in the eighteenth century. He built fake villages full of people pretending to be happy in order to impress visiting glitterati."

"Ah, I see. A bit like Center Parcs then?"

She studied me. "Hmm, I don't really see you as a Center Parcs sort of person."

Her searching gaze gave me an odd sense of unease. I realised how a hare felt being weighed up by a hungry wolf.

"I'd hate it," I said. "Too many people. My cottage is all the adventure park I need these days. I'm going to rewild it with watery bits and trees so I can sit in my pergola and watch nature take over. At least, I will once I've built my pergola. And bought some trees. I'll probably need something to dig the watery bits with as well."

"But apart from the watery bits, the digging, and the pergola...?"

"Good to go."

She smiled and said, "It sounds idyllic."

"You never thought of settling down? Trade in your apartment for a cottage somewhere?"

Her eyes took on a faraway look. "I fear I may well have forfeited any chance of that sort of dream."

I watched her for a moment, trying to decide if I should press. But the choice was taken from me when the car door opened and Eddie clambered in the back, lobbing his bag over the back seat.

"We ready?" he asked.

"Just waiting on the others," I said.

"Ah, I thought they'd be here. They were both at reception and Janet was just sorting out the bill."

"I'd better go and check." I glanced at my watch. "The clue will be arriving soon; we need to be ready."

I found them both still at the reception counter. The atmosphere seemed intense.

"Problem?" I asked.

"Oh, dear," said Janet. "I'm trying to pay the bill, but this very rude lady here," she pointed at the receptionist, "is saying Dylan has to pay for something called Adult Entertainment. We've had no adults in our rooms, let alone entertainers. I didn't even know they had them." She turned to the receptionist. "If you'd told me I could have had an entertainer in my room, I might have asked for a magician. I like magic. I dated an escapologist once.

He used to be able to dislocate his shoulders to get out of a straitjacket. One time, when I tied him to a chair—"

I touched her arm to cut short the story. "Probably best leave that for another day, Janet. I don't think that's what's meant by Adult Entertainment." I looked to the receptionist. "Are you sure?" I asked.

She slid a computer printout towards me. "It's all here."

I scanned down the list of billed items. On Dylan's bill, the list contained around twenty entries referring to the Adult Entertainment channels. "Dylan? It's perfectly alright, I mean, if that's what you… you know… if you find it… er, entertaining, in an adult way. But why all these changes of channel?"

"I didn't watch nothing," he protested. "I couldn't find nothing on the telly. All the channels were wrong."

"Wrong?"

"All in the wrong order. I mean, BBC One should be number one. Then BBC Two, because that's got a Two in the title, so it has to be at number two. Same with Channel Four. But channel one just had adverts for the restaurant and massages and stuff, then channel two had weather, so that made all the other channels the wrong numbers. You see?"

"But I still don't see why you watched all these Adult Entertainment channels?"

"I didn't. I was just re-ordering them all to make the numbers right. BBC One has to be at number one, and—"

"Yes, I get that." I turned back to the receptionist. "Look, I think there's been a bit of a mistake."

"We don't make mistakes, sir. We have a computer."

"I know, but—" My phone bleeped, as did Janet's and Dylan's. I glanced at the screen. The clue had just come in. "I'm sorry," I said. "We're in a bit of a hurry. Look…" I turned the printout back to her. "You can see he tuned to each channel for only about a minute each time. You can't make a separate charge for each one."

"We don't mind how long our clients watch a channel for. But premium channels are charged once they have been selected."

"But you can see he only tuned to each one briefly."

Eddie appeared at my elbow. "We gotta go," he urged, waving his phone at me. "The clue."

"I know, but this won't take a minute. Start trying to work out where it is with Robyn, and I'll be there in a minute."

I tried to return my attention to the receptionist, but Eddie wasn't having it. "I know where it is," he said. "I know the answer." He looked like a three-year-old boy with his first stick.

"Really?" I asked.

"Yes, really. Look," he thrust his phone at me.

"Hang on." I turned back to the receptionist. "Okay, how much is it?" I pulled my credit card out and handed it to her.

"That's ten channels at five pounds per viewing, that's…" She punched numbers into a calculator. "Fifty pounds. Would you like to pay for it separately or shall I add it to the bill?"

"Just put everything on the card. I'll sort it out later."

As the receptionist tapped at the card machine, I pulled my phone out and pulled up the clue.

"Good morning, Team Farmhouse Five. Here is clue three: Where Levara the leveret left him, the mighty huntsman stands, afraid of no one, not even the devil himself. All must hold his nose - Your team will be eliminated if the login has not been completed by midday, or you finish below the median. Good Luck."

"And you know what this means?" I checked again with Eddie.

"Yes, look, a leveret is a young hare and—"

"Tell me in a minute. Let's just get moving. Where are we heading?"

"Um, oh, hang on…" Eddie tapped his fingers to his chin. "It's somewhere near Branscombe."

"Somewhere near Branscombe? That's not quite as precise as I would have hoped."

"It was a long time ago."

"What was?"

The receptionist handed my card back to me. "Can I have your email address, sir?" she asked. "We're going paper-free, so we send your receipt via email."

"Yes, okay." I wrote it on a slip of paper, and she entered it into her computer. The machine immediately vomited enough paper to be able to gift wrap a double-decker bus.

"I thought you were going paper free?" I queried.

"We are. This is just a copy for your records. Have a nice day now."

I picked up the bundle of paper and we headed for the car, pausing by the driver's door.

I said, "Before we go rushing off to somewhere near Branscombe, can you just bring us up to speed with your reasoning?" I reached into the car and retrieved my map book.

"Right, so, I was down in Branscombe a few years back, 2007, I think. A sudden, unscheduled import event, and—"

"Hang on," I interrupted. "Branscombe 2007? That was when that ship, the Napoli, wrecked, wasn't it? I was sent down there as part of the police operation. Hundred or so shipping containers washed up on the shore."

"Yeah, as I said, a sudden, unscheduled import event. Anyway, as coincidence has it, a mate of mine came into possession of a load of LCD TVs about the same time. Latest thing they were, back then. He has a farm out near Manaton, on the moors."

"When do we get to the bit about the hunter with the nose? Only, the clock's ticking."

The sound of excited chatter caught my attention. A group of four men I'd spotted in the bar in The Camelot yesterday morning tumbled out of the main door to the hotel. The Money Boys, I remembered. They each held mobile phones in their hands and tapped as they talked as they hurried. One of them pointed a bunch of keys towards the car parking area and I heard a double bleep from behind me. A quick glance and I saw the hazard lights on a black Porsche flashing to indicate the doors unlocking. I remembered seeing what looked like the same vehicle in the car park of The Camelot the day before.

One of the curses of a long career in the police was that I'd been left with an obsessive interest in vehicle registration numbers. I squinted at the number plate of the car. It was the same one. More flashes and more bleeps pointed to a Ferrari, an Aston Martin and another Porsche.

"They were at The Camelot," Robyn said.

"Yes, there's also a few other faces I recognised. The Alter Egos, and there's a group of four who look like ex-military. There was also a table in the restaurant last night with what was probably a family, but they were studying maps and guidebooks."

"Might just be holidaymakers?" Robyn said, clearly not convinced by her own words. "They can't all be Wessex Chasers. I thought we were all being allocated specific start points now?"

"We are, but it looks like we're being grouped. It won't be the same clue location, for sure. But a twenty-five-mile radius has a lot of potential locations."

"Hmm, maybe it makes us easier to keep an eye, you know, to avoid cheating?"

"Possibly. But for now, we need to be getting on. Eddie, a bit more info might be helpful about now," I pressed.

"Yeah, well, I stayed at the local pub, a place called… The Huntsman, that's it. There's a sign over the door which says, *Afraid of no one, not even the devil himself.* The landlord told me the story of a mighty huntsman who'd been turned to stone by a group of witches when—"

"That's enough. Let's head there. You can fill in the details as we drive." I jumped into the car and said to Robyn, "There's a place near Branscombe, somewhere called Manaton. Can you find it?"

"Already on it. I checked against our list of likely places, and we have no sites in that area. Just get onto the M5 south and I'll program the satnav."

I turned the key in the ignition and the ever-reliable BMW engine started instantly. Then spluttered. Then came a big bang. Then it died.

"That's never a good thing," said Eddie. "Not with a bang, bangs are always bad news."

My mind instantly raced through scenarios involving breakdown trucks, conversations with puffed-up mechanics, and huge bills. I turned the key again and the engine immediately sprang into life. I paused, listening as it purred softly, like a prowling panther waiting to be released.

"That was very odd," I said.

"I heard a crash," said Dylan from the back seat.

"It was more of a bang," said Janet. "Like a pressure cooker exploding and throwing vegetable soup all over the kitchen you'd only just cleaned the day before, and then you have to open a can of cream of tomato for supper instead."

"No," said Dylan. "Not that bang. There was a crash too. Like the way a bottle of ketchup sounds when it falls off the table onto the floor because the table legs wobble. That came after the pressure cooker exploding, like a nanosecond after."

"I need to check." I turned off the engine and popped the bonnet.

After staring at the insides for a minute, I heard Eddie say, "You've no idea what you're looking at, have you?"

"Not really. It all looks to be here and there are no holes. Or ketchup." I closed the bonnet and went round the back. That all seemed as it should. I scanned the area and my gaze settled on a car directly behind mine. A dark blue Toyota Corolla.

My persistent policeman immediately recognised this as the one which had followed us to Dorchester the previous day. The tail we thought we'd slipped with our Maiden Castle stunt. The policeman took control completely now, and I looked around for signs of the two occupants. Nobody in sight. But the front of the vehicle was damaged. The nearside headlight was broken. My knees protested as I knelt down to examine the broken lens. Bits of glass lay on the ground, so it had clearly been broken in situ. But there was something else. A white, mushy substance muddled in the bits of glass and stuck to the remains still on the vehicle. I pulled a bit off on the end of my finger and sniffed.

It took me a moment to recognise the smell. Baked potato. How?

"Potato?" asked Eddie, arriving at my shoulder.

"Yes. How did you know?"

"Old trick, potato up the exhaust pipe." He pointed at the exhaust pipe of my car, which lined up perfectly with the broken light. "If it's done right, it can stop a car running, starves it of air. But done badly…" he pushed his foot at the light and another bit of glass fell to the ground. "Well, you don't want to be standing behind it, that's for sure."

I committed the Toyota's registration plate to memory. "We'd best be going."

"You start the engine again; I'll be there in a sec."

"Eddie?"

"Never you mind." He made a shooing movement with his hand.

I decided I didn't want to know and climbed back into the car. The engine started first time.

"All alright?" asked Robyn.

"Not sure. We seem to have gathered some unwanted interest."

Eddie jumped in the back. "Best be off now, fairly quick like," he said, folding his pocket knife and dropping it into his pocket.

CHAPTER THIRTEEN

SATNAV DECLARED THE DRIVE TO Manaton, although just twenty-four miles as the crow flies, to be forty-four miles by the fastest road. That put the journey time just under an hour. That would give us only about an hour to work out where the clue was, get there, and do the login. This was going to be tight, especially if the clue location wasn't easily accessible by car, like Durdle Door had been.

"That lot with the posh cars in the car park earlier, there's some money there. Who do you think they were?" I asked Robyn as I eased the BMW X5 into the motorway traffic.

"I was watching them in The Camelot yesterday," she said. "Called themselves The Money Boys."

"Bankers then?"

"Sort of. They all work for a big hedge fund company, Shye, Locke, and Grifter."

"How on earth did you know that?"

"I noticed the blond one with the beard, Digsworth, him with the phone, checking in last night. He used a Black Amex card, and I heard him say to charge it to the company account."

"Never heard of them," I admitted.

"Most people couldn't name any hedge fund companies, but this lot are the biggest. They have more money under management than HSBC."

"Ah, I forgot. You worked in the banking business, didn't you?"

"Not really, freelance. Data analysis. I had contracts with a few hedge funds and banks over the years. Not that lot though. They tend to keep everything in-house."

"I wonder where their clue was?"

"There must be hundreds of potential locations. A twenty-five-mile radius from Tiverton stretches from Sidmouth on the south coast to Minehead on the north."

Robyn kept the directions coming as we drove and in between, Eddie fleshed out his understanding of the clue.

"As I was saying," Eddie said. "A leveret is a young hare, and the witch was called Levara. I remember that because my uncle used to take me out lamping when I was a kid and—"

"You were a poacher?" I interrupted.

"Me? Nah, my uncle, Benny, his name was. I just thought we were out catching rabbits. I didn't know it was anything wrong. Not till he got nicked."

"What's this about a witch?" I prompted.

"What? Oh, yeah, Levara the witch. I remember it because I'm not keen on witches. There was this woman near us, she had tame crows and magpies. Gave me the willies, what with—"

"You've mentioned this before. What about this one down in Manaton?"

"Right, yeah, so, I was stopping at this pub down there, The Huntsman, and there's this sign over the door which says, *Afraid of no one, not even the devil himself.* Jacob, he's the landlord there, he said that was the motto of this hunter, Bowman, I think, who went hunting on the moors where the witches lived."

"What happened to him?" Janet asked.

"Oh, the witch got him. She pretended to be a hare and lured him in, then pounced. Turned him and his dogs to stone."

Robyn tapped at her laptop. "There's somewhere called Bowerman's Nose.

It's a rock formation close to this place Manaton. Oh, and a pub, The Huntsman."

"That's where we need to be then," I said. "How long?"

"Twenty, twenty-five minutes."

As she spoke the words, the traffic thickened in front of us at the point where the M5 narrowed into the A38. I peered ahead and noticed flashing hazard lights ahead. I guessed at a rear-end shunt where the lanes merged. My left hand twitched in an autonomic response, about to reach for the now non-existent blues & twos.

As if sensing my frustration, Robyn's hand touched my arm. I took the hint, breathed deeply and tried to calm.

It didn't work.

"Can we get off anywhere?" I asked.

"Nowhere near," she said. "It'll only take a minute. Look, the nearside lane is moving already."

A few minutes later, and we were filing past a three-car shunt in the outside lane. Normally, such a minor crunch wouldn't have caused this level of chaos. However, the occupants of the front vehicle were all dressed as clowns, with one of them setting about one of the other drivers with a large inflatable hammer.

"Well, there's a thing you don't see every day," said Robyn.

My programming to pull over and sort out the mess was almost overwhelming. I focussed forwards and asked, "How long now?"

"About two minutes less than when you asked me two minutes ago," Robyn said.

"Okay." I continued watching only the road ahead and tried not to hear her silent smile.

We arrived at the village of Manaton within minutes of Robyn's estimates. The lanes from the village to Bowerman's Nose grew narrower with each mile until the wing mirrors of the BMW were clipping the bushes on each side.

"We need to find somewhere to stop," said Robyn. "Bowerman's Nose rock is just up there." She pointed to a hill on our left, spasmodically visible between bushes.

I risked a couple of quick glances while trying to keep the car from collecting any more twigs. A large rock formation stood near the top of a gently sloping hill. From my brief glimpses, it looked no different to hundreds of other piles of rock scattered across the south west of England.

"Just there," said Robyn, pointing to a gravel cut just appearing up ahead.

I managed to pull the car into the cut just far enough off the road to allow other vehicles to pass. We piled out of the car and started up the hill.

"No security guards, and we don't need a boat. Looking good," I said.

"More hills," muttered Eddie. "Why is it always hills?"

"It's not always hills," said Janet. "Durdle Door was in the sea."

"Still had to go up a steep hill once we'd finished. I think it's discriminatory against people who have trouble with hills." He stopped and stood with his hands on his hips, staring into the distance and pulling deep breaths. "Don't know why they can't do one close to a car park or something."

"If you didn't do so much moaning, you'd have more puff for walking," suggested Janet. She marched past him like a Girl Guide leader on a mission. "You should try Pilates."

"Are they anything like pretzels?"

"What's the actual nose, then?" asked Dylan as we neared the rock formation.

I paused my climb, grateful for the momentary respite, and studied the formation. Bowerman's Nose stood, I guessed at a height of about six or seven metres and consisted of about a dozen huge rocks, which to me, must have been carefully positioned. The top three rocks did indeed give the impression of a head, with the topmost block protruding from the others.

"I think that's the nose," I said, pointing at the protuberance.

"That's not a nose," said Dylan. "That's his cap. He's wearing a baseball cap."

"What about the bit sticking out just below?"

"That's gotta be his chin, see, the next bit is his neck. You can't go from nose to neck."

"Maybe he did steroids, and he ain't got no neck," offered Eddie. "Like those American wrestlers. None of them have got necks."

"According to what I've read," said Robyn, "this was here in the fifteenth century. I don't think either baseball caps or steroids were around then."

"We need to be all holding his nose," I said. "So it's really important that we establish exactly which bit is his nose."

"About that," said Dylan. "I've been thinking—"

"In a minute, Dylan." I finished my climb and leaned against the rock-pile, trying to catch my breath. I stared up at the pile, rising above me against a clear blue sky. "Whichever bit it is, we can't reach it from here. It must be five metres up. Let's log our location and see what happens."

I opened the app and pressed the button for location logging. After a few seconds, a message appeared, *"Location correct. To complete, please upload a photograph on any phone of all five members of Team Farmhouse Five. All members must be touching the Nose. Your team will be eliminated if the login has not been completed by midday, or you finish below the median. Good Luck."*

"Well, the location is correct," I said. "But the bad news, it doesn't stop the clock until we upload a photo of all five of us holding the nose." I scanned the ground around us, vaguely hoping somebody had left a stepladder nearby.

"We could pile up some rocks," suggested Janet. "Like they did with the pyramids. They built ramps from smaller rocks."

"Except it took them a thousand years longer than we've got," said Eddie. He looked to me. "You got a tow rope in your car? We could use that to get up there."

"A tow rope?" I asked. "This is the twenty-twenties, not the nineteen-twenties. We carry breakdown insurance now, not tow ropes."

"It might not be what—" Dylan started, but Eddie cut him short.

"You should never leave home without a tow rope, a hammer, some wire, cable ties, duck tape and WD40. Standard toolkit."

"What about your mate in the pub?" I asked. "Has he got a ladder we can borrow?"

"You want me to go all the way down there again, then come back here with a ladder?"

"Do you see another way of doing this?" I pointed at the rock-pile. "Dylan might be able to climb up there, but not the rest of us."

"Excuse me," said Robyn. "I once climbed Pen-y-Fan in the Brecon Beacons."

"Sorry, I wasn't meaning…"

"Maybe we don't need—" Dylan tried before being interrupted by Janet.

"We went up Snowdon once with the Women's Circle Potholing Club."

"Potholing?" Eddie asked. "Up Snowdon?"

"Our Club Secretary is claustrophobic, so we have to do things with lots of open spaces or she can't join in. We didn't climb it though; they have a train. Forty pounds for ten miles. Could get the Orient Express for less."

"Meanwhile," I said, tapping my watch, "in the absence of ladders, tow ropes, or trains, how are we going to get all of us up to the nose?"

"I've had a thought," said Dylan.

"Hang on, Dylan. We just need to sort out who is going to go to the pub to scrounge a ladder or something."

"Yes, but—"

"How's a ladder going to help?" asked Robyn. "We can't get five of us up a ladder at the same time."

"How many ladders do you think your mate would have, Eddie?"

"I don't know. Oddly, that never came up in conversation."

"Somebody's going to have to go and borrow one. Or two, if he's got them."

"I'm not running up and down this hill all day, and certainly not with a ladder. Besides, you don't want me driving your car."

I looked at the others, then realised that it was going to fall to me. "Right, I'll go. Just where is this place, Eddie?"

"Don't rightly remember. But the village is no more than a few scattered houses, so just drive around a bit. You're bound to come across it."

"We haven't got time for me to just go wandering around hoping to stumble over a pub which may, or may not, have a ladder. We need another plan."

"You could ask at the post office," Eddie suggested.

"Where's the post office?"

"Ah, that's on the corner by… No, wait… scratch that, as you go into the village, it's on your left. Or maybe the right. It was a long time ago."

"This is impossible," I said. "We've got twenty minutes, and we don't even know where this pub is. Besides, surely nobody is going to be carrying a ladder with them. We must be missing something." As I glanced round the team, my eyes settled on Dylan. He was kneeling on the ground fussing over a huge, straggly looking dog, which could have been a cross between an Irish wolfhound and an alpaca. "Where did that come from?"

"This?" Dylan looked up at me. "Oh, this is Dog." He broke a piece from a bread roll and the animal gulped it down and looked up at Dylan with huge, grey eyes.

"Dog? Where did he come from?"

"Over there somewhere." Dylan pointed due south. "He's starving. Lucky I took some bread rolls from breakfast. He just came straight over to me while you were all stressing about the nose and ladders and stuff." Another chunk of bread followed the first.

"We weren't stressing—" I started.

Eddie interrupted my defence with, "Well, you were. A bit. Quite a lot, actually."

"It's not stress, it's… brainstorming. Throwing ideas around, honing a plan."

"Looked a lot like stressing to me."

"No. Well, okay, maybe a bit. But we still haven't any idea how we're all going to hold the nose. We can't even agree on which bit the nose is, and we're down to just fifteen minutes."

"It's all of it," Dylan said.

"What?" I asked.

"It's all of it. The nose. I've been trying to tell you."

"What's all of it?"

"The nose. This rock is called Bowerman's Nose. It's not called Bowerman, who happens to have a nose. It's Bowerman's Nose, all of it."

I stared at the rock. "It can't all be its nose. It looks like a person, not just a nose."

"The lad's right, Matt," said Eddie. "It's what it's called alright. Bowerman's Nose."

I looked at Robyn, she gave a shrug. "Seems right," she said.

I turned to Dylan. "Why didn't you say anything earlier?"

"I tried." He pulled the dog closer and rubbed the scruff of his neck. "Didn't I, Dog? I tried to tell them."

"Yes, well," I started. "Sorry, Dylan, we should have listened."

"We?" challenged Eddie. "I was listening, but you'd got your bloomin' sergeant's head on, and there's no shifting you once you're heading down that road. Like the time that—"

"Yes, Eddie, probably not the time to be bothering everybody with that stuff. We need to get on with this. Robyn, what was the clue again?"

Robyn swiped through a couple of screens on her phone. "Here we go, '*Where Levara the leveret left him, the mighty huntsman stands, afraid of no one, not even the devil himself. All must hold his nose'*."

"That seems we have to all hold the rock then? Agreed?"

Everybody nodded or muttered assent.

We tested several permutations of group shot against the stone giant but couldn't find one which showed the full rock with all of us in it.

"We need a selfie stick," said Eddie.

"My phone camera's got a timer," said Janet. "I use it when I'm boiling eggs."

"You use your camera to time boiled eggs?" Robyn queried. "Why don't you use your clock?"

"Because I don't want to know the time. I want to know when my eggs are ready. This goes flash when the eggs are ready."

"Can we get on with this?" I asked. "Janet, your system sounds perfect. If you can set up your camera timer and aim it at the rock, we can give it a go."

It took several attempts to select a suitable position for Janet's phone, but finally, we found the perfect rock on which to balance it so that it framed the rock, all five of us and the dog. We did a couple of dry runs with Janet pretending to press the button on her phone then hurrying back to us to take up her position.

"Okay," I said. "I think we're ready to go. Janet? You all set?"

"Ten-four, good to go. Roger that. I've always wanted to say that."

"Right, go!"

Janet ran across to where the phone sat on a nearby rock and pressed the button with precision then gave a little clap. She grinned like a five-year-old in a toothpaste advert and ran back to us to take up her position.

We all froze, waiting for the flash.

It didn't come.

We waited.

After a while, Eddie said, "What's happening? Are you sure you pressed the button?"

"Oh yes," Janet said. "We just have to wait."

"How long? Only I'm getting cramp in my leg, and I can't hold this smile forever."

"Six minutes," Janet said.

"Six minutes?" I asked.

"Yes, it's the perfect soft-boiled egg. Six minutes for two eggs."

"Why didn't you change the timer?" I asked.

"I can't remember how to do that."

"It's no good, I've got to stretch my leg." Eddie straightened up and did a little dance.

The camera flashed.

"There we are," said Janet.

We took a few moments to stretch limbs and tried again. Rather than attempt to reset Janet's egg-timer, we stayed with the six minutes, but didn't settle in our positions for the first five minutes. This time, the camera flashed when we were all in perfect shot and clearly touching Bowerman's Nose.

Janet retrieved her phone, and with a little help from Robyn, she uploaded the photograph. My app bleeped, and I checked the message: *"Congratulations Team Farmhouse Five. Location and picture accepted. Clue number four will follow tomorrow at 10:00. Your recommended starting point is rats.ocean.earth from where the next clue will be within a 25-mile radius."*

The team counter icon clicked down to 81.

"So, where's Rats Ocean Earth?" I asked.

Robyn tapped her phone. "Bodmin."

"Bodmin? That's not too far from home, only about an hour and a half, two hours tops. We don't really need a hotel."

"The problem with that idea," said Robyn, "is that if the clue is east of Bodmin, we could end up with a three-hour drive. Though, on the other hand, it could be on our doorstep."

"Hmm, not worth the risk. Okay, I guess we need to find somewhere near Bodmin to stay overnight, then."

I sat on a convenient rock and, for the first time, surveyed the view. The rolling hills of Dartmoor faded into a slightly hazy distance. Various outcrops of granite rose from the terrain at random points, though none so striking as Bowerman's nose. I looked again at the pile. It was very difficult to believe this was just a fluke of nature. Each piece looked like it had been specially cut to shape and positioned with great precision.

"Where did you say the dog came from, Dylan?" I asked.

"Over there," he said, nodding to the south.

"That's where Hound's Tor is," said Robyn.

"Seems appropriate," I said.

"I was reading about that," she said. "The legend is, that's where Bowerman's pack of dogs were turned into rock by the witch. And it was the basis for the Hound of the Baskervilles."

"Cool," said Dylan. "I've got a ghost dog."

"You haven't got any sort of dog," I said. "It probably belongs to somebody."

"I don't think he does," said Janet. "I can see the poor thing's ribs from here. And look at his coat. He's a stray, for sure. Look at the state of him."

The dog looked from Janet to me and somehow managed to make himself look even sadder in the process.

"A stray ghost dog," said Dylan. "I'll have to call him Yurei." He wrapped his arm around the dog. "Yurei? What do you think?" The dog brightened and licked Dylan's face. "Cool, he likes that. Yurei it is."

"That's an odd name," I said.

"It's Japanese, it means wandering ghost."

"You know Japanese?"

"No, silly, It's in the computer game Phasmaphobia."

I noticed Eddie wandering around the rock-pile. He kept pausing and staring into the distance.

"You alright, Eddie?" I asked.

"What? Oh, yes. Just not keen on all this ghost and witches nonsense. It gives me the heebie-jeebies."

"Well, we're heading out now, anyway." I turned to Dylan. "Say goodbye to Yurei, we're off."

"No," protested Dylan. "He's got to come. He's my dog."

"He's not your dog, Dylan. It probably belongs to a nearby farm or something."

"What farm? There's nothing out there, just more of this." He waved an arm around, taking in the area. "We can't leave him here."

"We can't take him," I said. "For one thing, we haven't got room in the car."

"I'm not going then," Dylan said. "We'll walk back, or hitchhike."

Janet knelt by the dog and stroked his head. "He's lovely. He can sit on my lap."

I looked at Janet, then at Yurei. Weighing up their relative sizes. "He can't sit on your lap, Janet. There'll be nothing left of you."

She looked up at me and said, "We're doing all this to save the stray dogs of the Little Didney Animal Rescue Centre. How's it going to look if we abandon this poor little man here?"

Yurei did a special sad face just for me. His ears drooped and his eyes pleaded.

"It's just not—" I started, then Yurei headed in my direction. He sat in front of me and looked up, tail beating the grass and eyes bright and pleading. "I'm sure Yurei will be…" Yurei's head cocked to one side, as if recognising his new name already. "I mean…" The head tipped the other way, and he gave the tiniest whimper. "Oh, for goodness' sake." I looked at Dylan. "But you're cleaning up any mess he makes in my car. Okay?"

"Cool, well done, Yurei," said Dylan as the dog ran back to him.

I shook my head. "Right, I suggest we get a bite to eat before we work out where we're going next."

"I ain't travelling with no devil dog," Eddie said. "You don't know what he's got following him." His eyes slowly scanned moors. "There'll be all sorts out here." He turned to me, his eyes wide and fixed. "When I was down here in 2007, I stayed at The Huntsman and Jacob Penrose, he's the landlord, he told me about some of the goings-on around here. There's Kitty Jay's Grave only just over there." He nodded to the west. "Her lover betrayed her, and she hung herself. There's new flowers on the grave every day, and nobody knows where they come from."

"You've been reading too many Lorne Turner books," I said. "I should imagine your landlord mate is just spinning yarns for the tourists. Good business."

"You can scoff, but he's got a haunted toaster."

"A haunted toaster? I don't believe this, get in the car. You can sit in the front. That way you can't see the dog, and you can even hold my hand if you get scared."

Eddie grunted something but headed down the slope to the car with the rest of us.

The Huntsman pub turned out to be less than a mile down the same lane. A gaudy painted sign, featuring a gnarled face, swung over an ancient, blackened oak door. I guessed the face was supposed to belong to Bowerman. We parked in what seemed an unnecessarily large car park, and Dylan took Yurei to a table on the small front lawn while we headed inside. The door creaked with just the right level of sinister as we stepped into an empty bar. Low wooden beams stretched across the room and were festooned with horse brasses interspersed with aged photographs in simple frames. I scanned a few. They seemed to be a mixture of portraits, or individuals in various settings.

We threaded our way through a selection of mismatched tables and chairs and reached the bar just as a man appeared from a door behind it.

"Eddie Bishop," greeted the man. "As I live and breathe. Seth told me you'd be dropping in. Pint of Otter?"

"Do you need to ask, Jacob?" Eddie said.

I looked at Eddie. "Who's Seth? And how did he know we'd be here?"

Eddie stalled. "Seth? Oh, he's just somebody I met last time I was down here."

"I got summat' for you, Eddie," Jacob said. "If you're interested, that is?"

"Not another briefcase full of whips and dildos, I hope. My missus went bonkers when she saw that. Took me ages to convince her I wasn't about to drag her off to some fetish club."

"A briefcase full of whips and dildos?" I said.

"Yeah, Jacob collects all sorts of things that his staying guests leave behind. Keeps it for a few months, then if nobody calls for it, he gives me first option before it goes on eBay." He turned to Jacob. "What have you got this time?"

"We had a TV film crew here a while back. Making a Sherlock Holmes series, and they came down here for the Hound of the Baskervilles' episode."

"Ooh, that's my favourite Sherlock Holmes story," said Janet. "It was set round here."

"Indeed it were," said Jacob. "There're some folks say Manaton was the village of Grimpen in the book." He pulled a pint from a pump marked Otter and slid it across to Eddie.

"We don't need your tourist talk, Jacob. So, what did this lot leave behind? A couple of umbrellas and a book about London bus routes of the 1960s like last time?"

"Yeah, sorry about that, Eddie. This is more of a surprise box. Lots of bits, mostly costume stuff, some cables, books, and loads of paper, looks like scripts. I think there's a microphone thing, but it's a bit bent."

"That don't seem worth much. I'll give you a tenner for the lot."

"Make it fifty. Those scripts could be collectors' items. They might have Benedict Cumberbatch's notes on them."

"He's not Sherlock anymore," said Janet. "He's off doing Hollywood now."

"There you go then," said Eddie. "Twenty, and that's it."

"I'll bring it out front for you." Jacob turned to us. "Now, can I get you folks anything?"

I ordered a pint of Otter and tried again with Eddie. "So, this Seth?"

"Old Seth Tyler," Jacob took over, as he poured a pint for me and another for me to take out to Dylan. "Bit of a one is our Seth. He never worries about which way up the bread falls, as long as it lands on his plate." He turned to Robyn. "What can I get you, love?"

Robyn clearly stiffened at the word *love*, but then overcame her instinct to challenge and ordered white wine for herself and Janet.

As Jacob poured the wines, he said to me, "D'you know, Seth sold me a so-called Alexa? Bloody thing only speaks Hungarian and no matter what I ask it to do, it only ever plays Hungarian folk music and tries to book me a hotel in Budapest." He pushed the wine to Robyn.

"Tell him about your toaster," Eddie said to Jacob, in a not-very-subtle attempt to change the subject. "He don't believe me."

"'Tis in the shed. Key's on the hook by the door, if you have a mind to visit it." He pointed to the main door. "Though, if you're gonna mess with it, you be careful to chain it up again after."

"You've got a toaster locked up in a shed?" I asked.

"Where else am I going to put it? Don't want it in the house."

"You could always just throw it away, if you don't want it," I suggested.

"Why is everything just thrown away when it's past its best these days?" asked Robyn. "We should be fixing things, not throwing them out."

"How do you go about fixing a haunted toaster?" Eddie asked.

"I tried chucking it out once." Jacob slid the drinks to Janet and Robyn. "Took it down the council tip over Bovey. Followin' morning, there it was back again. Sat on the kitchen counter like a vulture on a branch, just waiting to pick the carcass off yer soul." His eyes scanned left and right, as if searching for the toaster vulture.

"And this is haunted?"

"Stranger stuff hereabouts. There's Hunter's Tor just up there." He cast a nod northward. "They say that during a full moon Roman legionaries patrol the old Roman hill fort there. Not sayin' if it's true or not, but I heard clanking noises up there one night. Exactly like Roman armour."

"Isn't that where we were?" Eddie suddenly looked alarmed.

"No," said Robyn. "We were at Bowerman's Nose. Hunter's Tor is about a mile north of there."

"Bowerman's Nose?" queried Jacob. "No, don't need to worry about any ghost legionnaires up there. Just the witches."

After we'd collected our drinks and ordered snacks, we headed outside to join Dylan and Yurei at the table on the lawn. A gentle summer breeze whispered down from the hills, nudging at the grass.

"Come on then," Janet said to Eddie. "What's with this toaster? I had a haunted washing machine once. It used to say '*Help me, help me*' on the rinse cycle and then steal my socks. Did the toaster say anything?"

"No, it just makes pictures of a witch's face on every piece of toast. Nobody will eat it."

"Probably just a faulty heating element," I said.

"You try telling that to the truck driver who stopped for a breakfast with toast and then he picked up a hitchhiker on his way up to Okehampton." Eddie glanced left and right, as if in fear of being overheard. Then, in a lowered voice, "And neither him, nor his truck, were ever seen again."

"Um," I hesitated but decided to ask anyway, "how did they know he'd picked up a hitchhiker if nobody ever saw him again?"

"How do *I* know?" said Eddie. "I wasn't there, was I?"

A young girl arrived carrying a tray with our snack orders. As she placed them on the table, Dylan gave a stifled yelp, like he'd been stung by a wasp.

"What's up?" I asked.

"My food's wrong," he said. "The beans are touching the toast."

The girl scrunched her face in puzzlement. "But it's beans on toast," she said. "It's kinda how they come."

"No, no. I asked for beans *and* toast. Not *on* toast. It makes the toast go soggy. Beans mustn't touch the toast."

"I'm sorry," she said. "I don't understand."

"It's my fault," I intervened. "I probably ordered wrong. Could you please bring another one with the beans separate? I'll pay for it."

"I suppose," she said. "Shall I take this away?"

"No, leave it here, thanks. Somebody will eat it." I glanced at Yurei, already eyeing up the brunch mistake. As she turned back towards the door, I slid the plate to the ground where Yurei hungrily devoured it all in seconds.

"What are you going to do with him?" I asked Dylan.

"He'll live with me. I'll find some room for him." He thought for a moment. "I can get rid of the other armchair; I never use that anyway."

"You could take him to the Animal Rescue centre," said Janet.

"We're supposed to be doing this to help the Animal Rescue centre," I said. "Not bringing them more residents."

"He'll be alright." Dylan wrapped an arm around the dog's neck. "We're mates now."

The waitress brought Dylan's replacement, beans *with* toast, at the exact moment a battered white Transit van slid into the car park on a cloud of dust.

"Ah, that'll be Seth," said Eddie. "Can I borrow your keys?"

"You're not taking my car anywhere." I fumbled for a quick, but definitive conversation stopper. "It's only insured for me to drive, sorry."

"Nah, I don't want to drive anywhere, you wanted shot of my Prada leather coats, didn't you?"

"Oh, yes, here." I pushed my keys across to him.

"Cheers. Back in a jiffy." He headed over to the BMW.

The Transit van door swung open, and a small, round man clambered out. He moved as though walking was low on his list of enjoyable activities, and his bald head glinted with droplets of sweat.

Eddie opened the tailgate of the BMW and indicated the interior to Seth. They were too far away to hear what was being said, but it was clearly a negotiation of some kind. Waving arms, turning away, coming back, and lots of head shaking. Eddie finally closed the tailgate again and waved a dismissive hand towards the road. Seth stuffed his hands in his trouser pockets, looking for all the world like a stroppy schoolboy. He shook his head then kicked at a tuft of grass which was struggling through the gravel of the car park. Eddie turned once more, and negotiations resumed. Eventually, Eddie again opened the tailgate of the car and the pair of them loaded crates of leather coats into the Transit.

My sense of ease at having got shot of the contraband, however, was short-lived. Jacob appeared with a cardboard box the size of a large microwave and planted it on the next table.

"That's for Eddie," he said, and headed back inside.

I returned to watching the two by my car. It seemed the transactions had been successfully completed as hand shaking was followed by waves, and then another cloud of dust billowed around the Transit as it sped back out on the road.

Eddie closed the tailgate, then came back to our table.

"Well, that was worthwhile," he said.

I pointed to the box which the barman had left. "I thought you were getting rid of stuff? What're you going to do with that lot?"

"What? Oh, dunno." He lifted the lid on the box and pulled out a bundle of tangled, and fairly battered, extension leads. "I'll get a few bob for those." He reached in again and came out with a deerstalker hat. He planted it on his head. "What d'ya reckon? Elementary, dear Watson?"

"I don't think so. And how long am I going to have to cart this lot around?"

"It'll be gone faster than the hotel towels at a Tory party conference." He closed the box again. "You worry far too much. Have you ever wondered why so many men clock-out soon after retiring?"

"Probably because they've got friends like you."

Eddie chuckled and took a long drink on his beer.

As Dylan was due for another bail check-in, we decided it was probably best if we went back to Little Didney for the afternoon. We could catch a change of clothes and Eddie could clear his collection of extension leads out of my car.

CHAPTER FOURTEEN

TEAM BULLINGBOY CLUB

PERKINS' PHONE REFUSED TO STOP ringing. He'd ignored it twice already, but still it persisted. He looked at the caller ID. An avatar of an angry cat glared out from the screen. He'd thought it funny when he'd assigned this avatar to Sir Julius Combermere, but now it just filled him with terror each time he saw it. He gave in and with a slightly trembling finger, he stabbed answer.

"Perkins?" demanded an overpowering voice.

"Yes, sir."

"Where the devil have you been, man? I've been ringing you for the last twenty minutes."

"Sorry, I was… um… in the restaurant at the hotel. They have a rule about mobile phones during lunch and—"

"In the restaurant? What were you doing in the restaurant? You're supposed to be out there making sure these other teams are eliminated, not doing lunch like some millennial media consultant. There'll be plenty of time for lunch if I sack you for incompetence."

"Yes, sorry. I'm—"

"How are you getting on with putting trackers on all the cars? My contact in GCHQ says of the ones you've activated, most of them are now stationary, or just going to something called a Lidl. Whatever that may be."

"I think that a lot of the teams have already been eliminated, and it might be—"

"Why are you putting trackers on eliminated teams? That's a damned fool thing to do. Waste of governmental resources putting them on eliminated teams."

"They weren't eliminated when I put the trackers on. They must have—"

"'Od's pittikins, haven't we supplied you, and your bunch of scallywags, with every answer and means of winning this infernal competition? And yet you still can't seem to grasp the importance of this. I'd be better off employing a three-inch fool with his brains in his elbows."

"With all due respect, I feel—"

The phone went dead.

Perkins stared at the screen for a moment, then slipped the phone in his pocket and wandered outside. The car park of the Nirvana Motel had emptied significantly since breakfast. His own team had long-since gone off to their own clue location, the site of Stringfellow's first demonstration of powered flight in Chard. Since Combermere's tame chief constable had provided a list of suitable offenders from the Probation Office, Perkins' primary role was now basically that of liaison between Combermere, the Bullingboy Team crew, and the saboteurs. It certainly wasn't the career path he'd envisioned when he'd headed out from Oxford to start work as the Parliamentary Private Secretary to a senior front bench government minister. Trying to keep some sort of control over a bunch of miscreants recruited from the Probation Service's watch list of persistently re-offending petty criminals was his idea of hell. The very people he'd spent his life trying to avoid. And the fact that they were on a watch list of persistent re-offenders in the first place was hardly a testament to their skills in their chosen profession. He watched as Micky and Elvis fiddled with the front of their car, a dark blue Toyota Corolla.

Elvis noticed Perkins and straightened up. "Some sod's busted our headlight," he called.

Perkins drew a breath and held it momentarily before crossing the car park to see what the problem was.

Micky seemed to be trying to poke the broken pieces of glass back into the gap. He glanced up at Perkins. "You ain't got any duck tape about you, have you, guv?"

Perkins patted the pockets of his suit. "No, I'm terribly sorry, I seem to have come out without any. Maybe you could just carry on anyway? I mean, it *is* daylight, so it's not like you'll be needing your lights just yet. And we do have a schedule to keep."

"Yeah, about that," Elvis said. "Was we supposed to be followin' the BMW or the camper van? Only I kinda lost track." He tapped the side of his head. "I got this tune stuck in my head, dumfa dumfa dumfa, you know the one? DJ Chernobyl?"

Perkins shook his head. "No, I'm not familiar with that one."

"Bangin' it is. But I gotta confess, I wasn't really listening when you was talking. Soz, and all."

Elvis moved constantly as he spoke. It reminded Perkins of a marionette show he'd once seen on the beach at Bournemouth as a child. The operator had been very drunk, and the police had finally been called when Pinocchio started swearing at the children.

"I see," he said. "Well, you were supposed to disable the BMW, then follow the camper."

"Oh, yeah. We did that."

Perkins looked around the car park. "So, where is the BMW now?"

Elvis slowly scanned the car park, then said, "It's gone."

"Yes, evidently. And the camper you are following?"

Elvis repeated his search. "Yeah, that's gone an' all."

"Then may I suggest you follow the tracker we have on it?" Perkins studied his phone briefly. "Apparently, it's already near somewhere called Dunkery Beacon, not far north from here. Perhaps a little more haste might be in order?"

"Leave it to us, guv. We're on it already, ain't we, Micky?"

Micky nodded. "You can rely on us."

"Just one thing," Elvis said.

Perkins looked at him, his left eye twitching. "Yes?"

"Which way's north?"

Perkins' arm had already extended in the relevant direction even before Elvis had finished his question. Then, as he turned to head back towards the hotel, his phone bleeped to tell him a message had arrived. He opened it up. It was from Mr Nobody, Reeve's-Tabby's mysterious contact in GCHQ. The message read, *"Known starting locations so far for the clues in round four. Bodmin, Salisbury, Trowbridge. Will contact again if any more come through."*

He closed the phone and looked back to see why there appeared to be a fresh tirade of expletives from Elvis' direction. "More problems?" he asked.

"Me tyres've been slashed, look." He kicked a crumpled tyre with his foot. "That's five hundred quid's worth of Goodyear Eagles there. I'm gonna need some exes to get a new set."

Perkins drew a deep breath then let it slowly out again. "We have already discussed this; you are paid on results. To wit, the prevention of a team completing a round, and of which to date, you have so far failed to accomplish. Accordingly, your overheads are your responsibility alone."

"Yeah, but are we gonna get some money for a new set of treads?"

"No. There is no money. Not for treads, lights, DJ Chernobyls, or anything banging. There is no money."

"Huh, you don't need to get like that. We was just asking, like."

Perkins turned away and headed back inside, checking the message once again as he walked. Of the starting locations given, Bodmin was nearest. And he certainly didn't fancy visiting either Trowbridge or Salisbury. Decided then, he'd head for Bodmin and if his team were headed to one of the other start points, well, it didn't really matter. It wasn't as if they actually needed him. He continued walking to the fading sound of grumbles from Elvis.

TEAM THE ALTER EGOS

Bruce pulled his Batman mask over his head and reached forward to steady himself against the huge cairn. "I need to get some bigger eye holes in this," he said. "Can't see a thing apart from what's right in front of me."

"Just stay still," Clarke said. "It'll only take a couple of minutes."

"It might help if you kept your cape under control," Bruce grumbled. "They won't be able to see me in the picture if your cape is flapping all over my face."

"It's alright for you two," Diana said. "At least your capes keep you warm. I'm freezing."

Bruce pulled his mask up briefly to study Diana. "I didn't know Wonder Woman had nipples," he said with a grin.

Diana glanced down at her costume. "You'd have nipples too if you were wearing this get-up. Who'd have thought it would be so cold up here in August?" She nodded to indicate Bruce's crotch area. "And you can't talk. I can see you're not immune to the effects of a chill wind either." She gave a mischievous smile.

Bruce tried to pull his errant cape around himself.

"Well, it is the highest point on Exmoor," said Clarke. "I guess you have to expect a bit of a wind up here." He tugged his cape away from flapping at Bruce's head. "Are you ready with the camera yet, Peter? Only we're losing time."

"You have to all stay still," Peter complained. "It's hard enough doing this on a phone, anyway. The sun's too bright, I can't see the screen and every time I think I have, your capes flap all over the place and ruin it."

"Maybe take the photo from the other side," suggested Diana.

"Don't be silly," said Peter. "I won't be able to see you at all."

"I know, but I figured we'd probably all move round the other side with you."

"Oh, yeah."

Bruce, Diana, and Clarke shuffled around the cairn to the southern face.

"Interesting fact," said Bruce, as he sought to control his errant cape. "Did you know that this is the very spot which started the Joe Talon series of supernatural mysteries?"

"I thought that was a bit further up, on the coast," said Peter. "It was about a secret in some place called Crickley Hall. What was that book called?"

"The Secret of Crickley Hall?" offered Bruce.

"Oh yeah. That was Joe Talon, wasn't it?"

"No, you're thinking of James Herbert."

"I thought he did Dune."

"Now you're thinking of *Frank* Herbert."

"Oh, didn't he do... oh no, that was Terry Pratchett, I always get those two confused. Hold it there, I think I've got you all in." Peter clicked on his phone and studied the screen. "Better do another one." He looked up at the others. "Bruce, you might want to wrap your cape around..." he pointed to Bruce's crotch area and circled his finger in the air. "Only that which shouldn't be noticeable is making itself known by its absence. If you get my drift?"

Bruce looked down then hurriedly pulled the cape around himself. "It's this Lycra. It's very tight. Just take the picture, we're going to get timed out."

Peter fiddled with his screen again. "There we go. That's better, your reputation remains intact. Which is more than appears to be the case with certain bits of your anatomy." He grinned and tapped the screen again. "All good. We get our next clue in twenty hours and fourteen minutes. Give or take." He studied his screen again. "Thirteen now. Oh, and apparently we have a recommended starting location of picturing.pounces.joke."

Bruce tugged his own phone free from his Bat-utility belt and tapped in the words to the WhatThreeWords app. "That's Launceston, the castle."

"Lots of old stuff near Launceston," said Diana. "Tintagel, Plymouth, Power Isaac, and loads of old stones all over the place. We certainly won't be able to anticipate."

"Okay," said Clarke, "we'll go collect the camper and head off to Launceston today."

With capes flapping in the breeze, they trotted down the hill to Bruce's cry, "To the Batmobile!"

Their enthusiasm, however, was soon overtaken by the mere physical requirements of running over rough ground in full Lycra costumes specifically designed for standing still in at Comic-Cons and not for running in. Long before they'd reached the little car park at the end of the track, they were back to walking and trying to shed capes and masks.

As they approached the camper, Clarke noticed a problem. "Wait up," he said. "My X-ray super vision is telling me somebody has been up to no good." He pointed to the fuel filler cover which was not quite as flush as it should be.

"It's just come loose, that's all," said Peter.

Clarke moved closer and opened the flap. The filler cap lock had clearly been assaulted by something vicious. "Somebody's had a go at this."

Diana looked over his shoulder. "Were they trying to steal our fuel, do you think?"

"Maybe." Clarke ran his finger over the metal around the filler. "There's something here." He withdrew his hand and lightly rubbed his fingertips, squinting closely.

"What is it?" asked Bruce.

"Sugar, I think."

"You could taste it to make sure," suggested Peter.

Clarke gave him a scathing stare. "Seriously? It could be Novichok for all we know. You try it." He held his fingers towards Peter.

"Um, okay, maybe not. So, what do we do? Start it up and see what happens?"

"Probably not a good idea. The camper might blow up or something. I don't know how these things work."

"We've got breakdown cover with this," said Diana. "It came as part of the rental contract. I remember that."

"We haven't actually broken down though," said Peter. "They might not come if we say we haven't broken down, but we just think we might."

"We could drive it until it breaks down, then ring them," suggested Bruce.

"But what if they say we shouldn't have driven it if we suspected something was wrong and then they make us pay for a new engine or something?"

"Oh, for the love of Odin," said Diana. "Where's the paperwork? I'm just going to ring the breakdown people and see what they say."

Bruce reached into the vehicle and retrieved the rental papers and handed them to Diana. She chatted briefly to somebody, then gave the registration number and GPS position.

"There," she said, closing her phone case. "They said we did the right thing in not starting it, and that they're on their way. They have a special mis-fuelling service. They're going to drain it all out and give us enough fuel to get to a petrol station."

As they milled around the camper, awaiting the breakdown rescue, Bruce said, "Does anybody know someone who works in our Roaming Services department?"

"I know one person there," said Peter. "Trev, his name is. But he's a Star Wars nut."

"Jedi?" asked Bruce.

"No. He's into Jar Jar Binks."

"Oh dear, I'm not sure I can trust a Jar Jar Binksian. Anybody else?"

"There's Simon," Diana said. "He's a Trekkie, so he's okay. And he's in the International Alliance of Nerds."

"Cool, can you give him a call and ask if there have been any Ponzi Phones at this location? It's worth a try."

Diana called up the number and chatted briefly before turning to Bruce. "He says there were two Ponzi Phones at this exact location about an hour ago. They're now on the M5 heading west. They've just passed Exeter."

"Can you get the numbers?"

"I'll ask, hang on." She spoke briefly on her phone then pulled back to glance at the screen. "Got them."

"Great, text them over." Bruce climbed in the back of the camper and pulled out his company laptop.

Diana followed and watched him from the doorway. "What are you doing?"

"They have Ponzi Phone 10s. So I'm sending them an operating system update to OS23:1:002."

"But that's only for Ponzi Phone 12s. Won't that... ah... I see."

"Exactly, it will brick their phones. There we go, all done."

Diana's phone pinged and she glanced at the screen. "Simon's also sent me a list of their movements over the last week." She scrolled through the message. "That's odd," she said. "The locations are primarily hotels and the like. Not clue locations, by the look of it."

"That makes sense," said Bruce. "If these people were an actual team, they wouldn't be able to follow other teams. They'd be too busy following their own clues. These guys must be working for another team as sort of saboteurs."

"We need to find out which team then," said Diana. "I'll ask Simon if he can tie in any of the contacts from these phones to movements of others near clues sites."

A high-pitched beep-beep-beep sound alerted them to the arrival of the breakdown service. Bruce checked through the camper window and saw Clarke head over to greet the mechanic.

"If somebody's playing dirty, we need an edge," said Bruce. "I'm going to ring that other team. Who was it? Oh, yes, the Farmhouse Five. I'll see if they want to swap any more clues." He scrolled through his contact list and pressed call.

CHAPTER FIFTEEN

TEAM FARMHOUSE FIVE

WE'D JUST ARRIVED BACK IN Little Didney when my phone rang. Bruce from The Alter Egos. What did he want now? I motioned for the others to carry on and for Dylan to stay with me, then answered the call.

"Bruce?" I greeted.

"Hiya, Matt. Just wondering how you got on with the clues we exchanged."

"Ah, yes. The one to do with smugglers in the Caribbean, I'm not sure, but I think our start point tomorrow is in that area." I watched Dylan trying to persuade Yurei to exit my car. The dog had managed to spread himself across the back seat and was exercising a level of passive resistance that would have struck awe into the 2003 Stop the War protesters. I pulled a luggage strap out of the boot and handed it to Dylan. He looked at me as if I'd just handed him a dead kitten.

"Cool," said Bruce. "Your clues haven't come up yet either. Do you want to swap again?"

I still wasn't sure whether I could trust him. A working life dedicated to dealing with thieves, conmen, and fraudsters, had left me with a slightly skewed view of human nature.

I tried to suppress my natural inclination to suspect the worst, and asked,

"Are you sure this still makes sense? I mean, we're each helping a competitor. That just seems odd."

I glanced at Robyn and made an expression which I hoped conveyed, *"They want to swap again. What do I say to him?"*

She just nodded. Did that mean she understood or was saying it's okay? I glanced at Eddie, but he was more concerned with off-loading his dressing-up boxes and extension leads, and Janet was already on her way down the hill towards The Smuggler's Arms.

"It's only competition between us if we both make it to the final two," Bruce said. "And the probabilities of that are tiny, far smaller than being in the final with an unknown team. And if we do? Well, we'll know we did everything right."

"I suppose," I said, glancing at Eddie and Robyn to see if they objected, but neither seemed interested. I still didn't understand this probability business. I tucked the phone into my shoulder and tried to make a loop in the luggage strap, waving it at Yurei. Dylan's eyes suddenly widened in understanding.

"Cool," said Bruce. "What clues did you get then?"

"Oh, no. You first."

"Okay, ours was Dunkery Beacon. Maybe something you dip in your tea. On the high X, more will be seen. Dunkery, something you dunk, and X more, for Exmoor, and it's the highest point on Exmoor. Now you."

"Now me what?" I did a thumbs up to Dylan, who had finally secured Yurei to the luggage strap.

"Your turn, now you give us the clue you've done."

"Oh, right." I briefly wondered how he could be so naïve and trusting of a complete stranger. I could just spoof a clue and he'd never know. He'd surely assume it had never come up. I didn't. "We've just done Bowerman's Nose. A strange rock formation near Manaton. The clue was something to do with a witch called Levara and a huntsman not being afraid of the devil. Sorry, can't remember it exactly."

"That's cool, probably not too many clues about witches and devils."

"Just watch out for the haunted toaster."

"I ain't afraid of no ghosts. I have my sonic screwdriver."

"Never leave home without one." I closed the call and checked the luggage strap attached to Yurei. Yurei growled quietly and pushed closer to Dylan. "Yes, well, that looks secure." I made to pat the dog on the head, but a pair of eyes burning with the embers of hell suggested it might not be a good idea.

Dylan stroked him gently and tickled his ear.

"He's alright, he's never bitten anyone," Dylan said.

"You've only had him for an afternoon," Eddie said, setting his box on the ground. "He's probably got a trail of bodies all across the moors. Can't trust a ghost dog."

I locked the car, arranged to meet the others later, then took Dylan down to PC Muchmore's office behind Tiffin's Bakery and Cakes. Dylan entered the office first, and I heard a loud voice say, "No dogs in here."

Dylan froze in the doorway and his limbs twitched as panic started building. I slipped past him and said, "Hello, Albert. It's alright, he's just come to sign in for his bail."

Albert looked at Yurei. "Dogs don't do bail. Well, least not since Mrs Pascoe's little fox terrier broke into Pengelly's Pasty Shop."

"No, it's not the dog. It's Dylan, he's the one on bail."

Albert Muchmore scanned Dylan up and down. "Oh yes, you. You're the one who took my fax machine to pieces last week."

"It was making funny noises," Dylan protested.

"It's meant to. It's a fax machine."

"You still have a fax machine?" I asked.

"Not anymore," PC Muchmore grumbled. "Anyway, what're you doing here, Sarge? Sorry, Matt, I mean. It'll take me a while to get used to that. Thought you were busy chasing clues. Not been eliminated, have you?"

"No, we were nearby, so it seemed like a good idea to bring Dylan in for his bail attendance."

"I'll get the file." He pulled his not insignificant bulk free of the swivel chair. "You wait here, son." Then to me, "Keep him away from my desk,

Destruction of police property's a serious offence." He disappeared through the door behind the desk.

"You wait here," I said to Dylan, as I took the opportunity to be nosey.

For the last fifteen years of my career, I'd been stationed at Penzance. I'd often thought it would have been nice to have finished my service in my home town of Little Didney, but the size of the village hardly warranted a beat constable. Certainly not a Detective Sergeant. I moved a couple of papers on the untidy desk. A missing dog report, a boundary dispute between two neighbours, and some second home owners making a complaint about the smell from old Tom Trevellick's farm. No, this would have driven me mad in no time.

Muchmore trundled back through the door, clutching a manilla folder. He opened it on the desk and pushed a piece of paper at me. "Here, sign this."

"I'm not the one on bail," I said.

"I know, but he ain't coming anywhere near my desk or I'll end up spending the afternoon putting it back together. You can sign as his temporary custody officer."

"I'm no longer in the Job," I said. "Hang on." I took the paper over to Dylan and put a pen in his hand. "Just sign here." I held the paper against the door.

Dylan scrawled his signature, and I returned the paper to Muchmore. "There you go. Good for another forty-eight hours."

As I turned to guide Dylan out of the office, he handed me a door handle. "This came loose," he said.

I studied it for a moment, then looked at the place on the door where it used to sit. "How...? Oh, never mind." I turned to Muchmore and placed it on his desk. "Here, you'll be needing this when you want to get out."

We made our way to The Smuggler's Arms. Our plan had been to catch up on a few things we all needed to do, then have a quick bite before heading off to Bodmin in preparation for the next morning's clue.

Such are plans.

I opened the door of the Smuggler's and the noise from inside spilled out through the door and surrounded us. I stepped a foot cautiously inside and the noise increased. I paused to take in the scene. Party balloons and bunting graced every beam and wall, much of it clearly from the late queen's platinum anniversary and declaring 70 years of reign. One could always rely on old Sam Goodenough, the landlord, to recycle everything. Even when totally inappropriate.

A middle-aged woman in jeans and a green jumper closed on me.

"Sorry," I said. "I didn't realise this was a private function."

"Matt?" she greeted.

"Yes. Do I know…" I leafed through my mental mugshot book, trying to place the face.

"I'm Gwen," she said.

"Gwen? Oh, Gwen, yes, of course. Little Didney Animal Rescue. Nice to finally meet you."

She smiled at Dylan. "And you must be Dylan, and who's this lovely boy?" She squatted by Yurei and rubbed his neck. A dog treat appeared in her hand as if by magic and she slipped it to Yurei, who instantly sat and wagged his tail.

"His name's Yurei." Dylan shuffled nervously, and I instinctively looked around for anything prone to dismantling.

She straightened and touched my arm. "Come on in. I'll get you a drink."

"It looks like somebody's having a party. Maybe we'll just go down to the Harbour Cafe."

"No, this is for you. It's a thank you from the animals. Come and meet Teller."

"Teller? As in the magician, Teller?"

"Well, not quite." She led us through the packed bar and at each table we neared, people smiled up at us, or held up drinks in toast.

I could feel Dylan's stress rising with each table we passed until we finally spotted Eddie, Robyn, and Janet. They were seated at a group of four tables pushed together and, by the collection of glasses, they'd been here a while. Dylan immediately slinked into a seat next to Janet and ushered Yurei under the table.

Gwen guided me to a vacant seat then slid in beside me. My feet brushed against something soft under the table and I flinched back in surprise.

"Oh, yes," said Gwen. "That'll be Teller. I wondered where he was."

I peeped under the table. A pair of huge brown eyes shone back at me, and a wet nose pushed upward between my thighs.

"Ah," said Gwen. "Lovely, you've made friends with him already."

"Yes, he's very… big, isn't he. That's an unusual name."

"We rescued him and his brother, and we called them Penn and Teller. Penn's just gone to his forever home, but they couldn't take Teller. Bless." She reached down and rubbed his head. "He's a bit sad."

Dylan, and his chair, suddenly slid sideways towards Teller. I put my leg out to stop the chair and Yurei looked at me with eyes that could pierce titanium.

Dylan pulled the luggage strap closer, restricting Yurei's lunge. "There's a good boy, Yurei. See, he's a nice dog. He's a friend."

Teller placed his head on my thigh and looked up at me. He looked somewhere between a collie and a German shepherd, with maybe just a touch of wolf. Big brown eyes stared up at me, pleading with me for something. I hadn't the faintest idea what he wanted, so I rubbed his head and he pushed into my hand. His shoulders came just above the level of my knee and the soft, long white fur on his chest contrasted sharply with the dark brown of his back.

"You've made a friend there," said Robyn from two seats to my left.

"He just wants to find out if I'm going to feed him," I said. "They're genetically programmed to do this."

"Genetically programmed to tap up grumpy old coppers for food?"

"Less of the old. Are you going to eat those crisps?" I nodded towards an opened packet of salt & vinegar crisps.

"Help yourself," she said, pushing the packet towards me. "Drinks and snacks are all paid for."

"How?"

"We all had a whip round for the team," said Gwen. "Our way of saying thank you on behalf of the animals."

"So... all this..." I waved an arm to indicate the crowd in the bar. "This is all for us?"

"Of course." She squeezed my hand. "You're doing a marvellous job."

"But... we haven't really done anything. We've just solved three puzzles. The chances of us getting through are..." I needed one of Robyn's algorithms to tell me what our chances were. "Slim," I finished, lamely.

"You'll get through." She patted the back of my hand in time with each word. "We all have absolute faith in you."

"But—"

"Now, I must circulate." She stood and scanned the room. "Have you seen Reverend Featherstone? He was going to bring his Ouija Board of Fun game. Quid-a-go to raise funds." She disappeared into the crowd like a ghost into mist.

"No pressure there then," I muttered, to nobody in particular.

"Isn't it lovely?" Robyn slid into the seat just vacated by Gwen. "Everybody rallying round like this. It must be lovely to live in a community where everyone watches out for each other."

"Bunch of busybodies, mostly," grumbled Eddie. "A man can't even move his stock around quietly without some curtain twitcher wantin' to know what you've got in your boat."

"Is nobody even slightly worried that all this is for us, and yet our chances of winning this are about as likely as me being able to fold up a fitted sheet?"

"I've got hiccups," said Janet, then gave a hiccup as if to prove her point. She tapped her fingers to her lips, gave a little giggle, then took a sip of wine. Another hiccup, another sip, and her eyes scanned her companions at the table. "Oh dear. That's a tad more stronger than one might antisipect... expectirate... think." She held her glass up in a toast. "Hooray for the animals. Hic, oh whoops."

A pint of beer appeared in front of me. I turned to refuse it, but Gwen was already folding back into the melee. I took a very small sip and said, "To the animals."

A hand landed on my shoulder, and I turned to see a man with a ruddy face, orange slacks, and a yellow jumper draped across his shoulders. "Jolly good show," he said. "All power to the animals, what?"

"What?"

"I had a dog once. Berserker. That wasn't his name, just his demeanour. Went berserk at everything, the doorbell, the postman, the milkman. The postman and the milkman turned up at the same time once, it took me a month to redecorate the hall." He patted my shoulder and planted a bottle of champagne on the table. "Anyway, keep up the good work. Must dash, have to pick up a pie, it's Wednesday. Give my love to the doggies."

I watched him go and reached across the table to a bowl of cheesy puffs somebody had just planted on the table. Teller pushed his head against my thigh again to remind me he was there and that he liked cheesy puffs. I fed him one, and he crunched it noisily, while dribbling orange coloured dog-slobber onto my jeans. Yurei's head popped up from nowhere, demanding to know where his cheesy puff was.

A microphone crackled from a makeshift stage at the far end of the bar. "Hello, hello," Gwen's voice fought through the hubbub. "Attention please. Our band, the Dancing Queens, are about to start, so I want to invite our fearless champions, the Farmhouse Five up to the stage to join us."

The crowd between the stage and our table parted in a way that would have made Moses feel smug. Everybody seemed to be looking towards us. I tried to sink into my seat, but Janet was already on her feet, making shooing movements with her hands and calling, "How exciting. I hope they play Bohemian Rhapsody. That's my favourite."

"I think you might have the wrong—" I started, but she'd gone. Eddie grumbled to his feet and cajoled a reluctant Dylan to join him. I looked to my left, expecting to see Robyn, but her seat was empty. I scanned the room to no avail, then followed the rest of my team through the parting sea of smiling faces, suffering countless back-slaps as we went.

Once we'd gathered into an uncomfortable, and embarrassed huddle on the stage, Gwen took control and announced what she'd decided was to be our anthem. The Winner Takes it All. As the band started to play, Gwen waved her arms first to the audience, stirring the excitement, then to us in encouragement for us to sing along.

Over my long career in the Force, I'd confronted many an armed thug, stood in the path of fleeing vehicles, and even once faced down an enraged, and cheated upon, wife who was attempting to decapitate her husband with an electric bread knife. Yet still this was the most terrifying by far.

Not having the faintest idea of the words, I mouthed along to the noise made by the band while trying to smile and bounce enthusiastically. I feared I probably looked like I'd just been Tasered and tried to hide behind Janet. Not an altogether wise choice, given our size difference, but desperate times...

Eventually, the torture stopped, and we were allowed to salvage our shattered dignity and return to our seats. There was still no sign of Robyn. Teller was waiting for me as I sat down, and he immediately reminded me in no uncertain terms that I'd been neglectful in my cheesy puff duties.

"That was fun," said Janet. Her eyes darted round the table then popped wide in delight when she realised her wine glass had been refilled during her absence.

Dylan retrieved Yurei from the woman he'd been sitting next to.

"He's a very interesting dog," she said. "Dobermann?"

"Dunno." Dylan shrugged. "He just sort of turned up."

"It's not of this earth," Eddie said. "Ghost dog, is what it is."

I felt movement to my left and turned to see Robyn sliding back into her seat.

"What happened to you?" I asked.

"What? Oh, I had to make an urgent phone call." She reached for one of the opened wine bottles and half-filled her glass.

"Ah, more work?"

"Um, yes. An investment company. They want me to check the integrity of their data." She took a sip of wine and looked grateful for it. "It's all very boring really."

"You disappeared very quickly. You missed the show." Teller pushed his nose up between my knees and I fed him another cheesy puff. "One second you were there, the next gone. Like a ninja, whoosh." I made a whoosh gesture with my hand.

Robyn's eyes darted round the room. "I need some fresh air," she said. "Too many people."

"I could do with a breather too. I'll join you."

Robyn searched my eyes briefly, flicked a brief smile, then stood. "What're you going to do with him?" she nodded towards Teller.

I studied the dog for a moment. "I expect he'll stay here. Gwen will pick him up, no doubt."

But Teller was not going to be left behind. Not when his source of cheesy puffs was on the move.

The outside of The Smuggler's Arms was almost as crowded as the inside. The handful of tables were full, and others milled about the narrow street. People repeatedly wanted to shake our hands, buy us drinks or pat us on the back. We managed to find a quiet corner.

"This is madness," said Robyn.

"It's village life. Not much happens here, so people make the most of it when it does."

"I'm not good with crowds."

"I'm more worried about their expectations," I said. "We've had a bit of luck so far, but there's no way we can win this."

"Yeah, about that…" Robyn's eyes swept round the area as if looking for somebody. "I'm not sure I can see this through. Work, you know. I didn't realise I'd be so locked into this for such a time."

"Oh, I see. You do know if you leave, we can't go on? We all have to stay, or we're eliminated. You did know that, didn't you?"

"Yeah, but it's just that—"

"Ah, there you are," Gwen descended on us like a headmistress catching us smoking behind the bike shed. "Janet told me you'd popped out." She glanced down at Teller, sat patiently by my side. "I see he's taken with you."

"Not me so much," I said. "Cheesy puffs."

"Glad I've got you both. I would have asked Eddie or Janet but they're… how should one say…?"

"Both lit up like Christmas trees?" I offered.

"Yes, well, I suppose I could have asked Dylan, of course, but he's… you know, Dylan."

"What can we help you with, Gwen?"

"It's just that I don't know how this is going to work. When you win this competition, they will give the prize to you five of course. And that's only right, as it should be. But what happens then? Will you want a payment of some sort? For your troubles. And how long will it take? Only, we have just four weeks before we have to get out. Is that enough time? And the animals, how are we going to move them all? Oh dear."

Robyn drew a deep breath, paused, then started, "Gwen, I have something I must—"

I put my hand on Robyn's arm and cut through her words. "We're both a bit concerned that everybody is expecting some sort of miracle that we might not be able to deliver."

I felt Robyn's glare and squeezed her arm.

"I don't understand," said Gwen.

"We still have a long way to go, and there are a lot of other teams competing."

Gwen waved a dismissive hand. "Don't be silly. We all know you can do it. Rachel's thrown her rune stones things. They said you'd win, and Reverend Featherstone said he's going to give you a mention in Evensong tonight." She took my hand and patted it. "You just need a little faith, that's all." She looked like she was about to say something, then turned and hurried back into the pub.

"Why did you stop me? Isn't it best that she knows sooner?" challenged Robyn.

"I think we need to have a more private conversation," I said.

Her body stiffened, and she shifted to-and-fro a bit, as if unsure whether to go or stay. "Now?" She looked side to side.

"No, not now. Right now, we need to show our faces here." I motioned to the pub doorway. "We're heading to Bodmin later, ready for tomorrow's clue. We'll talk there."

"I was thinking…" She paused and studied my face. "You know, maybe it might be best if I just sort of slipped away now. Before anyone really notices."

"You really think nobody will notice?"

"Well…"

"When the rest of us are still here. You don't think they'll catch on fairly quickly that you've pulled the rug from under all their dreams? What on earth could be so important that you'd do that to everybody?"

"Look, you know as well as I do that we're not likely to win this. Does it *really* matter whether I disappear now or tomorrow? It's this work stuff, and anyway, they're going to have to face up to it one way or the other. This…" She waved a hand, indicating the chaos inside. "This is just insane."

"Okay, I'll make you a deal. Come with us to Bodmin. We'll talk there, and if what I say makes no difference, you can leave then. We'll try to go on until the point comes where the Quiz controllers, or bots, or whatever they are, ask for verification of your presence. We might get away with it. Deal?" I held my hand out.

She pulled her lips tight, and her eyes narrowed. The anguish at making a decision played across her face like it was subtitled. Or maybe that was just my copper's instinct for people trying to hide from questions they don't like.

Finally, and with a little shake of her head to dismiss her internal conflict, she pushed her hand forwards and took mine. "Deal."

Her hand felt warm, and oddly comfortable. We held contact for just two beats longer than required by formality. We both noticed, and at some unspoken cue, we broke contact.

"Thank you," I said.

"Well, alright." She turned towards the pub door, then back to me again. "But just Bodmin, right? I can leave then, yes?"

"If you still want to."

"Okay. I guess you're driving us up there." She headed for the door. "I need a drink."

I re-entered the bar to a scene which reminded me of the time I caught five minutes of Today in Parliament during a debate about MP's expenses. People were shouting, arms waved, and others seemed to be running around in pursuit of something, but I couldn't see what.

Gwen intercepted my momentary stupor. "Oh, thank goodness you're here," she said, a definite note of panic to her words. "I think it might be best if you gather your team and disappear."

"What's happening?" I scanned the room, taking in the chaos.

"It all started when we were about to start the bingo, and Dylan," she pointed to where he sat at the table with a scattering of bingo cards around him. "He just suddenly went all weird and ran round gathering all the bingo cards which Mrs Pomfrey had just distributed. He said they were all wrong and needed to go check them. I don't know what came over him."

"Oh dear. I'm sorry, he can get a little bit… trying. But he means well."

"And then his dog stole the Reverend Featherstone's Ouija Board of Fun and won't give it back. Nobody dares go near him."

"Ah, yes. He's new to us, and… he's not quite… um, socially trained yet."

"And Janet, well, I've never seen such a thing."

"Janet?" I queried. "What on earth's Janet done?" The thought of Janet offending anybody seemed surreal.

"I think she's been drinking."

"Well, yes," I said, confused as to why that should be a problem.

"I mean *drinking*," she mouthed the word rather than spoke it and at the same time circled her finger in the air. "We usually try not to let her *drink* so much," again, the word remained silent.

"I'm sorry, I didn't know. What happened? Is she alright?"

"Oh yes. She's fine, though I'm not so sure about the Reverend Featherstone. He's probably never had a lap dance before. Poor man."

I looked over again towards our table where Janet sat watching Dylan with his bingo cards. She seemed perfectly normal apart from a slightly glazed look and the fact she appeared to be wearing a vicar's dog-collar.

"Janet?" I mused. "Who'd have thought?" I found myself stroking the head of Teller, who was now sitting beside me. How do they do that?

"Normally, we try to distract her before she gets to that stage, and Mr Goodenough usually keeps an eye on her and waters down her sherry a bit, only he was helping me put out the fire at the time."

"Fire?" My head was now beginning to enter the dazed zone.

"An extension lead for the karaoke machine, never seen the like. Eddie got it for me. It just suddenly burst into flames while I was trying to set up YMCA."

"I'll gather up the team. I think it's for the best."

CHAPTER SIXTEEN

TEAM SABOTEURS

As Elvis strolled into the lounge of the Hotel Arnaquer, his usual air of supreme, but completely unmerited, self-confidence took a knock. His white Adidas trainers sank into the thick Axminster carpet, and the smell of old leather furniture and wood polish brought him to the edge of sneezing. He paused and tugged his grey tracksuit bottoms up a bit higher to cover the waistband of his Calvin Klein underpants. He felt obliged to make the effort when in somewhere this plush. He scanned the room and quickly located Micky. He was seated at a table next to the grand piano. Elvis waved an acknowledgement, then headed to the bar.

The barman looked Elvis up and down. "Good afternoon, sir. What can I get you?"

"A couple of pints of Stella and a packet of cheese and onion please, mate."

"I'm afraid we only have Stella in bottles." The barman placed two bottles on the highly polished bar.

Elvis picked one up and examined it. "That's 330 mili-whatsits, ain't it? That's a third, right?"

"It is indeed."

"That's cool. We can work with that." He held up his fingers and did some mental arithmetic. "Thirds yeah, we're gonna need..." he counted his fingers. "Six of those then."

"But it's a third of…" The barman realised he was probably going to lose this and finished with, "Certainly, sir." He collected another four bottles. "And it was a packet of cheese and onion crisps?"

"You got it."

The barman placed a packet of D'Abrille's hand cooked, Manchego and balsamic vinegar crisps next to the bottles.

"You ain't got no Walker's then?"

"We're right out, terribly sorry." He slid a pair of crested glasses to Elvis.

"No, ta." Elvis tucked the crisps under his arm and gathered up the bottles. "Won't be needin' them."

He sat opposite Micky and dumped the beers and crisps on the highly polished table. "They ain't got no proper crisps," he said, trying to get comfortable on the slippery red leather of the seats.

"My phone's dead," Micky slid his phone across the table towards Elvis.

Elvis picked it up and studied it. The blank screen refused to respond to any number of presses, swipes, or taps. "You've forgotten to charge, that's all." He gave it a quick shove and it glided smoothly across the table back to Micky.

"No, I ain't." Micky picked up the phone. "I 'ad it on charge in the car. It's dead, I tell you. Soddin' Ponzi Phones." He emptied his first bottle of Stella in one. "Why'd we have to have Ponzi Phones? Can't even get Zombie Convent Slaughter to work on it either."

"Because that's what they gave us." Elvis opened the packet of D'Abrille's hand cooked, Manchego and balsamic vinegar crisps and emptied them on the table. "Help yourself."

"Gimme your phone." Micky held his hand out. "I need to ring Sharon. Gotta make sure she don't forget my prescription."

Elvis pulled out his phone and pushed it across the table.

Micky picked up the phone and swiped at the screen. Then he pressed. Then he tapped. "Your phone's dead an' all."

"Give it to me." Elvis brushed crisp debris from his hands and tapped at the screen. "You've jinxed them, that's what you've done." He stuffed the phone back in his pocket. "Always said they were crap phones. Overpriced small dick substitutes."

"Why would anyone want a substitute for a small dick?" asked Micky. "Ain't a substitute a replacement for something you ain't got? Like if you ain't got a PS5 then a Nintendo is a substitute. Why would you want a substitute for a small dick?"

"What are you talking about? I don't need a substitute; I've got my old SimSun in the Toyota. You can borrow that when we're done."

They finished their beers and most of the crisps, then headed out into the car park. They stood under a group of beech trees that loomed over a hedge at the eastern end of the car park.

"Which car are we supposed to be nobbling?" Micky asked.

"Those four over there." He pointed to a group of prestige cars separate from the main parking area. "The Cayman, Ferrari Roma, the Porsche Carrera, and the DB12."

"*All* of 'em?" Micky asked.

"Yeah, they're all one team, but they all drive their own cars. Tossers. Here you go." Elvis tossed a spray can of black paint to Micky. "Paint out those two security cameras up there, I'll get the other ones. And, put your 'at and sunglasses on, in case anybody catches a glimpse."

Elvis scrambled up on a brick ornamental tree planter and sprayed the two security cameras. As he jumped down, he heard Micky call, "I can't see."

He hurried over to find Micky sitting on the concrete by the wall. His face was black.

"What happened?"

"I had the can round the wrong way and sprayed myself in the face. I can't see anything. I think I've gone blind."

Elvis knelt down beside him and removed Micky's sunglasses. "How about now?"

Micky blinked his eyes open in the late afternoon, low-hanging sun. "Wow. Okay, yeah, I forgot I was wearing those."

Elvis clambered up another planter and sprayed the cameras which Micky had failed to disable.

"Sorry," said Micky. "I thought I'd gone blind. We gonna do the cars now?"

"No, I'll do them. You can't go anywhere looking like that."

"Like what?"

"You've got a black face. You look like one of them minstrels in the old movies. You'll probably get yourself arrested for being a racist piss-taker. Wait here."

Elvis did a quick scan of the car park, then ran over to the quartet of high-end status cars. He hurried along the row of vehicles, spraying each of the windscreens in black paint. When he'd finished, he stood back to admire his handiwork, tossed the can in a nearby bush, then hurried back to Micky.

"Right, all done. Now we need to get you cleaned up before anybody cops a sight of you and sticks you on a plane to Rwanda as an illegal."

They scurried into the gents' toilets and set about trying to scrub the paint from Micky's face. After twenty minutes of scrubbing and soaping, Micky's face had gone from looking like a surprised gorilla to resembling an angry tomato, though still likely to cause consternation. They returned to the lounge bar and found a table in a corner. Elvis collected more drinks.

"We'll just wait here till the fuss dies down," said Elvis. "Then we'll get hold of Mr Perkins to sort out some more phones."

After about thirty minutes, the rising noise of a commotion outside proved too much for Elvis' curiosity, and he ventured out to have a look.

The Money Boys were standing around their cars and talking on phones. A tall, slim man in a grey suit, who Elvis guessed to be the hotel manager, was in deep conversation with one of the Money Boy team. The manager pointed to the cameras; the Money Boy pointed to the Aston Martin.

Elvis slipped back inside before they decided to point at him.

"They're having a mare about their cars," he said, settling back in his seat and picking up a bottle of Stella.

"What about these phones?" Micky asked.

"I'll give Mr Perkins a ring." He pulled out his own phone and called up the number.

"Why are you ringing me from your own phone?" was Perkins' greeting. "You're only supposed to use the phones we provided. They're secure."

"They're secure alright," replied Elvis. "Secure as a house brick. And about as much use."

"You've broken the phones? Both of them? How?"

"Nothing to do with us. They just broke all on their own. Won't turn on, nothing."

"Phones don't just break on their own. They're Ponzi Phones, top of the range. You must have dropped them or something."

"Oh, yeah, I remember now. We was juggling with 'em to relieve the relentless misery of our lives, and all of a sudden... what'dya think we were doing? You gonna get us some new phones or what? And not pieces of Ponzi Phone crap next time. Couple of SimSun X-flip 3000s would do nicely."

"How about you just swap the SIM cards to your own phones for the moment while I see what we can do?"

"That'll cost extra. Us using our own minutes. Minutes don't come cheap."

"I'm sure that can be arranged. Just send me the itemised bill. Now, have you stopped the Money Boy Team yet?"

"Yeah, sure. They ain't going nowhere for a while. Be lucky if they get back on the road this side of Christmas."

"I'm not worried about Christmas, only that they don't complete the next clue. Can you confirm that?"

"Job done."

"I sincerely hope so. And just a reminder, you do understand that our financial arrangements are purely dependent upon you rendering a team hors de combat *prior* to them logging in at a location, rather than subsequent to it?"

"Come again?"

Perkins sighed, then tried again. "You only get paid when you stop a team completing a login. You don't get paid if you disable them *after* they've logged in. Vis-à-vis, The Alter Egos this morning where they had completed their clue before you sabotaged their vehicle."

"Oh, yeah. But we couldn't do it before."

"Why?"

"They was in it, weren't they? They'd have noticed."

"I'll talk to you later."

"Wanker," Elvis grunted as he re-pocketed his phone. "What's that noise?"

"What noise?" asked Micky.

"Outside. Rumbling noise. That's getting louder." Elvis picked up his bottle of Stella and headed for the door.

Outside, The Money Boys stood at the edge of the car park, their suitcases beside them. The rumbling noise grew to a deafening level, vibrating through the building. A cloud of dust whipped up from the centre of the car park as the helicopter came in to settle. Once it had landed, The Money Boys walked over to it, and the door swung open. A young woman in a blue uniform jumped out to usher them inside. Two minutes later, the helicopter lifted into the air and flew off, leaving the fleet of cars behind.

Micky's gaze followed the helicopter as it flew over the hotel. "Well, that's bolloxed it. How're we gonna get paid now?"

Elvis tapped the side of his head. "Think, Micky, think. They ain't gonna leave half a million's worth of motors sat 'ere, are they? They'll send somebody to collect 'em, and we can pick 'em up on the trackers. No probs."

Even as he spoke the words, a van pulled into the car park, circled, then came to a stop next to the Porsche. The sign on the van read, 'C. Kleer, Windscreen Replacements and Repairs'.

"There ya go," said Elvis. "That'll be on its way in no time. We just pick it up later, and Bob's yer aunty's old man."

"Bangin'," Micky said. "Time to get a couple more beers down us then."

"What're you on? We still ain't stopped nobody today. We don't get paid nothin' if we don't stop nobody. Let's go see if we can find that crew with the Beamer. Might have to ring his lordship again to get a fix on them till we get some new phones."

CHAPTER SEVENTEEN

TEAM FARMHOUSE FIVE

I ROUNDED UP THE FARMHOUSE Five, plus *two* dogs now. Teller seemed linked to me by an invisible thread. I'd tried pushing him back to Gwen, but neither of them seemed interested in that idea. So now Teller settled in the rear luggage area, between our bags, while Yurei filled up the footwell in front of Dylan, guarding his Ouija Board of Fun. Fortunately, although Dylan was quite tall, there wasn't much of him in other directions, and he folded up quite comfortably on the seat.

Silence reigned in the car as I negotiated the winding Cornish lanes on the way to the A30. Once on the main road, I relaxed into the drive and threw the question, "Anybody care to explain what happened back there?"

More silence.

"Okay, Dylan? What was the thing with the bingo cards?"

Silence broken marginally by a sort of humphing sound.

"Dylan?" I tried again.

"They weren't right," came a sulky voice, eventually.

I knew I was going to regret asking, but, "Why were they wrong?"

"Bingo cards are supposed to be random. Random numbers." A hand appeared over my shoulder; it was stuffed with bingo cards. "These numbers aren't random, they cheated."

"Who cheated?" I pushed the hand back, clearing my view of the road.

"The people who made the cards, they cheated. Making *real* random numbers is difficult, they have to use special computers that use—"

"Hang on," I cut in, attempting to head off what I knew would be a very long and tortuous numerical cul-de-sac. "How do you know they weren't random?"

"Because they're all subsections of the square root of two."

"What?"

"The square root of two, it's like Pi, but different. Goes on forever. They use subsections to pretend they're random numbers, but they're not. Real random numbers can't be made by a normal computer because—"

"Yes, Dylan. I got that bit. But is it important? It's just bingo. And anyway, the little balls are random, so it doesn't really matter."

I heard Eddie groan, then mutter, "Here we go."

"Bingo balls are never random," Dylan sounded affronted, as if anybody would dare suggest such a thing. "There's a bias towards those balls with...bledeh bladeh..."

I tuned out the explanation and concentrated on the road ahead. After twenty minutes, we had to stop and let Janet out as she was feeling car sick. At least, that was her explanation. She disappeared behind a suitable bush and made some dreadful noises before returning with a pale smile and tousled hair.

"You alright?" asked Robyn, as Janet struggled back into the car.

"I think I may have eaten something funny," she said, fumbling with her seat belt.

"It must have been hilarious," Eddie said. "Besides, us all rushing out like that, we missed out on the cake. It was a chocolate sponge as well. I love a bit of chocolate sponge. Especially when it's all gooey and sticky, when the chocolate runs through your fingers as you try to eat it, and then—"

"Eddie," Robyn scolded, "stop winding her up. And anyway, you're just as much to blame."

"What do you mean?" he asked.

"Exploding extension leads?"

"Don't know what you mean."

"You ought to try offering those to the Taliban," she said. "They'd love them."

"If you lot don't stop arguing, there'll be no supper," I said across my shoulder.

As we approached the outskirts of Bodmin, Robyn pulled up a hotel guide on her phone.

"This looks tricky," she said, swiping through screens.

"What's up?" I asked.

"Everywhere's booked."

"It can't be competitors, surely? We must be down to lower numbers now."

"It's just seasonal," said Robyn. "This is the middle of Cornwall, in the middle of the holiday season and on the main road in and out of the county. Oh, hang on, here's one."

"With vacancies?"

"Looks like it. It's just off the bypass," she said. "The Benidorm Beach Hotel it's called. It's fairly basic, by the looks of it."

"The Benidorm Beach Hotel?" Eddie queried. "Not many beaches near Bodmin. Why call it that? Must be a good twenty miles to the nearest beach."

"And even further to Benidorm," I said.

"Who cares," said Robyn. "It's in the right area and it's got vacancies, let's not get picky."

"Okay, guide me there and we'll take a look."

Five minutes later, I pulled into the huge car park of The Benidorm Beach Hotel. Although car park was probably an exaggeration, as it was basically a large area of urban wasteland adjoining a small row of adjoining low-level buildings. A half-functioning neon sign announced it to be The Benidorm Beach Hotel, En-suite WCs and Colour Television. Another, more derelict looking building, lay about five hundred metres away, in the middle of the wasteland. It seemed to be a sprawling building, and probably quite elegant at some point. I parked close to The Benidorm Beach Hotel entrance, alongside a handful of other vehicles. One drew my attention immediately. A dark blue Toyota Corolla with a broken headlight.

"Looks like our friends are here," I said to Robyn, nodding towards the car.

She said nothing and just slid out of the door the moment the wheels stopped.

The nearest building had a glass door, as opposed to the simple wooden doors of the other dozen or so buildings in the line, and it had a small sign on the door announcing it as the Reception Office. Apart from that, they were all identical. It reminded me a bit of the racing stables at Porth Cullen. I'd been sent there once to investigate a missing racehorse, which turned out to be nothing more than one of the stable lads riding it into town to get a take-away kebab.

I pushed open the glass door and we found ourselves in an area about the size of a double garage. Apart from the door through which we had just entered, another faced us in the opposite wall, and just to the left of it, sat a large wooden counter. Littered around the walls were posters of palm tree fringed beaches and flamenco dancers. A couple of oversized and gaudily coloured sombreros punctuated the posters. Near the wall on the right, a man wobbled on an ancient wooden stepladder. He held a smoke alarm in one hand, an electric drill in the other, and a screwdriver between his teeth.

"Sorry," I said. "Reception?"

He nodded to the wooden counter, and I noticed a large brass bell sat in the middle of it. A sign next to it said, *'Please ring for attention'*.

I rang for attention.

The man descended the stepladder and came round behind the counter. "Buenos dias. How may I be of assistance?" He had a name tag pinned to his pristine white shirt. It read *Juan*, although his accent was far more Bodmin than Benidorm.

"Oh, I didn't mean to disturb you. We could have waited until you'd finished."

"Yes, but you rang the bell."

"I know, but… Never mind, we need some rooms for the night."

Juan scanned the five of us. "Certainly, how many rooms do you require?"

"Five, preferably. Do you have five rooms available? Dog friendly?"

"Indeed we do. Five rooms it is, and dogs are most welcome." He dipped behind the counter and came back with a white bowl containing a selection of boiled sweets. "Do help yourself while I find the keys." He bobbed down behind the counter. "Would you like consecutive, or with a space between?" His face popped up.

"It doesn't matter," I said.

"Or, I could do all at one end? Or the other? Oh, not the east end, they're all booked. I can do all at the western end?"

"Really, as they come. Make them random."

"As you wish."

"They can't be random," I heard from behind me.

"Not now, son," said Eddie.

"Random it is, then." The face disappeared again.

"It all seems very Spanish," said Janet. "I went there once. Lovely dancers, but I wasn't so keen on the food. Far too many legs and eyes for my liking."

"Here we are." Juan popped up from behind the counter again and dropped a handful of keys into a small wooden bowl. "Dip away."

It took me a moment to realise he wanted us to choose our keys. I pulled one from the bowl and read the wooden tag attached to it. Apollo, mine read. Eddie drew Maisie, but I didn't see what the others got.

"Unusual room names," I commented.

"It used to be a stables." Juan slid a laptop out from below the counter and began picking out letters on the keyboard. "I never got round to changing the names on the doors."

"Ah, and I have to ask, why The Benidorm Beach Hotel?"

"I went on holiday once to Spain, and there was this really posh hotel called The Benidorm Beach Hotel and I decided that, one day, I was going to own The Benidorm Beach Hotel." He opened his hands as if making a presentation. "And tada, here we are."

"In Bodmin?"

"Yeah, well, my old man died, and I got the stables." His face folded into a scowl. "My brother James got the house." He waved an arm in roughly the direction I'd noticed the dilapidated building. "Will you be wanting an early morning call?"

"No thanks. Where is the restaurant?" I scanned the room, half expecting to see a door I'd missed."

"Oh, sorry. We don't have a restaurant. We would have done, had I got the house, that had a lovely dining room. But no, James got that. Anything else I can help you with today?" A strained smile appeared briefly on his lips.

"Is there somewhere to eat nearby?"

"Nearest is a takeaway pizza place just over the main road, Gunther's Pizzas, it's called. Traditional Italian, they do a really good paella deep-crust, especially for our guests. If you tell them John sent you, you'll get fifty percent off a garlic bread. Other than that, you'll have to go into town."

I collected my bag from the car and went to find my room. Mine was the fourth door in the line and had a wooden sign in Comic Sans saying 'Apollo'. I turned the key and let myself in, slightly fearful at what to expect. I was pleasantly surprised. If this had once been a stable, it was now unrecognisable as such, and the size suggested it would probably be two knocked through to one. A small but functional bathroom snuggled behind a glass door and a tea-making area tucked in behind the main door. A huge king-size double bed dominated the room and faced a flat screen television over a narrow dressing table. I nudged Teller towards a rug by the window and he circled twice, landed with a whumph, then seemed to instantly go into a deep sleep. I hung up a couple of shirts, and took a quick shower. By the time I came out of the shower, Teller was now asleep on the bed. I tried to rouse him a couple times, but he was in a deep coma sleep. I gave up and headed over the road to Gunther's Pizzas. I resisted the paella deep crust and ordered a Margarita and a bottle of orange juice, then went back to my room. Teller was still asleep on the bed, so I opened the pizza box and went to the small kitchen area to find cutlery. When I turned back, the pizza box was on the floor and Teller had his nose inside it. I watched in amazement as a ten-inch Margarita disappeared faster than a Tory peer in a brothel raid.

"Pizza, is it then?" I said. "You needn't think that's going to continue."

I watched as he slumped back into immediate sleep, then slipped out and back to Gunther's Pizzas.

Teller still seemed to be asleep when I returned with my second Margarita, but I was taking no chances. Taking the pizza with me, I collected a knife and fork, then settled down to eat. I'd just cut into my first slice when I heard a knock on the door.

"It's open," I called.

"Ah, you already have pizza," Robyn said as she pushed the door shut behind her. "I brought sandwiches and beer."

"Where did you find those?" I asked.

"There's an offy just round the corner from the pizza place. Salad sandwich?"

"I'll stick with my pizza, thanks." Though I took the offered beer.

Robyn nodded towards Teller, spread out on the rug and dead to the world. "He looks content."

"He should be, he's just seen off a whole pizza."

She sat on the bed a short arm's length from me. "Right, let's talk." She cracked open her beer.

I nibbled stringy cheese from my fingers and said, "Yes, overdue, I feel."

She twisted round to face me, tucking one leg underneath her. "Okay, you've got your wish. I'm here to listen."

I'd been readying myself for this conversation for the last couple of days, and now I hesitated. "Tell me about your work," I said.

"My work? Well, as I said before, I do remote work for companies, data analysis, stress-testing systems etcetera. Boring really, but it pays the bills. Mostly bills for a place where I never sleep. Why do you ask?" Her eyes narrowed as she tried to read me.

"Just trying to put things into context. So, what's this sudden job that's causing you to bail on us?"

"Oh, it's just a financial company. In the City." She lifted the lid of her sandwich to examine the contents. "As I say, boring. But I have to pay the bills."

"On a place you never go."

She carefully replaced her sandwich in its plastic container and rounded on me. "What is all this? You said you were going to tell me something that would change my mind, and instead, I get all this policeman questioning nonsense."

"Which company?" I persisted.

"You wouldn't know them. It's a hedge fund company, Shye, Locke, and Grifter, if you must know."

"The same firm you said those guys back in Tiverton worked for? The ones with the flashy cars."

She looked surprised. "Yes, that's them."

"Bit of a coincidence?"

She stood, slammed the plastic sandwich container on the dressing table, and said, "That's it. I don't know what game you're playing, but I'm off."

"Just before you go…" I took a fair pull on the beer, then said, "what do you know about the Green Ninja?"

She froze, and the colour drained from her face. "Green Ninja? What makes you think I would know anything about a Green Ninja? What is that anyway? Some sort of computer game?"

"Maybe it's just coincidence that those boats were damaged in the Porth Cullen Boat Show the day you disappeared? Or that Krappi Burger had their slaughterhouse pictures everywhere the day after you were in email communication with them over Dylan's sacking?"

Robyn shrugged and hid behind her beer. "Coincidences happen, otherwise there wouldn't be a word for them."

"I might, at some stretch, believe that, but then there's the contaminated petrol in that Valdez Petrol station near where we were staying." I watched her carefully. Her eyes drifted sightlessly around the room, and she rubbed the back of her neck.

"It doesn't prove anything," she said, with a slightly resigned tone in her voice.

"But the patio heaters in the swimming pool last night? That was just careless. You didn't plan that one, did you?"

Her eyes flashed with a fire I hadn't seen in her before. "They're an abomination." She paused, trying to hold her control, drew a deep breath, then continued, "The planet is burning and suffocating in the rubbish we're pumping into the atmosphere and some clown thinks it's a good idea to create something which has a single, sole function, and that's to try to heat up the whole of outdoors! So yes, good cop." She thrust both hands towards me, wrists touching. "You'd better arrest me and lock me up before I try to inconvenience a coal mine."

"I can't arrest you, even if I wanted to. I'm no longer a police officer. I'm retired."

"Well, you don't behave that way. You carry on like you're Kojak and everybody's a crook."

I ran my hand over my head. "I know I'm thinning a bit, but Kojak? You could at least have said Starsky. Or Hutch. I was never sure which was which."

She looked at me like I'd just started speaking Chinese. "Aren't you supposed to be at home digging roses?"

"Not so keen on roses, too twee. I was planning on building a pergola. And how is this suddenly all about me?"

"Because you've spent so long looking for the bad in people, that's all you can see now. Poor Eddie, he's just trying to turn a profit here and there, and you keep on at him like he's Al Capone or somebody. And he's supposed to be your friend."

"Poor Eddie? He's a—"

"Sometimes the world isn't that tidy," she interrupted. "It's all sorts of grey, with most of us just trying to survive."

"Damaging other people's property is not about trying to survive, it's just—"

She cut me off again. "Of course it is. It's about the survival of the human species. Valdez Oil wilfully hid reports that proved they knew oil production was driving global warming. Yet still they drill, whilst having tame scientists and politicians on their payrolls to divert scrutiny. Krappi Burger destroys large swathes of rainforest to breed cattle yet still claim to be green, all because they pay a tiny fee to some crooked carbon offsetting tree planting scheme in Nigeria." She tried to drink from her empty can, then immediately reached for a second.

We sat in silence for a moment while she sipped at the new can, then she said, "Sorry. When John, my husband, was so ill, I promised him I'd make a difference. That I'd do something to make people see what's going on. The pollution, the greed which drives the destruction of our environment." She took another pull from the can. "But what do I do? I lose my temper and chuck a few patio heaters into a swimming pool. And now I've screwed it all up."

"To be fair, I had a pretty good idea it was you before the patio heaters went for a swim."

She lifted her head to face me, her eyes red and wet. "So, what are you going to do? Turn me in?"

The problem was, I hadn't actually thought this through. I'd only got as far as confronting her as being the Green Ninja, and with some vague idea of using that knowledge as leverage to persuade her not to run off. Typical copper's instinct, I guessed. Locked into a paradigm of turning minor miscreants to gain advantage over the bigger fish. Of course, the reality I'd neatly ignored was that Robyn was not some low-level offender to be turned. She was a driven woman with a conscience and a mission.

"No, I'm not going to turn you in." I spoke the words before I'd realised that was what I was going to say.

She cocked her head to one side, locked my eyes, and said, "Okay, what then?"

"That depends. Why were you planning on cutting out and leaving us in the lurch?"

"Because…" she paused to gather her thoughts and broke off a corner of her sandwich to feed Teller, who'd just woken up. "It's true that I have some business to attend to, but maybe not exactly as I might have led you to believe, sorry. It's… what shall I say… time sensitive. I can only attend to it at a specific place, on a specific day, and that's Friday. And I can't be in two places at the same time. And it's also true, as you clearly know, we're still up against another eighty or so teams, and the chances of us winning this competition are about zero, so, I figured best just rip the plaster off and get it done."

"And this, erm, business, is so important that it's worth destroying whatever chance we did have?"

Her expression hardened. "Frankly, yes. Maybe I can't save the planet, but I owe it to John to try. You'd do the same."

"I'm not sure I would," I said. "I don't think you can justify—"

"Bullshit. What would you do if a known drug dealer was cutting his drugs with Fentanyl just because it was cheaper and made more profit, even though people were dying? What lengths would you go to? As a policeman, where would you draw the line to stop him?"

"But that's not really the same thing. You can't make that comparison."

"It's exactly the same. It's just that we're talking about corporate offenders with lots of money, not just one man. And it's that difference which somehow makes them untouchable."

We fell into silence for a while. Robyn's ideas weren't new to me, of course. In my job, I'd had to deal with all sorts of impassioned individuals. But back then, I'd never had to make decisions. The law was clear, and we couldn't afford to think about the individual cause being protested, just the offence.

"What are you planning on Friday?" I asked.

"Really?" she said. "Do you think I'm that stupid? You'd be on the phone to your old mates in no time."

I deserved that, I supposed. "That wasn't the plan, but I understand your suspicion. I was wondering if we could find some sort of compromise. Perhaps, if what you're planning was… I don't know, maybe fairly harmless, I might…" I tailed off, realising I was just throwing half-formed ideas into the wind.

"You might what? You might turn a blind eye? How harmless would I have to be? Like writing a strongly worded letter to the chairman of Valdez Oil?"

"No, I was thinking… Okay, I wasn't thinking, but let's see if we can work this out. Are you planning on doing something which could cause actual harm to any individual?"

"Possibly."

"Not helping."

"Well what do you want me to say? I don't know, is the truth."

I pressed my hands across my eyes, as if somehow that would help me see a way through. "How about this, you tell me what you're planning, and I tell you if I can turn a blind eye or if I would have to turn you in if you went ahead?"

"How about, I tell you, and you simply make a promise to either help, or just let me walk away and forget we ever met?"

"You'd trust me to do that?" I asked.

She shrugged and dropped her head. "What choice do I have? I'm going to do what I have to do, and you're either going to either turn me in, or not. But yes, I would trust you." She looked up at me from under a flop of hair. "So? Do I get a promise?"

I raced through my options. If I didn't agree, she'd go off and do whatever it was anyway. I could turn her in afterwards, but it wouldn't stop her. If I agreed? I'd at least have a chance of talking her out of it.

"Okay, promise."

She studied me for a long moment. Probably trying to weigh up if I was genuine or not.

She eventually thrust her hand forward, and we sealed the deal.

"I'm going to hack the data files of the hedge fund, Shye, Locke, and Grifter," she said, with such a matter-of-fact tone that she could have just announced she was popping out for a loaf of bread.

"That Money Boy team?"

"Not them specifically, although I have already done that. I needed to get into their email system, so I set a worm in one of their phones. But I'm going to hack the company itself."

"What have they done? I'd never even heard of them until you mentioned it."

"Most people haven't, yet they manage more investment dollars than most of the world's biggest banks. Just short of $400 billion at the last count. These guys are the facilitators of the world's finance."

"Okay," I said, not really understanding.

She watched my expression, and obviously reading the depth of my ignorance, she said, "If you know a murder is carried out by a hitman, who is the murderer? The hitman or the hirer?"

The leftfield nature of the question threw me. "Well, they are both responsible. The hitman would be charged with murder. The hirer, conspiracy to commit murder, or solicitation of murder. It would depend."

"Exactly. The meat industry which deforests, the oil companies which pollute, Chinese companies opening new coal mines, the smartphone companies who use slave gangs to dig for cobalt, they're the hitmen. But Shye, Locke, and Grifter, they're the hirers. They put up the money. Yet, they stand at arm's length so their investors can claim ignorance as to where their money is being used. Just like the person who hires your hitman. They take investment money from pension funds, town councils, churches, charities, and well-off individuals to channel it as finance for the world's worst polluters. Yet the investors themselves can stand clear and claim plausible deniability of all knowledge of the destruction of a rainforest or the commissioning of a new oil rig in the North Sea on their behalf."

"And you're going to do what, exactly?"

"I'm simply going to open their client list. I'm going to bring into the light all these people who squirrel their investments away in the world's worst polluters, whilst at the same time virtue-signalling their green credentials. I'm going to expose the hypocrites who hide behind feigned ignorance. I'm going to put the client list on the internet for all to see, along with where the money is really being invested."

"And why does this have to be done now, rather than, say, next week?"

"Because Martin Locke, the main man behind the firm, is sailing his private super yacht into Porth Cullen for the boat show on Friday afternoon. Normally, hacking somebody like him would be next to impossible. Their systems are air-walled."

"What does that mean? Air-walled?"

"Parts of their systems don't connect to the internet. It means they can't be hacked from outside. You have to be physically inside their premises to hook up to their Wi-Fi."

"And how are you planning to achieve that?"

"Simple, his Wi-Fi security will be much lower on his yacht than in his offices in London. As long as I can get within range of his onboard Wi-Fi, all I need is a password. And, thanks to the carelessness of one of his traders losing his phone yesterday, I'm already halfway in."

"And that's it? All you're going to do is publish the names and investments? Nobody gets hurt, and no property gets damaged?"

"That's it."

"Then why did you say *'possibly'* when I asked you if anybody could get hurt?"

"Because I don't know how some people might react when their dirty laundry comes out. People do funny things when they're in a corner, they might lose their jobs, I don't know. You asked me to be honest. So, what is it? Are you going to stand in my way or are we going to cut a deal here?"

I shook my beer can gently. Empty. Robyn noticed my disappointment and passed me another. "Thanks." I cracked the can while my mind ran like an old movie on fast forward, showing me flashes of my life as a copper. The times I'd been thwarted from bringing down the real villains because they hid behind money and status. The countless times I'd been warned off by superiors who constantly reminded me that some targets were just untouchable. That *their* friends were higher than ours. The problem was, I fully understood Robyn's frustration and anger. I also understood I should be at home building my pergola and not getting involved in this mess.

I reached out and took Robyn's hand. She seemed to startle slightly. "I'm not going to try to stop you," I said. "Since leaving the Police Force, only a few weeks ago, I've been an accessory after the fact in the destruction of a police car, broken into private property, lied to a police officer, I've transported counterfeit goods, and now I'm harbouring a wanted criminal. And I've yet to collect my first pension payment."

She smiled. "Well, at least you're not getting bored."

"True." I nodded slowly. "I don't know much about this financial stuff, but nearly forty years in the Force has at least taught me right from wrong. And even I can see there's something very wrong about all this. So, I'm not going to stand in your way, but on one condition."

She withdrew her hand and frowned. "What's that?"

"That you work with me to see if there's a way for you to do what you have to, while staying in the team."

She took my hand back in both of hers. "You're a good man, Matt." She collapsed against my shoulder, and I instinctively put my arm around her.

"I think there's many a person might disagree with you there, but I'll take it."

"There's only one problem," she said.

"What's that?"

"I never did book into a room here. I wasn't planning on staying."

"Hmm. Do you think you should go and book in now, then?"

"It's very late." She wriggled her arm free to stare at her watch. "It seems a bit mean to disturb Juan at this time of night."

"I could take the chair." I nodded towards the small armchair by the window. Teller raised a sleepy head, then resettled.

"You could. But this is such a huge bed, silly to waste half of it." She looked up at me, her eyes didn't seem to be focussing.

"Where's your bag?"

"Huh? Oh, still in the car."

"I'll go fetch it. Help yourself to the shower."

I slipped out of the door and headed to the car. By the time I returned to the room, Robyn was already fast asleep in the bed. I showered and slid into the space left to me. Immediately, I felt the end of the bed wobble, then a weight settled on my legs. Teller. I tried to push him off with my foot, but he was doing such a good dead-weight resistance job that it would have been easier to move the whole bedroom three feet to the left and leave him there. I gave up and angled my legs around him. As soon as we got home, he was going back to Gwen.

CHAPTER EIGHTEEN

TEAM ALTER EGOS

"I'LL HAVE A KRAPPI BREKKIE Bun with a side of Krappi Onion Rings, please," Bruce asked the bleary-eyed man behind the counter.

"We don't start serving Brekkie Buns until seven o'clock." He yawned and his eyes appeared in danger of closing again.

Bruce looked at his watch. "It's two minutes to seven."

"Yeah, but we don't start serving Brekkie Buns until seven o'clock."

Bruce and the man stared at each other in silence for two minutes.

As the hand on the plastic cow clock on the wall hit twelve, Bruce said, "One Krappi Brekkie Bun with a side of Krappi Onion Rings, please."

"D'ya want to Super-Large that?"

"No thanks, just the normal."

"Super-Normal or Massive-Normal?"

"Do you have a Normal-Normal?"

"Yeah, but you'll have to wait. Normal-Normal's not very popular, so we only do them to order."

"Okay, I'll have a Super-Normal then."

"Mega-Size Onion Rings or Giant-Size?"

"Um, just Mega-Size please."

"Coming up." The man turned and gathered the order from the hotplates behind him. "There you are," he said, pushing the plastic tray towards Bruce. "All of us at Krappi Burger wish you a wonderful day."

Bruce studied his tray. "There're only two onion rings. I ordered the Mega-Size."

"That is the Mega-Size. If you'd wanted three rings, that's the Giant-Size."

"Oh, I see."

"You're welcome. All of us at Krappi Burger wish you a wonderful day."

Bruce took his tray and joined his companions at their table. "Whose idea was it to have breakfast in a Krappi Burger?"

"There was nowhere else nearby," said Clarke. "And we need to be on the main road because we don't know which way we're going yet. We did discuss this."

"I said I was never going to eat in one of these places again." Bruce lifted the lid on his Krappi Brekkie Bun and removed the very tired-looking tomato slice. "Not after seeing all those pictures the Green Ninja leaked."

"At least Krappi Burger are green though," said Peter. He picked up the menu card on the table. "See, it says here they plant a tree seed for every cow they kill." He squinted at the small print. "Apparently, their scientist said that a tree eats more Co2 than a cow gives out, and that makes them carbon neutral."

Bruce turned to Diana. "Did you hear anything more from your mate in Roaming Services? Simon, wasn't it?"

"Yes, he sent me a message last night. Apparently, those Ponzi Phones that were nearby when our camper was sabotaged, you know, the ones we bricked? Well, the numbers have been activated again. They must have put the SIMs in new phones."

"Bound to happen," Bruce said. "Where are they?"

"Currently near Bodmin. Apparently, they've been very busy recently with one other phone in particular. And which also seems to be visiting known clue locations."

"That must be the other team."

"Looks like. And that one has been travelling with three other phones, one Ponzi Phone and two SimSuns."

"That's got to be the team that's organising the sabotage, then." Bruce dipped an onion ring into the little plastic pot of yellow goop.

"We should report them," said Clarke.

"Who to? We have no contact details for anybody connected with this competition." He took a nervous bite of the gooped onion ring, squinted, and dropped it on a paper napkin. "We need to stop them ourselves. We are Super Nerds, after all."

"We have the power," said Peter, raising a clenched fist over the table.

"We have the power," said the other three in unison, and raised clenched fists to join Peter's.

"Who can save the world?" Peter said.

"The Super Nerds can," returned the others.

"Have you got the numbers of those phones, Diana?" Bruce asked.

"Yes, but bricking the phones with a dodgy firmware update won't stop them. They'll just swap the SIMs like the other guys did."

"We can change the IMEI numbers of the phones. We can run ZiPhone software remotely by triggering a dummy system update. That'll do it."

"How does changing the IMEI help?" asked Peter. "Surely, if their phones stop working because the SIM and the IMEI are no longer linked, they'll just change the SIMs to another phone again."

"That's the beauty. Changing the IMEI won't stop the phone working. They'll never know." Bruce tried to pick up his Krappi Brekkie Bun, but he'd left it too long. The combination of runny egg, oil saturated bread, and liquid cheese had done its worst, and the whole soggy mess just dripped through his fingers and dolloped onto his plate. He pushed it to one side. "The Great Wessex Chase app checks the IMEI of the phone against the number to make sure the right phone is on location for logging the sites. That stops contestants having duplicate SIMs on different phones."

"That sounds feasible," said Clarke. "That'll make it look like somebody else is trying to login. We can get Simon to run the ZiPhone on our Ponzi Phones, but what about the SimSuns? We can't get at those."

"I've got a friend in SimSun," said Diana with a wink. "He's on their Tech

Helpdesk, but he'll know somebody in their Network Section who can run it."

"Do you think you can get him to help?"

"He's a member of IAN, and once he knows it's to save the Tower of Doom, there'll be no stopping him."

"The power of the nerd," said Peter.

"The power of the nerd," the others all responded, holding up their cardboard coffee mugs in salute.

"We have a plan then." Bruce checked his watch. "We've still got a couple of hours before today's clue arrives, so I'm going to go back to my room for a shower, then find a Tesco Metro or something for a bacon sandwich. Meet back here just before ten?"

The others agreed and Bruce dumped his tray and Krappi Brekkie Bun in the bin by the door on his way out.

CHAPTER NINETEEN

TEAM FARMHOUSE FIVE

I AWOKE TO THE SOUND of Stairway to Heaven. That was definitely not the tone I'd set on my alarm. I reached blindly to where I thought the alarm phone might be and connected with a warm, furry head, which instantly began licking my hand. Dog. I had a dog.

I blinked my eyes open and struggled into a sitting position. Hotel type bedroom. Returning consciousness reminded me I was in The Benidorm Beach Hotel, which was itself in Bodmin. And that I had a lodger. My bleary eyes searched the room. The music was coming from the television, on which the screen informed me we were tuned to Classic Rock FM. The door to the bathroom was half open and the noise of an electric toothbrush buzzing merged with Jimmy Page's Les Paul guitar. I reached across to the bedside cabinet and this time found my phone. I forced my eyes to focus on the time. Just gone seven. "It's seven o'clock," I called.

The bathroom door opened fully, and a head emerged, buzzy toothbrush in mouth. "Sorry," said the head. "Did you say something?" Robyn removed the toothbrush from her mouth and stepped out of the bathroom, naked apart from a wholly insufficient towel which only served to highlight, not to cover.

I turned my head away. "I said it was seven o'clock. Who gets up at seven o'clock if they don't have to?"

"I usually go for a morning run. It's the best time. Sorry, I didn't mean to embarrass you. Safe to look now."

"No problem." I turned to look at her. The towel she'd been using had now been rearranged slightly, and sort of covered those parts intended.

"I don't often wear clothes when I'm in my own space, unless it's cold. I forget sometimes."

"Easily done, I expect."

"Fancy joining me?"

I paused momentarily to make sure I understood the context of her question. "Love to, but I forgot my running kit. I think I left it back in 1984."

Robyn dived into her bag and came out with some running clothes. "It's good for you."

"So the FME used to tell me, but my knees don't agree."

The towel dropped as she slipped into the shorts and T-shirt. "Sorry, too complicated to play hide and peek with a towel. Feel free to be embarrassed." She pulled on her trainers, straightened up, then glanced in my direction and grinned. "See you in half an hour." She disappeared out of the door.

I showered, dressed, and took Teller outside for a quick walk and morning ablutions. Being outside early in the morning, and before I'd flooded my system with coffee, was a new experience and Teller had much sniffing to do before we were allowed back inside. Once he'd finished, I headed back towards my room, and we met Dylan and Yurei on their way out to the sniffing zone. I grunted good morning to Dylan, and he responded in a similar vein while the two dogs sniffed at each other's rear ends.

Once back in the room, I made myself a coffee and settled down with a map to study the area. We were about ten miles west of Jamaica Inn, the site of the clue answer given to us by The Alter Egos. I scanned the map for other sites of interest within a twenty-five-mile radius of Bodmin. Quite a few archaeological sites lie around the area, along with numerous historical buildings. Both Tintagel and Launceston lay within the area, each with many individual potential locations. It would certainly be a risky commitment to relocate to Bolventor, the village near Jamaica Inn, on a hunch. Get it wrong, and we could be forty miles from the clue when it's revealed. But get it right, and we'd end up saving a lot of time.

Teller pricked up his ears and stared at the door thirty seconds before I heard the key turn and Robyn returned.

"Good run?" I asked.

"Not especially." She knelt to pet Teller who greeted her like she'd been gone a year. "When I don't know the area, I have to stick to roads, and that's never fun." She disposed of various items of footwear and clothing as she headed to the shower.

When she finally emerged again, almost wrapped in a towel, I asked, "Do you always go running this early? It'd still be dark in winter, surely?"

"Not usually this early, but I was feeling a bit sluggish after last night. The wine may have been a bad idea." She towelled herself with a nod towards modesty. But it was only a nod.

I purposefully studied the ceiling lamp as I spoke. "Wine? What wine? You brought beer with you last night."

"Hmm yes, confession. I might have had a bit of a session with Janet before I came to you."

"I see, that explains things a bit."

"To be fair, Janet's a bit of a bad influence. And anyway, I was feeling a little agitated yesterday. What with you getting all policeman-like and officious."

"My fault then?" I said with a smile and a flick of my eyebrow.

"No, it's not fair that you should take all the blame. I think both you *and* Janet should take equal responsibility." She caught my eye and smiled. Her face took on a brighter look, one I'd not seen on her before. She suddenly looked much younger.

"I've been thinking about today's clue," I said. "I think we should take a risk and head to Jamaica Inn. Remember, Bruce from The Alter Egos told us it was one of their clues."

She paused, halfway through buttoning her shirt, then said, "Makes sense. It could save us time."

I checked my watch. "I suggest we let the others know. Maybe get a quick breakfast and head off. We need to be there before ten o'clock."

A quick breakfast proved trickier than it should have been.

"Breakfast?" Juan asked, as if it was the strangest request he'd ever received. "There's a nice little cafe on Chapel Street. Lord of the Fries, it's called. If you go out of here and turn left... Would you be driving or walking?"

"Walking was the plan," I said.

"Ah, in that case, you turn right. That's because you can cut through the park. You can't do that in a car. Well, not since the one-way system was put in place, although you weren't really meant to before either. But everybody did. Do you find it sad that people misuse mini-roundabouts and just drive across them? All that work. Anyway, you drive past the estate agents, I can't remember what it's called, but it's the one with the green sign, not the one with the red sign. If you see the one with the red sign, you've probably gone too far, and you'll need to come back."

"Walking," I said. "We were going to walk, not drive."

"Really? Well in that case, you turn left out of here—"

"You said right, just now."

He held both hands out in front of him and studied them. "Did I? Sorry, I'm dyslexic." He pushed his left hand higher. "This one. You turn this way."

"That's left."

"Good, I was right the first time then. Now, where did we get to?"

"How long does it take to walk there?" Robyn cut in.

"About half an hour."

"Right, well let's scratch that one," I said. "Is there nowhere nearer?"

"There's Gunther's Pizzas, just across the road. He does a breakfast pizza of bacon, egg, and baked beans."

"I think we should just hit the road," said Robyn. "There's bound to be somewhere along the way."

"I think that's best," I said.

We all paid up our bills and headed out to the car park. I noticed two young men standing by the blue Toyota Corolla. Teller paused to stare at them, and suddenly, he looked more predator than pet.

It took me a moment to realise there was something odd about the car. It stood on four small piles of bricks where the wheels should have been.

The men turned and glared at us as we passed by.

"There's a thing now," I said. "I wonder who did that?"

I heard a groan from Robyn. I turned to look at her and she screwed her face up as if in agony.

"Really?" I said.

"Yeah, well. I popped into the offy to get some wine last night, and there was a gang of lads in there, obviously intent on making trouble. And I may have, sort of mentioned something about that Toyota being an undercover police vehicle."

"Clever call, I'm impressed."

"Umm, well don't be. Full declaration, I'd only got as far as thinking it might give them a fright and they'd piss off out of the off-licence so I could get my wine. I didn't really think through what they might do to the car. But hey-ho, it's an ill wind and all that."

I opened the back of the BMW to dump my bag in and noticed a cardboard box with a picture of a food mixer and text in Chinese.

"Eddie?" I said.

"Ah, yes," Eddie said from over my shoulder. "It's alright, it's not *actually* a food mixer."

"Oh good. I was worried for a moment that we might have a food mixer stowaway in the back of my car. Perhaps if you'd like to tell me what it is, rather than what it isn't, we might save a bit of time?"

"It's just a handy box."

"A handy box? You just happened upon a handy box, and you thought you'd bring that with us?"

"What? No, that would be silly. It's got stuff in it, but I was only saying, it's not a food mixer. In case you wondered why I'd put a food mixer in your car."

"Can we cut to the part where you give up trying to avoid the inevitable, and tell me what load of dodgy goods you've got me carrying for you this time?"

"Just a few watches, Omega Speedmasters. I told you the other day I'd got a batch coming in from China."

"I remember you trying to sell me one, but I don't remember anything about me helping you transport them."

"Only temporary, didn't think you'd notice. I've got a pal popping down from Bristol tomorrow for them. Soon as we know where we're going, I'll arrange the meet."

"And what about this other stuff?" I pointed at the box we'd got from Jacob in Manaton. "You told me that would be gone as soon as we got back to Little Didney."

"And it would've. I just didn't reckon on us doing a quick runner from there last night."

I drew a breath to speak, then sensed, rather than felt, Robyn's presence close to my left. I turned and caught her expression. It was one of admonishment, mixed with despair, and a little gentle scolding. At least, that's how it felt. She tipped her head slightly and fixed me with her laser stare, which said, *'remember how we'd discussed the way I treated Eddie like some big-time crook when all he's doing is trying to scratch a living.'*

I opened my mouth to argue with this unspoken scolding, but her face hardened into a gentle, but threatening warning that I shouldn't dare.

I shook my head slightly and turned back to Eddie. "Alright, but I know nothing about this. Deal?"

Eddie looked slightly shocked, and I heard a whispered, and self-satisfied, "There we go," from Robyn behind me.

"Yeah, deal," said Eddie, still looking like he'd just seen ET dancing the fandango in a tutu. I pulled a tartan travel rug over the boxes and tucked it round the sides.

Without bidding, Teller jumped in the back, and Yurei clambered into the footwell, complete with Reverend Featherstone's Ouija Board of Fun.

Once on the road, we drove for about twenty minutes. Then, with time to spare, we cruised the main road until we found a place for breakfast. Or brunch, as it would probably be now.

Just near Colliford Lake, and set back in a gravel car park, lay a small fast-food place called Sam & Ella's Eatery. A few white vans and other commercial vehicles littered the parking area, so it looked popular enough.

I opened the windows a few inches for the dogs, and we made our way to the cafe. A big sign on the door encouraged us to try their All-Day Breakfast, and proudly informed us that it was voted the, '*Best breakfast of the year by the Bodmin Journal of Woodturners and Model Aeroplane makers*'.

Inside, the place had a feel of somewhere between a British Rail station cafe and 1960s chic.

"I'll have one of those All-Day Breakfasts please," I asked as I arrived at the counter.

"Those finish at nine o'clock," said the bored-looking girl behind the counter, her nose ring jiggling as she spoke.

I looked at my watch. Three minutes past nine. "Then why do you call it an All-Day Breakfast?"

"Because one of these will keep you going all day. S'what they say anyway. I don't eat here me-self."

"Bacon, sausage, and eggs then?"

She wrote carefully on her pad. "Anything else?"

"Do you have tomatoes and beans?"

"Toms and beans," she muttered whilst writing, painfully slowly.

I glanced up at the list of ingredients in the All-Day Breakfast. "And hash browns?"

"Do you want fries with that?"

"No, but a couple of slices of toast? Oh, and some mushrooms."

We took our seats and the food arrived faster than it had taken the girl to write the orders down.

"I can't eat this," said Dylan.

I looked at his plate. Bacon, sausage, egg, beans, toast. It looked fine to me.

"What's wrong?" I asked.

"The knife and fork don't match. Look," he held them out for me to see. "The fork's got a flat edge to the handle, but the knife is rounded. See?"

I could see a minor difference, but nothing dramatic. "They look close enough to me," I said.

"But they feel wrong in my hands. That makes the food feel wrong."

We pooled our collective cutlery and managed to find a matching set for Dylan. I then watched as he carefully cut the edges from the toast where the beans had come into contact with it. He carefully placed the cutoffs onto a paper serviette, then wrapped it with a precision that would have caused an Origami master to go back to making paper aeroplanes. He slipped the package in his pocket, presumably for Yurei, then finally set about the task of actually eating his breakfast. One item at a time.

Robyn pulled out a map and spread it between the food plates. "I've marked on here any other likely targets within this area. Just in case it's not Jamaica Inn."

I leaned over the map as I nibbled the end off a forked sausage. A worryingly large number of red-inked circles graced the map. "There're a lot of places here."

"It's Cornwall," said Eddie. "You can't lob a stone around here without it landing on the roof of an English Heritage gift shop."

"There're also a lot of stone circles in this area," said Robyn. "Then we've got Tintagel, Launceston Castle, the Witches of Boscastle—"

"Don't want no more witches," muttered Eddie. "That last lot down at Bowerman's Nose, I'll swear they put a curse on my extension leads. Fire, that's witches all over."

I looked up at Eddie. "I seem to remember that witches weren't awfully fond of fire."

"That's why they use it. Well-known fact." He placed an egg between two slices of toast and bit into it. Yolk dripped through his fingers. "They've even got themselves a shop in Boscastle, where they swap spells and sell witchy potions to each other. If we gotta go there, we need to take an exorcist with us. Just sayin'." He cleaned his fingers with a paper napkin.

We finished eating and wrapped up the leftovers in a napkin for the dogs. Back at the car, Teller was instantly grateful for his treat, but Yurei far more suspicious, and thought it might be a ploy to separate him from his Ouija Board of Fun.

We let them both have a runaround, then made sure they were in the car just before the clue was due to arrive.

Exactly on time, all our phones bleeped simultaneously. I opened mine.

"Good morning, Team Farmhouse Five. Here is clue four: It's not in the Caribbean, but in the K6 the smugglers can get their money back by pressing button B — Your team will be eliminated if the login has not been completed by midday, or you finish below the median. Good Luck."

"It's the right one, it's Jamaica Inn!" I couldn't help the excitement in my voice. "It's the clue The Alter Egos gave us. It actually worked, and we're right on the doorstep."

I heard Robyn give a smug smile. A smile which wanted to say, *"You see, not all people are lying, conniving, villains out to deceive."* But I managed to get in first with, "Don't say a word. Not a word."

"It was never going to cross my lips," she replied.

I glanced at her as I pulled the car onto the main road. Another silent smile, only she seemed to be struggling to keep this one from breaking into a grin.

Ten minutes later, satnav informed me we had arrived at our destination.

We were here, and with nearly two hours to spare. A great result. Assuming, of course, that The Alter Egos hadn't tucked us up completely, and given us a completely wrong location for the clue. The perfect way to send a rival team off in the wrong direction and ensure they got timed out. We should have thought of that earlier.

"What if they've given us the wrong location?" I said.

"Here we go," said Robyn.

"What do you mean?"

"Only that I expected you to think of that before. It's a bit late now if they have."

"So, you think they might have?"

"No," she said. "After they gave us the clue, I checked the details. There is an old K6 model phone box there. You know, the red ones with buttons A & B? Add in the reference to smugglers, and there's no other place in Wessex, or even Britain, which would fit that clue."

"Why didn't you say anything before?"

"What? And spoil the fun of watching you panic?"

The first thing I noticed when we pulled into the Jamaica Inn was a row of eight coaches all lined up at the western end of the car park. All sizes, all colours of livery. Handfuls of people gathered around them as the coaches vomited even more tourists out onto the tarmac.

"Bloomin' emmets," Eddie muttered.

"That's alright," I replied. "We're not here to stay. Quick login and home for lunch." I made sure the windows were open enough for Teller and Yurei, then locked the car.

"We could stay on after we've logged in," said Janet. "It'll be fun. We might even see the man in the tricorne hat."

"Who?" asked Eddie.

"The ghost, he's famous. This is the most haunted place in Cornwall."

"Shush," I said to Janet. "Don't say anything about ghosts. You'll have Eddie running for the hills."

"I ain't worried about ghosts," said Eddie. "Stuff and nonsense. Witches now, that's a whole different matter. Did I tell you about the time some witch put a hex on my car?"

"I think you've mentioned it."

We threaded our way between throngs of chattering tourists, picking up smatterings of many accents and several different languages. We stopped in the middle of the outside courtyard, and I pulled out my phone to login to The Great Wessex Chase app. I pressed the location button and immediately received the confirmation. *Position confirmed.*

"Job done," I said. "Record time too. That will give us some leeway."

The phone bleeped again. "That'll be the photo request. Let's see what they want." I opened the message. *"Please use team member Robyn's phone to upload a photograph of team member Eddie touching the phone box."*

"That'll be the K6," said Robyn.

"Good job you didn't bail on us," I said softly to Robyn as we walked through the crowds of tourists.

"What's going on?" asked Janet as we approached.

The crowd grew noisier, and more dense, as we approached the phone box. We came to a halt in a wedge of people about ten metres short. I peered through and over the crowd. It took a moment for me to process the scene.

"Well?" persisted Robyn.

"It's a couple of pirates who seem to be having a bit of an altercation with a bunch of... I don't know... possibly ghosts?"

"Don't be ridiculous." Eddie pushed alongside me. "Well, I'll be... There's a thing you don't see every day."

"Any idea what's happening?" I asked a man next to me.

"Two coachloads, a bunch of tourists on a pirates and smugglers tour, and an outing of spookists doing a round of Cornwall's most haunted places. They all want their pictures taking at the same time and the coach drivers are on a schedule."

I looked at my watch, 10:45. Seventy-five minutes left to upload a photograph. I wandered out of the crowd to gain a better overview. I scanned the milling people who, with the advantage of perspective, appeared not quite as disorganised as they'd first seemed. There was a vague idea of a queue curled around and in on itself. At a quick guess, there appeared to be about a hundred people in the line. Years of managing football crowds and protest marches had left me with an eye for estimating crowd sizes. If everybody in the line wanted their photo taking at the phone box, and allowing even just one minute per person, that made a hundred minutes. And we only had seventy now before we were timed out. I felt the weight of defeat settling over me. I returned to the others.

"We have a problem," I said, and quickly explained my maths about the queue.

"Can't we push in front?" asked Janet.

"I think that's what this current punch-up is all about."

"Could we ask the management or something? It's a good cause, maybe they could do something."

"I doubt they'd believe us, and even if they did, it would probably take longer than we've got to find the relevant people and explain."

Eddie studied the tangled queue then said, "I'll get us in."

I watched as he made his way towards the front of the winding snake of humanity. He struck up a conversation with a young couple in matching yellow woollen hats. The exchange became more intense, then his wallet came out, and notes changed hands. The couple stepped back a bit and Eddie slid in front of them, He motioned for Robyn and me to join him.

We slid in alongside him.

"Oi, we didn't say nothing about other people," challenged the young man, the bobble on his hat punctuating his words.

"But it doesn't matter," said Eddie. "We're only taking one turn. We're all at once."

"We agreed on one person, not three. If there's gonna be three of you, we want three times the money. It's only fair. We want another… another…" He counted his fingers. "Another…"

"Another hundred quid, Darren," said his partner.

"Yeah, another hundred quid," Darren confirmed.

"But what about us?" asked a man behind them, who seemed to be trying to herd a flock of small children. "We've been waiting over an hour, and if you're paying them, you have to pay us as well. You're cutting in front of all of us. It's only fair."

"That's right," said another voice from further back in the queue.

"How well did you think this through, Eddie?" I asked.

"It normally works. Even got me into Wimbledon last year."

"Right," said Eddie, turning to face Darren. "Give me my fifty back then."

"No, that was a deal. Deal made is a done deal. No backsies, that's the rules."

"I think I can see this heading for another punch-up," I said. "Come on, Eddie. We'll have to think of something else." I nudged Eddie out of the growing scrum of irate pirates and ghosts.

"What about my money? Show them your badge."

"I'm retired, remember?"

"How about we phone in a bomb threat?" suggested Eddie. "We could do it anonymous, that'd get rid of 'em all a bit sharpish."

"It would also get rid of you for twelve months," I said. "The CTU guys don't mess around."

"When I worked for Fork 'n Chicken," said Dylan, "I had to dress up as a chicken to promote chicken nuggets."

"Oh, that must have been fun," said Janet. "I dressed up as a tree once when Porth Cullen Council wanted to chop down a 500-year-old oak tree to put up a statue of David Attenborough. A French Poodle did his business on my leg."

"Chicken costumes are very hot," said Dylan.

"Fascinating as this is," I said, "how is that of any use here?"

"Everybody wanted to take a photograph with me as a chicken. Then some teenagers stole my egg basket. They took it out of my wages."

"Right, we need a plan." I turned to face the others. "Ideas?"

"The lad's been tellin' you," said Eddie, looking dangerously enthusiastic. I learned to be fearful whenever Eddie began to show signs of enthusiasm. "People like having their photo took with some sort of character," he continued. "Look at Disneyworld, and the money people spend just to have their photo taken with a soddin' mouse. They don't even know if it's the *real* mouse or not."

"I'm not sure I'm getting this," I confessed.

"Easy," said Robyn. "If Eddie dresses up as something, all we have to do is get somebody to want to have their photo taken with him against the phone box."

"Okay, but where are we going to get a chicken outfit from?" I looked around in the vague hope I might see a stall renting chicken outfits by the hour.

"Well, if you're going to go looking for problems."

"What was in that box, Eddie?" asked Robyn.

"Just a load of stuff left behind in The Huntsman. I dunno really, not looked too closely. There was a Sherlock Holmes hat, oh, and a bunch of extension leads, but Sam Goodenough bought those for The Smuggler's Arms. I think there's a fancy makeup kit with all sorts of fillers and colourings. I could do you a good price on that if you like?"

"Eddie, I want you to think very carefully before answering my next question." Robyn fixed Eddie's eyes with a stare that threatened extreme violence. "Do I look like a woman who uses fillers and colourings?"

"Er, no. Course not. I was just saying that because that's just one of the things in the box, as an example, not that you need face fillers, or any fillers, or any makeup stuff, because… because you're just… right."

"Just right? You're saying I'm just right?" The flash of mischief in her eye passed Eddie by.

"Well, more than just right. Very right. Can I start again?"

A smile spread across Robyn's face. "Yes please. That box of stuff, didn't you say some of it had been left behind by a TV company filming near there?"

"Yeah, but I've not looked properly."

"Let's go look."

CHAPTER TWENTY

TEAM BULLINGBOY CLUB

THE BLACK RANGE ROVER SPORT tore up a cloud of dust as it slid to a halt next to the entrance of Camelot Fun Park.

Lothar was out of the vehicle even before it had stopped. He scanned the area in one take, then started towards the entrance kiosk.

A voice called, "You can't park there."

Lothar turned to see a man in a blue uniform and a peaked hat approaching.

"I think you'll find we just have," he said.

"That's the emergency exit," said the uniformed man, pointing at a sign which said Emergency Exit.

"You plannin' on havin' an emergency anytime soon?" Lothar asked.

"No, of course not."

"Well, if you do, you be sure to give me the nod and I'll be right there to move it."

The security guard opened his mouth to speak, but Lothar's expression warned against further discussion.

The doors of the Range Rover opened, and Perkins climbed out, followed by Clive and Barbie. The three caught up with Lothar at the entrance kiosk.

"Day ticket for four please," asked Perkins of the slightly shocked girl behind the counter.

She peered through her little window, trying to see below the level of the counter front. "No children?" she asked.

"No, just us."

"Twenty-four pounds," she said.

Perkins handed over a card and waited as the others filed past him. "Thank you, my dear." He took the card, tickets and receipt.

"And these are for you." She handed over four plastic bags decorated with a picture of a knight on horseback.

Pekins opened one of the bags. It contained a plastic sword, a cardboard wizard's hat, and a candy lollipop in the shape of a dragon's head. He closed the bag and hurried to catch up with his team.

"I believe these to be some sort of complimentary gift," he said, distributing the bags.

"Where're we going then, boss?" asked Lothar.

Perkins unfolded the sitemap which came with the tickets. He studied it for a moment, then pointed to a narrow trail path running between two groups of trees. "Just through here."

They hurried along the path, dodging a herd of chattering children coming from the other way, and arrived in a small circular area with a wooden ice cream hut in the middle. They stopped and stared around.

"Can't see no Arthur's sword here," said Lothar.

"Are you sure this is the right place?" Mario asked.

Perkins studied the map. "It's right here." He looked around as if it would appear the second time he looked.

"Give it to me." Mario took the map from Perkins. He scanned it quickly then asked Perkins, "Which way's the car park?"

Perkins looked all around slowly, then pointed his hand 180 degrees from where they'd come. "Um, that way?"

Mario stared at him, then said, "Idiot. It's a wonder you find your way home. Have you ever used a map?"

"Of course I have. I use the London underground all the time. I have the Tube Map app on my phone."

Mario stared at him a moment, shook his head briefly in despair, then said, "It's this way." He pointed to the left.

"Hang on, mate," said Barbie from the ice cream hut. "I'm just waiting for my sprinkles."

"I told you, I haven't got any sprinkles," said the man behind the counter at the ice cream hut. "You can have chocolate chips on your Super Cone instead."

Mario had to bend down to talk to the man in the hut designed to serve children, not giants. "I don't like chocolate chips," he said. "Not with ice cream. I want sprinkles."

The man looked exasperated. "Tell you what, I'll put some Smarties on it. How about that? We'll call them super-sized sprinkles."

"Will you get on," yelled Mario. "We're on a timer here."

"Just a moment," Barbie replied, then turning back to the man in the hut, "super-sized sprinkles?"

"Yes, for a super-sized cone."

"I like Smarties. They're like Candy Crushes."

"Good," said the man and handed Barbie his Super Cone with Smarties. "That'll be four fifty."

Barbie juggled ice cream from hand to hand while he searched his pockets and dumped a handful of change on the counter. "Gonna need a receipt for that, mate. I get expenses."

They set off through another little wooded path to find a clearing. This one with a ring of benches around the outside facing a paved central circle, in the middle of which lay a huge boulder with a sword sticking out of it. A metal sign attached to the rock read, 'Whoso pulleth out this sword of this stone is rightwise king born of all England'.

"I assume that's it?" said Perkins.

"That ain't even a proper rock," said Lothar. "It's just a lump of painted concrete."

Barbie grabbed hold of the sword and pulled. Nothing happened.

"I'll log us in," said Mario. He tapped away at his phone.

Perkins pulled up Combermere's number on his phone, paused to steel himself, then hit dial.

The answer was almost immediate. "This had better be good news, Perkins. I've just had to spend the morning with some blasted woman who wants to block the building of a new oil processing plant at Clevedon. All because a few fish will have to move and do their breeding somewhere else. Or it might have been butterflies. I wasn't really listening after the first ten minutes. You can find a scientist to debunk her when you get back."

"Yes, sir, I'll get right on it upon my return. We've just finished another clue, and everything's going like clockwork."

"I should hope so too, the money I'm paying out for this. I'll be lucky to break even."

"I understand, sir. I'll be sure to—" But the line went dead.

Perkins took a deep breath to re-centre himself, then looked over at Mario, who was looking a bit puzzled. "All alright, Mario?"

"Yeah, The Great Wessex Chase app glitched, or something. It didn't accept our location to start with, and then we had to upload the photograph twice. But it seems alright now."

"Jolly good, well let's get on then. I want to catch up on the cricket." His eye caught Barbie. "What's he doing?"

"Ah, yes," said Mario. "He managed to get the sword out of that stone thing."

Barbie held a distorted lump of metal in his hands. "It's not even a real sword," he complained. "How can the true king of England just have half a sword?" He held up the metal for all to see. It seemed to be a handle with only a few inches of a blade attached. Clearly, it had only been set into the supposed stone by just a couple of inches.

"Oi, what are you lot doing?" A security guard was heading across the clearing.

"I'm the true king of England, and you will not pass." Barbie held up the half sword and the security guard skidded to a halt.

"All right, fella," he said, "just take it easy."

"I'm the king. It says so. You have to call me sire."

"Er, yes, whatever you say… sire."

Lothar moved over to Barbie. "We need to go now. Put the sword down." Lothar turned to the guard. "He's alright. He just gets a bit over enthusiastic at times."

"He's busted the sword in the stone. He'll have to pay for that. What're the kids going to do now? We've got a school trip coming in an hour."

"He's sorry, aren't you, Barbie?"

Barbie nodded.

"Now give the man his sword," said Lothar.

Barbie thrust the sword towards the guard. "It broke."

Lothar gave a little wave and said, "We'll send you a cheque." He smiled, which on Lothar came across as a threat, barely concealed beneath a veneer of dire warnings and terrible consequences.

"Sorry," said Perkins. "We'll get you a new one." He turned to the others. "We need to go now. Come on." He hurried across the clearing and headed up the path. The others exchanged glances, then followed.

The security guard watched them disappear from view. Then, a few moments later, they all trooped back, this time led by a scowling Mario, crossed the clearing, and disappeared in the opposite direction.

CHAPTER TWENTY-ONE

TEAM FARMHOUSE FIVE

I CHECKED MY WATCH AS I watched the queue inch forwards, working out how long it took each group to move. Each time I calculated it came out the same. We were going to be out of time by at least twenty minutes. Janet and Dylan, who were holding our places in the queue, shuffled along a few more feet. Janet looked at me, an expectant look on her face as she silently asked how they were doing. I shook my head, and she gave a wan smile, then said something to Dylan.

I couldn't believe that even with the great advantage we'd had with the clue, that we were now going to be timed out.

I heard my name being called and turned to see Robyn and Eddie running back across the courtyard towards us. Both seemed to be carrying a bundle of something in their arms.

They arrived puffing like a pair of forty-a-day smokers who'd just run a hundred metres against Mo Farah.

"We might have a chance," panted Robyn, letting one of the bundles of cloth unfold in front of her.

A large piece of grey tweed flapped in the light morning breeze. It took me a moment.

"Sherlock Holmes," I said. I looked at Eddie. "Sherlock Holmes. You said the box of stuff was left behind by a Sherlock Holmes' film crew. I remember."

"Exactly," said Robyn. "Eddie can dress up as Sherlock Holmes and offer people the chance of being photographed with him next to an original English red phone box."

"But Sherlock Holmes had nothing to do with smugglers here," I said. "Or ghosts. Or even phone boxes, come to that. How does that help?"

"I know, but look," Eddie pointed at the crowd. "They're queuing up to have their photos taken against a phone box. What's that got to do with smugglers? Or pirates, ghosts, or Jamaica?"

"Eddie's right," said Robyn. "They're tourists. Don't try to understand the logic, or otherwise you're going to have to explain how an imaginary king and a mythical wizard drive the tourist economy of Cornwall."

As she spoke, she was helping Eddie into his Inverness Cape and hat. "There was even this." She held up a meerschaum pipe and planted it in Eddie's mouth. "All ready?"

Eddie nodded, and the hat slid over to one side of his head.

I checked my watch. "You've about twenty minutes. Just under."

"We've got this, haven't we, Eddie?"

"Elementary, my dear Robyn."

They hurried over to the phone box and Robyn spoke briefly to a young couple in the queue. I couldn't hear what was being said, but she pointed to Eddie, hovering near the phone box and pretending to smoke his pipe. The people seemed enthusiastic, and Robyn waited with them until their turn arrived, then motioned for Sherlock to join them at the phone box. She took the couple's phone while they posed with Eddie and took several pictures from different angles. A quick switch of phones followed, which probably went unnoticed by the couple, then she took pictures with her own phone.

It was all over in a matter of two minutes. As Eddie left the phone box, I heard people further back in the queue calling for him to go back.

"Did you get the picture?" I asked, as they both joined Janet, Dylan, and me.

Robyn swiped at her screen. "Yup, all done."

"Great." I glanced at my watch. "Fifteen minutes to go. You'd better upload them."

While Robyn fiddled with the app on her phone, Eddie said, "I'm just going back over there." He pointed to the phone box. "My public needs me."

"Eddie," I started, but he'd gone and was busy chatting with some pirates who were just coming forward to take their turn. I looked back to Robyn. "All good?"

"I think so. It seems to have been accepted, but I haven't got the confirmation back yet."

"That can take a minute or two." I looked back to Eddie, just in time to see an exchange of money and then him posing with the pirates by the phone box.

"Ah, here we go," Robyn said, studying her phone. "What? No, that can't be right."

"What is it?" I asked.

"Hang on, there must be something wrong. I'm going to refresh the app."

"What's it saying? Did they accept the picture or not?"

"Wait a second. Right, I'm opening it up again." She studied the screen. "This can't be right."

"Are you going to tell me what's going on?"

"We've been eliminated. Look." She handed me the phone.

"Team Farmhouse Five. Picture and location accepted. Your accumulated time is below the median average, therefore, Team Farmhouse Five has now been eliminated. We hope you enjoyed the experience."

I read the message several times. It said the same each time. The team counter icon clicked down to 21 as I watched.

"Eliminated?" asked Janet.

"We're not in the top 50% of accumulated time," I said.

"Oh dear."

***

As we set out on the ninety-minute journey back to Little Didney, the atmosphere in the car was subdued and tense as each of us processed the consequences of our defeat.

I rehearsed, over and over, how I was going to break the news to Gwen. I was hopeful she'd understood the futility of the project from the off, but I feared her passion for the animals in her charge had shielded her from facing the reality. My mind constantly thrashed over ways I might be able to make it up to her. Though, in what ways could I seriously be of any help? A copper's pension is liveable, but that was about it. Certainly, no leeway for supporting an animal sanctuary. Even the thought of taking on Teller was causing me stress. I had no idea how much dogs ate on a long-term basis. Or how expensive it was. And vet's bills? No, taking Teller on was probably going to be the limit of any financial commitment to animals.

The surprisingly light traffic and familiar road allowed my mind to drift a bit as I drove. Of course, we'd all known, deep down, that our chances had been slim. And in reality, we'd done exceptionally well to get as far as we had. We'd survived, where two thousand teams had failed. We should be proud, not downhearted. I wondered what the others were thinking. I guessed they were probably as stunned as I was.

"I don't suppose there's any chance of dropping by Exeter on the way, is there?" asked Eddie. "Just to pick up those E-scooters we spoke about. It's only just off the bypass."

"How is Exeter on the way to Little Didney?" I asked. "It's completely the opposite direction."

"Not completely opposite, just a bit of a diversion. We could go back on the coast road afterwards. Much more interesting than this road. We could make a bit of an outing out of it and stop off for a Devon cream tea. The upside-down ones."

"I need to get back," said Janet. "If we hurry, I can still get to my karate class."

"Getting back early suits me too," said Robyn. "I've got a big job coming up, it'll give me more time to prepare."

I looked at Robyn.

"What?" she challenged.

"Nothing," I said.

"Hmm."

"When have I got to check in again?" asked Dylan.

"Not till tomorrow, Dylan," I said. "It's every forty-eight hours."

"Cool."

"Is Exeter still on then?" asked Eddie.

"No," I said. "Exeter was never on in the first place."

"I'll cover the fuel. Plus a little sweetener on top."

"No sweeteners, no E-scooters. I want to get back now."

"Are we nearly there yet?" asked Dylan.

"No."

"I think we should all get together this evening," suggested Janet. "A sort of reunion. I've got a Murder Mystery Whodunit game we could play."

"That's a bit early for a reunion, innit?" said Eddie. "I mean, we're hardly going to be unpacked by then."

"I thought it might be nice, a bit of fun. Matt could be Detective Finder. I've got a detective's notebook."

"I think we'll probably all be a bit tired," I said. "Maybe next week? Or perhaps for a Christmas get-together. That might be nice."

Robyn said something under her breath, which I couldn't catch.

"Sorry?" I said.

"Nothing," said Robyn, then immediately followed with, "what was the name of that song by the Beatles? About picking up rice in a church?"

"You mean Eleanor Rigby?" I said. "What's that got to do... Oh, really? Oh, I suppose you're right." I half turned my head towards Janet while keeping eyes on the road. "That does sound like a fun idea, though, Janet. Maybe in a couple of days, once we get settled back?"

"I'll make a cake."

I returned to contemplative silence as I drove. Maybe the full impact of our elimination hadn't come home to the others yet, I reasoned.

We arrived back in Little Didney just after three. I dropped Janet off at her cottage on the outskirts of the village and the others at the top of the main street before heading out to my own place.

I showed Teller around his temporary home and found a tin of mince in the back of the cupboard. It had been earmarked for a spaghetti bolognese, but it was all I had. I decided I was probably going to be stuck with him for a while yet, so a trip to a dog food shop was going to be necessary. I found an old plastic dining set I'd kept in case I ever went camping again and emptied the tin in one of the bowls. I hadn't been camping in the last twenty years, so my chances of needing that bowl in the immediate future were slim. Teller looked at the food, then looked up at me.

"It's for you," I said, pointing at the bowl.

Teller looked back at the bowl, and suddenly, the minced meat had gone. I mentally moved dog food shopping further up my to-do list. I found an old blanket for him to sleep on and placed it near the sofa. Teller suggested that the sofa was probably more suited to his needs and settled down on that, managing to extend himself along the full length. Gwen had told me he'd been a stray. How did stray dogs know about sofas?

I took a lasagne from the freezer for my lunch and slipped it into the microwave while making tea. The microwave played its little tune, informing me lunch was ready, so I settled at the kitchen table with lasagne, tea, and the morning paper. I'd dived into an article on how the government's latest £20bn initiative on rebuilding the NHS had taken a hit because the company contracted to supply the new bespoke computer systems had just gone pop. Apparently, the whole operation had been dependent upon some fantastic new computer chip, which turned out to be about as real as a Black Friday discount. A government spokesperson had said, "Lessons will be learned."

I felt a nudge on my leg and looked down to find Teller doing big brown eyes and sad-face. I dropped a piece of lasagne down for him and it disappeared before it hit the floor. I moved dog food shopping to the very top of my to-do list, with a star against it. I also needed to get a book on how to look after a dog, as I had a feeling that Teller was taking advantage of my ignorance in this area.

After our lunch, I took Teller out into the garden to show him the areas he wasn't allowed to dig, or toilet. He cocked his leg against the only upright I'd managed to erect so far on my pergola, then dug a hole where I'd just patched the lawn with grass seed. I wondered how Dylan was getting on with Yurei. He'd seemed to slot into the role of dog carer a lot faster than me.

I decided to take a walk into the village to buy dog food and some sort of cheap bed to keep him off the sofa. I wondered if I should leave him here while I went, but then figured that I'd probably return to find my lawn looking like the aftermath of the battle of the Somme if I did. I gathered up a rope as a lead and some old forensic evidence bags and latex gloves to deal with accidents. Life as a police detective had taught me to never go out without plastic evidence bags and forensic gloves. As a result, I had a kitchen drawer dedicated to those which I'd accumulated over the years.

The village of Little Didney had a sparse selection of shops, but fortunately, one of these was a vets, which doubled as a pet supplies and food shop. I opened the door of Paws R Us and stepped inside, setting off a little buzzer. The vet herself was only in attendance on three days a week, with her assistant, Kaliegh, running the shop on the other days.

Kaliegh appeared from a back room on hearing the buzzer. Rather than greeting me with a friendly good afternoon, or even just, hello, she chose to open with, "You can't bring a dog in here."

"But it's a vet's?" I stood back to read the sign over the door to reassure myself I'd come to the right place.

"Not on Thursdays. On Thursdays, it's a pet shop. But we don't sell pets before you ask. So if you wanted to buy a rabbit or something, we don't sell them. Or tortoises."

"I just wanted to buy some things for my dog. He's new." I nodded towards Teller. "New to me, anyway."

"Oh, that's alright then. Only we get lots of people wanting to buy rabbits."

"And tortoises?"

"How did you know that?"

"Just a lucky guess. Can I come in now?" I asked.

"Yeah, but you got to leave your dog outside. We're only insured for animals when it's a vet's. Not when it's a pet shop."

"Not even if he wants to choose his own lead and bed?"

"You take them outside to show him, I s'pose," she reluctantly conceded.

I tied Teller to a lamppost just outside the shop and started back towards the door. Immediately, Teller signalled his disapproval by howling as if he were summoning the hordes of hell. I rushed back to him, and he quietened at my first touch. I gave him a gentle explanation of what I was doing and assured him he wasn't going to be abandoned to the demons of Little Didney's Harbour Lane. He seemed to accept my explanation until I turned away again, at which point he sounded like he was auditioning for the audio version of Munch's Scream. Okay, this wasn't going to work.

"Can you bring some leads for us to look at?" I asked.

"Leather? Synthetic? Rope? Natural Hemp? Rafia? Reconstituted waste fabrics?"

"I don't know." I looked at Teller. "What do you reckon? Leather?"

Teller's ears came up, and what could only be a big grin took over his face.

"He says leather," I said.

"Cool," said Kaliegh. She disappeared into the shop and returned a moment later with a selection of leather leads.

We chose a braided two-tone affair with bronze clips, then repeated the same process for a bed, blanket, a chew-ball and a sack of food. Teller looked very pleased with his presents. Me, not so much. Not only the expense, but now the fact that I was standing on a pavement with far more stuff than I could carry. I gave up trying to find a way of juggling everything and left it all, with the exception of the lead and chew-ball, in the shop for later collection and we made our way home.

I'd just arrived back and put the kettle on for tea when my phone bleeped at me. I glanced at the screen and the notification icon informed me I had a message from The Great Wessex Chase app. I ignored it and returned to making the tea. It was probably just some survey asking about my customer experience, or trying to sell me a time-share. All those entrants to the competition would represent useful, and saleable, data to somebody.

I took my tea, book, and summer white bucket hat out to my little table next to the pergola-to-be and settled down. Teller followed closely and sat exactly where I wanted to stretch out my feet. I opened my book and was just trying to remember where I'd got to when I heard my phone ringing back in the kitchen. I untangled myself from the chair, book, and dog, and hurried back. Of course, it stopped just as I reached for it. I checked the missed calls. Only one, Janet. She'll be arranging her Murder Mystery evening. Having spent forty years in the police, the last thing I wanted to be doing was to play detectives in my retirement. I knew that often retired coppers, especially those from C.I.D., went on to be private investigators, but the idea had never appealed to me. Once out, properly out. I eyed the phone again. I should really ring her back. Maybe it wasn't about a get-together? Maybe she really needed help? I mumbled a small curse aimed at Robyn for making me even think that way. But I still relented and pressed recall.

Janet answered after the first ring. No hellos or niceties, just straight in with, "We're back. Isn't it exciting?"

"Well yes, I suppose. But we *have* only been away a couple of days."

"What? Oh yes. I know that. But not that. I didn't mean back here. I meant back, back in the game."

"I'm sorry," I said, trying to work out if she'd been drinking. "I'm not sure what you mean. Back where?"

"Back in the game, silly. Didn't you get your message?"

"Game? Message? I haven't had any…" Messages, I thought. I'd had a message from The Great Wessex Chase. Was that…? "Hang on, Janet," I said. "Just checking something."

I opened up the app and pulled up the message tab. One new message. — "*Good afternoon, Team Farmhouse Five. Due to the elimination of a team found to be in breach of our rules, your team is the one with the fastest time of those eliminated in the last round. This makes Team Farmhouse Five eligible for reinstatement in the competition. This is subject to all team members replying "YES" to this message before 18:00 hours. After which time, the place will be offered to the next team."*

I looked at my watch. Just after four.

"Yes, that is good news," I said. "Have you replied?"

"Oh yes. I did that straight away."

"What about the others? Have you spoken to them?"

"No, I haven't got their numbers. Only yours."

"Right, yes, well. Leave it to me. I'll give them a ring and make sure we're all logged back in."

"Super. Isn't this fun?"

"Um, yes, Janet. It's certainly fun. I'll come back to you soon."

I disconnected and immediately called Eddie's number. Straight to voicemail. I left a message, then called Robyn. A computerised voice informed me that this number was unobtainable. What on earth does that mean? Not live? Missing? Or perhaps it's one of Dylan's imaginary numbers? I rang Dylan and his phone just didn't respond. No informative message or voicemail. Just dead.

Plan B, back to old school. I'd have to find each of them in the real world. I hurried out to the garden and gathered up my tea cup and book. George Smiley was going to have to wait. Teller trotted faithfully alongside as I headed for the car.

"Sorry, boy," I said. "You'll have to stay here." I opened the car door and Teller leapt into the driver's seat, a big grin on his face and tail thrashing like windscreen wipers in a thunderstorm. "Or you could just come with me," I said.

My first stop was The Smuggler's Arms, where Robyn was staying. The place was empty, not unusual for a late weekday afternoon. Old Sam Goodenough stood behind the bar with a hairdryer pointed into the sandwich cabinet on the bar.

"A hairdryer?" I queried as I approached the bar.

"Stops them getting soggy," he said. "A quick blow with this, and they'll get through to evening without the bread disintegrating. What can I get you?"

"Nothing at the moment. I'm looking for Robyn. She's staying here, Robyn Hedges?"

"Oh, yeah. Not anymore, she ain't. Paid up and checked out half-an-hour ago. Didn't even wait for her receipt to be made up or nothin'."

"Any idea where she was going?"

"Dunno. My business is selling drinks. Don't get time to worry about where folks are off to."

"I see. Well maybe I will have a small scotch. Perhaps you might remember while you pour?"

"It don't take very long to pour a single scotch," Goodenough said.

"Better make it a double then." I put a ten-pound note on the bar. "Keep the change."

He turned to press a glass under the optic of a Johnnie Walker bottle. "Happens I do remember now," he said. "She was askin' about bus times to Porth Cullen."

"What did you tell her?"

"Told her the bus stops up at top car park at five, thereabouts." He placed the glass on the counter and the ten-pound note disappeared.

I checked my watch. Fifteen minutes to five. "Thanks, Sam." I gave a short wave and turned to go.

"You'll not be wantin' yer scotch?"

"No, it's on me."

"Fair enough." He unclipped the Johnnie Walker bottle and poured the whisky back in. "Do you want a sandwich for your journey?"

"I would, only I've just eaten." I rushed out of the door and back to the car, where Teller was busy telling the world about his torture at being left alone for three minutes. "Move over." I pushed him out of the driver's seat again and we headed for the car park right at the top of the village.

As I pulled up in the gravel parking area, I spotted Robyn sitting on a low wall at the far end. A yellow suitcase next to her. I glanced up at the main road and noticed a green bus heading towards us. Robyn spotted it too and started making her way to the entrance. I stopped the car right by the entrance and Robyn started in shock, as if she were about to be kidnapped by some crazed lunatic. Maybe that wasn't too far off.

"Oh, it's you," she said, as I dived out of the car. "What on earth are you doing here? You taking a bus?"

"No," I panted. "Did you get the message?"

"Message?"

"Yes, from The Great Wessex Chase. We're back in."

"Back in? What are you talking about?" She turned to look as the bus pulled up to a stop and the door hissed open. She touched my arm. "We'll have to talk later. This is my bus."

"No, wait—"

"I can't wait, it's a bus." She pointed to the open door.

"Just hang on a moment, can you?" I called to the driver.

"Sorry, mate. If I'm late, I lose my bonus."

I moved to stand between Robyn and the bus door. "We've been reinstated. We're still in The Great Wessex Chase. Stay with the team and I will personally drive you to Porth Cullen when we're done. How's that?"

"How did you know where…" she paused as the penny dropped. "Ah, Sam Goodenough. I should have known better."

"Well?" I pressed.

Her eyes flitted from bus to me several times as she tried to decide.

"You coming or not, love?" the driver called. "Only I ain't got all day."

"We had a deal," I reminded. "Remember?"

She sighed and her shoulders slumped. She turned to the driver and waved her hand towards the road. "Go on," she said.

The door hissed closed, cutting off the driver's grumble.

Robyn turned to me. "I thought my quiet getaway was too good to be true. I should've known better."

I picked up her suitcase and we walked over to my car. "You're doing a good thing," I told her.

"Yeah, yeah. So, what happened?"

"I'm not really sure." I dropped her case in the back and closed the hatch. "Another team broke some rule or other. They've been chucked out, and we were the next closest time. Back to the Smuggler's?"

"Oh, hell. I checked out."

"I doubt that'll be a problem. Sam won't have let the room that quickly. Although, there'll probably be a surcharge for a short notice booking, or something."

"Do we know where we're going yet?"

"No, not yet. We all have to respond to the message before we're officially back in."

"Okay. I'd better put my SIM card back in." She pulled her phone out, flicked the back cover off, then found the SIM card in her purse.

"Why did you take it out?"

"I don't want to be tracked." She fired up the phone and logged into The Great Wessex Chase app. "I won't go back to the Smuggler's. I'll wait till we know before I check back in, we may be halfway across the country, for all I know."

"Makes sense." I pulled the car out of the parking area and headed towards the village.

"What about the others?" Robyn asked, dropping her phone back into her bag.

"Only Janet so far. I haven't got hold of the others yet. Eddie's turned his phone off, and Dylan's isn't responding."

"Do you know where they live?"

"Eddie, yes, but Dylan, I've no idea, which is why we're stopping off at the police office to have a word with PC Albert Muchmore. He'll know."

I pulled up in the parking space behind Tiffin's Bakery and Cakes. The door to the police station stood next to the back entrance to the shop. I stepped out of the car and looked at Robyn, who hadn't moved.

"I'll just wait here," she said. "I'm not very keen on police stations."

"This is hardly a police station," I said. "It's barely even an office. I'm sure the only reason it's there is that Albert's wife wants him out of the house. And he likes the unsold cakes from the bakery."

"I'll still give it a miss, thanks. I'll keep Teller company." She smiled and sank lower in the seat, as if wanting to disappear into the upholstery. Teller licked her face.

I knocked on the semi-open door and pushed it open.

"We're closed," came a voice from the back room. "Major police incident."

"What's that then, Albert?" I answered.

Albert Muchmore emerged from the door behind the desk. "Oh, hello, Matt, it's you."

"What's this major incident, then? I've heard nothing."

"We've had that Green Ninja fella round here. Let the tyres down on my official police bicycle."

"The Green Ninja? What makes you think she… um, they did that? From what I've heard, the Green Ninja is an eco-activist. Not much eco threat from a police bicycle, is there? I expect it's just kids."

"That's what the inspector said, but he's not on the front line here. Easy for them to say in their offices, away from the danger of modern policing on the beat. Anyway, what can I do for you?"

"That lad I brought in to sign his bail, Dylan, do you have his address to hand?"

Muchmore pulled a huge ledger from under the counter and opened it up. "What's he done now?" he asked as he leafed through the pages.

"Nothing, he's part of our team for this Great Wessex Chase, and I need to catch up with him." I watched as Muchmore turned page after page. "Is this not all on computer?"

"Yes, but I don't turn it on 'less I really have to. Takes so long to get it up and running and then it wants to update this, and logon that. I can't be 'avin' with it. Besides, I've forgotten my magic word again." His finger stopped scrolling halfway down a page. "Here he is. Flat B, 42 Pendragon Avenue. Want me to write it down for you? I think I've got a pencil round here somewhere."

"No, thanks, I'll remember it."

As I turned to go, Muchmore called after me, "If you see that Green Ninja, you tell him PC Muchmore's comin' for him. There ain't nowhere he can hide."

"I'll be sure to tell her... I mean him, or they."

I returned to the car, to find Teller sitting on Robyn's lap, presumably to make sure she didn't abandon him as well. We stopped by Paws R Us to pick up my dog kit on the way to Dylan's flat. We had to park a short distance away as Pendragon Avenue, which despite its name, was just a narrow alley with barely enough room for two people to pass, let alone vehicles. I found number 42, it was between number 12 and number 23, and pressed the button for Flat B.

"He's not here," came a voice, which sounded exactly like Dylan, from the window above us.

"Okay, so who's that in Dylan's flat?" I called up.

"It's... Zebedee. Dylan's gone out. He's taken Yurei down to the harbour." A loud bark came from the window. "That's not Yurei." Then more quietly, "Shush, Yurei." And loudly again, "That's Dougal. Zebedee's dog... I mean, my dog. I'm Zebedee."

"Dylan," I yelled. "It's me, Matt. I'm with Robyn. It's safe. Can we come up?"

"Matt?"

"Yes."

"Oh, come on up. The door code is 1234."

Walking into Dylan's flat was like stepping into an IKEA catalogue. Simple, functional furniture, and very little sign that anybody actually lived in the place. Apart from a pack of Coco Shreddies and an empty white bowl on a simple shelf over the countertop.

"Coco Shreddies?" I queried.

Dylan shrugged. "They're square, and they taste of chocolate. Perfect meal."

"Of course." I stroked Yurei's head as he came to say hello. "Did you get the message about The Great Wessex Chase?"

"My phone's not on."

"It's back on."

"No," said Dylan. "I keep it off."

"Sorry, I meant the competition, not your phone, the competition's back on. You have to confirm you want to continue."

"How can it be back on?"

"Some other team got disqualified for something. I don't know what, but it means we're back in."

"Maybe they had help from the interdimensional beings on M-Brain who know where all the sacred geometrical spaces are. I expect that's it."

"Yes," I said. "I suppose that's a possibility. Can you switch your phone on and accept the offer to rejoin?"

"What, now?"

"Yes, now would be good."

"I don't like having my phone on in the afternoon. That's when the CIA DARPA satellites are over Cornwall."

"Perhaps just quickly?" Robyn asked. "Just to get back in, then you can switch it straight off again."

Dylan looked up at the plain white plastic wall clock. "Hmm, should be alright by now. They'll be nearly over Devon by now." He opened the microwave, removed his phone and inserted the SIM card.

"Why the microwave?" I asked.

"It's like a Faraday cage. Blocks all radio frequencies and stops them monitoring me." His phone sprang to life and bleeped several times to announce incoming messages. "And you just want me to agree that I'm back in?"

"Yes. That's all."

"Cool." Dylan swiped through a couple of screens, tapped, then closed the phone and put it back in the microwave.

"It might be best if you keep it on," I suggested. "As soon as we get Eddie logged back in, we'll likely get a message telling us where to be."

Dylan studied his clock. "I'll put it back on in... thirty-three minutes. They'll definitely be clear by then. Do you want some Coco Shreddies?"

"No thanks." I patted my tummy. "Just had lunch."

As we left Dylan's flat, I tried again to get hold of Eddie. This time the call connected.

"Bishop's Banging Bargains," Eddie greeted, in a slightly strained attempt at received pronunciation. "How may I direct your call?"

"It's me, Matt. Didn't you get my message?"

"Oh yeah, I was busy setting up a deal with a Nigerian prince."

"Seriously? Has your cheese finally slid off your pizza? Have you never come across the words, scam, phishing, and what the hell do you think you're doing?"

"No, he's a proper prince. I've done business with him before."

"A Nigerian prince?"

"Yeah, Second Prince of the Kanuba people in Gombe. Brian, his name is. Lovely chap. He's got a load of drones at a ridiculous price. The Chinese bring them into Nigeria for surveying, but they're not very good at counting, apparently. You want one? They're great for spying on the neighbours. They're very popular with the boys in Dartmoor, just the right size for a 200 case of Benson & Hedges."

"Eddie, I need you to stop talking now. There's so much wrong with this conversation, I need to unhear it."

"You'll change your mind when you see one."

"On more pressing matters," I said, trying to get the conversation back on track. "Have you got a message from The Great Wessex Chase?"

"Yeah, it came earlier. I figured it was a con of some sort and deleted it. Why? You get one too?"

"Yes, but it's not a con. We're being invited back into the competition."

"Oh? Well, that's a turnup. We doing it then? Gettin' back in?"

"Yes, can you login to the app and accept?"

"Hang on…" The call went silent for about a minute, then, "All done. What now?"

"They'll send us our start point soon, I think."

"I'm in Exeter at the moment."

"Might be best if you wait there until we know where we're going. I'll ring as soon as I know."

I closed the call and turned to Robyn. "Looks like we're on."

"Oh… goody."

CHAPTER TWENTY-TWO

TEAM BULLINGBOY CLUB

"WHAT DO YOU MEAN, DISQUALIFIED?" Combermere's voice held an accustomed calm, which Perkins found even more terrifying than his normal rantings.

"I'm not sure I understand it properly, but all three of their phones went wrong when they tried to login. The Great Wessex Chase app said they were using unregistered phones or something then the app just disappeared."

"How can that be? You were supposed to make sure your team complied with all the rules."

"I really don't know. It might be a glitch. I don't really understand these things, but there's no way of appealing. We're out."

"Hmm, well, you wait there till you hear from me. Do you think you're capable of that?"

"Yes, but it wasn't really—" The line went dead. Perkins placed his phone on the table and pressed his hand over it, as if hoping it would disappear.

"How'd he take it?" Lothar asked.

"About as well as Richard Nixon opening his Washington Post in June '72."

"Huh?"

"He said we have to wait here."

"Oh, worse places to wait." Mario picked up his empty glass. "And if I'm not driving for a while, I might as well have another. Anybody want a top-up?"

The others all nodded or grunted assent, and he headed to the bar.

"Have we still got the gig?" Lothar asked.

"What?" asked Perkins, looking puzzled. "What's a gig?"

"Are we still on the clock? On contract?" Lothar tried again, but Perkins still looked puzzled, so Lothar said, "For fuck's sake, are you still paying us?"

"Paying you? Good Lord, no, not at the moment. You're not doing anything. The Master's not going to pay you for doing nothing."

"And another thing, what's with this Master business? I think you oughta cough and tell us just who we're working for."

"That's not the deal. He assured me he was going to ring back." Perkins looked at his phone. "And we're going to wait here until he does so."

"In that case, you're paying for lunch, and I fancy a nice fillet steak."

"Well, I suppose we can—"

"With onion rings," Lothar added. "And some of them curly fries."

Perkins conceded to lunch but resisted the requests for a bottle of Glenfiddich. Shortly after they'd finished, the phone rang.

"Perkins?"

"Yes, sir. Any news?"

"Right, now pay attention. There's a team still in this thing going by the name The Money Boys."

"Yes, I think we've come across them."

"Well, they're all traders for a hedge fund company called Shye, Locke, and Grifter. Martin Locke, the CEO, is in my club. He has a damned fine wine cellar too. Now, Martin didn't realise they were doing this, but he's had a word with them, and we've struck a deal. We're going to join forces."

"Join forces?" Perkins queried. "How would that work?"

"These chaps, The Money Boys, as they call themselves, all they're interested in is the money. They don't give a damn about the land, and they were going to sell it to a developer they had lined up if they won."

"I see, and you've persuaded them to sell it to you instead?"

"Exactly. We're going to use my contacts in GCHQ to make sure they win, and in return, they're going to sell it to me for half what it's worth. They get a guaranteed win; I get my hunting estate. You just have to ensure no other team comes close. I trust that is something within your limited capabilities, Perkins?"

"Of course, sir. Absolutely."

"And Perkins…"

"Yes?"

"Don't let me down again."

"But, sir, I didn't—" The line went dead.

Mario looked at Perkins. "Well? We on, or what?"

"Sorry," said Perkins. "You're not on the jig anymore."

CHAPTER TWENTY-THREE

TEAM FARMHOUSE FIVE

I DROVE ROBYN BACK TO my place, where Teller leapt on her like a long-lost friend. I tracked down a packet of Hobnobs in the back of the cupboard and made tea.

Robyn picked up the packet of biscuits and studied the label. "Hmm, vegan, well done." She smiled.

"I'd like to say I thought it through, but to be honest, I was just thinking of something easy to keep the wolf away for a moment." I waved towards the kitchen table in an invitation for Robyn to sit down. "Milk?" I asked, placing the carton of UHT on the table.

"And now you go and blow it," she said, shaking her head.

"Huh? Oh, yes, sorry." I picked the carton up, splashed a drop in my tea, then returned it to the fridge. "We'll sort out something more substantial as soon as we know where we're going."

She looked around my kitchen. "How long have you lived here?"

"Coming on twelve years. I lived in rented places before that. The Police Force tends to move you about a bit, so it was never worth buying somewhere before."

"You never remarried?"

I scanned my eyes over the room, trying to see it with the eyes of a stranger. Clean, functional. Maybe it could do with some pictures or something other than the takeaway menus, and post-it notes to self, which currently adorned the walls.

"Nearly once," I said. "The Job tends... tended to scare off potential life partners. Unless they're Job as well, of course. Even then... well, anyway, it just never happened. The career always took priority. It's what killed my marriage in the first place, and I was in no hurry to repeat that."

"Hmm, your career." She broke a hobnob into careful quarters and nibbled. "What was it, thirty years? And only Detective Sergeant. What went wrong?" Her eyes focussed on mine like a pair of laser gunsights.

I thought of telling her to mind her own business, but then I reflected on how I'd given her the treatment the night before. "A slight confusion of evidence. A local scroat, well known to us, had been robbing elderly people in their homes at knifepoint. I was a DI, out with a young detective, DC Graham Honeybun, his name was. We'd recovered a weapon from one scene and unfortunately, Honeybun hadn't changed gloves between bagging the knife and picking up a crowbar he'd found outside. I tried to cover for him, but it all came out. The DNA gathered from the knife was disallowed, and the scroat got off with a simple breaking and entering. Both of us were disciplined. I got dropped back to a DS, and the young detective was moved to the Met."

Robyn stayed silent for a moment, then just as she was about to speak, both of our phones bleeped simultaneously.

I swiped and tapped. *"Clue number five will follow tomorrow at 10:00. Your recommended starting point is bandaged.servers.monkeys, from where the next clue will be within a 25-mile radius."*

"Bandaged servers..." I started.

"I'm on it," Robyn said. "Hang on... Right, here we are, Camborne, it's the Retail Park. Just off the junction on the bypass."

"That's only up the road," I said. "Forty-five minutes tops. That means we don't need to stay overnight in a hotel."

"I'll give the Smuggler's a ring then. Hopefully, they've still got a room."

I pondered, then hesitated, then thought again, before saying, "No need to do that. I've got a spare room here. If you don't mind sharing it with a 1980s Space Invader machine?"

She looked at me and her eyes brightened. "Okay, as long as you don't mind hearing the sounds of a 1980s Space Invader machine playing all night. I loved those things."

"I'll find some bedding." I stood to go to the airing cupboard. "I warn you, it might not all match."

"I think I'll manage."

I cleared the cardboard boxes of books from the bed and laid the bedding out. Robyn followed me upstairs and took over making the bed while I phoned the others to make sure they'd received the message. Eddie said he was driving back anyway, so we all agreed to meet at the top car park at nine the next morning.

Teller managed to convince me he hadn't been fed since last Tuesday and was about to die of starvation if I didn't give him his favourite biscuits. I caved, then heard Robyn's voice behind me, "He'll get fat."

"He won't be with me long enough."

"You're still telling yourself that? Good luck."

I opened the fridge to peer inside. "Hmm, I'd offer to cook supper, but the only human food I seem to have is a pizza or a six-pack of Cornish Pasties, which I don't remember buying. Probably not a good sign." I closed the fridge. "Fancy dropping by the Smuggler's for a bite?"

"Not really. Sam's idea of a vegan menu is either salad or beans on toast. Although, he did offer me spaghetti hoops on toast once as a change. Tell you what, I'll pop down to the mini-mart and see what they've got. I could use the air, anyway."

While she was out, I settled at the kitchen table with a guide to Cornwall and an Ordnance Survey map and started listing potential sites within a twenty-five-mile radius of Camborne. Cornwall had a lot of old stuff. I gave up when I filled my first sheet of A4.

Robyn returned after about half an hour. She dumped a pair of cardboard boxes of shopping on the table and thrust a bottle of Chardonnay towards me.

"Do something useful and find a corkscrew for that." She emptied the contents of the first bag across the table. Mushrooms, potatoes, onions, and assorted spices. "Hope you like curry?"

"Love it."

"Just as well. Are you going to pour that wine, or just look at it?"

"Sorry, I thought we were having it with the meal." I took a couple of glasses from the cupboard and poured.

"I've got another bottle for that," she said, pulling one out of the second box. "Okay, you can go find something else to do now. Haven't you got a pergola that needs building?"

Half an hour later, I was enjoying one of the best curries I'd ever tasted. I was also feeling quite fuzzy around the edges.

"Who'd have thought vegetables could taste so good?" I said.

"I know." Robyn grinned. "Modern miracle. Makes you wonder how we ever managed before they came along."

After we'd finished, we shared the clearing up, and the last of the wine. Teller seemed nervous about the leftovers at first, but soon decided that curry was the best food ever and it disappeared in seconds. Somehow, shortly after that, we ended up playing Space Invaders in Robyn's bedroom. And shortly after that...

CHAPTER TWENTY-FOUR

THE SABOTEURS

"TWO GRAND FOR A SET of wheels?" Micky questioned, as they left the forecourt of the Bodmin Ezee Wheelz Centre. "And you'd only just forked out a monkey for the tyres yesterday."

"When you've got a nice motor, you gotta look after it right," said Elvis. "You can't just put any old wheels on a classic like this."

"Yeah, but two grand? You coulda bought yourself a nice little Fiesta for that."

"I don't want a nice little Fiesta. I like my Corolla. Besides, we'll get it back on expenses."

"Do we still get expenses if we ain't stopped any teams, then?"

"Yeah. I don't know. Probably. Look, just focus on the tracker, will you? I don't want to end up in any more farmyards like where you sent us yesterday. Brand new set of alloys and I don't want them all covered in cow shit in five minutes."

Micky squinted at his phone, watching a little red dot moving across a map. "It says they've stopped about a mile to our right. Left. Definitely left." He turned his phone through 180 degrees. "Right."

They pulled up in a lane just outside the gateway to the Hotel Bodmin Palatine. Elvis leaned forwards to study the place. A huge gravel driveway swept in a lazy semi-circle to arrive at the hotel entrance, a large, covered area with columns that wouldn't have looked out of place on the Parthenon.

"It's a bit posh," he said.

"Can you see the cars?" Micky asked.

"Not from here. They're probably round the back. Places like this don't want cars clutterin' up their front yards. Makes 'em look common."

"What we gonna do then?"

"We need a different plan. Ain't no point in nobbling their motors, not if they just go and get a chopper, like it's an Uber or something."

Elvis' phone started ringing. He pulled it out of his pocket and glanced at the screen. He grunted and pressed Reject. The ringing stopped, and he slipped the phone back in his pocket.

"That geezer Perkins again?" asked Micky.

Elvis nodded. "He won't leave it out. I can't be 'avin' with another nagging."

"If he thinks it's so easy, he oughta get down 'ere an' do it 'imself," said Micky.

"We need to get in a bit closer."

"What'ya thinking, Elvis?"

"Dunno yet. We need to do a reccy, get the lay of the land."

"Like in Call of Duty?"

"Yeah. Only without blowin' shit up."

Elvis tucked the car into a gravel cut under some trees and they set off across a field which led to the back of the hotel. They settled in the middle of an ornamental planting of pampas grass. They peered from the tall, thick grass like a pair of meerkats nervously watching a lion on the hunt for supper.

The evening shadows draped the rear of the hotel in patchy darkness. As they watched, an orange light appeared, indicating the opening of a door. A figure stepped through the light and into the shadow of a tree bordering an ornamental garden area. A sudden flare of light illuminated the figure's face as they lit a cigarette.

"Ain't that one of 'em?" Micky asked. "Looks like that posh twat who got all pissy about losin' his phone back in Tiverton. The one who drives the Aston Martin."

"Yeah, could be," agreed Elvis. "I've got a plan. Take yer hoodie off."

"Why do I need to do that? It's my disguise. I might get recognised."

"Who's gonna recognise you 'ere?" Elvis challenged. "I mean, it's not like Clapham High Street, where even the pigeons know who you are. Nobody knows you here. Now get yer hoodie off, you dopey twonk. We need it for my plan."

Micky did as he was told with muttered grumbles.

"Right," said Elvis, "you hang on to that, I'm going to distract him, then when I give you the signal, you pull it over his head."

"Why we doin' that then?"

"Because we're gonna kidnap him so's he can't do the clue. We cop for five grand and let him go next day. Happy days."

They crept through the growing shadows until they were within a few feet of their target. Elvis started to move again when Micky grabbed his arm. "What's the signal?"

"Signal?"

"Yeah, you said you were going to give a signal, then I jump him with my hoodie. What's the signal?"

"Um... I'll scratch my head like this." Elvis demonstrated scratching his head.

"Cool."

They separated and Elvis came round to the front of the man, but still keeping in the shadows. "You got a light, mate?" he asked.

"Yes, here." The man handed Elvis a box of matches. "We are a small, but resolute minority."

"Who?"

"We smokers. We, who are constantly persecuted for our little vice."

"Yeah, whatever." Elvis scratched his head.

"Are you not going to light up?"

"What? Oh, I ain't got no fags." Elvis scratched his head again.

"Would you like a cigarette?"

"Nah, I don't smoke." He scratched his head again and said loudly, "I'm scratching me head."

"As I see. Do you have—" The man's voice disappeared into a muffle underneath Micky's hoodie.

Man, Micky, and hoodie ended up on the ground in a writhing mess.

"What do I do now, Elvis?" yelled Micky.

"Don't use my name," scolded Elvis. He leaned into the man on the ground. "Though, of course, that ain't my real name. Just a fake name."

"I didn't know that," said Micky.

"What do you want?" came a muffled voice.

"We're kidnapping you, that's what," said Elvis.

"Why me?"

"Somebody paid us to, that's why," said Micky.

"I'll double it if you let me go."

"Yeah, you think we're gonna fall for that?" Micky challenged. "We ain't as stupid as we look… I mean, we're cleverer than we look. I mean…"

"How much are they paying you?"

Elvis thought quickly. "Six grand."

Micky looked up in surprise. "You said five grand."

"Yeah, I know, I was… Just shut up, will you, Micky. Let me handle this."

"Look, Micky, Elvis," said the voice from under the hoodie. "You let me go, and I'll pay you twelve grand, alright?"

"How're you gonna do that, then? You ain't gonna tell me you just got twelve grand just lyin' around in yer pocket."

"Of course not, maybe a couple, but I can transfer it to you. Bank to bank. Just get me out of this, and I'll have the money in your bank within a minute."

"A minute, fifteen grand?"

"Yes, but didn't we agree twelve?" asked the muffled voice.

"Get him outta that, Micky," Elvis instructed. "But keep a'hold of him."

The man struggled to his feet and Micky pulled the hoodie downwards, effectively pinning the man's arms to his side.

"Go on then, show me how you do this. Fifteen grand, right?"

Micky allowed the man to free one arm enough to reach his phone and open up his banking app.

"I just need your bank account number."

"What, so you can dip in and nick all me money?" Elvis said.

The man gave Elvis a puzzled stare and said, "Seriously?" He handed the phone to Elvis. "Here, just put your number in."

Elvis took the phone and entered his bank account number, then handed it back to the man.

The man tapped at the screen and said, "There we are then. All done. You can check your account balance."

Elvis checked his phone and when he looked at his account, his face drained of colour.

"I take it from your expression, the money arrived? Maybe you could let me go now? I have a table booked for eight and there's a Dom Pérignon waiting on ice."

"Yeah, well." Elvis reached out and snatched the man's phone from his hand. "I'm gonna keep that."

"What?"

"Don't think I ain't got you sussed," Elvis said. "Moment I'm gone, you're gonna press some button and whip it all back to you. So," Elvis waggled the phone towards the man. "So I'm just gonna hang onto this. Stop your game, thinkin' we came up with the turkeys. C'mon, Micky. They'll 'ave a nice couple of Stellas waitin' on ice for us in the pub."

Elvis nodded briefly, pocketed the phone, then they both ran back towards the car. Once there, they slid inside and breathed. Elvis fired up the car, and a spit of gravel from the new wheels signalled their departure.

"How's he going to continue the competition if you've got his phone?" Micky asked.

"Do I look like I give a shit?" Elvis asked, pressing the button to wind down the window. He tossed the phone out and said, "We're fifteen grand in pocket and his team'll be bounced out because a phone's gone. That means we can cop another five grand from that Perkins bloke for knockin' them out. Happy days." He closed the window and hit the accelerator.

CHAPTER TWENTY-FIVE

TEAM FARMHOUSE FIVE

I CHECKED THE FENCES TO my garden were Teller-proof and settled him on a blanket under a sunshade. I found a bucket and filled it with water, then left that and a bowl of dog biscuits under the sunshade with him. I had a suspicion that the biscuits wouldn't last the time it would take me to get to the car, but at least he wouldn't go hungry. Then, leaving ourselves plenty of time for problems, we picked up Dylan just before eight, along with Yurei and his Ouija board, which was now showing definite signs of wear. We dropped by Janet's house, where she was already waiting outside, and we were on the main road to Camborne just as the BBC pips sounded the hour.

The main road out of Cornwall on a Friday morning in the middle of summer should have been the number one place to avoid. Most of the weekly holiday lets have exit times of ten o'clock. And normally the A30 is beginning to resemble a car park from about eight. This morning, however, the traffic gods were on our side, and in just under half an hour, I pulled the car to a stop in the main parking area of the Camborne Retail Park.

"So, what are we going to do for the next hour and a half?" Eddie questioned as I turned off the engine.

"Better three hours too soon than a minute too late," said Janet. "That's what Shakespeare said."

"I don't expect he had to sit in a car in the middle of a shopping centre for an hour and a half. He was probably sat by a river with a jug of ale in his hand, watching the ducks."

"We could go and get a coffee," suggested Janet. "There's a Kupsa Koffee over there."

"What're all those people doing by that shop?" Dylan asked, pointing at a crowd across the other side of the parking area.

I tried to see what they were doing, but we were a bit too far away. "I'm going to take a wander over there," I said. "I could do with a coffee. Anybody else?"

Everybody decided to join me. I opened a couple of windows a few inches for Yurei, and we left him to guard the car and Ouija board.

As we approached, I noticed the group of people were forming an untidy queue outside a Ponzi Phone shop. A huge poster covering most of the window advertised the new Ponzi Phone 13. I scanned the poster and apparently the new Ponzi Phone 13 was due to launch this morning at nine o'clock. Above the window, the whole facia was one huge LED display screen with an advertising film playing. I guessed that the film rotated constantly, as most of the crowd weren't paying it any attention. They'd probably seen it twenty times already.

I watched it for a while, and it informed me that the new Ponzi Phone 13 had a new chip which ran even faster than the last one. Apparently, this shaved .002 seconds off the loading time of a typical webpage. I also learned that the new and improved screen had four more pixels than the Ponzi Phone 12, and that it now came with an optional titanium body and colour coded emails. The film went on to explain that it featured a smoother connection with Ponzi Book laptops, Ponzi Pad tablets, and Ponzi Smart Watches.

"Did you know that last year, Ponzi were sitting on $175 billion in cash?" I heard Robyn say from behind me.

I turned to her. "$175 billion?" I queried. "In cash?"

"In cash," she repeated. "That's nothing to do with their assets or working capital. That's just cash. Taken out of circulation and just sitting in their bank doing nothing. And did you also know that coincidentally, $175 billion is the exact amount which Jeffrey Sachs estimates would end world extreme poverty?"

"I guess you're not going to join the queue for the new Ponzi Phone then?"

"A thousand quid for a telephone?" She pulled her battered phone from her pocket. "This is fine for me." She studied it for a moment. "I can't even remember what make it is now. Something I couldn't pronounce. I do remember that."

I looked at my watch. "We've still got the best part of an hour before the clue arrives. I'm going to get a coffee."

The Kupsa Koffee looked like every other Kupsa Koffee I'd ever been in. Although, to be fair, my base sample was small. Strategically placed round wooden tables were scattered at precise intervals around the shop. At first glance, the tables looked handmade, until one looked closer and realised they were all identical. Identical random shapes, with identical flaws and imperfections in the wood. At carefully calculated positions sat the more casual seating. Sofas and armchairs, chosen to give the air of peace and relaxation. An intimate retreat in which to enjoy your coffee and ignore the world. As long as you keep buying.

Robyn asked me to order a Macchiato with oat milk and settled at a table by the window. Eddie was the first at the counter. The young man in a black-and-white striped apron greeted him with, "Hello, my name is Gary," pointing to a name badge on his apron which confirmed this, in case one was unsure. "We have a guest coffee today, all the way from Panama. It's a Gesha and tastes very much like an Ethiopian bean, which is very unusual. Would you like to try one?"

"Nah," said Eddie, studying the menu chalkboard behind the bar. "I'll just have a Nescafé. Make it Gold Blend, I'm feelin' adventurous. White, two sugars."

"I'm afraid we don't do Nescafé," said Gary. "Would you like a Cortado?"

"What's that?"

"It's coffee with milk."

"Yeah, that'll do."

"Wonderful. What name shall I put?" He held up a cardboard cup.

"Call it what you like," Eddie said.

"No, I meant *your* name. So we can call you when it's ready."

"It's alright, I'll wait."

Gary looked flustered. "I have to put a name on the cup."

"Really? Okay, call it Coffee."

"Just coffee? Okay."

Eddie paid, and I ordered for myself and Robyn then joined her at the table.

"Working again?" I asked, nodding towards the laptop she had open. "Whose day are you about to ruin now?"

She looked up at me and gave an impish smile. "Watch this space." She glanced through the window towards the Ponzi Phone shop opposite.

"What are you up to?" I sat and looked to see what she found so interesting at the shop.

"You see," she tapped at her keyboard. "The people who run these advertising display units, like that one over there." She pointed to the LED display proclaiming the wonders of the Ponzi Phone 13 which was now showing a countdown to when the shop would open. "They will have top line security to their own systems, but these things are just adverts, and they wouldn't think that somebody could be bothered with them. So, most of them have the default user and passwords, Admin, Admin." She tapped a single key. "Like this one."

I looked at the screen and it went blank.

"Very clever," I said. "But what does that—"

The screen suddenly sprang back to life. A film showed images of young African children digging. Very young African children. We saw men standing watching the children. Armed men. Words ran along the bottom of the screen, but we were too far away to read them.

"Did you do that? What's going on?"

"It's a film produced by the Danny Gola Trust," said Robyn, still tapping on her keyboard. "It's showing child slavery in the cobalt mines of the DRC. The very mines from which Ponzi Phones source their cobalt."

"You think any of those people will care?"

"Some. Better to light a candle than curse the darkness."

"You know I should stop you?" I said.

She turned squarely to face me. "Try it, I dare you." A smile played on her lips. I wondered if it was a threat or mischief.

Eddie sat down and placed a plastic tray of coffees on the table. Robyn snapped her laptop closed and shoved it in her bag.

"I don't like this place," said Janet, as she arrived with Dylan. "They make it all so complicated. Thank goodness I had Dylan here to help."

I glanced out of the window towards the Ponzi Phone shop. A group of people had gathered around the video display and there seemed to be much discussion happening. One or two people left the site but others took out their phones and filmed the screen and shop. Eventually, the shop door opened, and people swarmed in like ants at a kids' picnic. A few minutes later, a man in a suit appeared, stared at the screen for a moment, then disappeared back inside. Seconds later, the screen went blank.

By the time we were into our second coffees, a steady flow of people into, and out of the shop, had built. We relocated back to the car just before ten to make sure we were ready for a quick start.

The clue arrived exactly on time.

"Good morning, Team Farmhouse Five. Here is clue five: In the basement of the Ministry of Love, look through the eye of the 5 to see one — Your team will be eliminated if the login has not been completed by midday, or you are below the median. Good Luck."

I glanced at the team counter. 19. "Any ideas?" I asked.

"Sounds like a Barry White song to me," said Eddie. "Come with me to the Ministry of LUUurve, baby," he growled.

"No, it was in Orwell's 1984," offered Janet. "The Ministry of Love was where they had Room 101."

"101 is binary for five," Dylan said. "And 1984 would be five ones followed by six zeros."

"Orwell's real name was Eric Blair," said Robyn. "I don't know if that's relevant."

"Isn't that a TV programme, Room 101?" Eddie said.

"Hang on," I said. "What did you say, Dylan?"

"11111000000 is 1984 in binary."

"No, not that bit. 101."

"Oh, five is 101 in binary."

"That might be something," I said. "You can't have an eye of five, but 101. That's got a sort of eye, hasn't it?"

"Okay," said Robyn. "How is 101 any sort of clue?"

"That's easy," said Eddie. "The Stone of the Hole, or the Men-An-Tol, in Cornish. That's three standing stones, and the centre one's got a hole through it, so as when you look at them, it looks like 101. Down near Madron, it is."

I knew the site well. We'd had a call out there back in 1998. A group of hippies had decided that a UFO was going to land there at dawn on the winter solstice. Apparently they all needed to be naked because the Siriuns didn't believe in clothes. We'd only been sent there as the higher-ups had been spooked by the Heaven's Gate mass suicide the year before in America. This lot though, just put their clothes back on and drifted off home once it became apparent the UFO wasn't coming.

"I think you're right, Eddie," I said. "That must be... about forty-five minutes. Give or take." I checked my watch. "We'd best get on. Unless anybody has any other ideas?"

"Seems right to me," said Robyn. The others nodded assent and we piled back in the car and set out back the way we'd come.

The drive to Madron went without a hitch, and the parking area for the Men-An-Tol, a few minutes on. The small parking spot was already full with a police car, an ambulance and a fire engine. Not a good sign. I knew there were quite a few abandoned mines around this area, and it wasn't unusual for people to fall into them. We parked half on the verge a bit further up and set out on the final half mile trek across fields.

As we neared the Men-An-Tol, we could see a lot of activity with emergency responders much in attendance.

"What are we meant to do here?" asked Janet.

"The clue said to look through the hole and see one. I'm assuming that as it referred to the 101 being the three stones, we're supposed to look through the hole at one of the other stones."

"We might have a problem with that," said Eddie.

As we neared the stones, I could see what he meant. A very large, and mostly naked, man appeared to be stuck in the holed stone. A pair of firemen were crouched at each end of the man, with a paramedic kneeling by the man's head. A circle of police tape had been set around the scene by a young, and quite possibly, over enthusiastic police officer.

The young policeman stepped forwards as we approached. He held his hand up in best Hendon Police College regulation style and said, "No access to the public here. This is a secured area."

"What's going on?" I asked.

"It's an emergency incident," he replied. "You will need to keep the access points clear."

I looked around the area. We were basically in the middle of a field with no roads or tracks. Certainly, nothing which deserved the title of access point. I reached instinctively for my warrant card then realised I didn't have one anymore.

"I used to be in the Job," I said. "Until a few weeks ago, anyway. Over in Penzance, DS Dixon."

"Ah, yes. Nice to meet you, I'm PC Glover. So, this gentleman here has managed to get himself stuck in the hole of this stone thing."

I looked over at the stone again. The two firemen were trying to pull him through by his feet, but each time they tried, the man squealed like a teenage girl at an Ed Sheeran concert.

"He's a big chap. How did he manage to get stuck like that?"

"It's a bit difficult. He's German and his English isn't good," said PC Glover.

"I speak a bit of German," offered Robyn.

The young policeman looked nervous. His eyes flitted between Robyn and the man in the hole. "I suppose it will be alright, but try not to destroy any evidence."

"Evidence?" I questioned. "It's not a crime scene, is it?"

"We don't know yet, sir. There might need to be an investigation. I have to preserve the scene."

"Don't worry," said Robyn. "I'll try not to step in any blood splatters."

"What blood splatters?" PC Glover looked alarmed, then realisation spread across his face, and he returned to nervous smiling. "Oh, yes. A joke, of course." He held up the blue tape to allow Robyn to pass, and they both headed over to the stone.

Robyn knelt by the man, but they were too far away to hear what was being said. After a few minutes, she returned.

"You're not going to believe this," Robyn said.

"Go on," I said.

"He's got it into his head that going through the stone is a cure for impotence." She held a forced smile to stop a full-blown grin exploding. "He's also desperate that his wife doesn't find out. They're on holiday here, and she's back in their hotel in St Ives. She thinks he's gone out for a haircut."

"That's rubbish," said Eddie. "Going through the stone is for fertility, true enough, but that's for women. Not blokes. He'd be better off with a tub of Viagra. Unless he wants to get pregnant."

I looked at my watch. Valuable time was slipping away. We needed to tick off this site quickly. "I'm just going to log in," I said. "We're at the site. Hopefully, they'll only want a picture of one of us touching one of the stones."

"Don't count on it," said Robyn. "In the clue, they said look through the hole. I'm betting that's the photo they'll want."

"All we can do is try." I opened the app and marked our location.

The response was instant: *"Position confirmed. Please upload a photograph of team member Janet looking through the hole of the stone, using the phone registered to team member Matt."*

"We're in trouble." I turned to PC Glover. "How close are they to getting him out?"

"They can't. They've tried everything. They've even covered him in oil."

That was a mental image I didn't want. "So what happens now? He can't stay there."

"We've reached out to CASPN. They're the organisation who look after these places. The Fire and Rescue service needs their permission to cut the stone." PC Glover shrugged. "But they haven't got back to us yet."

I turned to look at the others. "Any ideas?"

"He needs to lose a bit of weight," said Eddie.

"Undoubtedly, but we haven't got time for that."

"He's at quarter to nine," said Dylan. "He'd be better off at twenty-five to one." He held a coin up to his eye and studied it.

I looked at my watch, 11:15, then I looked at Dylan. I decided not to ask, I had enough to worry about, without one of his conversations scrambling my head.

"They mustn't cut the stone," said Janet. "It's thousands of years old."

"But they can't just leave him there," I said. "And it seems they've tried everything else."

At that moment, another Fire and Rescue officer turned up with a large black plastic case.

Behind him, followed a second man wearing a Deliver-U-go uniform and carrying a black insulated bag. "Anybody here called Günter Heinig?" he called. "I have a Megasize Krappi Burger meal for a Günter Heinig."

"Ja, hier bin ich," came a strained voice from the hole.

I looked at the Fire and Rescue man who'd just arrived. "What's going on?"

"Don't ask me, mate," he said, unpacking a cutting machine from the case. "I was just back at the engine getting the cutter, when he turned up looking for our man."

PC Glover held the tape up for the Deliver-U-go courier to pass and escorted him over to the head end. As Günter's arms were on one side of the hole, and his trousers the other, PC Glover had to rummage through the German's pockets to find money to pay the courier.

Eddie said, "That's not likely to help much, is it."

A loud noise caught my attention and I saw the Fire and Rescue man had started up the cutting machine.

"Stand back, stand back, everybody," called PC Glover, a slight look of panic on his face. "All members of the public must move back behind the police security line."

"No, it's alright," said the fireman, shutting the machine down again. "Just testing the batteries. We can't do anything till we get the okay from CASPN."

The Deliver-U-go courier collected his money and set off back across the field.

Günter struggled with the plastic boxes his Megasize Krappi Burger meal came in, then called out, "Wo ist mein Krappi-Cola?"

I looked at my watch again. Time was ticking by, and this situation was not going to resolve itself before we were knocked out at midday. We'd had one lucky break yesterday. The chances of a second reprieve were about zero. Even if permission turned up for the rescue guys to cut the stone now, it would be too late. I'd seen these guys cut people out of all sorts of places over the years, and I knew it was always a very slow job taken carefully.

"What do we do?" asked Janet.

"Nothing," I said. "We can't do anything. We're screwed."

"Maybe if we hypnotised him he'd go all soft enough to squeeze him out."

"They need to put him at twenty-five to one," Dylan said.

"Twenty-five to one? I'm not sure what you mean, but twenty-five to one is thirty-five minutes past the time we'll be eliminated anyway."

"No," Dylan said. "He's in the wrong place, look," he handed me the coin he'd been playing with.

I studied the coin. It was a standard 10p coin, with nothing unusual about it. "I'm sorry, Dylan, I still don't understand. What am I supposed to do with this?"

"You put it in a slot and a fat German pops out," suggested Eddie.

"Not helping, Eddie," I said.

"No, look." Dylan took the coin from me and held it up towards the holed stone. "Like this, make it the right size to cover the hole."

Still not quite sure what this was supposed to achieve, I took the coin back and held it out in front of me towards the stone.

"Now move your hand to-and-fro until the coin just fills the hole," Dylan prompted.

I did as he said. "Okay, it's just covering the hole. What now?"

"Now you can see places where it doesn't fit. That's because the hole is not perfectly round. It's actually impossible to make a perfect circle because a perfect circle is a mathematical abstraction, and in the real world, where each point—"

"Dylan," I interrupted. "You can stop now. I think I'm getting what you mean."

By holding the coin just so, I could cover most of the hole, apart from two places. This meant the hole bulged slightly at these points. One bulge at around one o'clock, and the other at seven o'clock. If the hands of a clock were at these points, it would indeed approximate twenty-five to one.

"We need to turn him," I said. I pushed my way under the police tape, much to the dismay of PC Glover, and hurried over to the Fire and Rescue guys.

They looked up sharply as I knelt down beside them.

"You can't be here," said one man.

"I might know how to get him out," I said, looking at the man still working on his burger and chips. "The hole is slightly wider at these two points." I touched the one o'clock and seven o'clock points.

The rescue man peered closer. "You could be right," he said.

The paramedic shuffled round to our side of the stone, the side of the wriggling legs and trousers half down where the fire guys had greased him up. I was going to need therapy after this.

"The human body is widest in the plane of the hips and shoulders," the paramedic said. "And it's also the part that's the least compressible. We should try twisting him so his hips align with the widest points of the hole."

We each exchanged glances as we shared the realisation of what needed to be done. We were going to attempt to manhandle a mostly naked, probably at least 200-kilogram man covered in grease.

The fire rescue man took a small fluorescent spray paint can from his kit and sprayed orange dots at one o'clock and seven o'clock. "We're going to need everybody available to help." He looked at me. "Can you get your mates over here? Oh, and that copper, it's about time he made himself useful."

I hurried over to the others and explained the plan. Robyn knelt down by the head of the man and explained what they were going to do.

She popped her head over the stone and said to the paramedic, "He says he's about 220 kilograms."

"That's about... thirty-five stone," said the fireman. "It's going to be tricky."

Eddie peeped round the stone and said to Robyn, "Can you stop him eating for a minute? Only, he's just making things worse."

Robyn flapped her hand at Eddie. "Shush, it's probably comfort eating, he's very stressed."

"He's very stressed? He should be standing here seeing what I'm seeing."

"Right, here's the plan," said the fireman. "You three," pointing at the other fireman, the paramedic, and PC Glover. "You've got the head end. Us four," indicating himself, Eddie, Dylan, and me, "we're taking this end."

"Do I have to?" Eddie said, staring at the man's naked buttocks.

"And we're bringing him towards us," the fireman said.

I heard Robyn translating and mumbled noises from Günter.

"Sorry, mate," said the paramedic, dipping his hand into the pot of grease and applying it liberally to Günter's torso.

Once the grease had been applied, a pair of blankets were wrapped around the upper torso and the thighs. Hopefully, that would give enough purchase for us to hold him tightly.

"Okay, on my mark," said the fireman in charge. "We're going to lift and rotate towards me until his hips align with the marks. On three. One, two, and three."

We lifted to the sounds of German complaints from the other end, and once we had the weight, we turned.

"Stop," called the fireman. "Hold there." He peered at the marks. "A little more."

We turned again, stopped, and waited.

"That's about right. Now the tricky bit. Move towards me."

We all shuffled towards our side, while Robyn quickly applied more grease to the flesh on her side.

As I was concentrating on taking the weight, I couldn't see what was happening, but I did hear Robyn say, "It's working. He's moving."

We shuffled a bit more, then another command to stop. "Okay, we've just got to get the shoulders through now," said the fireman. "Get him to put his arms straight up and relax."

Robyn translated, then we moved again. This time we kept moving until just his head and arms remained through the hole. We lowered him to the ground, assuming he could manage himself from here.

Günter stayed where he was for a moment, panting as if it was him who'd been doing the lifting. Then he eased himself completely out and leaned back against the stone, still with trousers down round his knees, while he finished his burger.

Seizing the opportunity, I hustled Janet to the hole and persuaded Günter to move a little so that Janet could push her head through. Then I whipped round to the other side and snapped off a flurry of photographs.

"One for your holiday snaps, mate?" asked the fireman, as he packed away his kit.

"No," I said. "We're in that big quiz thing, The Great Wessex Chase."

"'Ansom, good luck on ya'."

I uploaded the photograph, then waited, breath held and expecting the worst. Nothing happened.

"What's wrong?" demanded Eddie.

"I don't know. The app hasn't responded."

"That's what happened last time," said Robyn. "When we were eliminated."

I refreshed the app. Still nothing.

The fireman stood up and heaved his kitbag over his shoulder. "Well, thanks, mate. We'd never have got him out of there without cutting if you hadn't come up with that idea."

"Not me," I said. "It was Dylan's idea," I nodded towards Dylan. "He's a bit of a genius, on the quiet." I smiled at Dylan, who shuffled and turned away.

The fireman went over to Dylan and slapped him on the shoulder so hard, I thought he was going to fall over. "Well done, mate. Proper 'ansom."

My phone bleeped and I froze.

"You gonna look or what?" Eddie asked.

"Yeah," I hesitated. I looked at the blank screen. I swiped once to open it, and it remained blank. Probably grease on my finger, I reasoned. Might be an omen warning me bad news lay within, I reasoned again. I realised everybody was watching me and swiped again.

The phone opened.

I went to the app and opened that.

"Congratulations Team Farmhouse Five, Location and picture accepted.

You have now completed the team rounds. Tomorrow at 10:00, will follow your final challenge, which must be completed by midday, or the prize is forfeit. Your recommended starting point is awaited.passively.landings, from where the final location will be within a 25-mile radius."

I looked at the team counter icon on the app. It showed zero. "Have you seen this?" I said. "The app is showing no teams left in the competition."

Robyn peered over my shoulder. "That's odd," she said. "It must be a mistake. We know we're still in it, so that's at least one. It must be a glitch. Don't worry about it."

She opened her phone and found the location. "Our start point is Stonehenge," she said.

"Within twenty-five miles of Stonehenge then," I said. "There's a lot of potential places around there. I don't think we can second-guess where it will be."

"It could even be Stonehenge itself."

"That's at least four hours' drive from Little Didney," I said. "We're going to have to do an overnight somewhere there."

"There's a village called Shrewton, just off the main road," Robyn said, reading from her phone. "There's a Sleep 'n Drive near there. They're cheap and cheerful, but the location is perfect. You could stop overnight there."

"You said, *you*?" I questioned.

"Yes, well. I have to go to Porth Cullen this afternoon. Business stuff." She caught my eye. "I did tell you. You offered to drive me there, remember?"

"Oh, yes. Of course. Right, let's head back."

We started off back across the fields the way we had come. It was a well-worn path, but it still held traps of occasional rabbit holes or spiky bushes to catch the unwary.

"What time do you need to be in Porth Cullen?" I asked Robyn.

She glanced at the others to see if they were within earshot. Satisfied they weren't, she said, "Martin Locke's boat is due in about three. He wants to be there for the Super Yacht flotilla. That'll be the best time to get into his systems. They'll be more focussed on settling his yacht into berth, rather than a potential Wi-Fi intrusion."

"Do we get to have a go on the super yacht?" asked Dylan, suddenly being there from nowhere. "I've never been on a super yacht."

"Super yachts, pfah!" said Eddie. "I've been down there to see them before. Think they're so posh, but it's just a trailer park on water. That's all they are. No different to that lot over at Rose Well park. But floating."

I stopped walking and turned to look at the others. "I'm dropping you guys off back in Little Didney, then I'm taking Robyn down to Porth Cullen."

"Hello, hello, hello," said Eddie with a grin. "Nice little getaway by the seaside?"

"No. It's… It's nothing like that." I turned to look at Robyn. She shook her head. Almost imperceptibly, but enough for me to see. That tiny movement was a clear instruction to not say a word.

"Look, I think there's something we should own up about," I continued, despite the under-breath pleas coming from my left. "But first, I need your word that this will go no further."

"Matt," said Robyn, out loud now. "This is not a good idea."

I flapped a hand gently in her direction. "Honesty. It's important. This involves us all, even if only at arm's length. It's not fair to ask that I potentially expose my friends to problems without being honest with them."

Robyn sighed. "I think you're wrong, but do what you think you need to do."

I turned back to the other three. "It's about the Green Ninja." I searched the faces, waiting for some sort of reaction. But nothing. "The Green Ninja, the person who's been doing this eco-activism and causing... well... problems around and about for some people who... who... Anyway, I think you should know, because it's only fair that you do, bearing in mind—"

Janet huffed and cut me off, "Are you going the long way round to tell us that Robyn is the Green Ninja?"

"I... um." My words muddled around in my head, refusing all attempts to arrange them into a coherent sentence.

Robyn rescued me. "How did you know?" she asked Janet.

"Tuesday night in that weird hotel," Janet started. "Some noise of splashes in the swimming pool woke me up just after midnight and I wondered who was swimming that time of night. Or maybe it was a murderer dropping a body in the pool. Then, when I left my room, I saw you coming along the corridor, remember?"

"Yes, but I told you I'd just been out for a walk."

"I know, and that's what made me suspicious as I saw water splashes on your shirt, and the faint smell of chlorine. That meant that you were linked to the splashes in the pool." Janet seemed pleased with herself. "It's a bit like in the Sherlock Holmes story, the Sussex Vampire, when Holmes notices a splash of water on the floor near the baby's cot. By examining the water splash, Holmes successfully solves the mystery."

"Right," said Robyn. "That's quite... Well, hmm, I see."

"And you didn't tell me?" I asked Janet.

"Oh, no. I didn't tell anybody. Not my business."

"But I knew anyway," said Dylan.

"What? How?" asked Robyn.

"Easy, I noticed you typing in your password on your computer. I like passwords. Passwords are never random. People try to make them seem random."

"My password? How does that…?"

"Your password is 477265656e204e696e6a61."

"Oh. Well, thank you for telling everybody that. I'll have to change it now. But I still don't understand?"

"It spells Green Ninja in hexadecimal code."

Robyn looked slightly dazed. "Yes, I just thought nobody... Well I never." She looked towards Eddie. "And I suppose you're going to tell me you knew as well?"

"Obviously. I have a nose for mischief. Have to have, in my line of business. There's always folks who are up to no good, ready to take advantage of a man's goodwill and natural generosity. Pays to learn how to spot them. Little signs and tells. Imperceptible to the ordinary person. Besides, you had green paint under your fingernails the day after that petrol station nonsense."

"So, basically, everybody knew, but nobody said anything?"

"Yeah," said Eddie. "Only, we didn't want to say anything 'cause we didn't want Matt to know." He looked at me and shook his head slightly. "Sorry, but you know what you get like."

"No, Eddie," I said. "Do tell me what I get like?"

"You know, everything's gotta be all legal and by the book. All that old bollocks. You'd've only worried."

"I don't believe this. I'm the professional detective here, and—"

"Retired detective," Eddie interrupted.

I glared at him. "Detective, *newly* retired. The only one here professionally trained to detect wrong-doing, and you all think I'm the only one who shouldn't know."

"Didn't want you to get in a stress."

"Oh, I think that boat has sailed and sunk already." I turned to Robyn. "Well, that's changed things. This has now gone from a single offender, through joint enterprise, to an organised crime group in twenty-four hours."

"What can I say?" said Robyn, shrugging. "I just have this magnetic personality, I suppose."

"Cool," said Dylan. "Are we going to blow up a super yacht?"

"No, Dylan," I said. "Nobody's blowing up anything. I'm dropping you all back in Little Didney, then we're going on to Porth Cullen."

"That's not right," said Eddie. "All through this thing, you've kept bangin' on about how we're a team, and we've all gotta stay together and whatsit. We're stickin' together now, seein' this through."

The others nodded in agreement.

Dylan held up a fist. "I am the Green Ninja," he said, in his best fierce voice.

"I am the Green Ninja," said Janet, waving a hand in the air.

"Oh, good," I said.

CHAPTER TWENTY-SIX

TEAM FARMHOUSE FIVE

THE PORTH CULLEN FISH & CHIP shop spilled tables out onto the pavement. It was just one of a dozen eateries fronting the harbour, each of whom had annexed sections of the pedestrianised harbour frontage to expand their seating arrangements for the duration of the Boat Show.

The plastic tables of the fish and chip shop fought for space with a Chinese restaurant on one side, and TV Chef Rupert Llewellen's Michelin starred restaurant Nouveau Sauvage, on the other.

Fortunately for us, fish and chips were significantly less popular among Boat Show aficionados than celebrity restaurants. We had managed to secure a table immediately, while next door queues formed along the pavement for a table at Nouveau Sauvage. I noticed several of their tables sat empty, but carried 'Reserved' signs.

And while the customers of Porth Cullen Fish and Chips tucked in and chatted animatedly, the patrons of Nouveau Sauvage seemed more interested in photographing their meals than eating them.

The other advantage was that the fish and chip shop had no problems with Yurei settling underneath our table. He waited patiently for lunchtime snacks.

"What do we do now?" Janet asked. "Are we going to sink some more of these boats?"

Robyn's face blanched. "Janet, shush," she said, head flicking side to side to see if we'd been overheard. Her voice dropped to a whisper, "We're not sinking any boats. Please forget all about that."

Janet's face dropped in disappointment. "We could just sink them a little bit."

"How'dya sink a boat just a little bit?" demanded Eddie. "That's like saying Hitler was just a little bit of a twat."

Janet put on her best fierce look and said to Eddie, "I was thinking like that big cruise ship a few years back, the Costa Coffee. It just sort of fell over next to Italy."

"You mean the Costa Concordia," Robyn said.

"That's the one. I knew it had something to do with aeroplanes."

"We're not sinking any boats," I said, as quietly as I could. "Not even a little bit."

"Send the lot to the bottom," muttered Eddie. "This used to be a busy fishing village, and now the fishing boats can't get a look-in and the families are all gone."

"I'm just getting into somebody's computer system," Robyn said. "That's all. No damage."

"Who is this bloke Locke, anyway? Ain't never heard of him."

"He runs Shye, Locke, and Grifter, one of the world's largest hedge funds."

"What's a hedge fund?" asked Dylan, slipping Yurei a treat under the table.

"Um," Robyn paused, clearly trying to find the easiest explanation. "It's a way for people to invest money without having to manage the day-to-day themselves. They also allow people to hide what they're doing."

"What, like under-the-counter money?" Eddie asked, a sudden sparkle of interest glinting his eyes.

"Possibly, but more normally for other reasons. You know when the trade unions say they'll never invest members' money into countries whose human rights records stink?"

"Uh uh." Eddie nodded.

"Well, they still do it, but through a hedge fund which hides what they're doing. And when your town council wants to invest in arms companies but realise it might not look good in their accounts? And when your 'green' pension fund wants to invest in an oil company because that's what's paying the highest returns?"

"And you're planning to steal the money?" Eddie looked positively intrigued.

"No," Robyn stated flatly. "I'm just going to publish the list of who's investing what and where. I'm going to bring the hypocrites and green-washers out into the open. Then people can decide."

"Oh." Eddie looked deflated. "It'd probably send a stronger message if you nicked it," he suggested. "I could help you put it to good use, you know, something vegetarian. I know this bloke—"

"No," interrupted Robyn. "Besides, that sort of hacking is way beyond me."

"What's the plan, then?" Janet asked, looking far too excited.

"I sit here with my laptop," said Robyn. "Then, when his boat pulls in, I hook into its Wi-Fi and from there, I can get inside his system and download the database."

"Just like that?" I asked.

"Just like that. I've already got the Wi-Fi password. When that pompous little prig, Charles Digsworth, one of The Money Boys team, and also one of the traders for Shye, Locke, and Grifter, lost his phone the other day, I was able to copy his data. Then this morning, I spoofed a text from him to Martin Locke, saying he would be in Porth Cullen and could he use the boat's Wi-Fi to do some work."

"So, what are we all doing here?" Eddie asked.

"I don't know. You tell me, what *are* you all doing here? This is just a simple little admin job."

The waitress arrived with our meals, and we settled to eating and idle chatter while keeping a watching eye on the harbour entrance, and tossing the eternally grateful Yurei the odd chip or two.

Just as we were finishing our meals, Robyn squinted at the sun dazzle coming from the sea and said, "There he is."

~ 261 ~

I followed her gaze. A huge silver and grey behemoth slid through the break in the sea wall and made its way into the harbour.

"That's enormous," I said.

"Looks like something out of a James Bond movie," said Eddie.

The beast manoeuvred round the sea wall, then slid into a bay at the far end of the marina.

"Oh, hell," said Robyn. "I should have realised."

"What's up?" I asked.

"I was expecting it to come up closer to the harbour. But I didn't realise just how big it is. There's no way it can get any closer."

"Is that a problem?"

"Yeah, just a bit," she said, biting back her anger. "I can't reach the Wi-Fi from here."

"Can't you just move closer?"

"I can't sit up there on the jetties with a laptop. That area's mostly for crew, they'd be sure to wonder what I was doing. I need a repeater. Are there any computer shops in this town?" She looked around the area as if one would magically appear.

"I think there's one up in the High Street. Bizzy Bitz, I think it's called." I pointed to the west. "Just past Nouveau Sauvage, there's an alley which cuts into the bottom of the High Street. Bizzy Bitz is about a ten-minute walk up there."

"Right," she said. "Don't let that boat leave until I get back." She smiled and set off.

The waitress collected our plates, and we ordered ice creams to justify hogging a table. A rise in the noise level from the next restaurant drew my attention away from my toffee ripple crunch. Three new customers, two young women and a forty-something man, had arrived and were being escorted to one of the reserved tables. The man, obviously in charge, guided the two women into their seats with entirely unnecessary help. His white linen shirt carried perfect designer creases, and his three-day beard highlighted an unnaturally perfectly tanned complexion. They'd hardly sat when two waiters arrived with champagne in silver buckets.

I noticed people sitting at other tables taking pictures of the trio and turned to Eddie. "Do you reckon that's the man Robyn's talking about?"

"Probably. He don't look short of a penny, that's for sure."

Another couple arrived, and the waiter showed them to the trio. The second couple looked like they'd been printed from the same machine as the others. The man looked familiar, and it took me a moment to place him. He'd been the one at reception who'd lost his phone. Digsworth, Robyn had called him. Much bonhomie handshaking and backslapping for the men, and double cheek kisses for the women. More obsequious waiters, more champagne.

I scraped the last of my toffee ripple crunch from the glass and caught a passing waitress for coffee.

I checked my watch. "She should be back by now," I said. "Hope she's managed to find whatever it was she wanted."

"It's a repeater," said Dylan. "It relays a Wi-Fi signal."

"Are they easy to find?"

"Mostly, but Robyn's going to need a battery-driven one. They're much harder to get."

A man, in cut-off denim shorts and a grey shirt, which had clearly seen happier days, stopped in front of our fish and chip restaurant. His hair was badly cut, but tidy, and he wore a beard which bordered on feral. He held a tin mug in his hand and walked by the front tables. A few coins rattled in the mug as he passed. I reached over and dropped a handful of change in.

"Paras?" asked Eddie as he dropped something in the cup.

The man nodded, but looked confused.

Eddie pointed to the tattoo of a winged parachute on the man's calf. "My brother was in."

The man nodded slowly at Eddie, then moved on.

"Your brother was in the Paras?" I asked.

"For a fortnight. Bounced out again when he sold the CO's Jeep on eBay."

Robyn suddenly appeared and settled into her seat with a sigh. "That was a mission." She dumped a couple of boxes on the table.

"Did you get what you needed?" I asked.

"More or less. Couldn't get a battery powered repeater, but I managed to get a battery pack and adapter for an ordinary one."

The sound of laughing from the Nouveau Sauvage caught my attention. The new arrivals there were tossing coins at the homeless man's cup as he tried to catch them on the fly.

"Whoa," said Robyn. "That's Martin Locke. And that guy with him is Charles Digsworth, the one whose phone I nabbed back at The Nirvana Motel." She sank down in her seat a bit as if that would shield her from view.

"That could be tricky," I said. "Won't they work out that the message didn't come from him?" I asked.

"Probably not. I doubt that Locke himself even saw the message."

"Let's hope."

"Well, it shouldn't take too long now for me to get in. Just need somebody to get close to the boat and plant the repeater."

"I can do that," I said. "What do I have to do?"

"You need to get as near to the boat as possible," Robyn said. "The repeater will try to lock onto the most powerful signal. If that happens, I can redirect it, but that all takes extra time. So it's best if the repeater gets closer to the target router than any others in range. You have to go out along this pier here," she pointed to the concrete pier running out from the harbour. "Then there are some steps down to the floating jetty where the larger berths are positioned. Locke's boat is towards the end of that. And you have to do it without anybody noticing you."

"Ah, I didn't realise that," I said. "That means sneaking and hiding, I guess. Might not be my best super power these days."

"I'll give it a go," said Eddie.

"Your knees are in a worse state than mine," I said. "I saw you in Wookey Hole the other day. The Daleks make easier work of steps than you do."

"I've got an idea," said Dylan. "Be back in a minute." He jumped up and disappeared into a side street.

We looked at each other.

"Well, I can't do it," said Robyn. "I need to be ready with the laptop."

"I could disguise myself as a housekeeper come to change the linen," Janet suggested. "Miss Marple did it in Greenshaw's Folly. She discovered who the murderer was that way."

"That idea might work better if we had a pile of fresh linen," said Eddie.

"We'll wait a moment," I suggested. "If nothing else, I'm curious to see what Dylan's up to."

I turned to look to make sure Locke was still occupied and not about to return to his boat. But there was no worry about that. Locke was currently posing with his arm around the homeless man while enthusiastic onlookers snapped photos of Locke giving the man a bottle of champagne. Facebook and YouTube were going to be busy.

A few minutes later, Dylan returned and planted a takeaway pizza in a box on the table.

"You still hungry after the fish and chips?" I asked.

"No. It's a pizza."

"Yes, I noticed that. Why?"

"Because pizzas can go anywhere. Nobody ever challenges a pizza, and nobody notices the person carrying the pizza. They only see pizza. Pizzas have special powers over humans."

I pondered that for a moment. Then I recalled reading reports of a professional hitman in London back in the eighties who used pizzas as a device to gain entry into otherwise highly secure buildings.

"You might be onto something there," I said.

Dylan beamed.

Robyn opened the lid of the box and Eddie said, "It's got pineapple on it. Nobody in their right mind is going to let a pineapple pizza into their gaff."

Robyn took her repeater from its box. It was tiny, about the size of a thumb drive. She plugged in the little battery pack, itself no bigger than a matchbox, then opened up her laptop.

"That all seems to work okay," she said. She lifted the pizza and slid her little gadgets underneath. It left a bump in the centre of the pizza, but it would certainly pass superficial scrutiny. She closed the lid.

"And this will work?"

"As long as it gets close enough." She slid the pizza box towards Dylan. "You're not going to take it apart now, are you?"

Dylan looked sulky. "I only do that when I'm stressed."

"Sorry, you still okay to do this?"

"No probs. I'll be like the Pink Panther, whoosh." He made a whoosh movement with his hand.

"Didn't the Pink Panther get caught by Inspector Clouseau?" Eddie asked.

"No, that's a common mistake," said Janet. "The Pink Panther was a diamond. The thief was the Phantom."

"Still got caught though, didn't he?" said Eddie.

Dylan frowned in thought. "Then I'll be like the Road Runner, in and out. Meep-meep."

"Won't they realise as soon as anyone opens up the pizza?" asked Janet.

"It doesn't matter," said Robyn. "It really only needs to be within close range for about ten minutes. By the time somebody discovers the repeater, decides what it is, and then disables it, that should be more than enough time."

"Remember, all you need to do is get it close, and leave it," said Robyn. "You don't have to actually go on board."

I pushed the serviette dispenser over to Dylan. "Wipe your fingerprints off the box then hold it with a couple more of these. We don't want this coming back to you later." I couldn't believe I was helping somebody avoid forensic detection at what was going to be a crime scene.

Dylan rubbed at the box with a serviette, then carefully picked it up using a couple more. "Meep-meep," he said as he set off.

"Are you sure that's altogether wise?" asked Eddie as we watched him head off down the marina pier.

"Probably not," I said. "But worst-case scenario, Robyn's out of pocket for the price of that toy and we wasted a good pizza."

"Wasted nothin'," said Eddie. "It was rendered useless the moment they put pineapple on it."

Robyn opened up her laptop and squinted through the sunlight obscuring the screen. "Nothing yet," she said.

We ordered more teas and watched Locke's group in the next restaurant. The waiter had just delivered Locke what looked like a painted fish finger with three potato wedges and a small flower patch. Many photographs were taken, along with a special shot of Locke holding the fish finger to his mouth and smiling.

"It's alive," said Robyn, shielding her screen from the sunlight with her hand. "He's done it."

"Have you got what you need?" I asked.

"Give me a minute. I'm in through their Wi-Fi and just getting access to their file system. Let's hope Digsworth hasn't changed his password in the last couple of days."

"Did it work?" Dylan panted as he reappeared. "I left it by the gangplank to his boat. It's a cool boat. It's got a huge satellite dish. I bet he can get American telly on that."

"I'm in," announced Robyn. "Here we go, files coming down. Got it. Well done, Dylan."

"Is that it?" I asked. "Can we head off for Stonehenge now?"

"Yes, I told you it would be easy. As soon as we get somewhere quieter, I'll upload it all to the Green Ninja blog pages and let the world see who's really enabling the polluters and arms dealers."

"Just to get our stories straight," I said. "If anybody ever asks, we all came down here, sat at this table, then went home. We all stayed together, right?"

"There's a turnup," said Eddie. "Matt giving advice on alibis. Never thought I'd see the day. You couldn't give me an alibi for last Tuesday, could you?"

"No. Now, is everybody clear on our story?"

Everybody nodded.

As we finished our teas and paid the bill, I heard the sound of police sirens. Piqued by professional curiosity, I stalled for a moment to see what was going on.

Two police cars arrived at the entry to the marina pier. Three officers made their way down the pier, the way Dylan had gone, while a fourth strung police tape across the entrance. The people in the Nouveau Sauvage switched their attention from photographing food, to aim their phones at the police cordon being set up.

"We should get out of here," said Eddie. "This has all the signs of being something Eddie Bishop should be a long way away from."

"You're probably right, Eddie," I said. "I don't see how it can be anything to do with us this quickly, but let's not take a chance."

We left the fish and chip shop and started out for the car park where I'd left the car.

We'd walked about five minutes up the road when a police car cruised by, stopped, then turned round and came back to us. Two officers jumped out and headed straight for Dylan, separating him from the rest of us.

One of the officers started firing questions at Dylan about where he'd been, while the second took control of Yurei.

"I'll take the dog," I said. "He'll be alright with me."

The officer handed the lead to me.

"I'm an ex-Job," I said. "DS out of Penzance. Anything I can help with?"

"No, sir. It's all in hand," he said.

A car driving past slowed down as it drew level with us. A blue Toyota Corolla with a broken headlight. The same one that had been tagging us since the start. I noticed two men inside. They studied us as they drove by. As soon as they saw that I'd spotted them, they sped up and disappeared.

I returned my attention to the policeman. "What's happening?" I asked.

"A suspect device was reported down on the pier, and we have an EOD team on route. This gentleman fits the description given by witnesses at the scene of somebody acting suspiciously."

I knew the procedure. Dylan would be one of dozens stopped and questioned. All he had to do was to keep calm, be polite, and they'd move on.

But this was Dylan.

Dylan had a natural talent for looking guilty. He could be sitting in church reading a parish magazine, but still give the impression he'd just held up a post office.

The officer talking to Dylan switched his attention to his radio and had a brief exchange with his control room. He then turned to the officer next to me and said, "This guy's out on bail for wilful destruction of property. We're taking him in for a proper interview."

"But he's been with us all this time," I lied, thinking about my pension. "You have no cause to take him in."

"We're very stretched, sir," the officer said. "I'm sure you remember what that's like. We have a potential bomb incident, and a reported sighting of a person known to cause damage to property. We just need to take precautions, especially after the incident here last week of damage to boats by that Green Ninja person. We'll just ask him a few questions under caution, and as long as that confirms your statement, and he's done nothing to breach his bail conditions, he'll be out by teatime."

"Where are you taking him?"

"Truro. It's where his bail court is."

"I'd like to act as his legal representative," I said.

"If that's what he wants." The policeman looked at Dylan.

Dylan asked, "Can I have Matt there with me?"

"I'll make a note on the arrest report."

"What about my dog?" Dylan looked at Yurei.

"Sorry, mate, you can't have a dog in the police station."

"Don't worry, Dylan," I said. "I'll look after him. He'll be fine. And just don't say anything until I get there."

"Like on Line of Duty?" he said. "No comment?"

"Okay, we'll go with that if you like. No comment. Wait for me."

They helped him into the police car, and we watched as they drove off.

"That's just buggered things up," said Eddie. "Can you get him out?"

"Depends. If they suspect he's done anything illegal, that would be classed as a breach of his bail conditions. If so, then they'll keep him overnight and put him in front of a magistrate tomorrow morning."

"And how long's that going to take?"

"Magistrate's court will start at ten, and even if he's the first on the list, and with no problems, he's probably not going to be released until midday."

"I'm so sorry," said Robyn. "I didn't mean for this to happen. I should've stuck with doing this on my own and not involved you all."

"It'll be alright," I said. "Even if it all goes wrong, the worst crime they've got is abandoning a pizza in a public place."

"What about the router?"

"Last time I checked, it wasn't a crime to put a router in a pizza box. He just needs to stay calm, and they'll have to let him go."

"Before we have to be at Stonehenge?"

"Let's hope."

CHAPTER TWENTY-SEVEN

TEAM FARMHOUSE FIVE

THE DRIVE BACK TO LITTLE Didney was subdued, but at least quick. I dropped the others off, then stopped by my place to leave Yurei in Teller's capable paws. Teller was overjoyed to see me, so I stayed longer than I'd planned to settle him down with Yurei. Once I was sure they weren't plotting an escape, I headed for The Smuggler's Arms.

Old Sam Goodenough was using the late afternoon lull to move some cases of spirits.

"Just the man," Goodenough greeted, as I entered the bar. "Give us a hand with this, will you? Only my back's playing up again."

I looked at the case in the middle of the floor. "Where do you want it?"

"Behind the bar here." He pointed.

I squatted and hefted the case up onto a nearby stool. "I recognise this one from somewhere." I paused to read the clearly homemade label. *Glen Fiddlich Single Malt.* "Interesting spelling," I commented.

"It's a sort of a guest whisky. Special customers only. Select like."

"You mean it's not actually legit?"

"Of course it's legit. It's a proper whisky, not like that factory produced blended nonsense."

I shifted the case to where he wanted it and straightened up. "I'm guessing that means whoever's distilling this is not licensed to sell it to you?"

"The paperwork hasn't quite caught up with it yet, that's all."

"And the taxes." I smiled.

"They get enough from me already. Do you want to try a dram?"

"Thank you, but make it a small one. I'm driving later."

Goodenough poured the whisky and slid it across the counter. "That'll be four quid."

"Oh, I thought you might… never mind." I fished out a fiver. "I need to ask you a favour."

"If you want an extension on your tab, I'll have to charge interest."

"No, it's not that. It's about Dylan, that lad who… hang on, I haven't *got* a tab with you."

"Yes, you have. Wednesday afternoon, at the little party Gwen, from the Animal Rescue Centre, set up here. Packet of cheesy puffs."

I remembered the bowl of cheesy puffs on our table that afternoon. "How have I got a tab for that? Everything was paid for by the collection they did."

"Not the cheesy puffs. Nobody arranged for them to be included. I'm just scraping by here as it is. I'd soon go bust if I start giving away prime hors d'oeuvres like I'm in the royal box at Wimbledon."

I gave up. "Okay, how much is on my tab?"

"Ten quid."

"Ten quid?"

"There was a packet of bacon Frazzles as well."

"And they came to exactly ten quid?"

"Just how it works out."

I pulled a ten-pound note out and gave it to him. It seemed to vanish before I'd even let it go.

"A favour," I reminded. "That lad Dylan, the one who dismantled your cash register."

"Aye, I remember 'im. Great dobeck that he is. What's he done this time?"

"Nothing, that's the point. He's a good lad, trying hard. Sam, could I persuade you to withdraw the charge?"

Goodenough sucked on his teeth. "And why would you be wantin' to do that then?"

"He's been picked up by the police on suspicion of something he didn't do, and he can prove it, but they want to keep him in just because he's already on bail."

"He should'a thought on that before he took my cash register apart." He turned his back and planted a 'Special Discount' sticker on a glass cabinet of pre-made sandwiches and rolls.

"The problem is, we need him for The Great Wessex Chase. Without him, we're out. That means that the Little Didney Animal Rescue Centre is going to fold."

He turned to face me. "You tellin' me you think you're going to win this?"

"I can't say that, but we're in the final. You'll also save yourself a lot of paperwork."

"What paperwork is that?" Goodenough asked, looking slightly worried.

"It's just that, well, I know how these cases go. Dylan's defence is based on his belief that the machine wasn't working properly, and he was just trying to fix it."

"It was all working perfectly well before he got his hands on it."

"I'm sure it was. But they'll need to investigate that, of course. That means they'll want to know what condition your cash register was in before he dismantled it. You know how they get with these things."

Goodenough planted his hands on the bar and furrowed his brow. "How *do* they get?"

"They'll want to see your cash records to double check those with what the cash register recorded. Not a big problem, they'll do a comparison to make sure the numbers tally. Just to confirm that it was working alright before."

"Sounds a bit unnecessary to me." He straightened up and pushed his hands into his back.

"I know, me too. But these forensic accountants are obsessive about detail. Especially when they're working for HM Revenue and Customs."

"Revenue and Customs?" Goodenough's eyebrows shot upwards. "What've they got to do with this?"

"They'll want to assess if there were any errors made on the taxes paid. Only a formality, of course. After they've been through your books and compared them with the cash register entries, they'll soon see it was all working properly, and Dylan will be fined fifty quid, and that'll be the end of it. But it's just a bit of a nuisance for you, that's all."

"Hmm. And if, and I'm not sayin' I will, but if I drop the charges, they don't have to do all of that?"

"That's right."

"Sounds like a lot of trouble. You know, for them. Not for me. I'm not bothered, you understand?"

I nodded.

Goodenough continued, "And I don't like to put people out. People who know me know that. I'm not one to put people out."

"So I've heard."

"Alright then, but it's for the animals. I ain't worried about no tax inspectors, but for the sake of the animals. I love animals. And dogs."

"For the animals," I said.

"How do we do this?"

I pulled a sheet of paper from my pocket. "I just need you to sign here."

***

I hurried back to my place, threw a pizza in the oven, and fed the dogs. While waiting for the pizza, I rang Janet.

"Oh, hello, Matt," she greeted. "Nothing wrong, is there? We haven't been thrown out again have we?"

"No, nothing like that. I've just managed to get old Sam Goodenough to withdraw the charges on Dylan over that cash register."

"Ooh, well done. How much did that cost you?"

"Nothing. He saw the wisdom of letting it drop. But I'm just ringing to say I'm going to Truro now to try to get him out and it may well take a while, so it might be best if you can drive Eddie and Robyn to that Sleep 'n Drive at Shrewton this evening. I know it's a long drive, but if you take it steady... I would have asked Eddie, but he's not supposed to be driving at the moment."

"How exciting. Henrietta will love going on a road trip."

"Henrietta?"

"My little car. She's a VW Beetle. I'd better change her blankets if she's having guests. Oh heavens, and we'll need some travel sweets. I think the Post Office sells them. We can't go on a road trip without Simpkin's Travel Sweets. And I'll make a Thermos of tea. Goodness, so much to do, I'll get on with it straight away." The phone went dead, and I stared at the blank screen for a moment before calling Robyn.

"Matt? Everything alright?" she asked.

I explained about Goodenough dropping the charges and then told her Janet would be driving them later.

"Is she going to be alright to drive that far?" asked Robyn.

"Yes, she's actually very good. She drove all the way to Great Yarmouth last year to meet up with a palaeontologist she met on an online dating site. They were going to go fossil hunting."

"Fossil hunting? In Great Yarmouth?"

"Yes, that's why I'm ringing you. She was meant to be going to Weymouth."

"Ah, that makes more sense. I assume her navigation skills need oversight? Is that what you're saying?"

"Yes, and could you just help her to check oil and water, you know, the basics?"

"Of course, no problem. We'll see you when you've broken Dylan out then. Good luck."

I closed the call and rescued my pizza.

Teller and Yurei explained that the food I'd given them not ten minutes ago had been just an appetiser, and what did I think I was doing eating pizza in front of them when everybody knows it's a dog's best food ever.

Once we'd eaten my pizza, I bundled the dogs in the back of the car, along with Yurei's Ouija board, Teller's chew ball, blanket, water, forensic bags, and a bag of dog food. Life used to be simple once. I could just get in a car and go. I checked the house was secure, then rejoined my furry friends and headed off for Truro.

Shortly after passing through Helston, I noticed I'd picked up a tail. The blue Toyota Corolla was tagging along behind me. They were probably thinking I was on my way to a clue with the rest of the team on board. I did nothing to shake them, and just drove steadily on to Truro.

It was nearly nine o'clock by the time I reached the city centre, and the evening had darkened under a low cloud. As I approached the police station, I turned off just before it, and into the small road which led round behind the building. From this side, the only thing which would differentiate this place from all the other office buildings here, was a sign by the open back gate to the small parking area. And in this light, as I'd guessed, it would be invisible. Unless they knew this was a police station, there would be no reason to think it was.

I pulled into the little car park and watched discreetly as the Toyota pulled up in the road opposite. I opened the windows sufficiently for Teller and Yurei, then locked up and found the rear door entrance to the police station. I pressed the button on the doors and waited while whoever was monitoring the cameras verified I probably wasn't a terrorist or Jehovah's Witness. A buzzing sound indicated I could proceed.

The desk sergeant greeted me with, "Good evening, sir. What can we do for you?"

"I'm Matt Dixon, ex-Job. I was stationed in Penzance until I retired a month ago."

"Ah, yes. I know the name. I wondered who you were when I saw you park outside. You do know that's police parking only?"

"I know, but it's late, and there were plenty of spaces, and I'm only just out."

"Hmm, I suppose we can overlook it this time. Just that we get all sorts trying to park here while they do their shopping at the Spar shop next door."

"You have a prisoner here," I said. "Picked up in Porth Cullen this afternoon on suspicion of breaking bail conditions. Dylan, his name is."

"Just one moment." The sergeant leant forward to read his screen. "Ah yes, here we are. Dylan Cooper, identified as a suspect in the leaving of a suspicious package. How can I help?"

"As he's only in custody due to the fact he's already on police bail, and I'm guessing the package turned out to be harmless, I'm rather hoping you can let him out? I've got a signed affidavit from the original complainant dropping all complaints." I pushed the piece of paper under the glass screen.

He took the paper and began to read it.

A door behind the desk swung open and a constable rushed out, settling his custodian helmet on his head as he walked. "We've got a problem, Sarge," he said.

"What's up, Andy?"

"Check your monitor." He pointed at the CCTV monitor on the desk. "Couple of wrong-uns out there having a go at a white Beamer in our parking lot."

The sergeant looked at me. "You'd best wait here, won't be a moment."

They both rushed out of the door. Two minutes later, the door swung open again and they returned, each controlling one of the two previous occupants of the Toyota, now handcuffed.

"Shan't keep you a moment," the sergeant said as he passed through and into the corridor.

After a few minutes, the sergeant returned and settled behind his desk again. "You might want to check your car before you drive away. Though, I think your dogs gave them a fright before they could do any damage. Those two actually looked pleased to see us. Now, Dylan Cooper." He picked up Goodenough's statement again. "This seems to be in order. I'll put it in his file."

"You can let him out then?"

"No, sorry, I can't do that. You'll have to have a word with the inspector. That'll be for him to decide."

"Can I see him then?"

"Not until six o'clock tomorrow morning. He's on the early shift and that's when he's due in."

I wanted to argue, but I knew full well that would go nowhere. A good desk sergeant had the intransigence of a donkey in a carrot field. And I also knew that had I been on the desk, and given the circumstances under which Dylan had been picked up, I wouldn't have let him out without a senior officer's okay either.

"I understand. I'd like a chat with Dylan though, while I'm here. He has put me down as his legal representative."

"Of course." He disappeared through the door behind his desk, and a moment later, he reappeared from another door just off a corridor leading away from the front desk area. "This way," he said.

I followed him down the little corridor to a small set of cells. He checked the window of the first one, then unlocked the door. "Just give us a yell when you're done."

I entered the cell. Police station standard. Small, functional, but I'd stayed in worse hotels.

Dylan stood as I entered. "Am I getting out?" he asked.

"Not just yet. Needs the DI's approval, and he's not in till morning."

"But I'll get out then, right?" He looked almost panicked.

"No problem," I lied. I really had no idea what would happen. Although Goodenough had withdrawn charges, that was by no means an automatic release. They may still decide they want him before a magistrate in the morning if they think he might have breached his bail conditions.

"What about Yurei? Is he alright?"

"He's fine, Dylan. He's outside in the car with Teller. They're probably tearing up my seats at this very moment."

"Cool. I never said anything," Dylan said. "Only no comment, like in the movies."

"Probably wise."

I explained how Goodenough had dropped the complaint and that the others were waiting for us in Shrewton. Then I told him to get some sleep as, one way or the other, tomorrow was going to be a busy day for him.

I called the desk sergeant to let me out, and he led me to the entrance of the station.

"Okay," I said. "I'll come back in the morning." I turned to go, then, "Oh, by the way, if those two you just dragged in are from that blue Toyota Corolla out there, then I also saw them cruising around in Porth Cullen earlier. Your officers who arrested Dylan will probably have it on their dashcam. They drove straight past us during the arrest."

"Thank you. We'll look into that."

I turned again, waved, and said, "See you at six."

I checked my car, but apart from a few fresh scratches near the door lock, it seemed they'd had no time to do any damage. I wondered what would have happened had they actually managed to get in. Both dogs demanded cuddles and treats before allowing me to drive the two hundred metres up the road to the Truro City Moto Lodge where I checked in for the night. Fortunately, they offered dog friendly rooms, a consideration which was becoming more relevant to my life day by day.

Once settled, I rang Robyn.

"Are you at Shrewton yet?" I asked.

"Just got here," she said. "Hotel's okay, a bit basic."

"All being well, it'll be the last of these. Back to normal next week, one way or the other."

"What about you? How did it go at the police station?"

"I have to go back in the morning to speak to the DI. He'll have the final say. I'm in a motel almost next door to the police station. Yurei and Teller like it. They have their own beds."

"That's not going to work," she said. "It took us just over four hours to get here. You'll never make it."

"He's on the early shift, gets in at six, apparently. It should be alright, and it's a bit shorter run from here than Little Didney." I tried to make it sound as convincing as possible.

I clearly failed.

"You don't sound convinced," she said.

"No point in worrying now. It's out of our hands. If they don't let him out, we've lost. If they do let him out, but take their time about it, we've lost. If the traffic's bad…"

We said goodbyes and I went outside with the dogs for their nighttime business. As I wandered the surprisingly deserted streets, I realised I was missing the company of Robyn. Strange, I'd only actually known her for a few days, but suddenly, I felt something was missing. I shrugged off the feeling and headed back, took a shower, and slid into a surprisingly comfortable bed. And then I felt a huge weight settle on my legs, and another against my side.

CHAPTER TWENTY-EIGHT

TEAM BULLINGBOY CLUB

PERKINS' PHONE RANG AND BUZZED. He watched its little dance on the table as the screen flashed Combermere's latest avatar of a furious Donald Duck. He ignored it and used his knife and fork to cut a neat triangle off his hot buttered toast.

He noticed the barman appear from a rear door and asked, "I wonder if I could have another pot of tea? This one was a little too strong for me."

"A little too strong? How can you have tea what's too strong?" he asked, as he came over to Perkins' table. "That's like sayin' you've got too much beef in your pasty." He picked up the tea tray. "Real Cornish tea, that. I'll 'ave to charge for a fresh pot."

"I understand," said Perkins. "Just charge it to the room."

His phone rang and danced again, and even though it was just an avatar, Donald Duck seemed particularly angry this time.

He patted the corners of his mouth with a neatly folded paper serviette, then picked up the phone.

Combermere's voice exploded out of the phone the moment Perkins pressed answer.

"Where the devil have you been?" he demanded. "I've been trying all morning to get hold of you."

"I've been having breakfast. It's still terribly early, and—"

"I'm not interested in early. I'm paying you to be there when I call."

"Yes, about that. I've been thinking—"

"Now, I'm assuming The Money Boys have made it to the final, so here's what I need you to do."

"I think I need to explain that—"

"I don't need explanations, Perkins. I need action. That's what I want, action. We need a good, strong, two-pronged attack. Stopping the enemy, and making sure these Money Boys get to the clue the moment my chum in GCHQ gives you the answer. Daphne holds the chase."

"Sir, I really must explain…"

"Well? Go on then," Combermere demanded. "Explain if you must."

Perkins drew a deep breath, gathered his conviction, and said, "The Money Boys were disqualified yesterday." He held the phone away from his ear and braced himself.

"Disqualified? What the devil are you talking about, man? How can they be disqualified?"

"One of them failed to check in. His phone was stolen." Perkins had already decided that was probably as much as Combermere needed to know. No point in prodding the angry bear by telling him how the phone had come to be lost.

"Why is everybody so damned incompetent? You had unlimited resources and yet still you make a misshapen chaos of it."

"It's hardly my—"

"Right, here's what I need you to do—"

"Sir," Perkins cut in. "I really must insist I speak." He paused, waiting for more vitriol to pour its way down the phone.

There was a moment of silence, then Combermere said, "Well? What have you got to say?"

"I'm resigning my position as your Parliamentary Private Secretary."

"Don't be a fool. What else can you do? Now listen, I want you to find out which teams are in this final and—"

"No," Perkins interrupted forcefully. "I have decided to leave London. I found this lovely quaint little village in Cornwall. It's called Little Didney, near where The Money Boys had completed their clue at Chysauster iron age village. There's a little pub where we'd arranged to meet after the clue. But they never arrived, and they've all gone home now, so I'm here on my own. And I think I might like to move here."

"Have you completely lost your mind? Enough of your nonsense. I've got 5,000 partridge and pheasant chicks on the way from Poland ready for the first shoot on the new estate. What am I supposed to do with those? Leave them stuck in trucks for five minutes and they all start killing each other. And the Poles will still want their money."

"That's not really my problem."

"Of course it's your problem. You're responsible for this mess. And the fact that my shares in Valdez Oil have crashed because of some data leak on the internet. Don't think that I don't know you're behind that, somehow. This is ruin, man. Ruin."

"I'm sure you'll find somebody else to blame. But it won't be me. You will have my resignation letter on your desk by Monday."

"Don't bother," snapped Combermere. "You're fired." The phone went dead.

Sam Goodenough returned from the kitchen with a fresh pot of tea. "I can see through to the bottom of the teapot. That ain't tea."

Perkins took the pot and poured some into his cup. "Perfect," he said. "Oh, and I'd like to extend my stay for a few days longer. I think I might do some house-hunting."

"There'll have to be a late booking surcharge," Goodenough said.

"Of course, I fully understand."

Perkins finished pouring his tea then cut another corner from his buttered toast and sat back with a faint smile.

CHAPTER TWENTY-NINE

TEAM FARMHOUSE FIVE

THE ALARM ON MY PHONE buzzed me almost-awake at five-thirty. At five thirty-one, Teller completed my waking process by licking my nose until I woke up properly. Yurei jumped onto the bed and settled down for his early morning snooze. I stroked Yurei's head with one hand, and with the other, reached for the remote control of the television and switched on to the news network. It was more a ploy to keep me from slipping back into sleep, rather than a desire to see what disasters were unfolding in the world.

Somebody who I probably should know, but didn't, had been voted off Celebrity Gulag Death Island, an MP had been caught taking back-handers from the Saudis over an arms' contract, and the stock market was in turmoil following a data leak on the internet. I was halfway through my morning shower when I connected the data leak with Robyn.

I came out of the shower, still towelling myself, and flicked through the fifty or so rolling news channels until I found one talking about it. Pictures of red price boards in the stock exchange backdropped a talking head explaining what had happened. An unprecedented leak of client data from one of the world's largest hedge funds was causing a massive sell-off of shares in oil, tobacco, and arms' companies. Statements were being rushed out by pension funds, town councils, trade unions, and others who were all busy trying to outdo each other in their protestations of ignorance as to the use of their funds in such dreadful companies.

I dressed and had a walk-through breakfast in the buffet restaurant, pocketing a few sausages for Teller and Yurei on my way, then checked out. I left my car in the police station again with the dogs guarding it and the Ouija board.

By five to six, I was talking to the early-shift desk sergeant.

I explained why I was there, and he pointed at a row of blue plastic seats and said he'd let me know when the DI arrived.

At six o'clock, I began to cycle through timings in my head. If the inspector arrived at, let's say six fifteen, we had a ten-minute chat and hopefully he agrees, then we'd need probably half an hour for paperwork and formalities. Call that seven o'clock. Stonehenge was about 180 miles. Three hours for 180 miles on the main artery through Cornwall and Devon in the middle of summer. That didn't look good.

I checked my watch again. Ten past. Maybe if I just took Dylan's phone? That was taking a chance that it wouldn't be him that was called to be in the picture. Okay, as a fall-back, that's the only option. Statistically, the odds of Dylan being the one for the picture were eighty percent in our favour. Not bad. Maybe I should just duck out now and take that chance? Leaving now would give me a good chance of getting there in time. But without Dylan. Then what if we needed his particular brand of expertise to solve the clue?

My phone rang. I glanced up at the desk sergeant and he gave a little nod indicating I was okay to answer it.

"Have you got Dylan yet?" Robyn asked.

"I'm still waiting to see the DI. He's a bit late."

"What do you think?"

"I really don't know. In theory, there's no reason why he won't be allowed out, but who knows? There's also a ton of paperwork, and they may decide they want to verify with Goodenough that he wasn't under duress when he signed the withdrawal."

"You don't sound very confident," Robyn said quietly.

"I was wondering if perhaps I should just come up with his phone. You know, take a chance that—"

"Matt?" I heard a male voice from the corridor. "Matt Dixon? There's a face from the past."

I turned to see a tall man in an expensive-looking suit. I guessed this to be the detective inspector.

"I've got to go," I said to Robyn. "He's here now."

"Good luck, keep us posted."

I closed the call and stood, walking towards the DI. I immediately knew I recognised him but couldn't quite place when and where.

He saw the puzzlement on my face. "Graham, remember?"

I struggled. "Graham? I…"

"Graham Honeybun," he said. "Green young copper when you knew me."

The penny dropped. "DC Graham Honeybun. Wow, that was a few years that went whizzing past. It must have been… Twenty years?"

"Twenty-two, but who's counting?"

"And now DI. Well done."

My eyes scanned the man. The years had looked after him. Twenty-two years ago, a young copper, some mishandled evidence and a career derailed. I should have felt anger or resentment. But although he had indirectly been responsible for my lack of advancement in the service, ultimately, it had been my own decisions to try to cover up which had led to my troubles.

"Come on through, Matt," he said, leading me to an interview room. "We've got a bit of catching up to do."

"I'd love to, sir," I said. "But I'm on a very tight schedule here."

"We can dispense with the *sir*, Matt. You're out, and this is a private room. Now, what's so urgent?"

I explained the situation regarding The Great Wessex Chase and the need for urgency as briefly as I could, while still touching all the salient points. He paused me halfway through to buzz through the desk sergeant and ask for the file. He scanned it as I spoke.

When I'd finished speaking, he said, "This is very tricky, Matt. We still don't understand why this pizza box had what appeared to be a Wi-Fi router in it. I suspect it might have links to this data breach since the boss of the company at the centre of this, had his boat moored close by at the time. However, as the bomb squad did such a nice job in destroying any forensic evidence available on the pizza box, or what was left of the router, we're at a bit of a dead end there."

"And Dylan was with me all morning," I said. "I gave a statement to that effect."

"You did indeed." He pulled a sheet of paper from the file. "I have it here."

"And you'll see from his file that he has no form for computer crime."

"Matt, I'll level with you. The witness statement we have is quite solid in putting your friend at the scene. On the other hand, we have no forensics tying Cooper to the pizza box, and even if we did, all we have at this moment is a potential charge of littering."

Honeybun paused and studied me. "I'm not sure what's going on here. Under normal circumstances, I'd go for keeping him in a while longer for more questioning and get to the bottom of it. But…" He sat back in his seat and twirled his pen through his fingers. "I owe you one, Matt. I also trust you. So, if you're assuring me that he was with you during the time in question, then I'm inclined to take you on your word. What do you say? Do you stand by your statement?"

"Absolutely," I said without hesitation.

Detective Inspector Honeybun closed the file and patted the folder. "Go and wait outside. I'll have him released immediately."

"What about all the paperwork?"

"Leave that to me. Now you get off and go win that competition."

***

Thanks to DI Honeybun's expeditious actions, we hit the main road east at just as the seven o'clock news started on the radio.

"Are we going to make it?" asked Dylan from the back seat where he sat between the dogs.

I checked satnav. "It's going to be very tight. Three hours, thereabouts."

The radio dribbled misery into the car with tales of earthquakes, conflicts and the price of imported tomatoes. I tuned it out until I heard somebody talking about the Green Ninja and a massive data leak.

I tapped the volume control on the steering wheel. A BBC interviewer was talking to a spokesperson for the Roman Catholic church. He was explaining that they were pulling all their investments out of the hedge fund run by Shye, Locke, and Grifter. He claimed the Catholic Church had no knowledge of the fact that they invested in arms' companies.

They then moved to a pension manager for Middleshire county council who refused to comment on whether they knew their employee pension funds were being invested in Valdez Oil's new exploration fields in the Arctic National Wildlife Refuge, followed by the head of the board of governors for Ethanhurst School for Young Gentlemen, who protested they knew nothing of the fact their funds were being invested in companies who utilised child labour in Chinese high fashion factories.

"Are they talking about what I did?" asked Dylan.

"You're not responsible, Dylan." I had to brake quickly to make room for a motorcycle determined to cut in front of me. "You were nowhere near there, remember?"

"Oh yeah, cool. I forgot."

My phone rang and I tapped the answer button on the steering wheel.

Robyn's voice filled the car. "How's it going?" she asked.

Yurei leaned forwards over my shoulder as far as his harness would allow. Searching for the source of Robyn's voice, his ears lifted. Or as much as his ever did.

"We're on the road," I said. "We should be with you about ten."

"That's cutting things very close. That's when the clue arrives."

"I know, but there's not much I can do. We might get lucky with the traffic and catch up a bit."

As I said the words, the motorcyclist pulled out again to hop the car in front. I noticed a grey van heading towards us in the opposite direction and it was immediately apparent to me that the motorcyclist had misjudged his timing.

"I've got to go," I said, my finger touching the button to close the call, at the same time as hitting the brake.

The car in front of me did exactly as I'd anticipated, and jammed on his brakes to give the motorcyclist room to escape the oncoming van.

The van coming towards us panicked and swerved to his left, but he'd overcompensated and clipped the grass verge. Clearly still in full panic mode, he jammed his brakes too hard, and the rear end of his van did a nice 180, clipping the front corner of the car in front of me.

I pulled quickly to a tight stop behind the car and just against the verge, while the motorcyclist sped off into the distance, completely oblivious to the chaos he'd just caused. I reached instinctively for the switch to put the blues on, but of course, it had gone. Hazards on then, I told Dylan to call 999 and to keep the dogs secure, then jumped out of the car. I went round to the back to get a warning triangle out, but there was already a tail of stopped cars behind us so there seemed little point. I checked the driver of the car in front of us, a young woman with two children strapped in the back. She responded to my questions but appeared shaken. As the airbags hadn't deployed, and with no obvious injuries, I hopped across the now static road and checked on the driver of the van. A young man, a paint-spattered T-shirt and jeans, and looking very dazed.

I opened the door. "You alright, mate?" I asked.

"Yeah, what? Where's…" He looked around and I followed his gaze, spotting a mobile phone in the passenger footwell. The screen looked broken.

"What's your name?" I asked. Step one in the injury assessment process.

"Trev, Trevor. What happened?"

"You've had a bit of a bump. Any pain?"

"A bit." He twisted his head and rotated a shoulder. At that, he flinched and swore.

It looked like the seatbelt had wrenched his shoulder. Could be a dislocation.

"Don't move until the paramedics get here. They're on the way," I said, trusting Dylan had done his job.

I glanced up the road in both directions. To the east, several people were out of their cars and seemed to be arguing. I guessed a rear-end shunt. There were no signs of anything more serious.

After a few minutes, I heard sirens approaching and a squad car arrived with two traffic officers. I gave a quick rundown on what happened and left him my details if they needed to contact me. Fortunately, they allowed me to leave, and we were back on the road again. Unfortunately, we had now lost half an hour on an already over-tight schedule. The only compensation was the fact that the road ahead was now fairly clear and I could pick up speed.

Dylan rang Robyn and explained what happened, and although I couldn't hear her words, her voice definitely sounded agitated.

At just past eight-thirty, we left the motorway at Exeter, and now we had nearly a hundred miles left, a good part of which was single lane road. We weren't going to make it.

I got Dylan to ring Robyn again to explain we were probably not going to get to the suggested start point before about half-ten, thirty minutes after the clue was due to arrive. I gritted my teeth and concentrated on squeezing as much distance into each minute as I could. That was when the car started to fill with dog farts.

I put up with the increasingly noxious gases building inside the car until, despite the magnificently German engineered ventilation system, it all became simply unbearable, and I had to pull over.

Yurei and Teller leapt from the car, and with minimal sniffing and fuss, made their deposits on the gravel layby in which we'd parked. I found a couple of evidence bags with which to retrieve the deposits, and we were back on the road.

As ten approached, we were only just nearing Wincanton. Still over half an hour away from Stonehenge. I asked Dylan to ring Robyn again to tell them to go on as soon as they solved the clue, and we'd catch up. Our best hope was that the clue would be on our side of the twenty-five-mile radius from Shrewton, and not the other side.

At ten o'clock exactly, both Dylan's and my phone bleeped, announcing the arrival of the clue. Dylan read it out, "*Good day, Finalists. Here is your ultimate clue: On St Michael's line, where circles turn within a circle, each must choose a stone and each stone must choose a team member. Do not login until a concert of the rings is complete. Login must be completed by midday, or the prize is forfeit. Good Luck.*"

Dylan's phone rang. He listened for a moment, then said, "They think it's a stone circle."

"I thought the same thing," I said loudly enough to be picked up by Dylan's phone. "But what's the reference to St Michael? Is that something to do with Marks and Spencer?"

Dylan listened again, then, "Robyn thinks it's St Michael's ley line. She's just checking on a map."

"And what's this about a concert?"

"I did a concert once," said Dylan. "I played the Stairway to Heaven on the recorder. I got detention for it."

"For playing Stairway to Heaven?"

"Yeah, everybody else was playing Frère Jacques. Oh," he paused to listen to his phone. "Robyn says it's Avebury Stone Circle. That's on the St Michael's ley line and it has two smaller circles in a big one."

"That was far too easy," I said. "Ask her if there could be anywhere else."

He conveyed the message, listened, then said, "Robyn said defo Avebury."

"Robyn said defo?"

"Well, nowhere else will fit, but she says she thinks it's too easy as well. They're leaving now."

"Okay. Avebury is up near Devizes somewhere. That's the other side of Shrewton. We're going to be really late. Can you put it into satnav?"

The road at this point was now back to dual carriageway, and traffic was light. I stepped up the speed a bit.

"Forty-four miles," said Dylan.

"It'll be a lot slower once we hit the minor roads," I said. "Can you tell them we're probably about an hour away?"

"We're going to be an hour late," said Dylan helpfully.

"I know, but we don't have any options. Let's just hope that whoever the other finalists are, that their location is more difficult than ours."

We made good speed until we had to turn off onto the smaller roads, where, although traffic was still light, overtaking opportunities were rare.

My phone rang again, and I answered it via the onboard sound system.

"Robyn, we're still about half an hour out," I said. "Are you there?"

"Just arrived. It's a huge area and I can't make much sense of it yet. These circles are vague to say the least. It just looks like bunches of random standing stones at the moment. I'm trying to find a good diagram on the internet so we can get our bearings."

"What about this concert business?" I asked. "Any ideas on that?"

"Not a one. I had a faint hope there'd be some sort of event happening here, music or something. But it's as quiet as silk panties dropping on a bedroom floor."

"You're on speaker phone and Dylan's listening."

"Oh shit. Sorry, Dylan."

"No probs, Robyn," Dylan said.

"We'll see you when we get there," I said, and we closed the call.

I managed to catch up a bit of time, and in the end we arrived just five minutes before eleven o'clock. That left us an hour to sort out the clue and log in. And all the time was the thought that whoever, and wherever, the other finalist team were, that they might complete theirs before us.

CHAPTER THIRTY

TEAM WHO?

WE PARKED UP NEXT TO Janet's VW Beetle and made our way to the site, and Robyn came over to meet us. She held her laptop under her arm, and the look on her face wasn't optimistic.

"We've got a problem," she started, as soon as she drew close.

"What's up?" I asked.

Teller leapt at Robyn and proceeded to climb all over her as she knelt to say hello.

"Yes, Teller, I've missed you too." She straightened up and said to me, "You won't believe this. Over here, look." She headed off towards a couple of standing stones where Eddie and Janet waited.

Dylan and I followed, struggling to keep up over the uneven ground.

Robyn came to a stop near the two standing stones. Yurei decided it was the perfect place to leave his mark, so he carefully put his Ouija board down and cocked his leg against the nearest stone. A fallen stone lay nearby, upon which sat Eddie and Janet. They both gave a tired-looking wave as we arrived and mumbled hellos. Robyn folded open her laptop into an oversized tablet.

"Right, we're currently in the centre of what was the north circle." She indicated a diagram on her screen. "Now, over there, just past those buildings and trees, is the south circle."

My eyes followed her pointing hand. Through a small gap between two buildings, I saw four people wandering around another group of five stones.

"What's the problem?"

She nodded towards the group of four. "Don't you recognise them?"

I looked at the people. Three youngish men and a woman, and they seemed to be wearing fancy dress.

"Difficult to see from here."

"You'll see better from over there," she pointed to a small road which separated the north and south fields. We moved to the road and a bit to the east where I had a clearer view past the buildings. "Just some hippy weirdos, I..." and then I recognised them. Batman, Superman, Wonder Woman, and Spiderman. AKA The Alter Egos, Bruce, Clarke, Diana, and Peter. "What are *they* doing here?"

"I don't know, but I'd guess they're the other finalists and we both have the same clue."

"Have you spoken to them?" I asked.

"No, they only arrived ten minutes ago."

"This could get messy. How are you getting on with the rest of the clue? We each have to choose a stone, or something, wasn't it?"

"Each must choose a stone and each stone must choose a team member," Robyn read from her screen. "And no, we're no closer to figuring that out."

"What about the concert business? Any more thoughts on that?"

"It could be Wagner's Ring Cycle," offered Janet. "I went to see it once in the Royal Albert Hall. It went on for fifteen hours. I gave up after half an hour. The Valkyries were far too noisy for me."

"I went to see Battlelore there," said Dylan. "They're a heavy metal band that does music about Lord of the Rings. Maybe it's them? That'd be cool."

"I don't think anybody's coming to do a concert." I looked around where we were standing. "You say this is the north circle?" I asked Robyn.

"Yes, we're in the centre. Strictly speaking, the actual circle is over there." Her arm swept a lazy semi-circle to the east where two more stones stood upright, and two others lay in the grass. "These three stones here are not part of the circle. They're central stones."

"That's all that's left of this circle?"

"Yup. And the other circle," she pointed to the south where The Alter Egos still wandered around. "It's similar. Just five standing stones left."

"Let's see how they're doing," I said.

We moved to the eastern edge of the north field where we had a better view of the southern circle. Or what was left of it.

I watched our opponents for a moment. They seemed as puzzled as we were.

"At least we know who the enemy are," Eddie said. "Maybe we could distract them. I'll go over there and pretend I'm in charge of this place and tell 'em it's closed."

"And what happens when they ask you a question about the site?" I asked.

"I just make it up. Nobody really knows about this stuff anyway. Even the experts are mostly just making stuff up."

"And so into the bin goes a three year PhD in archaeology."

"I'm just saying, it's an idea. Do you have a better one?"

"Let's start again," I said. "We have two problems. Firstly, who stands by which stone, and secondly, this concert business. My guess is that the reason the location was easy to find is because it's this part which is difficult to solve."

"It's impossible," said Robyn. "We don't have any ideas as to which stones are relevant. Or even which circle we're meant to be in. Do we each stand by a stone in this circle? Or the other one? If it's this one, then we fail on the part where each team member must have a stone, as there are only four stones here, and two of those are fallen."

"We go to the other circle then," said Eddie. "There's five stones there, so we can each have one and each stone will have somebody."

"That would seem to be right. But if those guys…" I nodded south towards where The Alter Egos were currently standing in the middle of the southern circle. "…have the same clue, then there would be an empty stone."

"Back to square one," said Robyn. "It can't be only the standing ones. Between the two circles, there are seven still standing stones, so that doesn't work."

"Maybe we have to count the ones in the middle?" offered Janet.

I looked at those. "There are three stones in the middle. That makes seven stones."

Janet pointed at each stone, counting on her fingers. "But if you only count the ones still standing, that makes four. And there are five of us. On the other hand, there are five stones still standing in the south circle."

"That might be it," I said. "But we only get one go. If we're wrong, we're out." I looked at my watch, it was now a quarter past eleven.

"But they've only got four in their team," said Janet, pointing at The Alter Egos. "And if they've got the same clue, both can't be right. Maybe there's something about the shape? Or the type of rock? I've got a book on rocks. I bought it when I was going to go fossil hunting once."

"So what sort of rock is this?" Eddie asked, patting the fallen stone on which he was sitting.

"That's a big rock."

"You read a book to learn that?"

"I only got to page eleven."

"Four plus five is nine," said Dylan. He was squatting next to Yurei and appeared to be addressing the dog. "And nine is the third square, which is cool, because the square root of nine is three."

"Thank you, Dylan. I think," I said. "I suggest we look at the stones to see if we can see anything significant that would make them different."

We examined the stones, but to me, they looked like stones. I turned to the sound of approaching people. The Alter Egos were heading in our direction, their capes flowing. Batman, Superman, Wonder Woman, and Spiderman. Neither Batman nor Spiderman wore their masks. I guessed the middle of the day in mid-August was probably not comfortable under a full mask.

They nodded acknowledgement of us as they wandered the stones of our circle. I heard muttering, but certainly no excitement in the voices which would indicate a solution.

I suggested quietly that we take advantage of their move to the north circle, to go and have a look at the southern one. This was met with nods of approval, or in Eddie's case, a mumble of reluctant acquiescence. We crossed the road and looped round the clutch of houses to the southern field.

The south circle consisted of five standing stones, all probably about twice as tall as me. Apart from the fact there were no fallen stones in this circle, or any central ones, I could see no real difference. I checked my watch again. Nearly half-eleven. We were rapidly running out of time and still no nearer an answer.

Five of us stood in a circle of five stones. On one level, it seemed obvious, until I thought about The Alter Egos, with their four members. If they had the same clue… This was just going round in circles. Bigger circles than the ones in which we currently stood. Sometimes, there comes a time when action, any action, is better than watching defeat slowly manifest in front of you.

"Okay," I said. "We're going to talk with the other team." I scanned the expressions on the faces in front of me. Puzzled, curious, dismissive. Dylan nodded and smiled. I waited for arguments, but none came.

"We clearly can't solve this, and in…" I looked at my watch, "…twenty-five minutes, the competition ends, and the prize is gone. Those guys don't seem to have any more idea than us, so maybe if we put our heads together, at least one of our teams will win it. We can hope it's us, but if it turns out to be them, then at least that's better than the whole thing being a complete waste of time. Thoughts?"

"Maybe we could do a deal," said Eddie. "You know, if we work it out between us, then whoever wins it, we split it fifty-forty to us, as there's Five of us and four of them."

"That doesn't make a hundred percent," said Dylan.

"What? Well, I don't know. Sixty-forty then."

"That's still not right. If you want to split it four ninths and five-ninths, that comes out at fifty-five forty-five percent. Nearly. It's actually two recurring numbers, which is quite cool. It's like Pi, or the square root of two. That one's weird because that's equal to the hypotenuse of—"

"Later, Dylan," I interrupted. "We haven't got time, or mental space for that now. I say fifty-fifty. That's fair."

"I agree," said Robyn. "Although, it's all fairly pointless if we can't figure it out, anyway."

"Right, let's do it," I said.

We started back up towards the northern circle. Just as we noticed The Alter Egos heading back our way.

"Do you think they've worked something out?" I asked, of nobody in particular.

Our teams met on the road which ran between the north and south parts of the site.

Batman nodded at me and said, "Matt, we meet again."

"Bruce," I returned. "I think that without the clues we've swapped, there's a fair chance we wouldn't both be here."

"Correct," Bruce said. "The question is, do we now swap what we know again?"

"You're suggesting you know something?"

"I'm suggesting nothing."

We faced each other in silence for a few moments. I felt as though I was in a scene from a spaghetti western. Except for the fact I was facing Batman.

"I suggest we start by comparing clues," I said. "Let's at least see if we're both working towards the same point."

"Agreed."

"How do we know we can trust you?" challenged Eddie.

"You don't," said Bruce. "But in…" he looked at his Batwatch, "twenty-two minutes, that question becomes hypothetical."

Eddie grunted, but offered nothing more.

I opened my phone. "Okay, as a sign of goodwill, ours first." I turned my phone to him to read.

Bruce took a moment, then nodded. "That's exactly the same as ours." He showed me his message as proof.

"Now what?" I asked.

"We pool knowledge."

"We've got as far as establishing that there are four stones in the north and five in the south, so as a team, we can only achieve the target of each having a stone and each stone having a team member in the south field."

"We got there as well, but with only four of us, it's the other way round."

"What about this bit?" Janet said, staring at her phone. "It's when they accepted our Men-An-Tol login. *You have now completed the team rounds,*" she read out. "How have we completed the team rounds when there are still two teams in the final? That doesn't make sense."

"Probably best not to worry about that bit, Janet," I said. "I don't think that matters now."

"Wait," said Robyn. "It might mean something though. This whole thing is very precise, and I don't think they'd say something like that without reason."

Bruce turned towards his companions, and they went into a small huddle. Seconds later, he emerged, and said, "We think you're right."

"Okay," I said, "what now?"

"We don't know."

Robyn swiped through her phone again. "What about this? When we got the final clue, it called us finalists, yet up until then, it had always called us Team Farmhouse Five?"

Bruce scanned his phone. "The same with us."

"Motive," I said. "We need to understand the mind of the person who set this up. It's always easier to solve a problem if you understand what, or who, created the problem in the first place. Like solving a crime. What is the perpetrator's motive?"

"People said he was a communist," said Janet. "But he wasn't. That was just the rich toffs who didn't like him because he wasn't like them, and he helped people. Like when our village hall heating broke down just before we were due to put on the Village Players' version of the Full Monty. The poor men were so embarrassed at rehearsal, you couldn't blame them, it was very cold. But he paid for the hire of industrial heaters for the opening night. It saved the day, and the men were outstanding." Janet seemed to drift away in thought at that point.

"Who are we talking about here?" asked Bruce.

"Oh, sorry," said Janet. "Thomas Lovett, the man who died and left his estate for this prize. He wanted people to come together, not fight each other. He was like his great, great," she counted on her fingers., "great, great, great... how many was that?"

I shrugged. "I wasn't counting. Is it important? Only we're running out of time here."

"She's talkin' about old William Lovett," said Eddie. "Thomas Lovett's great great whatever ancestor. The Chartist."

"What's a Chartist?" asked Bruce.

"A socialist, a union man," said Eddie "He was the first. Cabinet maker, born in Newlyn, he was, just down the road from Little Didney. It's said, he's the man what started the first unions in England."

"This is all very interesting," I said, "but how does this help?" I looked at my watch again. Fifteen minutes to go. Fifteen minutes to solve this, get to wherever we were supposed to be, and then login. We weren't going to make it.

"And what on earth has that got to do with a concert?" asked Robyn.

Dylan held up his hand. "When I was working in Krappi Burger, my Team Leader used to say that creating a perfect Big Krappi was a concert of tastes and colour. But he also said that Roger Moore was the best James Bond, so I don't really believe anything he said."

"Roger Moore?" Bruce looked shocked. "The man whose eyebrow acted better than he ever did. He wasn't even the best Saint."

"I know," said Dylan. "George Sanders was the coolest ever."

"Ehem." I tapped my watch. "Can we get back to the point here?"

"I think we're there," said Robyn. "This whole thing was set up by a descendant of the man who introduced the idea of collective action from workers to achieve better working conditions and pay. Working in concert, together?" She studied me as she spoke. "All together? Not in separate teams?"

"Four plus five is nine," said Dylan.

"Yes, Dylan," I said. "You said that earlier, but... Ah, nine, yes. That will be why it was the end of the team rounds. We have to work together, in concert, as one team to solve the puzzle."

Robyn patted my shoulder. "There you go. A concert of the rings."

"Nine standing stones." I cast my eyes to the two rings. "Each having their own person, and each person having a stone." I looked at my watch again. "We have less than ten minutes to make this happen."

"You take the five, we'll take the four," said Bruce.

"I'm assuming that when we're all in place, we all login at the same time?" I asked.

"That'd be my guess."

"We only get one shot at this," I said.

"I know, but what else have we got?"

I shrugged. "How do we know when we're all ready?"

"Good point," said Bruce. The easternmost stones of each circle are almost visible to each other through the gap between the buildings. You and I take those ones, then move a little further east until we can see each other. We'll signal from there. It'll only take a second to jump back to our stones." He looked at his phone. "We've got six minutes. Let's go!"

I ran to the eastern stone of the southern circle, then moved about ten metres east until I saw Bruce in the upper field. We waved acknowledgement. We both waited until our teams were by their own stones, with phones at the ready. We both raised our arms, checked our teams, then dropped our arms at the same time, running as we did so.

I touched my stone, hit the login button, and held my breath.

And we waited.

CHAPTER THIRTY-ONE

LOVETT PARK OPEN DAY

THE AFTERNOON SUN DAZZLED, EVEN through my sunglasses. I pulled my straw hat a bit lower and relaxed back in the folding garden chair, my feet stretched out on the grass.

"What time is it?" I asked.

"Nearly three," said Robyn from my left.

I reached my hand out and found hers resting on the arm of her own chair. "They should be starting in a minute."

"Do you want to move closer?" she asked.

"Nah, we've got a good view from here." I lifted my sunglasses and looked across the field. Lovett's Folly, or the Tower of Doom as it was now known, stood silhouetted against the bright sky, making it difficult to see detail. On each side, two armies lined up facing each other. Goblins to the left, Shadow Warriors to the right. Somewhere in that group, although I couldn't see from here, Bruce and his fellow Nerds readied themselves for battle. I felt a wet nudge against my right hand and reached out to stroke Teller's head. He pushed back into my hand.

"I'm just going to get another beer before it starts," I said. "Want one?"

"Hmm."

I took that as a yes and pushed myself out of the chair and scanned the field. The Wessex Craft Beer tent was about a hundred metres to the east, but Goodenough's Smuggler's Tent, only about fifty metres to the west. I chose the shorter distance in favour of the better beer. I could also then loop back past the Dolly's Ice-Cream van and pick up a couple of ninety-nines.

Goodenough stood behind a line of trestle tables in his tented version of The Smuggler's Arms. He had his back to the bar and was intently occupied with something on a table against the back of the marquee. An untidy queue tangled in front of the makeshift bar, while a trio of hastily hired assistants pushed foaming plastic glasses across the tables at the thirsty customers.

I joined the queue and nodded a greeting towards various people as they insisted on saying hello to me and shaking my hand.

A large loudspeaker on a pole just outside the tent crackled into life. "Attention, the Battle of Doom Tower is about to commence. This is a reenactment brought to you by the International Alliance of Nerds. The organisers ask that you keep all dogs controlled. Thank you."

A few people who had been standing around drinking and talking left the tent and headed in the direction of the Tower of Doom.

"Oh, there you are," a voice behind me said.

I turned to see Gwen bearing down on me like a cruise missile. I glanced around for a way to escape, but I was too late. "Ah, hello, Gwen," I said. "Lovely weather for the Open Day."

"I know, aren't we lucky? I was hoping to find you. There's a favour I'd like to ask you."

"Okay." The idea of a favour filled me with fear. The last favour I'd done for her had landed me with Teller.

"I wonder if you could do the introductions for our Fur Babies in need of homes parade?"

"I don't know. I'm not really one for public speaking." I shuffled forwards a few steps with the queue.

"Oh, but you're such an ambassador for our cause. I mean, look at what you've done." She waved her arms wide. "All this beautiful land for our rescue centre."

"It wasn't just me," I said. "There were five of us. And don't forget the Nerds. We couldn't have done it without them. Maybe you could get one of them to do the introductions." I shuffled forwards a few more steps.

"They're all busy with their battle thingy at the Tower of Doom. I'll just leave you with this." She thrust a purple folder onto me. "That's all the names of the fur babies needing their forever homes. Could you take another one? It would be great company for Teller."

"I don't think I could manage any more. He's a handful enough. Are you sure you want me—"

"We start the Fur Babies' parade as soon as the Battle of the Tower of Doom has finished. Lovely talking to you again, and thank you so much for doing this. Must dash, I have to find Janet. Her Pole Dancing team is putting on their show straight after you, and I need to make sure the St John's Ambulance crew are ready." She blended into the melee like tonic in a gin, and we shuffled a bit closer to the bar.

I heard another voice, "Should've known this is where you'd be," from behind me. This time a male voice.

I turned to see Eddie bearing down on me.

"While you're there, could you get me a pint of Proper Job?"

"Sure, I'd been wondering where you'd got to. How do you fancy doing the introductions for the Fur Babies needing forever homes section?"

"Love to, Matt, but I'm waiting on a call." He waved his phone near me so I could understand what waiting for a call meant.

"What are you up to now?"

"Got a fantastic deal on some Mongolian Glamping tents. They were due to go to Glastonbury, but they got stuck in Dover for three months while some customs clerk decided whether or not they contained Yak hides, or some other such Brexit garbage. Anyway, too late for Glastonbury, but good news for me, huh?"

"What are you going to do with Mongolian Glamping tents?"

"If you have to ask that, you don't understand the Millennial Generation."

"Probably not." We shuffled a few more steps in the direction of the bar.

"I thought we could start up a Glamping site down near the lake. Got some boats coming as well. Just paddle things, like they've got over Newquay."

I paused my shuffling and stopped to look at Eddie. "Actually, I think you might have an idea there."

"Well, don't look so surprised. I get lots of ideas." He tapped his head. "Always working, this is."

"I know, sorry. I didn't mean... It's just that most of your ideas are trouble traps. This one, hmm, it's not a bad plan. We'll have to put it to the committee, of course."

Since the end of The Great Wessex Chase, we'd set up a trust for the Lovett Park, as it was now called, and a committee to oversee the various interests of the nine of us who shared the ownership. Mostly, we all agreed. There was more than enough space for all ideas.

"I've already had a chat with Janet," said Eddie. "She's up for it. She reckons it'll be good for her Detective Mystery weekends she wants to do. Murder in the Glampy Tent Express. Get it?" He grinned.

"Unfortunately."

Eddie glanced at the queue. "I don't think I can wait. I'd better dash. I'm supposed to be helping with the cannons at the Battle of Doom Tower. I'm a goblin." He dashed off towards the entrance.

A loud cough from the person behind me in the queue made me realise I hadn't been moving forwards, and I hurried to catch up and close the gap which had formed in front of me.

I arrived at the bar opposite the point where Goodenough was still wrestling with something on a table at the back. He was grumbling loudly and hitting something with a small hammer.

"Problem, Sam?" I asked loudly.

He turned and glared at me, hammer in hand. "It's your mate, that gawky. He's only gone and taken my brand new, portable cash register apart."

"Ah, anything I can help with?"

"You can tell your mates down at the station that I want him arrested and locked up."

"I'll pass the message on." Fortunately at that point, a young man appeared in front of me to take my order. I collected the beers and headed to find Dolly's ice-cream van.

By the time I arrived back to our seats with a pair of ninety-nines and the beers, the Battle of Doom Tower had begun.

I settled in my seat and handed Robyn a beer and ice cream.

"You took your time," she said.

"Big queues." I found a treat stick in my pocket and gave it to Teller. "Apparently, I'm introducing the Fur Babies in need of Homes." I waved the folder Gwen had given me. "Oh, and I got an ear-bending from Sam Goodenough. Dylan's broken his till again."

"Ah, did you point out to him that the only reason he's got the beer tent concession is because Dylan insisted?"

"He wasn't in the mood. Where is Dylan anyway? I haven't seen him."

"He's over at the kennels building. He's helping the builder with the expansion plans."

"Helping?"

"That's what he said. I think he's just staying out of the way. He gets stressed around large crowds."

Robyn's phone rang, and she fished it out of her bag. She answered it and listened for a moment, giving the odd hmm, or really? Then she closed it and put it away.

"Everything alright?" I asked.

"I'm going to have to go. That was the front gate. There's some Polish truck just arrived with 5,000 partridge chicks."

I watched her go and took a bite from my ninety-nine. Teller planted his head on my lap and told me he'd never been fed and that he was the most neglected dog on the planet. I gave him another treat stick, and he took it with a gentleness that belied his size, and settled on the grass to chew it.

The sounds of battle drifted across the field towards me. The Goblin army was pushing a siege engine towards Doom Tower. The huge wooden construction wobbled as it rumbled across the uneven grass, then it appeared to hit a pit in the ground and toppled to one side, spilling like a massive Jenga pile.

I really must get around to finishing my pergola.

***

The End

Or

The Beginning of a new life for the animals?

Author Note

To take part in the competition yourself, just solve the entry clue and submit your answer at Luddington.com/competition for your chance to win a Special Hardback Limited Edition produced in aid of Valle Verde Animal Rescue.

I do hope you enjoyed this tale, if so, I would be grateful for a few words as a review on your favourite book-buying website or Goodreads. Reviews are very important to us authors and I always appreciate them.

Many thanks.

David

Find my books and sign up for the newsletter

IF YOU WOULD LIKE TO subscribe to my Newsletter, just enter your details below. I promise not to sell your email address to a Nigerian Prince or send you adverts for various biological enhancements.

I will however, at entirely random moments, send you a newsletter containing my writing updates, competitions, giveaways, general meanderings and thoughts on the latest Big Thing.

luddington.com/newsletter

Or to find out more about the author

To Follow On Facebook: facebook.com/DavidLuddingtonAuthor

The Website: www.luddington.com

Twitter: @d_luddington

TONY RYAN IS BEMUSED. HE thought he understood the way the world worked, but now, as a sacrificial lamb of the credit crunch he finds himself drifting... drifting into the clutches of the ever resourceful Pete who could find the angle in a Fairy Liquid bubble... and into the arms of the enigmatic hippy girl, Astrid, who's about to introduce Tony to rabbits, magic caves and the joys of mushrooms.

CHARLES TREMAYNE IS A SPY out of his time. After a long career spent rescuing prisoners from the KGB or helping defectors across the Berlin Wall the world has changed. The Wall has gone and no longer is there a need for a Russian speaking, ice-cold killer. The bad guys now all speak Arabic and state secrets are transmitted via satellite using blowfish algorithms impenetrable to anybody over the age of twelve. Counting down the days to his retirement by babysitting drunken visiting politicos he is seconded by MI6 for one last case. £250,000,000 of government money destined as a payoff for the dictator of a strategic African nation goes missing on its way to a remote Cornish airfield.

Tremayne is dispatched to retrieve the money and nothing is going to stand in his way. Armed with an IQ of 165 and a bewildering array of weaponry and gadgets he is not about to be outmanoeuvred by the inhabitants of a small Cornish fishing village. Or is he?

TINKER'S COTTAGE NESTLES IN A forgotten corner of deepest Somerset. It also happens to sit on a weak point in the space time continuum. Which is somewhat unfortunate for Ian Faulkener, a graphic novelist from London, who was hoping for some peace and quiet in which to recuperate following a very messy breakdown.

It was the cats that first alerted Ian to the fact that something was not quite right with Tinker's Cottage. Not only was he never sure just how many of them there actually were, but the mysterious way they seemed to disappear and reappear defied logic. The cats, and of course the Pope, disappearing literary agents, mislaid handymen and the insanity of Cherie Blair World.

As Ian tries to untangle the mystery of the doors of Tinker's cottage he risks becoming lost forever in the myriad alternate universes predicted by Schrodinger. Not to mention his cats.

Schrodinger's Cottage is a playful romp through a variety of alternate worlds peopled by an array of wonderful comic characters that are the trademark of David Luddington's novels.

For fans of the sadly missed Douglas Adams, Schrodinger's Cottage will be a welcome addition to their library. A heart-warming comedy with touches of inspired lunacy that pays homage to The Hitchhiker's Guide whilst firmly treading its own path.

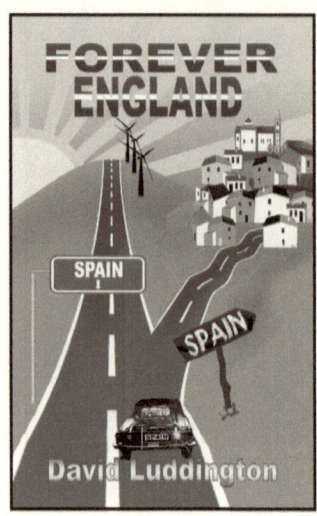

"...And there will be a corner of some foreign field that will be forever England."

ONLY THESE DAYS IT'S MORE likely to be a half finished villa overlooking a championship golf course somewhere on one of The Costas.

Following an unfortunate encounter with Spanish gin measures and an enthusiastic estate agent, retired special effects engineer Terry England is the proud owner of a nearly completed villa in a new urbanisation in Southern Spain.

Not quite how he'd intended to spend his enforced early retirement Terry nevertheless tries to make the best of his new life. If only the local council can work out which house he's actually bought and the leaf blowers would please stop.

Terry finds himself being sucked in to the English Expat community with their endless garden parties and quests for real bacon and Tetley's Tea Bags. Of course, if it all gets too much he can always relax in the local English Bar with a nice pint of Guinness, a roast beef lunch and the Mail on Sunday.

With a growing feeling that he might have moved to the 'Wrong Spain', Terry sets out to explore and finds himself tangled in the affairs of a small rustic village in the Alpujarras. It is here where he finds a different Spain. A

Spain of loves and passions, a Spain of new hopes and a simpler way of life. A place where a moped is an acceptable means of family transport and a place where if you let your guard down for just a moment this land will never let you go again.

Forever England is the tale of one man trying to redefine who he is and how he wants to live. It is a story of hope and humour with an array of eccentric characters and comic situations for which David Luddington is so well known and loved.

"Overall, this is a very warm and funny book. It is filled with wonderful characters and many laugh out loud moments." book-reviewer.com

"Genuinely funny, with many laugh out loud moment..." Matt Rothwell - author of Drunk In Charge Of A Foreign Language

Reading David Luddington is like "Like reading your favourite sitcom." —
Nigel Planer

RETIRED STAGE MAGICIAN TURNED PROFESSIONAL mystic debunker, John Barker, finds his sceptical beliefs under fire when he encounters a strange man who claims to be Merlin. After several unsuccessful attempts to rid himself of his increasingly unpredictable companion, John finally relents and agrees to assist in the man's crazy mission, to find the true grave of the mythical King Arthur.

Following a hidden code contained within the text of a soft porn novel, they gather a growing entourage of hippies, mystic seekers and alien hunters as they leave a trail of chaos across the south west of England. When the group comes to the attention of a TV Reality Show producer looking to make a fast profit out of harmless eccentrics and fading celebrities, John decides it's time to take charge and prove one way or the other, the identity of this mysterious person who claims to be a fictional wizard.

"Whose reality is this anyway?" is a warm-hearted tale of what it means to be an individual and to follow one's dreams. With his trademark cast of oddball characters and absurd situations, David Luddington once more transports us into a world where who you are is more important than what you are." — *Grady Harp*

"Like reading your favourite sitcom"
Nigel Planer

CAMP SCOUNDREL

Doing what it takes to survive paradise

DAVID LUDDINGTON

Author of the Best Seller - 'Forever England'

WHEN EX-SAS SOLDIER, MICHAEL PURDY, comes in front of the judge for hacking the bank account belonging to the Minister for Invalidity Benefits and wiping out his personal wealth, he braces himself for a prison sentence.

What Michael doesn't expect, is to be put in charge of a group of offenders and sent to a remote location in the Sierra Nevada Mountains in Spain to teach them survival skills as part of their rehabilitation programme.

But Michael knows nothing at all about survival skills. He was sort of in the SAS, yes, but his shining record on the "Escape and Evasion" courses was more a testament to his computer skills than his ability to catch wildlife and barbecue it over an impromptu fire. Basically, he was the SAS's techy nerd and only achieved that position as a result of a bet with a fellow hacker.

Facing a stark choice between starvation or returning home to serve out their sentences, the group of offenders under Michael's supervision soon realise that the only way to survive is to use their own unique set of skills — the kind of skills that got them arrested in the first place.

"Like reading your favourite sitcom"
Nigel Planer

The **BANK** of
GOODLINESS

Shadeys Bank needs to clean up its image,
a country vicar needs a new career.
It could be a match made in heaven.
Or Hell.

Shadeys Bank

DAVID LUDDINGTON
Author of the Best Seller - 'Forever England'

WHEN SHADEYS BANK LOSES YET another C.E.O. to a major scandal, they are desperate to show they've reformed. Who better to present their redemption to the world than a country vicar with a reputation for being annoyingly good?

Reverend Tom Goodman is ousted from his job as a country vicar for allowing a homeless family to stay in the church hall. Meanwhile, a major bank is trying to rescue its image after the latest in a long string of financial scandals.

It seems like the perfect match and Goodman is hastily appointed as the bank's new C.E.O. All they have to do now, is promote him as the new face of Shadeys Bank whilst at the same time, keeping him away from the day-to-day business of dubious banking.

However, Tom Goodman has other ideas. He's not going to be satisfied with being used as an empty puppet for a PR stunt. Unfortunately for Shadeys, Tom is planning on actually making a difference.

And so begins an epic battle of wills. The might of a multi-billion pound bank versus a seemingly naïve country vicar.

No contest.

"Yes Minister meets The Vicar of Dibley."

ROSE WELL HOLIDAY PARK NEEDS a hero.

This once shining icon of the Great British Holiday Camp is dying, and the last residents are more interested in preparing for a zombie apocalypse or fighting off imaginary UFOs than playing Crazy Golf or Bingo.

In addition, a foreign bottled water company is attempting to force a sale so they can seize the last asset of Rose Well Park, the Rose Well Spring. The famous spring water claimed to bestow great health and longevity.

And then there's the bomb...

What Rose Well Park could probably do without, is a hero whose belief in a better tomorrow far outweighs any of his past achievements. But William Fox is all they have.

Armed with nothing more than an undying sense of optimism and a box of books about alien conspiracies, he slowly draws up his plans to make Rose Well Park famous.

"Dad's Army meets X-Files"

• *Woozle: Noun*

A presentation of evidence by citation only. A woozle occurs when frequent citation of publications, lacking evidence, mislead individuals, groups, and the public, and nonfacts become urban myths and factoids.

AGEING ROCK GOD, JIM SULLIVAN, is heading for the quiet life on his newly acquired, tiny island, off the coast of Cornwall. That is until he sends a letter to the King of England, announcing his intent to declare independence from the UK and appointing himself king.

Determined not to cede one inch of British territory, the UK government despatches low-level Foreign Office researcher, John Cabot, to put a stop to Sullivan's ambitions.

What they didn't anticipate was Cabot's tenacity for unearthing information they'd rather he didn't, or Sullivan's relentless, but completely unfounded, optimism in his own ideas.

Armed with nothing more than a guitar and a spreadsheet, can these two stand up to the might of the British Empire?

No contest.

Nigel Planer
"Another bunch of swarthy characters who strike out on their own against all the odds and eat a lot of pub food. Classic British comedy. It's Passport to Pimlico without the passports. And not in Pimlico. Luddington does it again."